BARCELONA DAYS

ALSO BY DANIEL RILEY

Fly Me

BARCELONA DAYS

Daniel Riley

Little, Brown and Company
New York Boston London

Little, Brown and Company
Hachette Book Group
1290 Avenue of the Americas, New York, NY 10104
littlebrown.com

First Edition: June 2020

Little, Brown and Company is a division of Hachette Book Group, Inc. The Little, Brown name and logo are trademarks of Hachette Book Group, Inc.

The publisher is not responsible for websites (or their content) that are not owned by the publisher.

The Hachette Speakers Bureau provides a wide range of authors for speaking events. To find out more, go to hachettespeakersbureau.com or call (866) 376-6591.

ISBN 978-0-316-36216-0
LCCN 2019948241

10 9 8 7 6 5 4 3 2 1

LSC-C

Printed in the United States of America

For Sarah

"Eruptions and cataclysms and plagues and the colliding of planets were the only real, the only inevitable events, and the human activities that happened to lie in their path, and which are destroyed with such blind ease and ignorance, were of as little real importance as the doings of insects. How effortlessly they had all been burnt up! How pointless all our passions and complications and the intricate structure of our little society now seemed!...How microscopic, how minute, were the feuds, the passions, the pleasures and the vanities of the small anachronistic community of Saint-Jacques!"

—*The Violins of Saint-Jacques*
by Patrick Leigh Fermor, 1953

"Barcelona is something else, isn't it? There you have the Mediterranean, the spirit, the adventure, the high dream of perfect love. There are palm trees, people from every country, surprising advertisements, Gothic towers and a rich urban tide.... What a pleasure it has been for me to meet that air and that passion!"

—letter to a friend, Federico García Lorca, 1926

I.

Before Volcano

"To you and me," Will said, lifting his wine, a local something, butcher red. The label said it was from Penedès, just down the coast, and it featured a bull with roses where its horns should be.

"To 1-2-3," Whitney said, lifting her glass to match, and they clinked a heavy *clink,* and it rang out around the dining room like a good idea.

Heavy chatter blew about like smoke, ninety-nine percent of which neither of them could understand. They couldn't even tell whether it was Spanish or Catalan being spoken most of the time. Written signs they could distinguish: the extra *J*s and *X*s and liquid double-*L*s that had tempted their Scrabble brains for the last four days. But with the talk, they were hopeless—they weren't wired for translation.

They'd strolled in without a reservation, typically impossible, they were told. But given that the booking at the bar was already a *mitja hora tard,* the hostess sat them there at the edge of the dining room under the condition that they might be asked to get up at any moment. It was good enough for Will and it was good enough for Whitney. They were compatible like that, key-cut for one another.

There was no wine list except what was written on a chalkboard above the bar, and so they'd put their faith in the hostess not to rob them blind. Now they sipped from their glasses and took each other in. Will with his wide edges, his twice-broken nose, his shaggy mop lightened by a lifetime of sun and salt. Whitney with her silver eyes and brows thick like lipstick, her freckled cheeks crisped from a Memorial Day weekend pounding the sawed-off sidewalks of the metropolis on the Mediterranean. They knew each other's faces; they were seven years known. They knew the battery of inflections inside and out. But they'd never seen in the other's what they saw just then: the set jaws, the knotted throats. The frame-up of fuzzed uncertainty and cold nerves. What they knew the looks to mean was that it was finally time to confess.

"You or me first?" Will said.

Whitney exhaled and blinked deeply. Her hand found her hair, dark and wet as ink. She loosened the belt of her coat to let the air in. She had beads of sweat on the sides of her nose that caught the overhead lights. It had been a longer walk to the restaurant than they'd anticipated. But it would be worth it—it had been recommended by Gwyneth.

Whitney didn't have to say it, and still Will understood that it was his turn to go.

"Well, okay then," he said, and halved his glass. "I guess, uh, I guess the first one then....The first one I met at a party. She came right up to me. We talked. We went—"

"Whose party?"

"A young-lawyers thing. The ones I never go to."

"But you went this time."

"Well, how else?"

Whitney sucked in her lips.

"I couldn't tell anyone, remember?" Will said. "I didn't tell Mark. I didn't tell Dave or Jay. No websites. No apps. Not even the one with the bees. So: one of those happy hours."

"And so she walks right up to you and does what?"

"She asks me what firm I'm at."

"And you tell her: *I work for a media company.*" Whitney did the voice that sounds nothing like Will: Christian Bale's Batman as a contracts associate.

"She asks me where I went to law school, if I know so-and-so. Connections are made."

"And she just assumes you're available."

"There's a reason I hadn't been to one of those things in years. There's a reason people go."

"And so you drink your drinks, and how does it get to where it gets?"

"We drink our drinks. She seems to have come alone, like me. She—"

"Was she blonde?"

"I don't know."

"You don't know?"

"You're so weird with that."

"Was she?"

"She was...like *that,* I guess." Will pointed to a woman in the dining room. "Mostly blonde, dark at the roots."

"And supersmart too, I bet."

Will leaned back on his stool and sat up straight, bared his teeth like the grimace of the grimace emoji. "Look, I know this is weird, and if you don't want to do it this way..."

"No, I know.... What can I say? I knew I would be bad at

it. I'm jealous of hair color. I'm jealous of the conversation as much as the fact that you went home and fucked her."

Will's eyes tracked to the bartender to see if he'd noticed. Nothing. The staff wouldn't be bothered even if they understood. "And I was funny that night," he said, looking back at Whitney.

"Oh yeah?"

"Funniest I've been in a while. It's interesting how everyone thinks I'm funnier than you do. I'm the 'funny guy' at the office."

"I think that says more about your office."

"Point is, she's having a good old time with me."

"You talk about defamation lawsuits. You talk about libel and IP."

"TV, movies, music."

"You don't even listen to music," she said.

"Not true."

"You listen to legal podcasts when you run..."

"I know new bands. I've gotten into some deejays at—"

"Some *deejays*? I was only out of town for a month."

"I know it's been seven years, but I remember what it's like to talk to girls, all right? I did okay before I met you."

"So you impress her with your CD binder from high school?"

"With tales of concerts in Hollywood. With the names of venues. The Roxy, the Troub—" He registered her nausea and cut himself off. "Whatever, it worked."

Whitney picked at a cuticle. She reached for her wine. "So you, what, close out and hop in a cab?..."

"We go to another bar."

"Oh! Another drink."

"Another couple drinks," he said.

"What a lush. So you wind up canoodling in a booth with sexy candlelight."

"We avoid the darts flying over our heads and laugh about an obnoxious Australian woman shooting pool."

"And she takes you to the bathroom right then and there because she can't resist."

"Do you want me to tell it, or do you want to?"

She opened her hands, an invitation to proceed freely.

"We finish our drinks, hit the street. I think that's basically it."

"So, what, you just start heading home? You think you've struck out?"

"We exchange phone numbers. I start walking toward the subway. I hear a voice and look up and she's in a cab and asks me if I need a ride to her neighborhood."

"Smooth."

"I guess it was an unnecessary step. There was a straighter line."

"But she wasn't gonna risk you judging her by making her move at the bar."

"Anyway, I get in the cab."

"You get in the cab."

"And take her straight to our place," Will said.

"No you didn't . . . "

"Right to bed. Let her root around in your closet. Let her admire the photos of us on vacation."

"It was a good rule," Whitney said. "I'm glad we made it. I couldn't have dealt with someone at the apartment."

"You had it so much easier," Will said, finding her wandering eyes. "A month on the road. A month in a strange city. A month of being able to bring them back to your hotel. . . . All while I'm forced to take cabs to *Brooklyn*."

"Oh no," she said. "Where?"

"I don't know, not far."

"Bushwick," she said.

"South Williamsburg."

"By the bridge..." she said, smiling again now.

"Nice place by the bridge," he said, smiling back in confirmation.

"So she leans into you in the cab."

"She leans in. She grabs my wrist. She places my hand on her leg."

"Oh-kay, then.... Stockings? Skirt?"

"I don't know—skin, shaved."

"Bare legs," she said. "A warm night."

"Not that warm..." he said.

"So bare legs for Young Lawyers Night. Man, being a girl is hard."

"We eventually get there. We head upstairs."

"No pretense of dropping you off somewhere else."

"Pretense gone after the bare legs."

"And so she walks you past the first of three roommates..."

Will smiled again. He loved her. The precision cuts. The smothering judgment.

"*Two* roommates," he said. "But both supposedly at work. Another lawyer. A hospital resident."

"No wonder the bare legs, then. A rare night with the place to herself."

"They're way up in a big building. They have a narrow balcony and a nice view. She dumps some ice in a couple glasses and makes two vodka sodas."

"Of course," she said, chewing on some bread now, feeling lighter. "Perfect."

"You love this," he said. "Every detail is everything you'd hoped."

"Don't stop now. You're on the balcony..."

"We look at the view of the bridge, and then I guess it just happened from there."

"Nope," Whitney said. "The whole thing."

"We don't need to do the whole thing."

"Step-by-step."

"Well, when it's your turn, you don't need to go step-by-step."

"So you're on the balcony, you're making her laugh—the funny guy—and she looks up at you with her wet bovine eyes and begs you to kiss her."

He tapped the tip of his nose and swirled his wine.

"The poorly colored hair dried out from a brutal winter," she continued. "Bounced up with some heat tools. A little too much makeup concealing lines she swears weren't there yesterday. Maybe from overdosing on Netflix and Ben & Jerry's in bed..."

"Nah," Will said, "way too young for wrinkles."

Whitney shifted on her stool. She knew his buttons and he knew hers. Younger, smoother. It halted her momentum, even though what he'd said wasn't true and he could tell that she could tell. Whitney lifted her glass and then dug in deeper.

"She can't figure out what about her isn't fully lovable," she said. "Why dragging home a strange man from a cheesy networking event and giving it up after three hours and four drinks might not be girlfriend material."

"I think she'd been in a long relationship. Something left over from college."

"And what about you—what had you been in?"

"I'd been in a long relationship myself. But out of it recently. Looking for a young lawyer to hang out with, 'cause I figured that's what she'd want to hear."

"So you kiss her on the balcony, under the stars. She's short or tall."

"She's short. She's pretty little."

Another button. It drove the color to Whitney's cheeks and the blood to her temples.

"Wow. A little petite blonde buzzing bee. Lucky you, right out of the gate."

"There were plenty of strikeouts. I went to bars around the apartment. I'd sit there, order a beer, bring a magazine. Wonder if there was any possible way to talk to a stranger and not be creepy. I saw a girl waiting for a date who'd clearly no-showed. Thought about saying something, swooping in to save the night—but decided against compounding her and my embarrassment. Picked up a slice of pizza and went home instead. It's a challenge, for me at least, when you take all the tools off the table.... All the ways people actually meet, and I'm stuck at happy hours with junior associates."

"But I didn't use the apps, either," she said. "And it wasn't so hard for me."

"Terrific. Let's go, then. Your turn."

"No way, José. You're making out on the balcony with your petite blonde legal beagle."

"And it goes like it goes."

"This is the first woman you've slept with besides me since college. It couldn't have been that boring."

"We move inside. It's cold. We move to her room."

"Even though the roommates are gone."

"You remember what it's like—fear of the walk-in. It's

there even if it's not rational. I could tell she didn't do this very often."

"And so you head to her room. It smells like Zara. Dresses from Anthropologie hung up on a rolling rack in the corner of the converted third bedroom. Scarves over the lights and *This Is Water* on her bedside table."

Will grinned with a swelling in his cheeks. An unbidden love for this woman.

"Two pairs of neon Nike Flyknits kicked in the corner," Whitney went on. "The Lulu leggings with the cutouts that show off some thigh and make her feel sexy."

"Actually, that's what she was really wearing all night."

"Bare legs, I thought."

"Who knows?" he said, grinning again, the heat really humming in his cheeks now.

"Well, bring us back to reality, then.... You're in her room. You're drinking vodka sodas on a twin bed squeezed in next to the steam pipe."

"She puts on The Weeknd and blushes and whispers in my ear that it's what she masturbates to."

"Come on."

"With headphones, though," he said. "The roommates."

"And so a silencer for the vibrator?"

"I didn't ask. Maybe she's old-fashioned."

"So things are getting less subtle," she said. "Good for you two."

"And then things go from there."

"More, please. Clothes come off. She's got a tight little bod and big tits and an ass that floats like it's filled with helium. She laments the fact that Equinox hasn't opened a location near the bridge, and so she has to work out by the office on her lunch break."

"We were a fair match," he said. "Nobody had a right to be too disappointed by the other."

"But, c'mon, your hands are back on her thighs. It's what she's wanted since she spotted you at the event. It's what she had in mind in the cab."

"Right, we screw around."

"What's her underwear like?"

"What do you mean?"

"The women in my classes are older than me—I know what rich 38-year-olds around Union Square wear. I know what my friends wear. What about the youths?"

"She's, like, four years younger than us."

"So Victoria's Secret. Hot pink. Straps and hearts. G-string."

"Light blue something. Not much material."

"You're saying you wish I wore that."

"It was all that was going through my head."

"You wish I dressed like a stripper beneath the Céline."

"I've been searching for the right way to say it for years."

"So you get her out of the straps and hearts and strings. She thinks she's in a *Fifty Shades* movie. She's practically gonna come from the soundtrack alone. Meanwhile you've got your tongue in her pussy and a finger in her ass."

"Jesus." Will looked to the bartender again, searched the dining room for their waitress. Of course nobody was paying attention to them. Of course nobody cared. They were as inconsequential to their surroundings as they'd been their whole trip.

"And she's totally shaved, I'd assume?"

"Whit, I dunno."

"Oh, you don't remember that either? You didn't notice?"

"If I had to characterize the experience, I would say that

she had gotten ready for the night with the intention of being naked with someone."

"Completely waxed, then."

"It reminded me of college," Will said, smiling now. "Before I met you."

"And so what about Will, then?" she said, plowing ahead. "What does he get out of it?"

"What he'd expected?" he said. "She kept asking if it was okay, and if she was doing it all right, and if there was anything she could do differently."

"Hot."

"After a little while I went back to doing what I was doing and things started driving toward maybe-sex."

"She can't believe how lucky she's got. Someone who knows how to handle himself. Meanwhile, you're certainly ready for maybe-sex. A stranger for the first time in seven years."

"And honestly?" he said. "It was around then that I started thinking about work. It was getting late and all I could think about was what needed to get done before noon, and how much I hated every last element of that work, and how terrible I was bound to feel in the morning."

She breathed deeply through her nose. "If nothing else about this story is true, I know that detail is."

"And so as I'm sort of drifting to tomorrow's to-do list, just kinda going about whatever business, she says to me, 'You have great hands,' and—"

Whitney burst. She laughed like she hadn't all trip, a little squeaky wheel of delight. Her eyes asked for more. More more more.

"And the music keeps breaking," he said, picking it up again. "Cutting in with ads for stores around where she went to college. Must've been tied to the zip code where she signed up for her non-premium service. Ads for grocery stores in upstate New York."

"Colgate. Hamilton. Skidmore," she said.

"Sure," he said.

"You didn't get a good look at the sweatshirts crumpled up in the closet?"

"Do you want me to pick one?"

She rolled her eyes. "So the music eventually cuts back in. It keeps her in the mood. She's still gearing up."

"And, yeah, at some point she just kinda says it sweetly, she gets up in my ear again and whispers, 'Do you want to have sex?' "

"Very polite lawyer bee."

"And so we have sex."

"How?"

"The normal way."

"She's on the bottom."

"She's on the bottom, she's on top."

"The normal *ways*," Whitney said. "She has the night of her life. She's making a real show of it since no one's on the other side of the temporary walls for the first time in months. You make her come seven, eight times."

"Here's the part I've been waiting for, though."

"Uh oh."

"Here's the whole point of everything up to now," he said, shifting on his seat. "It's happening, there's all the normal stuff, she seems to be enjoying herself. The album's running through again for the second time and another ad's playing for three-for-one something or other. Then she sort of scoots up the bed and gives the impression that she might turn over and face the other way."

"She wants you to fuck her from behind."

"Hold on. We're just sort of going through the motions, nothing crazy, she's still on her back, but we go to shift things up. It's all happening slowly. But then, without warning, the whole right side of my face just *cracks*—like it's been hit by a two-by-four or something. Somehow this knee's come gunning for me. This limb, connected in no way to the hips beneath me, has come whooshing like a propeller blade, smack in my face, and *hard*. Kneecap, leg bones. All at once, my face is hot and damp. Eye and cheek throbbing, nose gushing."

"Oh my god!" Whitney, alight. Whitney, in love. Those gleaming teeth. Those wide wet elastic lips.

"She's mortified. She hops up. Throws on a robe. I ask for directions to the bathroom and end up in a closet. I must be bleeding out like a pig all over the place. I find the bathroom, close the door, get a good look at myself, naked and pasty and pathetically out of shape. Just the sight everyone wants to see after imagining themselves doing all the right things in bed. It looks like I've murdered an animal in the sink, there's so much blood. I get some toilet paper up my nostril. Clean up as best I can. Watch my dick shrivel in the mirror."

"Your clothes are in the bedroom."

"It's not the most comfortable three minutes, getting dressed again."

"God, I legitimately feel terrible for her."

"I say goodbye."

"You kiss her good night. You mitigate the humiliation, I hope."

"No kiss. It's late. There's been a lot of drinking and mouthing around. There's some thick breath. I don't know how okay I make her feel about the whole situation. I sort of hold her hand and shake it and tell her there's nothing to be sorry about."

"You *shake* her hand goodbye?" Whitney said, pressing her palms to her cheeks like the Munch. "Oh, Will..."

"I know. I was rusty. I was out of practice. But, hold on, there's more. When I get to the front door, I can't manage the right combination of the deadbolt with the other two locks while standing there in the dark. Then I hear this creature scratching with keys on the other side of the door, and we screw each other up again and again until ultimately I'm standing there in front of this mousy brunette wearing a backpack stuffed with bricks, and a Nalgene bottle clipped to the strap with a carabiner. One of the roommates, I presume. The hospital resident. She can't take her eyes off me. And it sorta gives me butterflies, if I'm honest. This impression I seem to be making on women all over the city all night. What I've forgotten, of course, is that I basically have a bloody tampon sticking out of a hole in my face. Naturally I offer her my hand, too, and *we* shake. She looks reasonably mortified. For her friend mostly, I'm sure. I could be a home invader, for all she knows. I wish her a good night. I ride the elevator down and watch my face warp in and out in the dented reflection of the doors. I looked like one of the Picassos we saw yesterday.... I step out in the cold night. I hail a cab. Return home from the strange land across the river, my head pulsating, my face all bloody..."

"And your balls gone blue."

"Nice," he said. Will snorted and finished what was left in his glass. "Foreshadowing, for what it's worth?...I didn't come with anyone."

"Wow," Whitney said, shocked and saddened in equal

proportions. "That's terrible. Foreshadowing, for what it's worth?...The same can't be said for me."

What timing! The waitress was at their shoulders. She apologized for the delay. She pointed to the chalkboard above the bar with its inscrutable Catalan. Through her broken English and their pathetic Spanish the three were able to agree on the simplest order: whatever the chef suggested. It was the sort of friction-less decision that might cost them a fortune. But the risk was less than picking out the names of dishes they couldn't decipher. They understood the waitress to be asking about food restrictions, and they both shook their heads no, and it was a thing, like so many things, that was radically compatible between them. It was precisely the reason why they'd gotten engaged.

When Will proposed, he managed to do the thing he'd worried would be impossible: he actually surprised Whitney. They'd been together for seven years. They'd shared spaces and they'd lived apart. They'd traveled long distances to visit one another for a night, for three hours. They'd left parties to talk on the phone. They'd Skyped across oceans. They'd moved in together, into a studio apartment of their own, no roommates, no bathroom split among people they weren't sleeping with. They'd bored their single coworkers, accepted their role as the practically married couple among their wider searching set. When they'd been introduced to new partners of friends, those fledgling pairs looked to them to share the laws of enduring chemistry. They obviously knew something about sticking it out. After all, they'd been together since college.

Senior spring, but still. They'd met in the gardens. They'd seen one another before, but had never spoken until then. Which was at least half by design. For by the afternoon they came into each other's lives, Whitney had been operating for some time at a frequency that she and she alone was tuned to, moving about campus with urgency and purpose, and a well-honed indifference to student life. She was just ready—had been ready all her life, maybe—to get up and out and on with it. Just as she had been with her first exit, when she left home for school. It was time now to get going with the life she'd been looking for all this time. Consequently, she seemed then to carry herself like someone with a hard-won secret or a past forged by fire, or at least like someone with several somethings figured out. It was the thing that attracted Will to her so very much that first afternoon—that she possessed a knowledge of herself like no one else he knew, like someone in *at least* her mid-twenties.

Whitney would joke with Will for weeks and then months and then years that they couldn't have met a day earlier. That it was serendipitous timing, the only way it could've worked out. Until that afternoon, she'd argue, he wouldn't have been ready for her—submitting his sweat-stained T-shirts and milkshake addiction and lack of a single credit card to his name as evidence of the lack of requisite maturity. But deep down, Whitney knew that it was really she who had needed every last hour up to that point to complete her transformation away from where she'd come from and who she'd been.

There would be a grand dispute in the years that followed about who smiled at whom first. But what is undeniable is that the screenplay Whitney was reading that day was a screenplay Will knew by heart. And when he told her so, she told him to prove it. He asked her to read a setup, and when she did, he delivered Michael's lines to Kay: *This one time, this one time I'll let you ask me about my affairs.*

What made the whole thing spark, though, wasn't that he'd answered correctly, but rather how embarrassed Whitney had been made by his earnestness. She burst into laughter, the squeaky wheel of delight that he'd soon learn meant that the comedy was actually tickling her nose. Still, she picked another scene and read another prompt, and though he knew those lines too—knew them like breathing—he refrained this time. Will had proven that he'd understood. And that successful navigation of the challenge—that restraint and that pivot—was what prompted each of them to draw for one another, for several warm hours, much of the map of their separate lives apart up until then.

He left her there in the gardens that afternoon because he had to meet some friends for dinner downtown, near the house they shared. There was a March Madness game on and their school was playing, did she know that? Of course she knew—but she let him tell her himself. They had won in the first two rounds of the tournament. They were in the Sweet Sixteen thanks to the junior star, JJ Pickle, who had led them deeper into the postseason than the program had ever been before. But besides JJ Pickle, Will and his housemates were certain the winning streak had been preserved because they'd each eaten a fried-chicken sandwich during both the first half and the second half of the first two tournament games. It was important to do their part again tonight, she surely understood.

She liked that he walked away from her that day, that he left her there in the long shadows that hadn't been present when they'd first started chatting. She liked that he didn't ask for her number, even if he'd meant to. She could find him, just as he could find her. But of course, after all those years of never crossing paths, they bumped into each other at a bar that very night. Maybe she went downtown knowing that there was a chance. Maybe she went downtown knowing that that was the point. They'd dispute that intention, too, for weeks and then months and then years. But if running into each other out of the blue again wasn't a clear enough sign from the universe that they'd better go home together that night, then they didn't know what was.

When Whitney woke up beside Will the next morning, she surprised herself with how purely at home she felt in his bed. She wasn't concerned by the light coming through the beach towels he'd nailed to the window frame in lieu of blinds, nor by the laundry lining the baseboard that made it impossible to tell whether the floors were carpet or hardwood. The only thing that bothered her even a little that late-March morning was the realization that they had just six weeks left of college to make up for all the lost time. She rested her head on his chest. She watched his eyes flutter to consciousness. But even as she stretched her mind to its vastest limits, it would've been impossible for Whitney to comprehend that it would be Will, and Will alone, for the next seven years of her life.

The waitress plopped down the first dish: garlic shrimp and fried eggs. They were starved, but they ate patiently. They didn't know how many dishes they were in for. They hadn't any idea what was coming.

"Well, go ahead then," Will said. "Your turn."

"Okay," Whitney said, cautiously. "Um…it happened early."

"I don't doubt it. The whole thing was your idea. You were hungry."

"I didn't do anything to prompt it, it just…"

"That face, that body, that California light...*who could resist?*"

She shook her head faintly. "More like: locked inside a hotel during a lovely sunset, hiding in the corner of the restaurant, drafting notes."

"Stretched out long and lithe on the striped yellow beach beds of a hotel on the water," he continued. "A handmade sign that says, 'I may be engaged but I'm DTF.'"

Now she was the one looking around at the staff, looking for anyone listening. She forked a shrimp. "Alone in the hotel restaurant, not even late, but the place has the feeling of it being late, the way everything does out there. The restaurant's cleared out by nine-thirty. I've got a glass of wine and a shooting script that needs to solve a location fuck-up. Flooded basement in a bar they scouted for weeks."

"You told me about it. I assumed you figured it out and went to bed."

"That was the plan," she said. "But I'm no longer alone in the restaurant. There's a man at the bar. He's ordering a drink. He flips over a shoulder and catches me staring.... The guy looks like Adrien Green. The guy *really* looks like Adrien Green. Turns out it's Adrien Green."

"Come on."

"At the bar. All alone. Waiting for a drink. And he smiles at me."

"You spend forty-eight hours in L.A., single in the world for the first time as a functional adult, and your first night out you run into one of your top five dead or alive?"

"I thought for a minute you'd sent him. A 1-2-3 welcome gift."

"I should've thought of it," Will said. He was wearing

the shock in his face still. He shook his head. "So does he do the smile?"

"He does the smile," Whitney said. "You can see all of his teeth. The big rubbery gums. He does the whole thing in a flash—*GQ*-cover-serious to mischievous little boy—and I start to feel my skin, like, getting turned inside out."

"All right, fewer *Tiger Beat* sensations.... So you go up and tell him about your predicament."

"The flooded bar or the fact that I've only got thirty days to hit three?"

"You tell him you need to ask him for a favor..." Will said.

"Weirdly, he gets his drink and walks straight over to me," Whitney said. "Stands right there and keeps smiling. Asks what I'm working on. Asks if he can sit down."

"Do you tell him that you're a professional woman with an important job that can't be disrupted by German-English movie stars of a certain woman-melting age?"

"I tell him about the show and he says it's exactly the sort of thing he wishes he got asked to read for more often. That it's just another strike against an agent who hasn't given him anything good to look at lately."

"By this time he's sitting?"

"He's sitting, and I guess I'm pretending that he's just another person staying at the hotel who's come down for a nine-thirty nightcap."

"But you don't tell him that while you're a perfectly responsible twenty-nine-year-old woman, you have zero control over your heart, mind, and pussy in the presence of a bona fide celebrity?"

Her face was overtaken by a wide wine smile. She really did love him. "I think it became clear by the end of the encounter. . . . But no, at that moment I acted as though I was just another industry executive who spends her life in meetings around famous people."

"You don't tell him to forgive you, but you know everything about every woman he's dated, every film he's gone out for and failed to land, and how every critic described his cock when he unzipped his pants in the gigolo movie?"

"*A burnished bronze bell clacker,*" she said.

"*A hazard in a lightning storm,*" he said.

"I edged up to it. We talked about streaming services. We talked about shows he liked. He talked about the mutant thing and the new PTA. I finished my drink and told him I'd seen a couple audition tapes of his. For something that never got made, from when he was fresh off the boat. *West End straight to here,* he'd said on the tape, and they asked him where he was living and he'd said *a couple blocks off the park in the East Village.* So I told him I lived right there these days."

"By yourself, all alone," Will said.

"It never really came up," Whitney said. "But I got the sense that he wouldn't have cared, either way."

"So it's all just as you'd hoped it'd be out there. Shooting scripts and audition tapes and Adrien Green."

"We had another drink. He slid around the booth to look at the scenes I was reviewing. He gave some suggestions I didn't ask for, and at some point his hand fell into my lap."

"Just like that."

"A nice little rhyme to your and my experiences."

"Bare legs, too?"

"Jeans for me. But I got the picture. He paid for the drinks."

"So it's his room or yours, then?" Will said. "I still can't believe this."

"Here's the thing," Whitney said, smiling helplessly again, "he wasn't even staying there. He was just making a dutiful little sweep of the hotel bars after a charity dinner he'd attended nearby."

"God, why didn't I think of that? Get off the subway after work, scour the Standard and the Bowery. See if any beautiful bundles of nerves seem lonely?"

"So he comes up to the room," she said. "He plugs in his iPhone and puts on some English band from the eighties. He flips through the books on the coffee table...he actually *uses* all the stuff they set out to make the room look cool."

"And from there it's from there."

"I...I guess that's right. How much detail?..."

"I don't need to know much, I guess. I mean, I've seen the guy shirtless in every magazine we work with. And I've fucking seen him full-frontal on an Imax screen."

"He was shorter than I expected, if that's any consolation."

"Shorter than me?"

"Well...maybe still taller than you, but I was expecting the oversize muscle-bound mutant. Six-five or something."

"Did he sleep over?"

"That's a...that's a question that's hard..."

"You just fucked all night."

"We stayed up for a while."

"Jesus," Will said. "So what do we mean here? What are we talking?"

"Well, we just kinda kept...I dunno."

"One after another in a hotel room on the beach," Will said.

"There were a couple, a few," Whitney said. "And then a shower."

"He fucked you in the shower."

"Then a couple more hours, I dunno."

"Whitney. I got a bloody nose and a black eye, and you played out your all-time fantasy."

"Look, it wasn't anything. He's mostly an idiot."

"Who was nominated for an Academy Award. Who has a cock that every late-night host and male lead in Hollywood has paid homage to with envious jokes."

"Look, it was too big, if you want to know the truth. It was gross."

"Whit!"

"I don't know what you want me to say!" She was laughing now. Pink in her cheeks, guilt gleaming in her teeth. "I'm telling you the truth—it was way too big, it wasn't for me."

"You're saying you could barely get your mouth around it," he said.

"Will," she said.

"It's so gross, but you can't stop hopping aboard for another ride. Light comes up and it's time to go to set, and hearts are still pouring out of your eyes as he strolls out the door and says he can't wait to see you again."

"It was one night. He doesn't give a shit about me," she said. "I never heard from him again. It was purely sexual."

Will strained his hair through his fingers, his face practically in the *gambes*.

"Seriously, that's all it was," she said. "It's the whole point of what this was about!"

"I hope that counted for all three. I hope that gave you

the nice rounded-out experience you were looking for when you suggested three instead of one."

"That's not fair—we agreed on three together."

"I'll take that to mean it didn't count as all three."

"Look, I'm not exactly loving hearing about yours, either," she said. "But I didn't say all that to hurt you. I just, I'm telling you the truth, 'cause those are the rules, and what's the point of lying at this stage? It was one night with this one guy."

"The longest night with the biggest movie star with the biggest dick."

"*A* movie star with *a* big dick."

"*It was purely sexual.* Christ," he said. "The explanation that puts everyone at ease."

"Well, guess what?" she said. "You're up. But I've got to go to the bathroom first."

"Ask the waitress for another bottle of wine if you see her," he said.

Earlier in the year, they turned twenty-nine within a couple weeks of one another and celebrated with an all-expenses-paid trip back down to school. Whitney had been invited to give a talk at the arts-and-media fair where she'd learned about TV jobs in the first place. But the trip also served as an anniversary of sorts. It was the overnight-blooming spring of that part of the country, during the same time of year when they'd first met. The spring of the basket-ball tournament. The spring of the Masters. The spring of Thomas Wolfe's plump adjectives. This was why they'd chosen to go to school where they'd gone. They'd both vis-ited then, and walked right into the marketing scheme—the trees plugged in like strands of neon, the students slung out half naked on the quads, classes outside, classes dismissed.

And though they'd skipped previous reunions, and felt in almost all ways beyond it, they were heavily tethered still, too. They didn't miss opportunities like this one—to feel the feeling of that place again, over and over. It was, after all, their point of origin. It was where they'd found each other during the time of year when they'd changed their lives for good.

On their first night back on campus, Will parked at the edge of the gardens, where he knew there was a break in the hedge. They were on their way to dinner, she didn't know what he was doing. No one was allowed in the gardens after dark—same rules as ever. But it had never kept anyone out. It was one of the unofficial graduation requirements, sex in the gardens. They'd missed some of the others but had checked that one off before the last day of classes. She'd brought a blanket and worn a skirt and no underwear. Now, as then, they strolled into the gardens hand in hand. There were no lights except the bright blue emergency beacons. They found the path by squinting and consulting the yellowed map in their heads. Whitney bent at the waist to sniff the flowers. Will stared up into the royal canopy of the sky and at the stars that pierced through crisply. There was an underwater darkness. They found the clearing, the wide-open grassy hill where students liked to lie out and read or toss a baseball around. And in the vicinity of where they'd first encountered one another, Will slowed his steps and dropped to a knee.

He had a ring in his hand—the ring his mom had given Will that he kept in a shoebox in their closet, the ring Whitney had never known about. Her fingers flew to her mouth, a gesture Will had never seen Whitney make before. She started crying and she lifted Will to his feet. She hugged him and he could feel the dampness on his chest, the quake in her bones. But he couldn't tell if she'd said yes. She was getting snotty and he held her face in his hands and asked her what she'd said. She nodded but didn't say it and he took it to be good enough. He slid the ring onto a finger of her shaking hand, but it was too big—for her ring finger and any other. And so he pocketed the ring. They would have forever to get it right. It was the perfect surprise. It was exactly the right place and exactly the right time. And though he couldn't make out her face in the darkness as they walked back to the car, he figured she must've looked as happy as he'd always hoped she would.

They decided not to tell anyone that night. Not while they were down at school and not right away when they got back to New York. It was tacky to post something so meaningful to social media. Besides, they'd need to tighten the band first. Till then, the ring could go back in the shoebox in the closet. They talked about telling their parents or at least a couple friends, but they pushed it to the end of the weekend and then it was a very busy week at work, one of the busier weeks of the year for each of them. And before long it was another weekend, and it had been nine days of silence. Of late nights at the office and early mornings at the gym. Of no meals at home together and not much chatter. No conversation about a potential date or venue. They'd talked about locations before, in the abstract: somewhere on the coast in California, somewhere in the neighborhood in New York. But there was something that obviously hadn't locked into place the way it should.

One night that second week back, he asked her about it. She denied anything was wrong. They fought a little bit about the full sink of dirty dishes and the pileup of laundry in the corner of the studio. A week later, in for the night on a Friday, they drank whiskey and lemonade, and as they drained the cocktail shaker they finally cut to it. She was worried. Not just about her, but about him. They were meant to be together, she was certain, but there was something that had been gnawing at her, she said, low-level gumming her guts for years. They were still young. But they'd spent their twenties together. They'd gotten old prematurely. What happened if that suppression of twenties-dom reared its head someday down the road? If all the crazy, if all the lost nights, if all the solitary searching and shame they'd skipped right over bubbled up and buried them alive at a future time and place TBD? What then?

He knew her well. He knew what she was really saying. "You're worried I'm gonna want to fuck other people," he said.

She didn't answer right away. She had tears in her eyes and she looked at him cautiously. "I'm worried about you, I'm worried about me.... We're still ... changing. We're still becoming who we are. We still have some things to figure out, don't we?"

"I'd never do that to you and you'd never do that to me," he said, still caught up on the first part.

"That doesn't mean it doesn't hit me here," she said, placing painted nails on her stomach.

"So what," he said.

"So nothing," she said.

And they danced around it for the rest of the night, and the next day and the day after that. And neither of them told anyone else anything. But then one night while they were screwing around, teasing each other's bodies, bringing each other to the edge, they started saying it aloud. For fun at first, just speaking the words, making one imagine what it would be like if the other were with a stranger. To be single for a night, a weekend, a couple weeks max. To bury the question for good. To go out and have one last time, or maybe two, or at the absolute max three. It was like someone had cracked open the window and let the outside in, a razor-sharp breeze in the bedroom.

No one knew about the engagement still. Another week passed. There was an elaboration of the fantasy. Busy days at work, but a rush to get home. More sex than they'd had in years. Personas embodied. Strangers come between them. He asked her if they should finally tell their parents. She said it was probably a good idea. But nobody called home. Not yet.

Another few days. Her bosses asked her if she could spend a month in L.A. To keep an eye on the production of a pilot she'd helped to develop. On previous trips out west she'd stayed with Will's folks, but this was different. This was the most critical trip of her nascent career. She had to be in Santa Monica. Close enough for when they needed her when they needed her. They'd put her up in a nice hotel. It was the perfect opportunity, she told him. It would be one month, five weeks max. Late April to late May. A discrete period. Away from here. Somewhere else. Both of us with one month to work out what needed working out.

He was stunned. He couldn't believe she was serious. She saw the hurt in the lines around his mouth, and she flew across the apartment to his side, assuring him that she was just kidding, she didn't mean it, it was only a game for the bedroom.

He told her he thought maybe she was right, and that he could do it if she could do it. Only, could she really do it?

She was the one who kicked him in the shins when his eyes followed a pair of yoga pants across the street. Who flicked his forehead when he smiled too long at a barista. Who twisted up the bedsheets when he described the summer associates fresh out of Stanford and Yale, lawyers who were so much younger than she was now, leggy redheads and petite blondes.

Four or five weeks. She thought about it. She could handle it if he could handle it, she said. She was pretty sure she could.

"One, then?" he said.

"One it is," she said.

And with their minds sweating a little at the prospect, their hands and mouths found each other's bodies right there, and she wound up bent over the couch, her dress pushed up around her waist, her hair gripped tightly in her fiancé's fist.

Then one became two and two became three. Three was the only number that made sense, they decided. A variety of experience, a triangulation. A system that enabled each to take a swing right out of the box. That wouldn't necessitate an assessment of whether the he or she across the bar was good enough for the one and only shot. Two meant too much comparison and contrast, an attempt at the full spectrum of possibility as defined by two points on a line. But three—three provided depth and shading and roundnesses. Three meant opportunity in three dimensions, three dimensions of a lifetime of experience crowded into a month of secret living.

Whitney in L.A. Will in NYC.

1-2-3, they'd call it.

1-2-3, in emails and texts and occasionally over the phone.

1-2-3, they said in front of a friend before Whitney left for California, and the friend was none the wiser.

They wouldn't tell a soul. They wouldn't tell one another until the end of it all, when they'd go somewhere special to reveal the scheme in full. They would take a trip, Memorial Day weekend. After it was wrapped, after the month-plus apart. They'd get on a plane and drink in the details of a foreign city and then, on the final evening, fill each other in on the plot points of their lives while they'd been living on opposite edges of the continent. Together, on their trip, they would walk the streets and see the sights and fall in love all over again. And on the very last night, they would sit across from one another and eat strange food and hopefully not barf from envy and rage as they spilled their secrets about what they'd done and who they'd done it with.

The flash-fried rice balls followed Whitney back from the bathroom to the bar.

"What if I told you there wasn't a Number Two?" Will said.

"I'd know you were lying," she said, sitting down. "I see it in your eyes that you want this one to hurt."

"I don't want it to hurt. I'm the one who asked you to marry me. I'm the one who was fine with everything as it was."

"And so it's all my fault, all this. You get to chase twenty-five-year-olds around the East Village—that burden? I'm responsible for holding your feet to that fire?"

"I'm just saying, I didn't need it. And I'll never need it again. But let me preface this by saying I don't think you're gonna like Number Two."

"Petite-er, blonde-er."

"I slept with Kelly Kyle."

"*What?*"

"It happened once, not much to report."

"*What the fuck?!*"

"Hold on, hold on, look . . ."

"There was *one rule*. One *cardinal* rule. No one we *knew*. No one who knew both of us. No one we fucking *work* with."

"Hold on. Kelly left. She put in for a transfer. Her last day was a few weeks ago."

"I said: no friends, no coworkers. Not Lily. Not Christina. Not *Kelly*. I remember literally *naming* her."

"Look, I'm sorry, but we don't work together anymore. I knew better than that."

"There was a reason it had to be strangers."

"Don't make this more than it is. You know the disadvantage I had. You were in a city all alone with endless options, all working in *the industry*. You were surrounded by movie stars and people you had a million things in common with. I was stuck in our apartment, couldn't bring anyone home, couldn't use the bee app, couldn't meet people through work. I either had to creep at bars or, I don't know what. How do people meet other people without their friends or phones?"

"I just wish it wasn't someone I've *met*," she said. "Someone I can *picture*."

"Trust me, I can picture Adrien Green better than you can picture her."

"The day we ran into her and her boyfriend in the Rockaways."

"That was, like, three years ago."

"Those perfect giant round tits. That line that no one's supposed to have running right down the middle of her stomach."

"Whit, I don't know what to say. Want me to skip this one? I'm sorry this upsets you. I'm sorry it's easy for you to say *It was purely sexual* but not to hear it."

"It *wasn't*, though," she said. "That's the whole thing. You had history. She was, like, your work wife..."

"Jesus, no she wasn't. This whole thing is exactly as fucked as I thought it would be," he said. "I'm glad it's over and I hope you got what you needed."

"*What I needed?* There it is again! You're such a prince for letting us do this. You're such a noble innocent for your sacrifice."

"How 'bout you dive into your Number Two, then?" Will said.

"What did you tell her about us?"

"I said you were in L.A. and we were on a break."

"And what did she say? Was she surprised?"

"She didn't ask for more. People's relationships are complicated. She said she hoped we figured out what would make us happiest."

"Do you think she told anyone?"

"I asked her not to."

"And what about that guy—is she still dating him?"

"They broke up a while ago, I guess. She's been single and struggling with it. That was part of why she's moving back to Chicago. Nothing keeping her here. Some friends. But she's from there. Figured it was the right time."

"So, how?"

"Her going-away drinks. I wasn't planning on it. I wasn't scheming."

"You have a few beers and just stay later than everyone else," Whitney said.

"That's definitely one thing I missed out on by being with

you all this time," Will said. "I missed staying out hours later than I wanted to, chasing the slimmest chance around town, burning through cash, and coming up empty-handed at four in the morning in a weird neighborhood."

"But not this time," Whitney said. "You knew this one was in the bag."

"C'mon," Will said. "I get along with lots of the women I work with."

"And none more than this one. All those happy hours at Johnny-O's."

"Cheapest beers near the office. So what? We liked to go for beers after work."

"All those long hours and late nights. You must've wondered about it."

"What are you doing? What are you trying to pin on me?"

"I just mean there were a lot of drinks over three years. A lot of shared bitching about coworkers and clients. It's not like it's out of the realm of possibility. It happens to people. It *has* happened to people..."

Will fixed her with a disbelieving stare. "There was a woman, my age, at work for a stretch, with whom I occasionally drank beers, because she was actually down *to* drink beers. That's it."

"And that's all it is to me, too. But there was something longstanding. There was something in the air, is all I mean.... You never fucked her before?"

"I can't believe you're doing this."

"Might as well get it all out now. I'm just asking the questions while I have the opportunity."

"You didn't have to react this way," Will said. "This was the thing I worried about most the whole time. You coiling back down into that snake pit and getting me for the same old fucking thing I've more than paid for. You could've held on for twenty more minutes, gotten to the end of all this, and decided to be okay with it, but instead—"

"You're the one who broke the rules," Whitney said. "I'm just trying to lend a little context to the encounter."

"Well, now you know," Will said. "You're up. Go on, Number Two."

"You head home with her from the party," Whitney said, undeterred. "Where does she live?"

Will scraped his fork around the plate. He chewed slowly and the volume of the dining room crashed over them.

"East 80-something..." He swallowed and watched the light change in her face. "Look at that fucking grin. It's exactly what you'd hoped, isn't it?"

"It makes me feel better."

"You're such a fucking snob."

"Close to the Met because she loves art so much?"

"Closer to York."

"Even better."

"So I head up there with her after the thing. We're both pretty beat. I, unlike you, don't have it in me to spend eight straight hours going at it."

"But you get her clothes off. You get to see those glorious tits."

"The apartment smells like kitty litter. There's three or four half-drunk Juice Press bottles in the fridge."

"More please."

"White carpeting with scattered wine stains. A stand-up AC instead of an in-window unit. I don't know. Mailings of summer offers from SoulCycle. A membership application to The Wing. A fridge with a dozen Save the Dates. One of those little word-magnet things spelling out a lyric from 'Formation'—"

"I love you," Whitney said, cutting him off. "I'm sorry I lost it for a second. I know you, I trust you, I didn't even mean what I was saying. I know you didn't do anything intentionally hurtful. I recognize that you're one of the good ones. I'm sorry."

"If there's anything I've learned this month," Will said, "it's that this thing here is good, okay? You're good to me, I'm good to you. That's it."

"I know," she said swallowing hard, serious very suddenly. "I feel the same way. I love you, and I want to do this with you, and I'm sorry about a minute ago."

"I love you, too. But do me a favor and think back and count. How many times with Adrien Green?"

She failed to quell the rush of blood to her face. She failed to suppress the grin that knew the precise answer. "It's hard to count. What's the number you're looking for?"

"How many times did you stop and start again?"

"I don't know."

"You're lying. I can see how crystal-clearly you know the number."

"Enough..."

"Four, five..." he said.

"Nine?"

"*Nine?!*"

"Twelve?"

"Whitney!"

"I don't know. Six. I don't know!"

"So a new record," Will said.

"I guess it felt like a record."

"*It was purely sexual.*"

"Something to shoot for, then," she said, placing a hand in his lap.

"*It was too big, it was gross.*"

The waitress dropped off a single cube of pork belly.

"So, what," Whitney said, drawing her hand back to her knife, "you snap her bra off with one free hand and dim the lights with the other?"

"The whole time I'm thinking of you," Will said.

"Give me a fucking break."

"You and the petite blonde who broke my nose—I can't get either of you out of my mind."

"I'll bet Kelly gives effortful head."

"I don't know."

"I bet she watches herself in the mirror above the bureau that's caked in foundation dust. I bet she watches porn for tricks and practices on her hairbrush."

"All based on a conversation at the beach three years ago?"

"I've met her other times. I met her at that holiday party. You glean things."

"It was all fine."

"You do it this way and that. You shove your face between her legs. She says, *You have great hands.*"

"All I wanted to do was go to sleep. I couldn't stay up any later. I was thinking about work again."

"You run your tongue along the heart she's shaved into her bush."

"It didn't look like she'd been up to much down there for a while, if you really want to know. Unlike Number One, she did not appear to be expecting company. Based on the mess of mail, and the cat box, and whatever was going on with that situation..."

"So between the downstairs nothing and the downstairs

everything of your pair, you really did catch the full spectrum we thought wouldn't be possible with just two, huh?"

"The missing variety of seven years out of the game," he said.

"You ask her to ride you so you can watch her bounce," she said. "So you can stare at that line on her stomach."

"I don't even know what this line is you keep referring to."

"You know the line. Which is why you try out all the positions, to get a good look at every inch of that body. You flip her around. You smack her butt. You pull her hair—not too hard, though, 'cause, remember, you're one of the good guys."

"She faked a couple big crescendos."

"And we've already revealed the fact that you certainly didn't get there."

"While I was buttoning up my shirt, she asked me if I wanted her to try again. I told her that it was okay, it had been great anyway. Her face scrunched up and she told me she could just add it to the list of things she'd failed at recently. I started getting dressed a little faster. I didn't love where this was going. She said she was leaving New York because it had spit her out and left her with nothing to show for her years there. She was heading home and she knew she'd never leave Chicago again. A few hours earlier, she'd told everyone at the party that going home was the thing she was most looking forward to on earth. Now she's crying and I can't find one of my shoes, and so I hand her the tissue box on the floor near the headboard. She doesn't take it. Just lies there, with the covers up to her waist and tears in her eyes, her tits slipping off the tabletop of her chest, just kinda pooled up there in her armpits. Man, they look like a pain in the ass to deal with. Just, the whole scene...I felt terrible."

"But you leave anyway."

"I leave and tell her I'm sure I'll see her again before she gets out of town."

"But you don't."

"I don't."

"Poor Kelly."

"Your Number Two, then," Will said. "Please."

"You're not just framing it all this way for my benefit?" Whitney said. "The bloody nose. The tears. The boredom through and through."

"I guess you'll never know."

"But it's useful for me to know before I head into this one. Just to help me calibrate my telling." She sipped from a nearly full glass and considered the volume of liquid. "We'll never finish the second bottle."

"What are you talking about?" he said. "We have half that chalkboard left."

They took a break and teased each other about their eating and their drinking. A breather before diving into Whitney's second, and each of their thirds. The server brought the new dishes at an accelerated pace. Spiny urchin shells stuffed with whipped uni. Razor clams. A pair of ruby-red langoustines. A bowl of fried potatoes. They were getting fatter. Their teeth were turning pink. The overhead fan had stopped for some reason and they were starting to sweat through their clothes.

He'd never felt the sensation of her belonging to him more than he did just then. And that same feeling of possession was overwhelming her in the moment, as well. Whatever they'd devised for themselves, it had worked, it was working. He wanted to break the new record she'd set. She wanted to make sure he never had an up-close look at another woman's pubic hair again.

"Go on, then," Will said. "Number Two."

"He was old."

"Forty."

"Fifty-five."

"C'mon."

"One of the things they wanted me to do while I was out there was make a last-ditch play to get this novelist to let us option his first book. It's not my favorite thing, but John read it in college and it changed him or whatever, and he'd failed to get this guy to go with us before."

"A novelist."

"It's a boring story," she said. "But he's lived in the Palisades for twenty-five years. Has two grown kids with a first wife. Published those first couple books, wasted some time with screenplays that were never made. But John saw a series in his debut. The guy's nice, nice-looking, still has his hair. . . . But this *house*. I'd never seen anything like it. Exposed beams and ceilings and glass walls, and just *lush* like I didn't know it could be in L.A."

"A novelist," Will said again, and Whitney rolled her eyes.

"The book's not even *good*. I did it as a favor to John. I drank the guy's coffee. I made an appeal. I knew he had no intention of working with us. I could've left, but I wanted to tour the house. These warm rooms where the light splashed in. Bookshelves on every wall. His kids were handsome and didn't look like the sort who were doing blow in Hollywood clubs at fourteen—but what do I know? The ex-wife was an actress. I said she looked familiar even though she didn't, and he said she was on some network shows in the nineties.

He was tan, nineties-handsome himself. I don't know, there wasn't anything in particular about it, except I was running out of time out there, and I've always been curious what it'd be like to be with someone that age. He didn't want to do the show, and I could care less, but I thought I'd make his day. It was simple as that. I didn't want to leave yet. I really wanted to get another look around. I really wanted to see the upstairs."

"So you fucked *the house*."

She laughed. She looked uncomfortably full. "I guess that's right."

"You asked for an extended tour."

"I just went upstairs and he followed me and I guess I sat on the edge of the bed and he sat on the edge of the bed and nobody said anything, and then it just happened. No booze. Conventional as can be. I imagine with guys like that, they either get divorced and bang hookers, or they just kinda pack their dicks away and try to be a halfway-decent little-league coach for a while. I got the distinct impression that he was the latter."

"The un-Adrien-Green."

"It was perfectly pleasant."

"That's kinda gross, though. That's fucking old."

Whitney shrugged. "It was warm upstairs. He knew enough about what he was doing. He'd lived over there most of his life, you know? He'd been married and he'd probably dated plenty of beautiful women. The sort who are just...around. He was probably more confused than anything. Halfway through, he needed to catch his breath and I sorta did the work on top."

"But you got there anyway. Nice and primed from a record-breaking effort."

"You couldn't even call it the full thing that I'm used to, though."

"Un-Adrien to the max."

"It was like, I dunno, sliding down into a bath or something. Different than I'd had in a long time. Definitely not bad, definitely not better."

"Whereas the other one's what?"

Whitney thought about it. She wanted to get it exactly right. "Glass shattering?"

Will rubbed his face in an exaggerated fashion.

"I had my eyes closed and didn't really look at him much and wondered after the fact if he'd maybe felt used. It really was, like, we couldn't have been less connected. But it seemed to work for him. I guess I know what I'm doing, too."

"Please tell me you used a condom. The way you're saying it, this doesn't sound like a condom situation."

"I don't know," she said, and she felt Will's eyes boring deeper. "I don't think we did. But it's fine. I got tested when I got back to New York. Everything's fine."

"You let a fucking stranger old guy, who lived in L.A. in the *nineties,* come inside you?"

Will put his forehead flat on the bar.

"It all worked out okay," she said.

"You can be fucking careless sometimes," he said without moving.

"And you made some decisions I don't love....But we made it through unscathed."

Will sat up again. "What were you thinking? Seriously?"

"I wasn't, I guess. It didn't even occur to me. I didn't have much time. I had to take what was in front of me. Just like you. I know you think I had it easier, but that's just not the case. The rest of the trip was production all day, every day. I just wasn't thinking too hard about it. Sorry."

"An old guy with a nice house," Will said.

"Just like a young guy, but old," Whitney said.

"What did the novelist have to say for himself afterward?"

"He thanked me in this deeply gracious and depressing way. The whole thing was a little surreal. Maybe it didn't happen."

"Adrien Green wakes up your body and you can't wait to put it to use again. You find the first living breathing thing with a garden and a custom modern home on the Westside."

"I'm twenty-nine years old. Every day I get older, my body gets grosser. I'm on the clock. Besides, it wasn't right away after Adrien. I was running out of days."

"Okay..." he said, swallowing. "So what about Number Three, then?"

Her brows flexed, extremely anxious-seeming all of a sudden. "You first," she said.

"Well..." he said, pausing and dropping his eyes to his plate again. "I have another confession to make. And you might not like this one, either."

"Oh, Will..." She looked like a different person than she had ten seconds ago.

"You might want to finish that wine."

"Who?"

"Just finish it."

"*Who?!*"

The bartender and the waitress turned toward them. They'd finally made them notice.

Will dragged some strange noodles around a dish of burgundy goo. He couldn't tell if the contents came from land or sea.

44

"There, uh, there wasn't a Number Three," Will said. "Sorry. I... know what the deal was. But I was a little shook after all the crying. No Three for me, unfortunately."

Whitney stared at him blankly and her breathing shifted.

"I know it's not what we said," he continued, "but I figured of all the options, you'd be better with fewer rather than—"

"I didn't..." she said, cutting him off, and swallowing hard, seizing on something, some window of opportunity. "I didn't find three guys, either.... Just two."

They sat there on their stools in silence, letting the revelations linger. They looked all at once drained. Paralyzed, almost, by their symmetry. They reached beneath the bar and squeezed each other's hands. They kneaded each other's fingers and knuckles and palms, and it felt like something they could do for the rest of their lives.

"This is good," Will said, smiling disbelievingly.

"This is exactly why this is meant to be," Whitney said, snorting with an incredible relief.

They sat there in the thickness of what they'd done and what they hadn't done. The way they'd operated in the world without one another, yet in unison nonetheless.

"Adrien counted as two, anyway," Will said.

"And Kelly, then, too. A penalty for breaking the co-worker rule."

"*Former* coworker."

"It all worked out," Whitney said, eyes wet now, eyes red.

"And it did what you were hoping it would do?"

"I don't know what to say," she said. "I guess I just... needed this so that I never had to wonder again."

"Now we know," Will said.

"Now we know," Whitney said, smiling sadly, uncertainly. "Thank you."

They drank from their glasses, but couldn't touch another bite.

"Oh, one final confession..." It was Will. "I should tell the whole truth before we leave, and admit that I downplayed it—all of it, unfortunately. Each was, in fact, the best I've ever had."

Whitney laughed, an overwhelming release of pent-up tension. "I downplayed it, too."

"I don't think that's possible."

" 'A new record,' " she said.

"*A new record*," he said. "Jesus."

A piece of chocolate cake arrived, as though their waitress had understood where they'd wound up. And with the cake, the check. All that food, chef's choice, for half as much as they'd expected. What a meal. What a final night. What a way to cinch up the experiment. It went as well as they could've hoped. A vacation. A revelation. An eradication of the gnawing questions.

And now they were ready. They would leave in the morning. They would return once again to the apartment they shared, to the places where they existed both separately and together, to the country and to the life. They would be married in ten to fourteen months, on a cliff or in a meadow or near the windows of a restaurant that didn't cost too much to buy out. They would pick up the societal soldering iron, and carefully, consciously, fuse themselves together for good. They'd acted as they'd intended. They'd done what they needed to do. They'd played by the rules and they'd come clean. Now they would walk to the Airbnb, wake up early, catch a cab to the airport, and settle into their seats for the plane ride back to New York. The trip was finally over. It was time to go home.

Holudjöfulsins

The blackness is first, the puff of pumice and methane and ash, the dense clouds gathering over the vent, thick as balls of yarn. The breath condenses when it touches the freezing northern sky. A diffuse hot rain falls all around. Then there is fire, the first sprigs of neon pinking the undersides of the black mass. Orange threads from the overflowing cone extend in all directions. With the sound of the sky splitting in two, there comes, unsubtly, a rising red column, the dense vertical, the ultimate expulsion that seems, at its height, not to be lifting from the earth but rather pouring from the clouds like molten steel in a mill. The column holds on its true plumb for eternity-spanning seconds before it slips from its height, wavering like a slackened line, and falls as red rain back to the mouth of the volcano. The fountain reduces itself to a stewing boil and the overspill comes slower, a steady slip of the rim, orange and black icing streaming down the slopes, creeping to the valley floor and ultimately to the sea. There is for half an hour a deafening rumbling of thunder, matched in volume only by the sizzling of the lava at the surf's edge. Ash falls like pillow-fight feathers.

There is ash all around. Ash, and then steam, rising from the waves that pound the ragged shore.

The fire subsides in the evening, but the ash tumbles out tirelessly for days. It rises in ever-replenished walls of soot, puddling up in the heights above the vent. And then it spreads. Wider. Farther. Drifting as swiftly as a scent into unoccupied air. The ash moves on currents in the sky. It passes into the virgin emptinesses of the troposphere. It finds new altitudes, new canopies, new expanses of sky when there is nowhere else to go. The ashcloud speeds across the reach, darkening land and sea, a blanket of blackness stitched extra tight, indifferent to the lives of the living things below.

II.

Volcano Barcelona

Sunday

Will and Whitney woke up an hour later than they'd planned. Instead of setting an alarm, they had relied each morning of the trip on the fade-up of the sunrise that flooded the apartment. The place was spacious, twice what they had in New York at what they knew to be half the price. They were Airbnb-ing their own studio while they were away, after all. Here there were big simple rooms with not enough furniture and a sound system the owner had struggled to demo at check-in. Tall ceilings and wide windows onto the street. Sky and trees and strung-up laundry on rooftops— and towering above them all, the rainbow-scaled Nouvel in the neighborhood to the north.

The apartment had been a placid base camp for four days. It had been still. No sharp edges, no nerves. But this morning they'd shot up in a panic, their hands grasping for phones. They'd blown the grace period for the international flight. They'd be cutting it close even if they somehow got out the door in fifteen minutes. Before Will had rolled over in bed, Whitney was across the bedroom, dirty laundry flying from the floor of the closet into her butterflied suitcase.

Will was still flat, staring at his phone.

"What are you doing?" she said. "Let's go."

"I think our flight's canceled."

"What?"

"They emailed a few hours ago. I just got the notice. Red strike through the time of our flight. But doesn't say *postponed*. Let me call."

He was put on hold.

"How the fuck is it so dark out?" he said to Whitney, who was rushing still.

The wait for the next available team member was " ... for-ty min-utes."

Since entering the working world, he'd suffered those in his life who lived to discuss their airline-loyalty programs. Recently the subject had elicited more genuine excitement among friends and colleagues than movies, politics, sports, or streaming. *Platinum. Agate. Elite.* The systems had their languages, their incentive structures, their marginal benefits. Will knew picking a loyalty program was the prudent thing to do, but he worried it would only make him more boring than he suspected he already was, joining his colleagues in their deadly speech-codes of *medallion-qualification miles* and *fare classes*. Nonetheless, he coveted the ultimate benefit: the assurance that at a certain level of status, every phone call, no matter the hour, would be tended to by a real live person. A new dull passion was worth it if he could guarantee getting a human being during an emergency.

"Our flight is canceled," Will said. "And I have no status."

"I know that," Whitney said from the bathroom. "If anyone knows how little status you have, it's me."

"*I*" he said. "*It's I.*"

"*It's me,*" she said, certain at first, but feeling that certainty halve, and then halve again.

They'd have to go to the airport and get the answers direct. And so they packed as quickly as they could. They tended to move at similar speeds, on similar schedules. They woke up with each other and tried to turn out the lights at the same time. They had read that there were such things as larks and owls and sometimes one of each fell in love at their own peril. But they seemed to be calibrated in almost all the ways that mattered.

Outside it was socked in. They hadn't noticed the full extent of the weather. It reminded Will of the foggiest days at the beach growing up. Soft streetlights were boring through the haze at low heights. But no suggestion of sky. Way up was a yellow glow that slipped down a gradient into white, a thick white that threw one's relationship to space all out of whack. It was like looking out the window of an airplane during a banked turn and not knowing which way was the sun and which way the ground. Wobbling through the fog toward the cab made Will think of the word *yaw*. He should've been a pilot. The whole effect of the low light had him queasy and tripping over his feet.

They made the thirty-minute drive in twenty. The streets were empty. The boulevards were slick. The curbside at the international terminal was cluttered with passengers who looked like people with nowhere to go. Inside it was worse.

The international terminal was stacked up hundreds deep at the desks. The dense fog. This weather, apparently. If it was all just some system glitch—if everything was indeed good to go—there was no way they'd get to the front of the line in time to get an answer and make their flight. And so they found a roving representative and asked her what was going on.

"You haven't heard?" the woman said.

Will reached uncertainly for his phone. He hadn't expected the reason to be something they could've heard about.

"There's been a . . ." the woman said.

"Cancellation?" Will said.

"Computer crash?" Whitney said.

"There's been a *volcano*," the woman said. "The volcano in Iceland that"—she made an eruption with both hands— "a few days ago. It is worse now. It kept going. They thought it is small, but now it is big. The cloud it made, it is into Europe. London, first, yesterday. Today, France and Espanya. The howdoyousay . . ." She trickled with her fingers.

"Rain," Will said.

"Ash," Whitney said.

"The ash. There is no way for planes to go. Because of the ash."

"A volcano," Will said.

The woman squinted at him. She seemed skeptical still that they hadn't heard.

"We've been on vacation . . ." Whitney said, by way of explanation. "We tried to take a couple days away from our phones . . ." The truth was that they had skimped on international coverage. Or rather that Will had insisted they not pay for the exorbitant daily roaming. And so they pulled up their maps and email only when absolutely necessary. They'd spent yesterday distracted anyway, fixated on their dinner all morning and afternoon, and had passed out after the confessions like a pair of tension knots poked by needles.

"The volcano has been a problem before, but never like

this," the woman said. "Is what they say on TV. No flights. Barcelona. Madrid. Paris. London. Not like this since nine-eleven."

"No flights," Will said, still catching up. "How are we supposed to get home? What are we supposed to do?"

"This is..." the woman said, gesturing to the crowds, to the chaos in evidence, to the wider crisis that was obviously greater than the concerns of Will and Whitney's small, specific circumstances. The lines in the woman's forehead suggested that she needed them to start thinking in grander terms, beyond themselves. That if they were going to understand and she was going to be permitted to carry on with more pressing matters, they would need to calibrate to the scale here. "There is no news. No instruction. You can see yourself. You can wait in line to speak to someone, but the only thing we know right now is no flights."

"But how do they handle the rebooking?" Will said. "The cost of—"

"Don't look so..." Whitney said, cutting him off, impatient. "They're not gonna make you pay for new tickets, okay?"

"So, tomorrow, then?" Will said, ignoring her, and reaching for the woman's shoulder as she slid away from them.

"It is impossible to say," she said, halting again. "Maybe today. Maybe three days. Maybe a week. They say the volcano still..." The hands again, erupting.

"Iceland," Will said.

"Incredible, no?" The woman smiled and her eyes drifted to the ceiling, to the wavy ribs of the roof, to the luminous architecture. There was a light glowing beneath the woman's skin. There was wonder in her face so plain that it lifted her chin.

"I still don't totally understand what we're supposed to do," Whitney said.

"Maybe you wait in the line like the others?" the woman said, smiling and turning to leave finally.

The shape of the problem was letting itself in. Whitney thanked the woman and started rolling her bag to the end of the check-in line. They'd given themselves over to it. Will turned on his network coverage. It drew a foreign carrier that appeared in the upper corner of his screen. He dialed customer service and the wait was over an hour now. He hung up and opened a browser. The volcano led the news on the *Times* and on the *Guardian*. The volcano was trending in pole position on Twitter. Pictures of the volcano. Pictures of the ashcloud. Retweets of up-close images and faraway images, taken by farmers and fishermen and satellites. Everywhere the cauliflower plumes. Retweets of maps. Retweets of thoughts and prayers. Retweets of groundings in Munich and Milan. Holudjöfulsins, it was called. *The Devil's Hole.* They scuffed forward in line.

Will messaged the owner of their Airbnb through the app. He asked, on the off-est chance, if she had availability for tonight. Right away he saw the response bubbles. She said the apartment was not available, but that according to the information she had, the new renters may be in the same trouble as Will and Whitney. They were coming from Athens. There were no outs from Barcelona, but no ins, either. Will and Whitney were welcome to return to the apartment until she got word that the others were in fact en route. It was, Will remarked, the same convenient arrangement that had worked out for them at the restaurant the night before.

It turned out to be as bad as the representative had

suggested. The woman at the desk even showed them a map on her display. The picture looked worse than the map on CNN's site. More aggression in the spread. Greater-seeming impenetrability. The way the winds had swung it, England was sealed beneath an even thicker ceiling than usual. From there it followed a path down the Atlantic coast of France, over the Pyrenees, and into Spain, widening like a mudslide as it went. The effects Europe-wide were greater than they had understood, too—more damage, greater disruption. A second tine of ashcloud had blown north over Scandinavia; groundings in Oslo and Copenhagen and Stockholm. It looked like it would reach Russia the same time it hit Portugal. Maybe today, even.

The best the desk agent could do was add Will and Whitney to the list in the system. The purgatory to which they'd collectively been condemned. Because of their fare class, the agent was happy to report that they would be placed in Clearing Zone 6—which was, she explained when Will asked if that was good or bad, at least ahead of Clearing Zones 7 and 8.

"So...come back tomorrow?" Will said.

"Oh, no no. No no no. The line, of course, is on the computer. Not a real standby at the airport. I'm not allowed to guess on these things. But if I have to share, the earliest would be two days. What they say on the news is two days to...five, six, seven days."

Will and Whitney looked at each other and their eyes widened. All around them travelers were pacing, raising their voices with the agents, gesturing with their hands in hyperanimation. Wordlessly, Will and Whitney met the moment at last, accepting that there was nothing to be done, that no amount of effortful human unpleasantness could get them on an airplane today. Whitney pursed her lips and gave a little puff of resignation, the way she'd seen the women of Western Europe do it. She'd been practicing for days, and here, here it came out before she'd even thought it, like speaking a foreign language brainlessly for the first time. It pleased her immensely and she felt convinced that things would work out okay for them in the end.

They thanked the agent. They hailed a cab. They rode back into the city beneath the infinite edgeless sky.

The Greeks had indeed been grounded, the owner of the apartment messaged. They were canceling their trip to Barcelona altogether. The apartment was Will and Whitney's for at least a few more days, then.

It could have been so much worse. They had jobs, of course, but they had an excuse now. An international incident. A seismic event of superseding magnitude. What could anyone say? They had the limitless Wi-Fi of their adopted apartment. They had laptops with conversion plugs. Coworkers would cover for them, at least for a couple days. And it wasn't as though they had left children back home with their parents. No cats or dogs or tropical fish. No pending lawsuits or shooting schedules that couldn't be monitored from the couch of the rental. The houseplant in their studio might die, but they could ask their renters to water it on their way out the door and to just leave the keys at the bodega on the corner. There was nothing left for them to do but extend the trip and pray the internet never cut out. What a convenient week for the world to end.

Before they left the apartment again, they emailed their parents and their bosses. Will held his breath as he checked for an email that he knew deep down wouldn't have come through early on a Sunday morning. Whitney spent an extra-long time drafting an email of her own, and then posted a picture of the view outside, a picture in natural gray scale that struck a contrast with the view she'd posted the day before, all blues and greens and creams of lucent May. The ashcloud was white in spots and yellow in others, but at all times shadowless-seeming. No dimensions, no curves or ends or holes through which they could spy the heights. The light was soft, the whole world diffuse. It was uncanny but not exactly ominous. It was like winter. Winter but with the ideal temperature. She posted the photo of the view with the volcano icon and the grimace emoji.

They read more about the volcano on their way out the door. How it had last erupted in 1961. How scientists had been waiting impatiently for it to go again for decades. It was a thing Icelanders somehow lived with. Ash and rock and orange-hot lava occasionally spilling into farmland like batter into a cake sheet. There were evacuations from the valley at the volcano's base and from the fishing town on the water. There was likely extensive destruction. But miraculously no one had died. Not yet, at least. The villagers near Holudjöfulsins had somehow known in advance and fled. It was the one everyone had suspected would be next up. And now it would be finished soon. The experts were fifty percent certain that it would be over tomorrow. But the ashcloud would take days to dissipate, maybe even a week. They couldn't predict the winds.

They had a free Sunday at their disposal. In their four days, they'd done the things in Barcelona they'd heard they had to do, which meant now they could really start seeing the city. Let Clearing Zones 1 through 5 go on ahead of them and wait out their purgatory at the airport. They'd gladly stay trapped in the city center. They walked down to El Born to toast the convenience of their inconvenience. They chose a bar on a tree-shaded plaza because of the almonds in the window. The server said the almonds were for the cooks, but she brought some over anyway. They ate almonds and cheese and tomatoes and drank glasses of Moritz near a projection of the soccer match. Barça was on the road, in Bilbao, and it looked even worse there. The cameras were heavily fuzzed as they shot through the particulate. It looked the way a sporting event does after fireworks or flares. Whitney couldn't believe they were putting players out in it, those invaluable pink lungs. They'd never have allowed such a thing when she played. It got worse as the minutes ticked up. And when Barcelona scored, Will and Whitney could tell only by the pitch of the announcer's voice. There was nothing to see until they cut to a secondary camera on the sideline, and the striker who'd claimed the goal jammed a thumb in his mouth in tribute to his baby.

Before they left the bar, they made a list on a napkin of things to do with their bonus time. The Miró museum. The van der Rohe pavilion. A stroll up to Gràcia. That wine bar in Poble Sec they'd tried to drink at the one night it was closed. The restaurant in Sant Antoni they'd failed to get through the doors of when they stopped by without a reservation. Maybe even return trips to Parc Güell, La Boqueria, and that beach bar at the far point of Barceloneta, the one that looked to serve only orange spritzes and pink langoustines. But would establishments even be open during the volcano days? Would it be appropriate to lounge down by the beach? It wasn't as though the city had been hit by an attack or flooded with protests, but would anyone want to be out? It was the question they wondered aloud once they'd stalled their list and popped their last almonds into their mouths: Would the ash make it more like a city during a storm or a city during a war?

Whitney recalled hearing about a Sunday evening party that she'd been bummed they hadn't had the opportunity to attend. Something that had been recommended to her by a TV writer she'd met through work. It was a dinner, hosted by an American artist who'd lived in Barcelona since his flying days in France, that had taken place almost every Sunday—rain or shine or ash—for forty-five years. There was a website and everything. All you had to do was send him an email RSVPing, and bring twenty euros a head to cover the cost of the booze and the home-cooked meal. Guests apparently came from all over. It was a deliberate gathering of strangers, Whitney had heard, and the whole thing was to mingle with new people. The artist was some kind of functionary of the sexual revolution in Europe, she recounted to Will at the bar. He'd started porno mags in Amsterdam and Edinburgh. If you go, Whitney had been warned, show up on time and head out early; it gets weird when the regulars reach the witching hour.

"So, what do you think?" Whitney said.

"Sounds like a lot of talking to people we don't know," Will said.

"Yes, that's the point."

"And they don't care that we won't know anyone *at all*?"

"I can't tell if you're being deliberately thick. That's what it's about. All these travelers from all over. A few locals. Some expats—if they still call them that. It's a couple hours, nothing crazy."

"If you want to go," Will said.

"But do *you* want to go?" Whitney said.

"I'm sure it'll be great. These are the things I'm always suspicious of but never regret having gone to. Just to be super clear, though: You want to spend a whole night making small talk with strangers?"

"You didn't seem to have trouble making small talk with strangers when they were first-year associates in pencil skirts."

"That is true, yes."

"...when they were all paralegals buzzing hot in the cheeks, on X and Y and Z."

"Are those your names for party drugs?"

"...on E and F and G."

"You're right," Will said. "No problem then, no problem now."

"...ready to walk right up and put their sticky little mitts on your arms and chest, presuming without a doubt in the world that a guy like you's not hanging around unless he's ready to get down right then and there."

"Desperate times called for desperate blah blah. Though you realize this is a little different. This is talking to people just because.... No best-sex-of-my-life at the end."

"No bloody noses," she said. "No tits in armpits."

"What makes people get up in the morning if at least the *possibility*'s not there at the end of the night, right?"

"Maybe this is the same sort of idea," Whitney said. "I hear all the old people are there to fuck each other anyway. All those aging free-love swingers."

"Good, then," Will said. "I'll get to see you in action. Now that I know you've got a taste for vintage."

She could've smiled, and she may have tried, but it faded in the same instant. Last night was important for them.

They'd survived it. But it was raw still. It wasn't quite all the way to lightness. At least not like it had been at times the night before, and not like it might be down the road. There was serious trauma still. But they were okay. They'd survived the dinner. And then they'd gone home, and taken it out on each other.

He'd been rough with her. He'd wrapped his fingers around her throat and held on longer than he knew he should, reminding himself at the critical moment to slacken his grip: *easy*. . . . He made sure to mark her up. Surfaces. Cupped palms, smacks that stung. He stuck his hand in her mouth and hooked her teeth and lips, unhinged her jaw. He pulled, he pressed. She'd done the same to him. Used him like she'd used her pair, let herself be used like they'd used her. They brought strength into it. Made sure there was a hairline fracture of uncertainty about whether they maybe hated one another. Pressed and pulled. Over the line. To the point of *stop*. To the point of *not so hard*. The windows were open and it was warm out. The ash had created a vacuum seal, a sheet over the city. But they hadn't known it yet—the ashcloud had slipped in under cover of darkness. Their bodies were wet when they were through. There was heat in their hair. Dampness at the neck and forehead. Sweat sliding down the pane of her stomach, around the well of her belly button and the risers of her hip bones. Her pubic hair was dewy. Her crack was damp. They grew slicker as they lay there. He'd finished inside her. Not the way they normally did. But she'd fastened him in with her legs and practically made it end on command. She could make him do what she wanted when she wanted it done. Not like the others. She knew how to do things to him and he knew how to do things to her. They fell asleep above the covers in a locked, logical tangle. A tessellation. They hadn't bothered to set an alarm.

They went to the party. It was a fifteen-minute walk, in the vicinity of La Sagrada Familia. Across palm tree–lined boulevards, beside fountains and light-rail tracks, up narrow alleyways with bars and tabacs and copy shops and pet stores. The grinding of espresso machines, the upshift of motorbikes, the steady laughter of large groups drinking at tiny tables on the sidewalks. The sky was low and lit up yellow. The core of the cloud cover was dark, but the smothered presence of a late-spring sun persisted gauzily into the early evening.

The entrance to the party was through an iron gate in a narrow archway that opened onto a courtyard shared by the building. It was like a secret park. There was a small pool for children and dogs. Benches beneath palm trees. A modest garden and a faded soccer goal spray-painted onto the brick wall at the far end. The courtyard was teeming, but it was difficult to tell if everyone was there for the dinner. The apartment nearest the street belonged to their host, and enough nice-looking people were spilling from his atelier— out the doors and down the steps into the courtyard— to convince Will and Whitney they'd found the right spot. Each guest had a plastic cup of wine in hand, a plastic cup or a bottle of beer. Drinks were in buckets of ice. Whitney led Will by the hand.

"Do we check in, then?" Will said, and Whitney shrugged like how would she know.

They walked around slowly. The courtyard was such a surprise, the sort of thing they never would have noticed if they'd been simply walking by, if they hadn't had reason to dip in. So many of the buildings they'd strolled past in the previous four days, especially in the planned sections of the Eixample, had an identical footprint. Four sides and four chamfered corners—perfect octagons—taking up one block each for the entirety of the vast neighborhood. The heavy diagonal corners were matched by diagonals on the sidewalks and streets, creating exceptionally wide intersections. It was inconvenient for pedestrians, but the plan was beautiful, and the buildings looked even better, Will and Whitney knew from their maps, from above.

Inside many of the buildings was a hollowed-out center, a courtyard with a range of attractions. This one had its garden and pool, but also enough space, evidently, to accommodate a hundred strangers. There were lemon trees. There was a pea-gravel pit. There was a squeeze bag of wine resting on someone else's steps. The signs on those steps—in Catalan, in Spanish, in English—asked that guests respect the private property of the neighbors, that Sunday was a day of peace and quiet for everyone else. The weekly dinners, it occurred to Will and Whitney, must've been a nightmare for the neighbors.

An English woman with long gray hair and blue glasses asked if they were part of "the Gram Thing." When Whitney said she didn't know, the woman explained she meant the thing that she herself had resisted for years before attending a lecture of his at the university and falling in easily with his congress of former students. Whitney explained that they hadn't met Gram yet, that they were merely stuck here because of the volcano, that they weren't aware that Gram possessed a following of note. And so the woman introduced Will and Whitney to some others, who, like her, were British developers or architects or artists who worked primarily in

Spain. Personal homes in Barcelona and Madrid and Valencia, et cetera. Who, too, professed to be very much part of the Gram Thing, if they caught their drift, which Will and Whitney still did not. Will asked a middle-aged man with a brand-new baby how he was coping so far. "The baby's fine, but the birth part, that was like watching your favorite pub burn down," he said, gesturing in the direction of his wife's vagina.

The couple introduced Will and Whitney to a restaurant owner with a French accent, and identical male twins with matching Scandinavian hair and glasses, and a Catalan separatist with a yellow-ribbon lapel, and a short, curly-haired Italian classics professor who talked excitedly at Will and Whitney about their university years in the American South, how he'd long fantasized about taking a road trip to mythical jazz and blues destinations, to New Orleans, to the Delta, to the Mississippi crossroads where Robert Johnson made his deal with the Devil. An older man with hair like soap suds crashed in and introduced himself as Josep, then shooed anyone inside who hadn't yet checked in with Gram. There was the business of saying hello and verifying attendance, but also soup was being served, the first of three courses. They squeezed past several small groups, strangers clearly getting to know one another, based on the biographical details they picked up. They all seemed at least twice Will and Whitney's age.

The atelier apartment was up a half flight of stairs from the courtyard, and the door was a retractable wall of glass that ran on runners like a gate in a loading dock. The main room was overstuffed. Several queues competed for space. To the right ran a line to a kitchen island with a checkered tablecloth, where a younger man ladled white-bean-and-kale soup out of an industrial-size pot into wooden bowls. To the left, a shorter bathroom line pressed against the floor-to-ceiling bookshelves with titles in countless languages. And in the center of the room was the line to check in with Gram. From Will and Whitney's position, only glimpses could be caught of Gram, the edge of his generously follicled head, a free arm gesturing with a golf pencil in hand.

Above the main room was an open loft—the bedroom, they presumed. Another set of stairs led to a basement. Will and Whitney kept tucked into themselves, their faces scouring like a pair of searchlights. They pointed out dozens of unframed paintings hanging over the edge of the loft, floating there above the gathering in the kitchen. They squinted from distance at the books on the shelves. Fifty feet of travel guides. Sicily and Bordeaux and Yugoslavia. Lapland and Baden-Baden. Thick and thin spines, West and East. There was conversation all around in Spanish and French and German and a brightly colored collage of heavily accented English.

The couples peeled off. The line grew shorter. They were nearly up.

"Genevieve, François, meet Lily and Tomas," Gram boomed to the couple before them in line. "Lyon meets Dortmund. You must know someone in common, right?"

Then it was their turn. The mustache was thick and white and wide, wider than his wide face, wider-seeming than the hips that spilled over the edge of the stool. He leaned back against the stool, wrapped in an apron that matched the tablecloth, checkered red and white, with a loopy *I Love Lucy* script that said Screw Me, I'm the Chef. His cheeks were red, his skin was tan, his hair was gray in spots and yellow at the edges—the color of a used cigarette filter. He watched Genevieve and François disappear into conversation with Lily and Tomas, then turned his half-moon glasses on them.

"Two under *Will Granger,*" Will said, holding two twenties outstretched.

"Put that away," Gram said. "I'm not a whore. You don't need to pay me up front."

He peered down his nose at them through his glasses.

"It's a joke," Gram said. "It's a joke that I'm too lazy to make funnier. There's nothing to worry about. I don't recognize you. First time?"

"If we haven't made that clear enough yet," Will said, smiling cautiously.

"Well, there are plenty of folks here who can show you the ropes. But it's not meant to be a night of strict rules. Just one rule, really." Here he pointed his pencil at Whitney. "You must always be talking to a person you didn't know before tonight. If I catch the two of you off in the garden by yourselves, I'll ask you to leave. Or Josep will. Or Caterina. Easiest rule there is. Make friends. Drink drinks. Soup, then chicken, then dessert, courtesy of . . . Curtis." He screwed up his face. "How cute."

Curtis was behind Gram in the kitchen, and he lifted his wooden spoon at the sound of his name. He had jean shorts on and a white V-neck T-shirt and hair down to his shoulders, tied back with a red bandanna.

"Curtis is from Brisbane and staged in Perpignan last season. He's crashing here while he writes away for his next internship. Lucky us. Anyway, you're all set, and it's a pleasure to have you in my home, Will Granger and Whitney Cross. Will and Whitney, young blood, did you meet Genevieve and François when you were in line? Or better yet, I see him coming up the steps, the tall American, the basketball player. *Jack!* Jack, come here. Jack, meet Will and Whitney..."

Will couldn't believe it. There, ducking beneath the bottom edge of the retractable door, was a face he'd known and loved, but hadn't thought of in years. There, scanning for something essential, attempting to distinguish among the three competing lines in the room, was none other than JJ Pickle. Star of the basketball team during their time at college. Three-time first-team all-conference. Breakout of the first weekend of the NCAA tournament Will and Whitney's senior year. Top scorer in program history. And here he was, with an empty 250ml beer bottle that looked like wax candy in his hand, searching for another drink, searching for the bathroom.

It was as though he didn't hear Gram at first, so Gram called out again: "Jack!" And JJ lit up at the realization that it was he whose attention the host was seeking. "Jack, my boy, this is Will, this is Whitney."

JJ was trapped by two bald men with rimless glasses and dark jackets. JJ, who towered over them, mocked a fake handshake across the divide. Will turned to Whitney and said, "Unreal." And she said "What?" like she really didn't know.

When the men with the glasses cleared out, the three of them were body to body. JJ was five inches taller than Will, a head and neck taller than Whitney. He took her hand and said her name again and he said "Jack" and their hands bobbed between them like one or the other might ask another question. Whitney squinted like she maybe recognized him from somewhere, and he squinted like he maybe knew her, as well. But at the word *volcano* behind them, Whitney cleared her throat and dropped his hand, and he eventually turned to Will. Will didn't say his own name, but rather, "Believe it or not, we went to school together. All three of us."

Jack's mouth was open like a cave, eyes slit and turned down like a tickled baby's. "No way!" he said, emitting a low roll of uncomplicated joy. He squinted again at the two of them and put his hand on Will's shoulder, then took another long lingering look at Whitney.

"Hold on," Whitney said.

"We graduated a year ahead of you," Will said.

"I love it!" Jack said.

"You're..." Whitney said.

"And you've been playing here ever since college, right?" Will said.

"Well, not here the whole time," Jack said. "Norway, then Germany, then..." He trailed off and stooped his dark-haired head. "And, weird as it is, I guess I can't claim that anymore. It's all through, as of last night. It was supposed to be my last game, but it was canceled 'cause the other team couldn't get in on a plane."

"Last game of the season?" Will said.

"Of everything. Of all basketball, forever. Twenty-five years and *done*."

"As of last night?" Will said. "You're kidding."

"We weren't gonna make the playoffs, so they just decided to call it. No makeup game. Over just like that."

"You're on a team right here in Barcelona, then?" Will said.

"Not the big one, not the one like the soccer team. The smaller one just north of the city."

"And so, what, as of twenty-four hours ago, your career is over?"

"You play professional basketball in Europe..." Whitney said, still lagging.

"Did. Six years. I was scheduled to fly home in the morning. But with all this, who knows?"

"We were supposed to fly out this—"

"So how'd you end up *here*?" Whitney said, cutting Will off.

"Well, I guess...I've been in Barcelona for two years. I was thinking this morning, and realized I'd done basically the same thing every day for my entire time. Even when my brothers visited: practice and games and practice and games.... Once, I was supposed to go on a weeklong trip with some of my boys, but Coach decided to cancel our days off. Emergency practices after a couple bad losses. So my buddies stuck around town, and actually came to this party and had a fun time. I just felt like I was always missing out, so figured one last Sunday—why not?"

"We'd heard good things too," Whitney said, "but were supposed to be gone by now."

"It's weird," Jack said, still lost in what he'd been saying. "I haven't had a night out without practice in the morning since..."

"Wait, so this is literally the first night of your retirement?" Whitney said. "Your first free night in years?"

"I mean, I went home for summers. But it was still every day at the gym then, too. Every day of shooting, running, lifting, swimming in the lake."

"Chicago?" Will said.

"Yeah, exactly..." Jack said, squinting at Will's knowingness.

"I went to my share of games," Will said. "I remember the lineup intro is all..."

"By his *share of games* he means every game," Whitney said.

"What a gym, huh?" Jack said.

"Are you here with anyone else?" Whitney said. "Teammates? *Girlfriend*?"

"Just me," he said. "Pretty last minute. Looked up the website. Sent an email just an hour ago. But the cook over there, he was manning the list and follows the team. Said he played at uni in Melbourne. So he squeezed me in."

"Anything for JJ Pickle..." Whitney said.

His eyes fell to the crowded floor. "And that's a thing I'm trying tonight, too, actually.... It's sort of embarrassing, but I thought I'd give it a go.... Trying it out as *Jack* tonight. First time since, I dunno, since elementary school."

Jack smiled at Whitney and Will saw in her eyes what she was seeing—not JJ Pickle, but a handsome American athlete who had just confessed to being equal parts insecure and famous, at least enough to want to change his name.

"And did *you* know it would be an old-people swingers' party?" Whitney said, brightening with the wine.

He laughed. "Oh man, you're the second person to say it. Maybe I haven't been here long enough. Or I'm talking to all the wrong people. I've just been with this girl, who's the only other young person I've seen so far, but she mentioned it, too. I had no idea."

"Maybe we're seeing things that aren't really here," Will said. "Maybe they're all just, like, extra European."

"And here I thought I'd come away with some knowledge from my time over here. Some sense of how to tell the difference between Germans and Spaniards and swingers," he said, grinning again and squirming in place and indicating with a thumb that he still needed to find the bathroom.

They each took a sip of their wine as they watched him walk away.

JJ Pickle. Six-foot-five shooting guard. Number 30 in your programs, No. 1 in your hearts. Will had been to every home game for four years. Three of which included the "Nothin But Netter from the North Shore." An overlooked prep prospect, jilted by the bigs for his lack of being able to do anything but shoot, and picked up without much fanfare by their little program late in the recruiting process. Coach was from Chicago. He'd played in the backcourt at Immaculata with Mr. Pickle. Coach knew what to say to get Chicago kids down south.

The team wasn't supposed to do much. No players over six-nine anywhere on the roster. They played a pro-style small ball before it was popular. Five shooters on the court at all times. Make threes or die. Outrebounded two-to-one most games, but able to beat the best if JJ Pickle got a hot hand. He scored fifty in a conference road game his freshman year. Fifty-five in the home opener the following season. Twelve threes in the finals of a Thanksgiving tournament on a Caribbean island, creeping the team into the top twenty-five for the first time in program history. A perfect game his junior spring: fifteen for fifteen from the field, eight for eight from the line. Will was in The Weevil for that one. Six rows back, standing on the wooden risers, his eyes level with the rims. Packed in shoulder to shoulder—sweating, stuffy—tilting his face to the rafters to breathe cleaner air, lifting the foam pickle he wore on his hand with each JJ swish, just like everyone else in the gym.

He couldn't jump. He'd never dunked in a game before. At the end of his junior year, just before the wind-down of a route, JJ took an outlet pass on a fast break and, all alone, planted his feet in the key and leaped straight up, like measuring a vertical, extending toward the rim with the ball on his fingertips and easing it over the insurmountable edge in what would be widely derided on the internet as the saddest slam dunk in the history of basketball. Sliced and diced and made viral. A meme for the weakest version of something awesome. Will had been there. Will had lifted his pickled hand and cheered for the seemingly impossible. It didn't matter; JJ was a shooter. And they were winning. He led them late into March during Will and Whitney's senior spring, JJ shooting his way through the opening round of the NCAA tournament, the program's first tournament win in two decades. Then an upset of the tournament's top seed in the second round. JJ with eleven threes. Six from the corner, three from the elbows, two—including the game winner—from ten feet behind the top of the arc.

The buzzer-beater landed JJ on the cover of *Sports Illustrated,* flipped wrist held high, frozen above his head, the arm posture of textbook form. Inside, the magazine had Photoshopped a foam pickle over his shooting arm; Will knew he had the issue in a cardboard box somewhere at home. They won another game that run—the same night Will and Whitney met, in fact, the game Will had left the gardens to watch downtown. They'd slept together for the first time that night; the two events were tied inextricably for all time. It was a win that would be JJ's last in the tournament, as teams finally figured out how to guard him, to smother him, to force his middling handle in the double-team. They were antibodies that would neutralize him not just in that Elite Eight game but all the following season—when, with the pressure rising for a replication of their Cinderella success, they failed to be anything but a smudgy

Xerox of the magic that had made a brief household name out of *JJ Pickle*.

Will reminded Whitney of all of it when Jack went to the bathroom. The parts that Will knew well, the parts before Jack's time in Europe. Whitney had been an athlete, too— a college athlete even. But the day she'd quit was the day she'd lost interest in sports as anything other than a factory of human-interest narratives or ripe worlds in which to set a series. And so Will explained that to stand even a remote chance of playing basketball professionally in the U.S., you needed more than JJ's single special jump shot; NBA players were expected to pass and rebound and play defense, too.

They stood together, just the two of them now, squeezed on all sides by the chatting masses, whose engagement made Will and Whitney only more susceptible to expulsion. They were suddenly worried they might be spotted, flagged, booted for breaking Rule No. 1. They needed Jack to come back at once. They moved across the room to give the illusion of an essential destination. They moved as slowly as possible toward a bookshelf.

They overheard conversations about the volcano. New predictions that it would be a disruption of six days, or three days, or two weeks. That not only would there be no flights, but no sign of breaking light, either. A sort of hot humid winter was what they all were in for. Will and Whitney keyed into loud theories from the academics who asserted that though nobody would wind up dead, fingers crossed, it would feel like a sort of raid-alert state. Life would go on, but with limited ins and outs, limited exchange between the city and the state, the heart and the extremities. They really believed themselves to be trapped, the conversations made clear. And it would force each country, each metropolis, to act ever more like itself, shaded inward, selfishly, nationalistically. They spoke of it with a panicky catch in the throat, those graying art-adjacent capitalists, those conscientious proponents of liberal democracy, who lived their lives with freedom of food and language and transport, taking for granted the fluid membranes of the Schengen Area. But the ashcloud would bring a temporary halt to all that. The shape and the shadow resembled that of an old-fashioned European crisis, one not so close to them in time but close enough, and with a weight of ever-presence, of psychic occupation.

As the conversations evolved, the guests began speaking of the ashcloud as though it had been in their lives for months. There was a pitch shift—Will and Whitney both heard it—as the talk turned to the logistics of a battening down. There was a raw energy among the guests, nostalgia almost, for the safe parts of the wars that had come before, the wars that they themselves had not experienced firsthand, but that they had dreamed of all their lives. To be trapped on the edge of the sea...no goings and no comings. A packed, pressurized containment. The comforts of claustrophobia. They craved it. It would be like getting stuck in a cabin during a snowstorm, someone said, but with plenty of wine and cigarettes. Which is when Whitney finally whispered it to Will: "They're getting a thrill out of this." She said it into his ear: "It's like how people get before a blizzard at home. They're literally getting turned on by the prospect of being stuck."

Jack made his way back across the room to them. He had updates too, they could tell.

"You should see the photos in line for the bathroom," he said. "I recognized some of the actors and musicians. But if the others I didn't recognize are just as famous, he seems to have met a lot of interesting people."

"As a sculptor?" Will said.

"Sculptor now," Jack said. "But other things before, I guess. Fighter pilot? Record producer? The whole thing with those porn magazines? That girl I mentioned before was telling me about it."

They glanced in the direction of Gram. He was still on the stool, kissing the cheek of a woman his age with streaked hair and roomy skin the color and consistency of parchment paper. He kissed her other cheek and said something in Spanish, then kissed the first cheek again and said something in German. Then he kissed her deeply on the mouth. They both laughed and he checked something off his list.

"I guess he's still sculpting," Jack said. "That girl I mentioned, she actually models for him. She's around somewhere. I think she maybe stays here while she's visiting."

"Like a nude model?" Whitney said.

"What she said was that she was picked because of her feet."

"A foot model!" Whitney said, tipping the rest of her wine down her throat.

"Said she stays here and gets her days and her nights to herself, aside from a few hours in the afternoons, when she has to sit in the studio and let him sculpt her feet."

"C'mon..." Will said, smiling. "Which one is she?"

Jack stood up straighter and scanned the room like a lighthouse.

"She must be outside," Jack said. And they settled into a conversation about other people they'd met at the party, their interesting jobs, but how Jack's was obviously the most interesting of all to anyone, though he was ready to stop talking about it. This ending for him was all pretty fresh, he said, and if he let himself think about it too hard he might puddle up right there on the floor. They got in line and grabbed their wooden bowls of soup and then settled outside on some stone steps in the garden. Which is when they heard a voice behind them in clean California English.

"Drink, big boy? Anyone need another glass of wine?"

She was the youngest woman at the party, anyone could see. And the first part was meant for Jack, they confirmed, when they saw her neck craned in the direction of his face, half of her mouth in a torqued suggestion of a smile, the other half flat with indifference.

"There you are," Jack said. "These two, they're from the States, too. We actually went to college together, believe it or not."

"Not," she said, and her face was blank—still and uncompromising. Her hair was long and white and fell practically to her waist. It was pushed way up off the top of her head and down her back. It gave the impression that she'd just faced down a heavy breeze. Her eyes were a sparkly cool blue that seemed almost sensitive to light. Her cheeks were full like a child's, baby fat around the eyes and jawline, smooth as spread butter. She had a nose that was an afterthought on her face, the sort of thing a sketch artist might render with a flick of the wrist. She was wearing a white terrycloth something that was either a bathrobe or a kimono or a dress. It plunged at her chest and it was very possible she was wearing nothing else. Will's eyes fell to the soft folds at her neck, to the missing collarbones beneath the thickness of her throat, and down the lines of her robe. Whitney's eyes fell immediately to the girl's feet, to the pair-of-interest in their leather slippers, to those twinning points of contact with the courtyard bricks.

"Me neither," Will said, finally. "I don't believe it, either."

The young woman smiled and then shifted the empty plastic wine cups she'd collected to a single hand, in order to free up the other to shake.

"Leonard," she said.

"Will, actually," Will said.

"No, *I'm* Leonard."

"And I'm Whitney," Whitney said.

"*Leonard*'s an unusual name," Will said.

"I've met a number," Leonard said.

"Well, for a woman, I mean. I'm sure you've heard that before."

Leonard shrugged with her lower lip. "Wine, anyone? I'm making the rounds."

"Sure, thank you, if it's not too much trouble," Whitney said. "Another white."

"Two," Will said.

"Three, please," Jack said.

And she took the stairs into the apartment.

"Okay, then," Will said.

"It's her last name," Jack said.

"Leonard?" Will said.

"She introduced herself to me as Jenna. I'm pretty sure it's her last name."

"She must like you more," Will said, and he felt Whitney shift beside him.

"How old is she?" Whitney said.

"She said she just finished her junior year abroad."

"Of course," Whitney said.

"A year in Paris," Jack said.

"But you said she models for him?" Will said.

"Takes the train down here sometimes, I guess," Jack said. "I didn't ask too many questions."

"What a baby," Whitney said, scanning for her inside the apartment, finishing another cup of wine. "Still in college. And wearing a Prada dress and Gucci slippers."

"She's gotta keep the moneymakers safe," Will said.

"Do you think she has sex with him?" Whitney said, her eyes still inside the atelier.

Jack's mouth slackened, like he hadn't really considered it before, and then he laughed into his soup—a single snort.

"I mean, that must be what's going on," Whitney continued.

"I hadn't thought about it," Jack said. "That's...that's an age difference. That's one way to meet someone, I guess..."

"What about you, then?" Whitney said, hypnotized almost, still waiting for Leonard to reemerge in the cracks between the guests in the crowd.

"Hmm?" Jack said.

She snapped her attention back to him, the spell broken, and teethed the edge of her cup. "How'd you find people to pair off with? I mean, while you were playing, if you weren't coming here every weekend?"

Jack still looked confused. But Will knew where this was headed. He could see that her eyes were glassy, and greedy for juice.

"In Norway, in Germany, in Barcelona—how did it work with...how did you pick up women?"

"Oh, I don't..." His eyes dropped again, uneasy as a child under interrogation. "I didn't spend too much time going out to bars or clubs or anything like that, if that's what you mean. Sometimes I met people, you know, the normal ways, I guess?"

"Groupies? Dating apps?"

"I'm not gonna lie...my life has been pretty boring. Gym in the morning, nap at one, practice in the afternoon. Two meals a day at the facility. Pretty beat at night. I'd tag along with some of the local guys every once in a while, and there were girls here and there, but—"

"Nothing serious in all those seasons?"

"Summers, sometimes? Back in Chicago, when I had a little more time."

"Old high-school flings," Whitney said, grinning again. "The prodigal All-American..."

"Jesus, let the guy *breathe*," Will said, flinching his eyebrows.

"I'm just curious how it all works when you're a famous basketball player, is all."

Jack smiled sheepishly. "Life's mostly the same as anyone's, I guess. You work out, try to get better every day. You travel. Some locals really care, but most don't have any idea who you are and don't give a shit about the team. One thing, though, is that no matter where I went, I always seemed to find myself involved with some girl or another passing through from Evanston or Winnetka, 'cause how else could it go for me?"

"See, here I was fishing for the difference between Scandinavian girls and Bavarian girls. But you're talking the gradations between Lake Forest and, what, Wilmette?"

"Hey, look at you," he said, smiling, his cheeks flushed more than even a moment ago, out of practice with his drinking. "Definitely can do that. But maybe I can do the other ones, too..." He had a big mouth that stretched wider than his teeth were set. And his head was undersize for his body, for his shoulders and his legs. "Actually, here's one thing I learned from all my travels, if you really wanna know."

"I do."

"After a couple vodkas, after some dancing to remixes of 'Sorry,' every girl everywhere apparently wants the same thing."

"Gelato?" Whitney said. Will shook his head and stared into his soup bowl.

"Even better, though? My best trick? A big bed. A big bed to head back to. Each new place I lived. I never had to say much, just kinda said it because it was true, but it was always good enough.... I'd say, 'I'm gonna head home because I've got practice in the morning. And I especially can't wait to get home'—and leave you, fill-in-the-blank-beautiful-lady, here at the bar—'because I've got this *bed,* it's the most comfortable bed on earth, and it's calling my name, *lo siento,* good night, señorita.' And guess who was interested in checking it out just to, ya know, confirm the claims?"

"You preyed on their exhaustion!" Whitney said, covering her mouth in case there was kale in her teeth, enjoying it all as much as she'd hoped. "On their lust for soft pillows and a downy comforter and a chance to get to sleep an hour earlier than they'd planned."

"Worked since high school," Jack said. "These long legs? Those big games? It was the only thing I ever successfully negotiated from my parents. A big bed where my feet didn't fall off the edge. I'd show them pictures of Jordan's bed, of Longley's bed. You ever seen pictures of Shaq's bed?"

"Round," Will said, looking up. "Fifteen, twenty feet across."

"Bingo," Jack said. "Big bed, doesn't take much to get girls interested."

"I've never heard of anything like that before," Whitney said. "Are you sure these women didn't think you were just speaking euphemistically?"

Will flipped to her again, as though she might notice, as though her focus weren't elsewhere.

"I got a king in eighth grade," Jack said, missing Whitney's line entirely. "No one had ever seen anything like it. And our house, we have this big old mess. No one knew where anyone else was most of the time. All six of us could be home, or maybe no one, you couldn't tell. Even if it was my older brothers' friends who were around, the girls in their classes? All it took was the *curiosity.* They just wanted to see what a really big bed looked like in a teenager's overstuffed little room. To sprawl out and take a breather."

"I'm picturing a Halloween party at the Pickles' and a bunch of cute older girls dressed up like Rockford Peaches and Racine Belles."

He laughed hard. "Pretty much!"

"And you're sure this wasn't about something else?" she said. "Maybe, like, the fact that you were the star of the school, on your way to becoming a pro athlete? Might be a causation-correlation mix-up, no?"

"Is that something we were supposed to learn in college? I think they maybe let me skip that class."

"Then again, the more I think about it, the more I can totally picture it: *I'm much more interested in my bed than I am in you,* the big man on campus says. A classic Big Bed Neg. Make her feel like dirt—but *chosen* dirt."

He shrugged blamelessly. He knew only what he knew. He was getting exhausted, besides.

"Let me ask you this, then…" Whitney said, holding her soup spoon in front of his face like a microphone, like a beat reporter in the locker room. "Norway, Germany, Spain, Chicago: What's the difference once you get them *in* the big bed?"

"Hey," Will said, standing now and shading his body so that his back was to Jack. "Why don't you have another drink, huh?"

Whitney's grin faded and Will looked at the sky, the low ceiling dialing darker. Jack sipped what was left of his soup and let the question hang there unanswered.

"Well," Whitney said, turning back to Jack, "for the first time in my life, I can safely say *my* interest is piqued, too: How great can a bed really be, anyway?"

Will narrowed his eyes and offered to collect the bowls, snipping the thread before it could unspool further.

"Three whites, then…" It was Leonard again, back down the steps, as Will turned to carry the dishes inside.

"Perfect timing," Will said, looking at his fiancée looking at Jack.

"Can you take a load off?" Jack said to Leonard. He'd grown looser still. He had nowhere to be in the morning, nothing to be up for ever again.

"But the animals in there are thirsty," Leonard said.

"It's wine," Jack said. "They know how to pour wine."

Whitney scooted over on the steps and patted the bricks beside her.

Leonard pressed the butt of her robe down, leaned over, and gathered herself into a comfortable-looking assortment on the top stair.

Whitney's eyes watched Will's widen as they fell down Leonard's dress. She made a face at him like a mother makes at a child who's throwing food. Will returned an expression that said: *You would've done the same thing.*

They'd set the rules. They'd lived their lives apart. They'd come back together and then they'd failed to go home. It was either as simple as flipping a switch off or it wasn't.

"So," Leonard said. "What brings you guys here? You couldn't have come voluntarily…"

Whitney explained. Will filled in the gaps.

"I'm stuck, too," Leonard said. "There are worse places, obviously. But I've never stayed here for more than two nights in a row before."

"And sounds like you're not looking forward to it?" Whitney said.

"I've been abroad since September," Leonard said. "My mom came to Paris for Thanksgiving and my dad came for Christmas. But I haven't been home that whole stretch. The term ended Friday. I shipped my stuff out. And I decided to come down here to just chill for a minute, before flying back for good. I knew I had a place to stay. Two days. Maybe a night to myself in the uni housing down in Barceloneta. But now this."

"Now this," Whitney said.

"I just have to get home," Leonard said. "I never really felt it all year, but now I need it. The first plane out, I'll pay for it. I told them whatever it takes, I'll pay."

"We tried to bump up," Will said, "but not enough miles. We didn't even try to pay our—"

"I don't mean to suggest it's *my* money that I'm throwing around," Leonard said. "It's just…it's urgent. And my parents understand."

"Listen to us," Whitney said. "Torn up about being stuck for a few days in Barcelona."

"No offense," Leonard said, "but you just got here. I'm dead. I've gotta get out of here."

"I understand," Whitney said, blinking, a little wrong-footed. "I get it....Do you wish you'd stayed up there, then? Do you wish you'd been stuck in Paris instead? I studied abroad there, too, actually..."

"*Mes affaires sont toutes disparues. J'ai nettoyé mon appartement...*"

"Not that I..." Whitney said pinkly. "Not that I ever spoke all that well to begin with."

Leonard smiled. She'd tested the fence, and Whitney could tell it had gone just as she'd suspected it would.

"My stuff is all gone," Leonard continued. "I'd cleaned out my place. I'd done everything there was to do. I thought it'd be two days down here, then a flight. Turns out the cloud pushed right up behind us off the Channel and followed us down....I keep picturing the boulder in the beginning of *Raiders*. I thought there was a chance of missing it. But it was the same down here starting last night. Cancellations on the whole board. Every airline, every flight. I went to the airport, but it was clear no one was going out."

"But you have a place to stay, at least?" Whitney said.

"He and I have an arrangement. But Curtis, the cook...I don't know, he's in the room I normally stay in, so I'm in this weird walk-in closet thing. The reason it usually works is I get my room, I get my stipend, he gets what he needs. Everything's just different this time."

"If you don't mind me asking...you're a model?" Whitney said, and Leonard turned to Jack accusingly.

"He's a sculptor..." Leonard said, when Jack betrayed nothing. "But he has a thing for feet."

"A thing," Whitney said.

Leonard shifted on her step, yawned, and settled into the explanation: "It's gone the same each time, pretty much. I pack a bag for a couple days. I show up. He's either around or he isn't, but the door's unlocked. He leaves a key and a note with the hours when he'll be ready to work. Two to six, say. That's when I meet him in his studio, downstairs. He'll start by taking my hands in his hands. He says it to me aloud, so I know what he's doing, like a doctor. That he's feeling for the bones and the veins and the muscle. For the way everything comes together. The way the fingers taper. And then he sculpts a hand, maybe. Sometimes it's an arm. One time he asked if I would remove my shirt and I told him I wouldn't. And he got testy. And then ashamed. And then offered to pay me twice if I'd forgive him. And when I wouldn't, he offered me five times the usual, and then he asked all over again if I'd take off my shirt, and by that point it was worth it. No touching, though. He understood. But that's all beside the point. All those studies, all those exercises, they were just a warm-up for the feet. That was always the last part. I'd sit in a wooden chair, wearing shorts or pants or a dress— he'd usually specify in a letter beforehand. Sometimes the letter would have instructions about nail polish. Red or black, or whatever. Sometimes he'd ask for a pedicure and scrubbed feet. Other times he'd say, *Walk outside before leaving Paris, walk in the park without shoes on. Don't wash them. Keep the grass stains and the mud.* He'd specify: *From Buttes-Chaumont ... from Parc Monceau.* And he'd do the same thing as he did with my hands. He'd grab a foot, he'd tell me what he was looking for, the bones, the arch, the invisible hairs, the joints of the toes. He'd close his eyes, his breathing would shift. He'd arrive at some sort of understanding in his head and then return to the clay. He'd move back and forth between my real feet and the fake feet. And it'd take not much detective work to see that he was hard the whole time. The way he walked. The way his pants strained. Last time I was here, he had the clay in his hands, and he asked me to rub my feet together. You know, just kinda roll them around like you would to keep your hands warm. He flinched, and right there at pocket height was this giant wet spot....I don't know, things changed after that."

The three were fanned around Leonard: Will on his feet; Whitney swiveled on the axis of her spine; Jack slung out, legs stretching to the bricks at the bottom of the steps. Their eyes were fixed on Leonard's mouth.

"I say all that just to explain why I'd like to limit my stay this go-around. A final little thing for some cash has turned into this indefinite residency with, like, a world-renowned foot fetishist. Anyway," she said, gesturing faintly, "that bell you hear means the chicken's ready."

"We'll come with," Will said, helping both women to their feet. "Stay in line with us?"

They moved inside. Will dumped the bowls in the dish bin near the retractable door. They found themselves at the end of the snaking line, sipping their wine.

They were paired, two by two, Whitney and Jack, Will and Leonard.

"So," Whitney said to Jack, "what's next for you, then? Once we're free, I mean."

"I have my plane ticket home. That's as far as I've got. It still hasn't fully set in."

"You mentioned brothers?"

"Yeah, everyone's still there. Two older brothers and a

younger sister. We have a family import business. Meats and cheeses and stuff. We're the halfway point between over here and the fine-food stores in the Midwest and the South."

"I worked a summer in one of those in Dallas," Whitney said. "I know the very 'cheeses and stuff' you mean."

"Nowak's? Bisset's?"

"It was in our little town, actually. Haney..." Whitney said. "You really know all the names?"

"I'm not kidding when I say it's everyone in my family. My grandpa started it after the war. Grandma ran it after he died. Dad took over. Now, my older brothers work at the warehouse."

"And what about you, then?"

"I dunno, I just don't think I could do it. It always seemed like an inevitable thing, but then I left, and now it's hard to imagine. Plus, I'd be fourth in line. Dad's not going anywhere. My brothers are already banking their time. They'd start me on the loading dock. That's the rules. I mean, I'm twenty-eight. I don't know if it's my life anymore."

"What about your sister?"

"She's an astronomer. In grad school at U Chicago. The genius. Works at an observatory most days, up near the state line. Looks at stars. Figures out, I dunno, the speed of the expanding universe, or whatever."

"Does she need a lab assistant?"

"See, you're making me nervous now...I'm realizing just how unprepared I am for getting home, just how little I've thought it through."

"I'm sorry, I don't mean to pry. I'm just—" She held up her wine cup and smiled a smile that said more prying will come. "He gives me a hard time about the questions," she went on, flipping her head in the direction of Will.

"I obviously always knew it would end," Jack said. "I just never knew how to prepare for it. Once you start thinking about it being over, that's when you're through for real. No coming back."

"So you banish the thoughts for as long as humanly possible."

"Till the volcano goes off, at least..."

"Precisely." She smiled again. "I wonder if I ever signed for an order from Pickle Imports."

"Pickle *Products,* actually."

"'A Family Tradition...'"

Whitney's neck was beginning to hurt. The craning, just to hear his soft voice over the din of the room. A mechanism he maybe employed to stand out less than he naturally did. She smiled up at the giant, up at the strange predicament he'd found himself in. This life in which for years he'd been the very best at a thing, only to be thrust right back into the old way now, with no new experiences, no new degrees, no new contacts in any of the professional worlds that valued valueless things.

"I need to stop blah-blah-blahing about basketball," he said. "I know Dallas...Haney...but you don't have an accent?"

"It never took," she said, leaving it at that.

He smiled, possibly understanding. "Okay, then.... And I know you two are from New York. But I haven't even asked you about what you do."

She explained that she helped develop television shows that were meant to be talked about.

"No kidding!" He looked genuinely lit up. "I wouldn't have said it, but the one thing I've always wanted to do is write a screenplay, believe it or not."

"Not," Whitney said, smiling.

"Yeah, me neither," he said, missing the joke. "I actually tried to write one this winter. Didn't go well."

"Funny, I tried out for the basketball team this spring," she said. "Same result."

"I read some books about how to do it." He'd missed it again. "Found this guide in this used bookstore in Poblenou. I learned the formatting. I started listening to this podcast these two guys do. I dunno, it's not like it's something I really should be able to do."

"Sometimes good stuff comes when people don't know what they're supposed to do."

"This time over here, I watched so many…six years, all alone, I mean. I've memorized a lot of movies."

"I know the type…" Whitney said, sensing Will behind her, but hearing only Leonard's voice. "I'm picturing you in all these romantic European cities, sitting in the dark with your laptop watching the same scenes from *The Matrix* again and again."

"More like *Inception* and *Interstellar.*"

"Ah. Should've pegged you."

"What's that?"

"You are not alone in your appreciation, is all. It's sort of become a problem. I don't know what you've been working on, but if you want some unsolicited advice, I'd keep it simple—simpler than those. How 'bout an American athlete abroad, sticking out, sore-thumbing it in foreign cultures, a new team every year? *Lost in Translation* but with a six-foot-whatever point whatever?"

"Shooting guard," he said, smiling. "Go on…"

"He's in a new city every season. The American player

who's been traded more than any other. This specimen of physical perfection..."—she watched his eyes flinch—"...trapped inside, hiding from fans, watching movies, and eating..."

"Grilled chicken. Grilled chicken in every country."

"See, keep that stuff in a notebook," she said. "And then one day, there's this American woman. She enters his life. Maybe she's older... like Bill Murray's character."

"I've never seen it. I should admit that now."

"Maybe she's younger, then. Like..." And Whitney flicked her head back toward Leonard, whom she could hear yapping nonstop at Will still. "An American athlete abroad and a young American passing through. An affair... she makes him a worse player. She wants to bring him home with her. Reintroduce him to life's earthly delights, whereas he's committed to the sacrifice of training, to that discipline. He has to choose between the commitment he's made to his sport his whole life, versus the pleasure of giving up, of giving in to her, of just deciding one day to be happy....So, maybe he does. They run away. They kill somebody. They find the fifth dimension in deep space and learn that time is a subjective construction..."

His face was carrying a charge. His mouth was slack again with anticipation.

"Figure out the ending first. Not everyone agrees, but that's something I'd recommend."

"An airplane heading home to America through an ash-cloud..."

"Okay," she said, "but who's on it?"

They were at the serving table. Curtis carved off some roast chicken for Whitney and then for Jack. Whitney forked her slice and held it up to Jack and made a face like:

Aren't you so happy now? He gobbled it off her fork and Curtis frowned and then served her a second helping.

Behind them, Will and Leonard had been struggling to find a single overlap in their L.A. maps. Something had changed in Leonard since their first encounter outside. She'd disappeared for wine and come back chatty—looser of jaw, sparing no detail, seemingly, of her first twenty-two years on earth.

She was from the Palisades, she said. Rustic Canyon, she said, which "some slummingly classify as Santa Monica." Leonard had been in "private school, K through 12," she said, "near the country mart, near the country club." Her father "knocked up my mom when he was a caddy there, where she'd bought a membership just to have a quiet place to drink and not be slobbered over by someone without money. . . . Little did she know," she said. Her mother did "business in Asia, overseas for weeks at a time, Japan in the nineties, China in the aughts." When her mother was away, it was "just the two of us, me and Scott." They were right there, "not far from the Rockingham circus, even closer to the Lewinskys, right smack at the center of the bull's-eye, circa nineteen-ninety-whatever—or so I'm told. I was, like, a baby."

Home was "as weird as it sounds" and school was "filled with the names you'd expect," which made her feel "like even more of an outsider than I already was," with an absentee mom and a dad who "probably loved Riviera more than he loved me—and neither of them even worked in the industry." She rattled off her GPA and test scores and the places she got into and the places she didn't, and said "the one exception was that I was exceptional at French." But they "never went to Europe, never went to Paris," she said. So she spoke French on just a couple occasions only in the wild, on a trip to Vietnam, "in some cafés in Hanoi— it was literally life-changing."

College was a way to "get out of the canyons," she said, and "finally get to France." She'd gone to school with "the same people for thirteen years," she said, and summer camp in Malibu with "the same Westside Jews since middle school." At NYU, though, everywhere she looked were "the same kinds of JAPs, and in many cases literally the same exact ones from home." She read French. She enrolled in the school of individualized study. She listened to hip-hop out of the *banlieus*. She could move easily, she said, between "the clip of Parisian and the slang of North African immigrants." It went on and on and Will nodded along, wondering at times what Whitney and Jack were talking about so happily.

Life in the dorms, Leonard said, was an extension of everything she'd already experienced back home, only set in "the miserable winter grays of lower Fifth Avenue." The heat never worked in her suite. Her roommate fucked her boyfriend in the room while they thought she was asleep. When she complained, the roommate had her boyfriend build a shower curtain around her bed, hanging a contraption from the ceiling that collapsed on them "while he was pounding her in the ass one night, and I was on the other side of the room, wearing headphones and—get this—reading *Madame Bovary.*" The other two members of the suite lasted only until December (suicide attempt) and March (midterm scandal), granting her the opportunity to move alone into the cursed room, "with its stench of bong water and depression, and its view of the Empire State Building."

She lived the next year with a girl from the Valley, in an even more destitute suite, "giant by lower Manhattan standards," but with "a seemingly direct pipeline for bugs from the boiler room." She found a first-year analyst at Morgan Stanley to spend time with, mostly so she could "be alone at his apartment." He worked "twenty-eight hours a day and full-time on weekends." He required "three blow jobs a week, that was it." But if he was stressed about something at work, he might "try and fail to make me come..."

It was the line on her lips as she reached the carving station. They'd covered a lot of ground in the distance from the door to Curtis's chicken.

And so, she said, she would go to Paris for a year to "figure things out." It was her escape, she said, the only thing that had "made life tolerable." Arriving in Paris in September and walking around on the first afternoon was "the only time I've cried over something from feeling good." Her apartment was near the Canal, "near enough to the classrooms, near enough to the good places." She'd lived with two foreign roommates, "a German couple," she said. She went to clubs at night. She chose "a *nom de fête.*" She met "a boy." She met "another boy." She followed his band on tour to Brittany and then Bordeaux. She felt her interests "coming into focus in ways they wouldn't have back home." The place was "alive to me," she said. The place was "filled with my people." And it was affordable, she said, "half the cost of New York—New York truly is the worst." She could "never go back." But then the year ended. It was time to leave. She just knew. Suddenly, she said, she "couldn't spend another day there." So she boxed up her apartment and fled, "chased down here by the ashcloud, like I said before."

"*Et bien,*" she said, wiping her nose manically, clearing

the rim of a nostril, and joining Whitney and Jack back outside on the steps: "*Me voilà, donc.*"

The four rearranged themselves in a different shape than before, and they ate quickly. It wasn't much food, after all that time in line. Jack's legs ran like handrails down the steps. Leonard contorted herself between them like an ampersand, and flipped her hair so that it spilled onto the lap of his jeans.

An older couple wearing silk scarves approached the steps, and the man lowered his glasses to ask, quizzically: "*Je ne sais quoi?*"

Leonard stared back at the man, then turned to Whitney as though he might mean her. Leonard looked back at the man and said, "Me neither."

"From Le Grenier," the man said, in French-tinged English. "Jenna Saisquoi, no? We talked for some time maybe a month ago, after one of your shows. My wife, Celeste. And I'm Maxime? We shared a drink at Le Grenier..."

"I'm...sorry..." Leonard said. "I think you must have me confused with someone else."

Maxime turned to Celeste and chuckled, not in confusion, but in clear comprehension.

"No, no," Maxime said. "I'm sorry. Carry on. You know what they say: *Once you turn fifty, anyone under forty looks the same.*"

"I hadn't heard that," Leonard said, and smiled without unsealing her lips.

"Well aren't you a sweetheart," Maxime said, grinning widely at having caught her out. "Can we take your plates in for you? We're heading inside now, anyway."

The four waved them off graciously, and the couple disappeared into the apartment.

"Well," Leonard said, and everyone seemed to understand, and they stood, and they followed her in. As they passed into the light, Will pinched Whitney in the ribs, an acknowledgment that whatever this was, and whoever all these people were around them, they were part of the thing they'd noticed before, only now they were getting deeper.

Back inside, there was more wine. And Curtis had disappeared the pots of roasted chicken and replaced them with new wooden bowls of ice cream and berries. They sat beneath the bookshelves, their numbers dwindling now that it was creeping later. Curtis emptied another box of beer into the bucket of ice. Will and Whitney found themselves talking to the British architects again. They talked about politics, about the exit negotiations, about the new American president, about the elections in Holland and France and the Continent's swift lurch to the right.

But all conversations in the room seemed to eventually return to the volcano. You obviously couldn't return to London, the architects said, but there were still trains running east. They thought they'd head that direction for a few days until it cleared, go somewhere they hadn't been before. Bosnia, maybe. Serbia. They'd disappear into the mountains for a while, wait for the skies to clear. Gram overheard them and declared it a marvelous idea. He parted the crowd and stood on the couch beneath one of the grand shelves, and selected a slim volume in a blue jacket that looked like it could've been printed in the copy shop they'd passed on the walk up. It was a guide to the Balkans, to old Yugoslavia, written by Gram himself. The book had been published, he explained, by Likken Zuigen, the Dutch publishers who'd put out his first magazine. The borders might be different, he said, but the particulars no doubt held true. They could have the book, so long as they brought it back someday, he said. It would ensure their attendance at a future dinner party.

The first overt things Will and Whitney noticed were the hands. It may have started earlier in the night, but it caught their attention when Gram gave the British woman the guidebook. His hands fell to her hips. His hands traced around her lower back and he shifted behind her like a golf pro, giving a full-body demonstration of how best to flip the pages. His arms spread over her arms, showing off the maps, showing off photos of Gram in grainy black and white. His hands lay upon her hands. His face was in her hair. Her hips pressed back into him. Her husband watched, pleased.

All around them, unlimited wine, plastic cups in long supply, Will and Whitney drinking to speed things up, as a way to get through the ice-cream course quicker. There was music now. Rock 'n' roll in Italian. The conversations turned up to drown out the guitars. Jack and Leonard were in line for the bathroom, ignoring the books and photographs, locked into each other instead. Standing there like two different species, one practically twice the size of the other. Will and Whitney stood silent, watching them. They couldn't hear what they were saying, but Jack had Leonard laughing. He was acting out something physical, hands in the air, up on his toes—the saddest slam dunk in history. She pointed to a book on a shelf. He turned and looked, but instead of reaching for it himself, he lifted her at the waist. She was featherweight. Her legs dangled like soda straws and her shoes slipped to the floor. Her park-stained feet, nails painted the requested color of the session, hung there like prized hooves. She reached for the book and the inner edges of her breasts announced themselves to the room. They fell straight down, concealed only by the indifferent fabric of her dress. She pulled Jack's ear and he brought her back to Earth. She opened the book and showed him something. He laughed and she laughed, and then, as though forgetting about the bathroom, they disappeared up the stairs to the loft.

What had just been hands in the room was fully bodies now. No one was crossing the line yet, but there was a coziness all around, in the couches beneath the bookshelves, against the counter in the kitchen. New friends who'd spent a glorious gray evening together beneath the ashcloud, humming pleasantly with wine, buzzing ceaselessly with conversation, and the promise of being trapped in the city forever. It was time for Will and Whitney to go.

They approached Gram cautiously, wanting nothing less than to spark a fresh lecture. Will offered him the forty euros again. This time, after a brief and half-hearted protest, Gram handed him an envelope and asked him to write their names on it. There were already dozens of names, crossed out, Sundays for months, maybe years. Names of every nationality, like one of those posters with all the ways in the world to say *hello*. While Will filled out the envelope, Gram took his turn with Whitney. He wrapped an arm around her delicate, freckled shoulders. He complimented her eyes and her brows and her skin. Gram was still wearing the apron. He'd long lost his glasses. He told Whitney to come back anytime; Will, maybe one out of three of those anytimes, ha ha. It was a joke that prompted Whitney's polite laughter, which led to a heartier embrace. She made a final appeal with a smile that meant goodbye, and Gram kissed her on the cheek, and then the other cheek, just as anyone would bid farewell to a friend at a party in a city such as this one.

As they made their way to the entrance, they heard a soft

"Hey" and then a louder "Yo!" They turned to the sound, up to the loft that hung over the main room. Jack and Leonard were waving at them. "Are you leaving?" Leonard said. And they nodded and waved goodbye and Whitney blew a kiss.

"Hold up," Leonard said. "We're coming with."

Which is how they found themselves through the iron gate and out onto the street, mere hours after entering, but with seemingly a shift of seasons in the air.

"Where to?" Leonard said. She seemed recharged again, loose-jawed.

"Don't know," Whitney said. "We were just gonna head home, I guess."

"Walk with us, at least," Leonard said. "I needed out."

"It wasn't so bad, was it?" Jack said.

"It was only beginning," Leonard said. "It was going to get weird so fast. It's a nice night. No need to be stuck there as the party really gets going for the olds."

They walked three blocks in the wrong direction at first, and they were at the edge, suddenly, of one of the parks at La Sagrada Familia. It was already later than they'd realized, eleven-thirty, and the church was closed for the night, but bathed in the golden spotlights that kept the drip-castle spires visible at all hours. The cathedral was, Whitney had read, Gaudí's dying obsession, his lasting appeal to God to look after his one true love, Catalonia. A dark familiar feeling seized Whitney, as rarely happened anymore—a vestigial reminder that Sundays were meant for appeals for salvation, for family, for laundered skirts and blouses, not for getting drunk and staying out late with strangers. The feeling lasted only as long as a nervous tic, and then it was gone. Around the cathedral were Costa Coffees and Burger Kings. Open late for different travelers than the ones they'd just spent the evening with. The brightly lit vacant chains gave her an altogether different sense of dread.

"Wrong way," Leonard said, course-correcting to the Passeig de Sant Joan. The pedestrian walkway led toward the water, ever so faintly downhill. It was a long way, but they all seemed to have a sense that it was the *where* worth heading to. The passeig saved them from the pedestrian-unfriendly corners of the blocks in the neighborhood. Instead, they had a straight line to the sea. When the walkway disappeared, they looped around the Plaça de Tetuan to the wide boulevard leading to the Arc de Triomf and the entrance to the parks. Whitney took a picture of Will in the glow of the red-brick arch. Jack and Leonard were cozy shapes at the edge of the frame. She was pleased to have something to remember them by, to remember the night by, when it was all just a surreal story that Will and Whitney laughed about one day in the future.

They caught up to Jack and Leonard on the stone avenue of the park, lined on either side by sodium lights. They crossed into the Parc de la Ciutadella and happened upon several Sunday-evening dinner parties stretching later even than the one they'd escaped. There were balloons tied to lights and crepe paper in the trees. There were children still playing soccer in the low yellow light. There was no *quit*. Not yet. There was so much night left.

They passed beside the zoo. They heard animals rustling the trees, scraping their sides on the stone partition that kept the big cats out of the park. They crossed the train tracks—the heavy cargo rails that led into the Estació de França, that divided the planned part of the city from the old-world beach tenements of Barceloneta. They found stairs to a burned-out clearing and a modest pedestrian footpath buried beneath fresh spring foliage. At least three of them had no idea where they were going, yet they worked like a platoon, unquestioning, pressing collectively onward, ten steps at a time in the direction forward.

On the other side of the tracks, they smelled the ocean. There was a breeze in their faces, a breeze that was doing to Whitney's hair what appeared to have been done to Leonard's earlier. It punched Will in the gut when he realized just how close the water was: hundreds, not thousands, of feet from them now. They crossed the street and there, in the darkness—a gradient of blues, of midnights and Yves Kleins—were the sky and the sea. Immediately before them, palm trees stitched into the concrete of a promenade at even intervals. Between the palms were long flat backless benches. And then a railing before a modest drop-off to the sand and the water. There were bodies huddled up on the beach, clusters in the few skeins of knotted moonlight that permeated the ashcloud. Will and Whitney stood at the rail, watching them, breathing in the breeze, but Leonard was already on her way up the promenade, Jack in tow, heading toward the enormous gold-scaled sculpture, the fish, the *peix,* the Gehry.

They marched two by two, up beach, even farther up beach, past a port and some closed fish restaurants. Then, emerging from the blackness as though it were the only place for hundreds of miles, there appeared before them a softly lit cube on the sand, open-air, with windows and doors missing. It looked like what was left when the inessential blocks had been yanked from a Jenga.

Leonard led the way, and without a break in stride they

had four seats at a corner of the bar, two and two again, Will and Whitney pointed toward the water, toward the bonfires on the beach, toward the midnight volleyball and soccer games near the surf. The only other people at the bar were a pack of Swedish teens sitting in the corner sharing large bottles of beer and watching commercial-free music videos loop on a projector screen.

Leonard asked what everyone wanted and ordered in better Catalan than the three of them could muster combined. They sat there for a moment in the silence of realizing that they'd covered plenty of ground already. That they'd already imbibed more collective chatter than was responsible for strangers in a first encounter. So they did what was particularly useful in cases of the sort, and they talked about college. Whitney revealed to Jack that she too had been an athlete at school, if only for a season, and really just for a couple weeks. She showed him the gnarled scar beneath her kneecap. She described for Jack and Leonard her final couple semesters, when she'd finally locked into her most effective mode on campus: solo, solitary, script-obsessed. And though she left out what had come before all that, she felt its presence right there, beneath the surface of the bar, like the fat part of an iceberg.

Will told Jack and Leonard the story of the gardens, how he and Whitney had met, as wild as it was to recall now, the night of Jack's Sweet Sixteen game his junior season. It was the kind of school that was just big enough for that to be possible—for the three of them to have all been there together, but to have never overlapped. Jack couldn't believe it, but he loved it. He kept slapping the bar.

Leonard looked bored and so they paid up and she led them to a club. Will and Whitney would never have known about such a place themselves. It was a mile down the beach in the direction of the blackness, a twenty-minute walk. They followed the beach and kept the ocean to their right. They passed a fighting couple, then a stray dog, before arriving at a lonely office building sprung from a plain of asphalt. The office building functioned normally during the day, but at midnight it opened its top floor to music and dancing. Leonard spoke Catalan to the doorman. He let the two girls behind the rope but put his palms on the chests of Will and Jack. Leonard hooked the doorman's bicep and spoke something persuasive into his ear, and then he let them in, too, but with a finger that said: *Just this once.*

They took an elevator to the top floor. The ceiling and walls were covered with screw-in light bulbs, whites and reds and blues, that pulsed with the beat of the DJs at center stage. At the bar, Leonard explained there would be an unbroken string of thirty-minute sets until eight in the morning. The bright green numbers at the cash register said *01:32.* They were early. The drinks were surprisingly inexpensive. Will and Whitney drank tequila. They drank beers from tiny bottles. They drank vodka mixed with Red Bull. They'd been exhausted, but now they felt further from sleep than they had six hours ago.

Leonard and Jack were easy to keep an eye on. Jack's head grazed the light bulbs on the ceiling. They moved from the dance floor to one of the wings, and then to the stage. Will and Whitney danced together near the bar, dancing like they never did at home. They faced forward, moving side by side. Everyone faced forward, bodies toward the DJ. It was the crowd-facings of a political rally. They didn't look at one another, they looked at the person working the faders and the knobs. Everyone but Jack and Leonard, at least, who locked inward instead. Jack bent over a little awkwardly. He must've had his legs spread to lower himself to her height. She fit between his legs and he was low enough then for her to sling her arm over his shoulders, one hand on the back of his neck. Will and Whitney watched them dance. Will and Whitney could sense each other watching them dance. They could see, out of the sides of their eyes, the other shift toward them like the face of a flower to light. They could feel the other drawing in with curiosity, with concern, with whatever the feeling was when you need to see something and can't stop looking.

They hadn't gone out dancing for years—not since Will was in law school, probably, when the two of them would burn off the endless hours of Will's case law and Whitney's assistant work with friends who were in the same boat. They'd eat falafel and suck down shots on MacDougal and spill out onto the streets in an all-points-Lower-East stream to the underground rock 'n' roll bars below Delancey. They'd squeeze in together and dance themselves dripping, until their shirts and pants and dresses sweat through, until somebody lost a shoe. And then they'd wander back, waiting for the cheapest slice of pizza to present itself, so that they might eat a few bites and give the crust to a bum dog, and then head to the law dorms, and hope that the bars downstairs had called it for the night, so that they—the two semi-strivers in question—might be able to fall asleep now that they were through, now that their fun had been had, instead of being forced to listen to all the same keening pop melodies they'd danced to a few hours ago, before it had been time to catch their Zs.

This wasn't quite like that. This was electronica. This was another language that at least Whitney didn't speak. This was a face-off among the DJs, but also a propping up of one another, passing the beat like a baton. People moved spastically in tight quarters, like they were trying to dance their way out of a Porta-Potty. For Will and Whitney, it had kept feeling better until all of a sudden the music made no sense, and it was as though the link had failed between the cheap booze they kept buying and the way it manifested itself in their blood. There was nothing left to do but look around and realize it was a strange place where they didn't belong. Not just because they were illiterate to the music, not just because they didn't have any money left, but because, it occurred to them as bluntly as a crashing wave, they were the oldest people there—they were practically *thirty*.

Before they left, they found Jack and Leonard in line for the bathroom. They would've ordinarily let the night be the night and gone off forever without a trace—their MO at weddings, at dinner parties, at gatherings where they didn't have the time or energy to make new friends. But there was no telling how long they'd be trapped. It might actually be nice to hang out with someone else in the coming days. And so they all exchanged contacts, and Will explained that he wasn't always on the network—that he tended to keep his roaming turned off, it was so expensive—and that the best way to be in touch was probably via email. They learned from Leonard that before she'd left Paris, a whole impossibly long day ago, she'd thrown her phone into the Seine. It was the end of something significant, Leonard explained, and she couldn't possibly need it anymore.

Will and Whitney and Jack nodded like they understood completely, and then the couples detached and Will and Whitney found themselves riding the elevator down alone, and then spilling outside onto the asphalt, where there was a line fifty deep, now that it was four-thirty in the morning and time for people to really start coming out for the night. Will asked Whitney if she wanted to take a cab, but she said she'd prefer to walk along the water, to let some of the booze run its course while the music in her brain and body dialed down.

They wound up back at the long flat benches, at the palm trees, at the edge of Barceloneta. The sky was lightening, if vaguely. To the left was the Gehry fish. To the right was that giant hotel, out there on the point like the sail of a sixteenth-century galleon. The light was changing, but it was a matter of grays. The sun was coming up, somewhere behind the blackout shade of the ashcloud. But there was no color, there were no cones at work, just pencil shadings, just gradations. They'd made it to dawn. They had endured.

They slumped there on one of the backless benches, Whitney's head on Will's shoulder, Will's shoulders pushed way up to his ears. They had stayed out, they had been interesting enough, they had done something new and un-expected and wholly unlike themselves. Whitney rubbed her fingers through Will's salt-crystalled hair. And though she knew that what he wanted most just then was for her to say it first, to concede her desire to finally go home, she resisted, which he knew she would, which only confirmed for him just how well he knew what was going on in her head, too. Instead, she stood up, in silence, and wondered if he was really going to make her say it, she was too exhausted for words, and he must know what she wanted, anyway.

They let each other dangle there, they deferred the curtain. He needed her to say it, to name it, to be the dull one, to be the bore—just for a change of pace. He needed to prove his interestingness, his ability to last. They played this game at home sometimes. Who would call it quits first? Who would be the first to go down for the night? They would sometimes fall asleep with the lights on, they were both so stubborn—lights bright, a mutual abeyance. Most of the time, though, Will would pass out right out of the blocks. He was, after all, as deficient as he suspected sometimes, limited in all the ways he feared. Tonight, for once, he had been convincing as the sort of young American who stays out late in Barcelona. He had played the part, and it had even felt easy at times.

At the party, she had been never less cool than the coolness of her career. Which meant she hadn't had to be from anywhere in particular. She hadn't had to speak, as she sometimes did, on behalf of the legislature and laws of the state where her parents happened to live. She hadn't had to answer questions about Aikman or Cruz or JR. She could simply be American, and quite beautiful, and young enough still. And so she wouldn't be the one to concede. But she knew that he wouldn't either, resisting with every fiber in his bones being the one who ended the unending night.

So instead, she just started back in the direction of the apartment alone. She was barefoot now; her footsteps were light and Will didn't hear her go. Which was why when he turned around to finally call it, to officially say the words, he saw that she was well down the alley, practically halfway home.

Kýr

The black-hot jelly burned through the valley with a speed all its own. It was slow compared with the geyser that had lit the canopy the day before. It was slow compared with the spread of the ash above, the tephra and the smoke. The liquid fire, rather, crept like a slurry down the gentle slopes of the volcano—in one gravitationally destined direction toward the sizzle and the steam of the sea, and in the other toward the flats of the farmland.

The farmers and fishermen had evacuated without incident but had left behind their homes, the possessions they couldn't pack away, the permanent things that were too heavy for itinerants. They'd unlocked the fences and encouraged the animals to run. The horses and the pigs had been wise enough to flee, the ducks and geese swift enough to fly. But the cows had stayed behind and grazed as ever, in the shadow of the ridge of their eternal home.

A cow called Blár, alone and unafraid, approached the edge of a lazy stream, liquid in abundance like she hadn't encountered since a trip to the far side of the mountain for a festival in her youth. A festival for which she'd worn flowers

109

on her back and a bell around her neck, and been paraded through her town and the next and the one beside that. They'd marched her to the lake in the hills and she'd drunk from the lake until she was full, and then they'd marched her back in the bright light of a summer midnight, and she'd slept as never before.

She saw the stream approaching, and she hooved up to its edge, even as she felt a great heat all around. As she lowered her mouth to drink, the liquid splashed her legs, and she cried out at the shock of it. But slow as it rolled, the stream was still much too fast for Blár. The hide of her forelegs separated from the muscle, and the muscle peeled from the bone. Her legs crumpled, and her chest and face fell into the fire, cutting her agonizing bellow like an ax, a severing of the sound. There was a final desperate jerk as her flaming head reached for the sky, and a new noise came out this time—an atavistic sound—that resembled most closely the bark of a dog. Embroiled in fire, short on breath: a death cry.

The ash fell soft as snow all around. The sparse trees of the valley burned like stovetop flames. The air grew hot, unbearably so, each movement in the vents of Holudjöfulsins like the door of an oven opening up. The volcano was finished but the consequences kept coming, kept working over the land, kept running their course. Lava and ash, on earth and in heaven, spread with impunity and took on all comers.

Monday

They slept until noon, but it didn't feel like sleep at all. The apartment had been wide-awake when they got home—lamps on, ash-light through the open windows—and the rooms had been lit up with daybreak. But before they could summon their zombie reserves to lower the blinds, they'd passed out half-clothed, smothering their faces with pillows and sheets for six restless hours.

Now it was the exhaustion of a transatlantic redeye all over again. The grime in Will's stubble, the slime in Whitney's pores. The burning red rings sapping the liquid from their eyes. They'd grumbled and they'd showered and then they hit the street feeling their legs and bodies and heads abuzz. The faint stench of sewage found their nostrils. They hadn't been hungover in the afternoon in years. They hadn't been hungover in the morning since 1-2-3.

It was too late for the commuting crowds and too early for the lunch rush. But there were more working-age people who didn't seem to be working than they'd seen anywhere in the world besides lower Manhattan. A grave unemployment rate, protests and drum circles at Plaça de Catalunya, panhandling on La Rambla. They passed the unworking in droves, and that didn't even count the old men who seemed to stroll—alone, driven toward fixed points—three to a block. These were not the European men of graphic T-shirts and jungle-cat jeans, of shiny sunglasses and tangles of jewelry in chest hair. These were the old dignified Catalans. Of reserved judgment and austerity. Of loafers and slacks and moth-eaten cardigans. Cardigans for all seasons. Cardigans for every occasion: for separatist rallies, for lunches of ham and espresso, for football matches late into the evenings. Hunched forward ever so, reading materials clamped and concealed behind their backs. Fresh copies of *La Vanguardia* and treatises with names like "L'Idea de Europe." They were like French philosophers without the pretension; like English farmers without the melancholy of the countryside; like Italians of the breezy north without the worship of textiles. These were men who hadn't realized that they lived on the Mediterranean Sea until development for the Olympics had brought their city back down to the waterfront. Of average-est height, of average-est wealth, of average-est ambition—they were a vision of resolve and of pleasure worth pursuing. They loved coffee, they loved wine. They loved to read the print edition of the newspaper.

Will and Whitney followed a few of them up the mountain. One peeled off into an empty bar. Another disappeared into a café where he was greeted with roars. A third, with a leashless Labrador retriever, slipped through a small door on the lower slope of Montjuïc that led, they could see when they peeked, into a courtyard like Gram's. From there, the road steepened abruptly. A transition to sea-facing buildings, of more modest verticals with drying lines. Will and

Whitney felt themselves lean back with the road, as steep as a pedestrian could handle. They found the stairs. A hundred to the top. They gained altitude in large gulps. They felt their legs burning and the urge to break, to turn back to look, but denied themselves that pleasure in exchange for the payoff at the top.

At the clearing, they made faces at each other for their heavy breathing, for the seizure of conversation, for the crimson in their cheeks and the veins in their foreheads. They were still drunk, they were still reckoning with the booze and the strawberry tinge to their acid reflux. They barely even remembered ordering Red Bulls at the club.

The view was north, astonishing, into the bowl of the city, the strip of sea-blue to the right, the baked oranges of the roofs like pointillist pastels. Each building stood at its near-uniform height. The Gótico jumble nearer the beach, the orderly octagons of the Eixample well off the water— the city plan. Everything looking itself, in harmony, with the exception of the great cathedral, whose completion seemed eternally forbidden.

The mountain, Montjuïc, was lush. A gondola fell down its backside toward the water. Buses delivered tourists to the castle at its crest. Will and Whitney ordered espressos from a stand in the clearing at the top of the steps. They didn't say anything that wasn't essential. They were exhausted, sweaty, a little sick of hearing each other inhale and exhale. They passed the public swimming pool where the diving at the 1992 Olympics had been held—two-and-a-halfs off the platform in the foreground, the sweeping panorama of the city behind. Will bent himself around a barricade to take a crummy photo with his phone. The ashcloud had sealed impenetrably over the lambent blues of those famous diving shots. The ashcloud had trapped the whole of the city under tinfoil.

They found the line at the Fundació Miró, their destination. They hadn't been able to squeeze it in during their shorter stay, so they had put it on the napkin list. The building was all flats and crescents, unshowy curves in glass and concrete that looked composed of the limited building blocks of a play set. The structure spread leisurely out from the entrance into a series of spacious rooms and terraces. The floors were made of a buffed brown tile. The whole place seemed deliberately run-down, architected to take the piss out of the expectation of the sort of art-induced reverie Whitney was always seeking. Here, there was no pinch of anxiety about saying the wrong thing or stepping into the wrong room at the wrong moment. It was no wonder there were children everywhere, lounging on the floors, making their own art to match the artist's. Children spreading out into wider shapes in larger rooms still, some drifting off to sleep. In the new world beneath the volcano, life had been paused indefinitely for Will and Whitney, but it had gone on for everyone else here, which meant work, which meant school, which meant field trips to art museums, and to this place in particular. It was their home, their city, their *museu*—it so very much belonged to them.

They paid for their tickets and drifted in different directions, into separate rooms. Rooms of arcs and moons, of primary colors. On the canvases, Will detected a shakiness of line, a shimmer from the application of paint that betrayed a human hand. There was a serenity to the works, an in-suck that imparted a quiet on body and mind that approached, for Will, the lift he got half an hour after a run.

But that pleasant helium lasted only until he ran smack into something he wasn't prepared for.

On the far wall of the farthest room, alone and in strange still windowless light, a perfectly pleasant mural transported Will suddenly to the lobby of his office, to the abstract monstrosity that hung on the accent wall opposite the security check-in counter. The mural at Turtle Bay Tower was meant to signify to all employees that right here, in this most select office building, there existed abundant exposure to external culture and a well-balanced life: a life of humanism, a life of art. The mural was also meant to more literally represent a map of the hubs and spokes of connectivity between the media conglomerate and the law firm that represented it globally—cartographed right there on the wall for all who gazed upon it. The mural had become the centerpiece of Will's interminable days at work, passing it six or eight times each morning, afternoon, and evening, depending on how often he went for coffee or food or fresh air; depending on how often he felt even one more minute at his desk might result in sudden capitulation to death.

He wasn't supposed to be a lawyer. *Lawyer* had been a dirty word in his house growing up. And yet one lazy grade after another in the weed-out courses in college had led him through the laundry list of pre-professional tracks he knew he'd never possessed the facility for anyway. And so it was for all the wrong reasons—he'd followed a beautiful new acquaintance into the lecture hall, on the off chance that they might spend the semester studying together—that Will wound up in the undergraduate Constitutional Law lecture in his final fall semester. And it was perhaps only fate showing its face that the afternoon he received his first eviscerating critique in an Intro to Screenwriting course he also received near-perfect marks on his conlaw midterm. The mastery of the facts, the creative application of available materials, had more in common with the work he did in summers building houses with his father than anything he'd encountered in the classroom before. Like an attorney, Will's father was hired to execute on someone else's objective, but he got his reputation for the way he solved the puzzle. Even his father's motto—*We're expensive, but we're slow*—sounded to Will like a lawyer's boast.

Will had spent every summer of college at home, at the beach. Where he could cut lumber and pound nails with his shirt off, and get back to something tangible, something he knew he could start and finish with pride. He got tan in summers. He had flings with toasted bunnies who sold sunglasses in downtown Sela del Mar. He rented and re-rented his favorite DVDs from their video store, and bought the scripts that the clerk recommended. But it was also during each of those long sparkling summers, in a sun-daze of contentedness, that Will grew convinced of what he suspected to be true when he was away at school: that being from Sela del Mar was the single most interesting thing about him. He longboarded around campus. He played club volleyball. He surfed warm weekends out on barrier islands. And as he struggled to find his footing in the classroom, his association with California became his primary antidote to anonymity. Still, the fact of having found no clear passion or path forward had become a singular fixation for Will, like a pulse in a rotten tooth. He was happy to go home for every hour of every break, to disappear into the luxury of that escape— and for a while, it was enough. But as the finish line crept closer, he knew he needed a real plan for the exit.

It was during that final fall, on a trip to the chain bookstore outside town to pick up scripts for *Taxi Driver* and *Rocky* and *Chinatown* and *Jaws*, that Will spotted an LSAT prep book on his way to the checkout counter, and dispassionately added it to his stack for good measure. The morning of the exam, he assured those he recognized that law school wasn't something he'd actually pursue, it was just to see, just to cross his Ts—just like everybody else was probably doing there, right? But at Christmas, after returning from an early-morning surf beneath the flight path, he logged in to the test portal and discovered he'd scored a 174.

He knew at once that it was a mistake. That his exam must've been exchanged with someone else's. He'd never sniffed 174 on the practice tests. He'd never approached the ninety-ninth percentile in anything in his life. Some poor someone out there was scratching his or her head, wondering what he or she had done to deserve such an inexplicably compromised fate. As compared to Will, that walking embodiment of the benefit of the doubt, who tempted himself in that instant to believe that maybe, just maybe, he'd earned it—and that he was maybe even destined to succeed in life after all.

He had been blessed from the beginning, he knew. Born at the beach. With the salt, the light, the perpetual glory. The three-bedroom house with the stucco veneer, a ten-minute walk from the ocean. That little house. That little porch. The screens on the windows and the screens on the doors. The brown carpet. The yellow kitchen. The shed with the tool bins. The work truck parked out front. The drawers stuffed with VHS tapes. The video-store membership card like a key to the kingdom. They had spring, summer, fall, and winter. Rain, Camp, Fire, and Fog—their seasons, his seasons growing up. His father worked outside year-round in Red Wing boots and Gramicci shorts. His mother lived in a comfort zone of three or four degrees Fahrenheit. He built houses and she sold them. They had one child. Lucky him. Lucky Will. It had been the case all along.

And now, after so much searching, he had found his escape pod. No more failed attempts at the things that were too hard—that he had no business trying, that he was just too not-good-enough at. He knew enough about movies to know that they were simply the dreams of a naive teen skater with a camcorder and a video-store card. And he hadn't even yet met the someone whose knowledge—whose understanding of what it really took, of what it really was to be great—would put him and his knowing-ness to further shame. He felt fortunate then, so early on in life, to understand the difference between what was possible for him, and what wasn't. He felt fortunate that even at twenty-one he could see himself the way he truly was. He would go to law school. He would be a lawyer. And he would be good at it.

Those were the last days before Whitney. The days before love and law school and internships, and the public defender in New Haven, and the First Amendment firm in Washington, and then ultimately back to New York. He worked in magazines now. Or at least *for* magazines. Advising on libel and defamation, but mostly processing contracts. *What must we do to not get sued?* was the question often presented to Will—along with an attached contract and a claim by a contractor, or a manuscript and a quote from the litigious founder of a sham start-up.

He had liked it fine at first. The stakes. The peripheral yet critical work helping to prop up a fragile American institution. And he had had a handle on it for a while, too. Steady. Cool. Californian. But two and a half years of pressure and volume had squeezed him, deadened him. Heat and acid congealing right there between his throat and his heart. He'd been in the job for just thirty months. Not long enough to quit—he couldn't quit. But it had been longer than he could remember since a day at the office had not placed that anvil on his chest. The braided symptoms of anxiety and rage.

On recent working weekends, Will had marveled emptily at the uncanny scale of the computer-generated splotches of color on the lobby mural. Standing there slack, with a tossed salad in a plastic trough, Will would slip deeply into the mural while the jaw he inherited from his father pulsed tensely in his cheeks. He would just hang there, hating every inch of the fucking thing, then crash through the mechanical arm near the security desk before it chirped wide. Which direction was it all flowing? Was his work making him hate the art? Or was the art making him hate his work?

Will stood before the Miró now, contemplating these questions, and heard sharp, audible breaths from somewhere. It took him a moment to realize they were his own. He had been so relieved, that seeming eternity ago, when he'd found law as a warm and friendly way station, that he never once considered the long-term implications of a career in contracts. But that fucking mural—sensing it even where it wasn't—confirmed for him his most private concern: that his thoughtless career choices had led him into a trap of inescapable dullness. He must quit. But he couldn't quit. He needed the money badly. For loans, for living. No one who had been hired right after the crash threw away a job so hastily. He needed to keep up with Whitney, anyway. He needed to stay above water and not plunge into the deep end with all the people around him who had even worse debt than he did. There wasn't anything he could do just now.

And so he would wait. He would wait for feedback on the screenplay. The thought of his script provided instant relief. He'd sent it out before the trip. It was a secret; Whitney knew nothing about it still. He would hear back soon from the producer. And the new escape pod would present itself. A new life that moved just a little slower. A life of more cafés, more afternoon naps. He couldn't quit just yet. He couldn't succumb to the provocations of the mural. He would be patient for now. He would persist.

At the other end of the museum, Whitney smiled as she turned another corner. She loved being inside museums. She believed they could change your chemistry, if even for a short spell. After visiting a museum, she felt civically lifted, the same sensation that flooded her after voting. She felt at home with the generous width and limited depth of her knowledge, with the undergraduate's foundational base. She kept up with reviews in the *Times* and *The New Yorker*. She paid full price at the Met and took advantage of her MoMA corporate membership. She felt comfortable confirming her best guesses with the labels on the walls. There were connections that went back.

Her father told people she'd been named for a mountain, but her mother insisted she'd been named for a museum. Her mother would drop little truths like that, as though she were the only one who knew the real story, as though her version of their shared life superseded his. Her father flew commercially, the reason they'd wound up in Dallas in the first place. He was bighearted but unconditionally deferential, conceding any fact—including the origin of his daughter's name—in order that he might get out the door faster, his head still clear for flying. His stretches away meant Whitney's mother was often alone with a messy house and a full-time job and a shy but self-sufficient daughter and a handsome but hell-raising son, who sucked up the lion's share of her attention, the energy of a solar system. Whitney's mother had had a life before them, she made sure they knew. A life that reared its head with the names of museums in far-off cities, and a habit of going alone to the movies once a week, and an insistence to Whitney that she not waste her time on a liberal arts degree, as she had, lest Whitney find herself trapped in the same endless cycle of dissatisfaction.

They'd moved to five different pockets of Dallas–Fort Worth by the time Whitney was even thinking about college. Her mother switched schools more than football coaches, searching out new teaching opportunities for herself, but claiming all the change was on behalf of Whitney's brother, who could never seem to find the right "situation," whose violence on the playground would rear its head "unexpectedly," even though physical fighting was the only way he communicated with Whitney for years. But for all the focus on her brother, Whitney knew even from a young age that it was her mother who necessitated the sudden ejections, the hard pivots, the whiteboard wiped clean. She'd never stopped wanting the better something for herself that she was certain she was owed for all the sacrifice. She told Whitney all her life that everything she did was to make her and her brother's life easier. But the effect of her rule—for Whitney, at least—was almost always to make it harder.

At schools in Euless and Arlington and Richardson and Haney, Whitney navigated toward the unobtrusive middle, tacking neither too high or too low, leaving knots of near-friendships in her wake. Daylight hours, then, were devoted to schoolwork and soccer. And in the evenings, on the personal television that her parents gifted her as an alternative to the 24/7 live-sports marathons her brother insisted on, Whitney could commune nightly with the wisdom of MTV, of the lives lived out there, away from the Webers and the Whataburgers and the overwatered yards of her cul-de-sac. Growing up, she'd never given herself entirely over to home. She'd never even let the accent in—choosing to mimic her mom and dad and MTV VJs instead. Her parents had only landed there eventually, she reasoned. They didn't have it in their blood, and so why should it be required of her? But New Orleans and Chicago and Paris—her favorite seasons of *Real World*—what would it be like to turn herself into not a cast member necessarily, but an extra in a city like one of those someday? A young woman in the background reading a book in a café? A slightly older woman in monochromes clacking down a sidewalk in heels? There was something grand out there, she knew, something her mother and father had seen in their prehistory together, in their years stationed overseas, that she must experience herself. She'd had the flushing sensation, even before she could name it, that she must not get sucked down, that she must make something of herself.

Whitney turned another corner in the museum. There was a detonation on the surface of one of the Mirós. She approached it slowly and mouthed the word "Pow!" She'd seen this one before—maybe in a textbook. Maybe in one of the many courses she'd taken near the end of college. Her mother's insistence that she not study liberal arts hadn't guaranteed that Whitney would do so, but it hadn't exactly had the effect her mother intended, either. Literature and classics and art history and film. There were things that could happen to you with art, she knew. Things it could do to your body.

It started for Whitney with the sparse illustrations in the Bibles in the backs of the pews. As much as they moved house in the sprawl, the airport and the church were the sole fixed axles around which their life revolved. At DFW, her father was unburdened. At St. Luke's, her mother was able to sit still. From the illustrations, it progressed for Whitney to the stained glass that stretched from the altar to the narthex. And then, of course, to the sculpture of Saint Teresa that rooted itself beneath the bleeding Christ on the cross. Teresa in ecstasy. Teresa in religious elevation, the sort all boys and girls at Sunday school were instructed to aspire to—through study, through practice, through prayer. After taking the wafer and the wine, Whitney would, for years, steer wide on the way back to her seat to extend her glimpse of the face of the woman whose heart was pierced by the news of the angel, his sharp little golden spear.

At first, there was fear. It looked as though Teresa was in pain—scared, even. When Whitney had asked her mother about it, her mother showed her the photo they bought from the top of Splash Mountain on a family trip to Disney World. Whitney looked terrified, but her mother reminded her how she'd felt at the bottom, the fit of giggles. Whitney lived for that feeling. If that feeling was findable again by focus, by willing it through prayer, that was something worth pursuing. That was something she could think really really hard on before bed each night.

For a time, she'd convinced herself that she'd found

glimmers of that ecstasy in MTV, her oasis, her own little golden spear to the heart. And then, for years, she thought she felt flickers on the soccer field—rapture in a boomeranging cross from the wing, in a blistering strike from outside the box. But the shards of light that the older women had promised were gradually lost on her, as many of them later confessed they had been lost on them. Her effort faded. It had been a silly pursuit anyway. It wasn't until a stopover in New York on their way to a club tournament one spring in high school that Whitney's faith in the promise was restored.

It was her first trip to New York. She was intimidated by the assault of stimuli, suffering a blizzard of sound and light. She liked the pizza and the pretzels and the dogs that looked like their owners. She liked the hotel and the room service and the bellhops in the lobby. But after just the first day, she was eager to escape. Which was when her mother took her on a walk through the park and up to the museum that was claimed as her namesake, depositing Whitney inside all alone for an hour while she met a friend Whitney had never heard of before. All alone, Whitney wandered the concrete floors, as chilly on the inside as outside, until she came upon a room containing a series of paintings by two American women that did to her body the thing she'd long abandoned hope for. Her blood beat in her wrists and her ankles. Her throat flushed. She felt her pores open and a scrim of slickness on her skin. She loved whatever these things were, loved them absolutely. She wanted to cover the walls of her room with those paintings as soon as she got home. She knew they were made by women the instant she'd spotted them.

After that trip, she started searching for those surges

of reverie in more accessible places—like the back seats of Pathfinders and basements with Cowboys pennants. She pursued them at sleepaway soccer camps and parties after school plays, in the hot tub at Jake Devine's and in leaf piles behind Nick Harris's grandma's. And still, it was never all the way what she was looking for. She'd steadily, incrementally, mapped a transition away from Sunday school to occasional encounters with boys, but she couldn't quite find the feelings in her body that she craved most intensely.

It wasn't until she went to Paris her junior fall that she rediscovered art, rediscovered museums, rediscovered what it could do—led back into it all by a beautiful new friend. After landing awkwardly on campus, after leaving the soccer team unceremoniously, after making a mess of her second spring and summer, she'd just never fully locked in. But the experiences abroad elevated her into the milieu she'd been searching for all along on campus—this castle of sorts she'd known had existed, but hadn't known where the door was. She moved from painting and sculpture to literature and film, schooling herself in classic narratives and then contemporary, in emotional beats, in beginnings middles and ends, in the craft of tension and satisfying payoffs. These works of art, these stories, were the places, it turned out, where she finally found the reveries she'd been searching for since she was old enough to take communion. She could have a hand in creating for others those sorts of emotional and physical responses, an alumna told her at the arts-and-media fair senior year. And so it was in the long afternoons of reading at the museum café on campus that art fused with books fused with movies and TV—and then ultimately with a boy named Will. And just like that there was a whole new galaxy of feelings worth pursuing, feelings that might hopefully never run out.

But it just wasn't happening for her here today. She was too distracted, maybe even drunk still. Whitney turned the corner to find a class of elementary school children spread out across the floor, hunchbacked and crane-necked, fixated on the paintings, working hard at their own works. Handprints, sparrows, suns with faces. The children were making a real effort to see something special on the walls, even if they didn't fully understand. She looked at the paintings with them. She waited. She concentrated. It was like she was being muted. By plastic. By glass. By ashcloud. She watched their little faces searching. She felt trapped suddenly. There were no windows in the corner where she'd wandered. It was boiling hot. The light was stale and the tiles were brown. She needed air, even volcano air, even air filled with fire and smoke.

She stepped out onto the terrace with the sculptures. Play-Doh colors, the pinched-form figurines. She looked out over the bowl of the city and tried to imagine the basin soaked in a golden light. Her eyes found the water. They found the unfinished cathedral. Everything was bathed in a blackness of shadow. She coveted nothing more in that moment than a crack in the clouds, even the briefest glimpse of the city in its full radiant glory. She even tried praying— *what was she doing?* It was dark still. She wasn't important enough, powerful enough, talented enough to affect things like that. She knew. And so she slipped into a familiar spiral. She thought back to several mistakes she'd made at work this year, several people she perceived she'd disappointed recently, all the people she'd failed to let herself get close to growing up. She thought of the disappointment her parents had expressed when she quit the soccer team, the financial burden it had brought upon all of them when she forfeited her scholarship, all because she couldn't stand playing a single day more. She thought of the ways in which she'd wasted those first couple years on campus, hobbling around on her bum knee, failing to fit in, fearing nothing more than being found out by the young women who so very much belonged. She thought of the errors she'd made back then—the blinding fuckups, the miscarriage—and the subsequent escape abroad. She thought of Paris, she thought of the pivots she'd engineered, the reorientation to the heading that finally made sense, that had led directly from there to here. She thought of all the things she was responsible for now, and how she wasn't qualified to be responsible for any of them. She thought of all she'd never be able to achieve.

She thought, then, of Will. Of Will fucking other women. It sent a hot shock down the length of her esophagus. She hated him just then, but he'd done nothing wrong. It had been her idea. She imagined Will fixated on the tops of their blonde heads between his legs, Will's mind in those moments filled with every thought but a thought of Whitney. She thought of being naked with the strangers of her own. She thought of the openness of her body those evenings and afternoons, the ease with which her clothes had come off, how much she'd worried about being naked with someone for so many years, and then one day how ordinary it had become.

The city was frozen still beneath the ashcloud. She turned on her roaming and checked her email. She had several. She read them. She felt her nipples pressing against the padding of her bra. And then she felt a searing shame that she'd been growing aroused on the terrace all alone in the grim ash. She wandered back inside holding her head, her hangover suddenly chirping like a smoke alarm.

When they found each other inside, they inferred that they were both through with their museum-going experience, and wandered into the courtyard café without either suggesting it. Whitney said she was growing queasier by the moment, so Will ordered a couple beers. He popped the caps and stuffed the bottles in his jacket pockets and the two of them spilled into the dense-shade park that adjoined the museum. Cypresses and palms and damp mud, damp without a concession by the ashcloud to some drying light. They sat on a bench in the park that had softened with the weather to the texture of a cashew. The mud near their feet had a skin like ballpark cheese.

"What do you think happened to them?" Whitney said.

They'd resisted until then. Neither had acknowledged the resisting, but it had been present in their silence all afternoon. They had bangings in their brains, they had dry tongues and fatigue. They hadn't minded the lack of small talk on the walk up, since each was focused merely on completing successive footsteps, on suppressing nausea, on following their slow-rolling shepherds in cardigans. But they'd known that the other had been thinking about the question and the likely answers.

"What happened to who?" Will said.

Her face forfeited nothing and made it clear she wasn't in the mood to be teased.

"I mean," he said, "it was probably going where it looked like it was going, right?"

"Whose place?"

"Well, I doubt they went back to Gram's at six in the morning."

"What do you think his apartment is like?"

"Probably not that different from the place we're staying. Those guys don't make *so* much money. He's living alone. He's not there half the time. A big bed and a big TV? Some chicken in the crisper and a tub of protein powder on top of the fridge?"

"They make me feel old," Whitney said.

"You and JJ are practically the same age."

"But he still has that thing where, I dunno, he's been playing a game since graduation."

"That sounds like a mixed bag, though, doesn't it?"

"I just mean he's still functionally twenty-two. Did you see the way he held his spoon? Did you see the way he looked up at the buildings and the trees on the way to the beach? It's like he's been in college for a decade."

"So what?"

"So we're too old for them."

"I didn't realize we were auditioning for something."

"Just, don't you ever think about how quickly we're getting older?"

"How 'bout we don't have to talk about them anymore?"

"It just gets under my skin. I don't get it in the winters, for some reason. But every spring, there's a new neighborhood I feel out of place in. Don't you? First it was the Lower East Side, then it was Williamsburg, now I don't even feel like I can eat dinner around our fucking apartment, everyone's such a baby. The ever-replenishing supply of fresh-faced models in the neighborhood."

"*We get older, they stay the saaaaame age . . .*"

"All looking at me like *I'm* the one who's lost. *I fucking live here!*"

"Who gives a shit? You don't get some relief from it? Every year, as more things are shut off, as there are more things we're not meant to do? At least it's clarifying. Think about it: we'll never have to check the Lower East Side box on StreetEasy again. That's not so bad. I like knowing there's stuff I can't even fantasize about anymore. Pro surfer—gone. Lead guitarist, hedge-fund dipshit, wunderkind of any sort—gone gone gone. Makes me at least come to terms with what's never ever gonna happen."

"That bums me out. I wish you didn't feel that way." She sat on her hands, stared off into the bowl again. She didn't say anything else. And so he tried it out for the first time in a while.

"In that case, maybe I'll finally write a script....Put all that dumb prep work to use. I realize it goes against what I just said about knowing what you can't do, but maybe it's, I dunno..."

"You sound like Jack."

It slapped him, and it surprised him that it stung.

"How's that?" Will said, flinching.

"That's his big next plan, so he says. That's his second act."

"Aren't we all a bunch of cliché assholes?"

"It's not as easy as it looks."

Will snorted and twisted on the bench. He hated her. "You're telling that to me or you're telling that to him? It better not be to me."

"It's more than just downloading Final Draft, is all I'm saying."

"Are you taking it out on me because a petite blonde

twenty-two-year-old made you feel twenty-nine last night? Is this your pressure valve for all that?"

The beers had gone straight to their heads, resuscitating the booze still sloshing around their soft pink brains.

"So you're agreeing that I'm old," Whitney said. "That's what you're saying?"

"What are you doing?" Will said, squinting through burning eyes. "Is this fun for you? I don't know how we found her in a random-ass park in Barcelona, but I'm thrilled this Whitney decided to show up. Self-loathing Whitney. Envious Whitney. My favorite Whitneys through and through."

"No bags under her eyes, no veins in her hands? Water balloons that sit up on her chest like she's wearing a bra when she isn't? Isn't that what you want? Isn't that what anyone would want? If that's what you want, go for it—you have my permission."

"You forgot all the to-the-manor-born elements of her upbringing, too," he said. "All the easy thoughtless connections to art and culture and money and moviemaking. Friends with the sons and daughters of Hollywood royalty. We didn't even talk about all that stuff yet—everything she told me in line for dinner. All your favorite old buttons. This explains a lot, actually. This at least explains the silence on the walk over here—"

"You weren't talking, either."

"—feeling nice and good about yourself after a night out with a girl who was raised with everything you weren't. Here I thought you were just hungover."

"I feel fucking fine now, thanks. Maybe you don't, but I'm—"

"Then what are you talking about?!"

"They barely even blinked when we left," she said. "In

that club we were nothing more than, like, a breeze that passed through the place. Nothing changes whether we're there or we're not. We don't change anything for them or anyone else."

"Thank you for joining the party, Insecure Whitney! We were wondering where you were hanging out. Jesus, Whit, who gives a shit?! We're not even supposed to be here. This isn't our place—you get that? We're here on bonus time. We're not meant to make some big impression that changes the fucking lives of some strangers. And if being the coolest kids at four in the morning at a nightclub in Barcelona is important to you, I think we've been living the wrong life for a while—working the wrong jobs, hanging out with the wrong friends, and certainly dating the wrong people."

She squeezed her eyes tight and held her hands up in concession.

"You're right, you're right....I know that. This isn't our life. But isn't that the *point?* We *are* in bonus time. We *aren't* supposed to be here. Which means it isn't like real life, it doesn't have to be precisely the same as it always is, you know? It's this parallel thing happening. And it's, like, a test, or something. The universe telling us: *Go do the things you wouldn't normally do. Find out if there's a version of yourself you like more.* It's seeing if we'll take up the offer."

"I actually have no idea what you're talking about. I hear the words, but it's like your brain has gone scrambly. You're saying: *Drink one more drink at the club? Stay out one more hour?* You're saying: *Follow those two home and watch them fuck?*"

"Don't be an asshole," she said. "All I mean is here we are in bonus time and we're, you know, going to museums. It's not the most excit—"

"It was your fucking idea! You wrote it on the napkin yesterday!"

"I should've known better. I should've known it wouldn't be what I needed it to be. We should've deviated from the plan. We should've followed one of those old men down a path somewhere, wherever they were going, wherever that led."

She closed her eyes again, touched her longest fingers to her temples and rubbed clockwise.

"This is so dumb," he said. "You sound like a fucking study-abroad pamphlet: 'Get lost in Florence.' 'I just *love* losing myself in the alleys of Toledo.' Whatever, man—do whatever you want."

"Maybe we bump into them again tonight."

Her eyes were still shut. He turned his body on the bench again and looked at her, disbelieving, waiting for her to return to the time and space where they were sitting.

"Is this jealousy?" he said. "Is that what's going on? You're jealous that the chick with the famous feet gets to go home with the basketball star, too?"

"Please don't put it in those terms," she said. "I wasn't until now."

He smiled. "God, you're so easy. You're almost thirty years old and you're easy as ever. And I can tell you're not even *actually* bothered by it. You just *want* to be bothered by it, because it's more interesting. Let's wrap this the fuck up, all right?"

"I'm sorry. I know. I mean, I don't know. *I don't know!* I don't know what's going on right now. I woke up drunk and buzzing in the face and my whole body's fucking throbbing. And I got this chill out on the museum terrace. My mind started wandering to some unhelpful places. I'm just...feeling anxious. Like: *You're wasting an opportunity.* Like: *You've been granted something spooky, and you're in a museum while the world's waiting to see how you respond to its big provocation.*"

"Maybe we should've stuck together in there. I didn't realize how perilous it was gonna be. I saw a painting that made me want to quit my job, if that makes you feel better. It started speaking to me and said that I could never set foot in my office building again. It convinced me that I need to look for a job that traffics in less fine print."

"Or maybe you just need to work somewhere that doesn't require you to go in both days on the weekend."

"I can't do it yet," he said. "I need to do it, but I can't do it without the money lined up."

She nodded and leveled her eyes out at the basin. "Think about it, really.... She's here for twelve hours...she gets one man off with her feet, then she goes home later that night with a nice tall handsome guy who also happens to be a pro athlete. What is that? What are we being told here? What is the volcano saying to us?"

"I think the volcano's saying that sometimes real-world shit goes down. Sometimes volcanoes erupt. Sometimes events transpire and consequences are imparted. This isn't biblical, as much as you want it to be. This isn't a bulletin from the heavens."

The sky was brightened by a light source deep in its recesses. It gave the impression of an El Greco seen through sunglasses.

"But what if it *is?*" she said. "Maybe this is a sign that we should be paying more attention to something."

He shook his head again.

"Like, what if we're stuck here until we come to terms

with some implicit truth about ourselves and change something essential?"

"Ah, right—trapped here until we live a day being kind to everyone we encounter," he said. "We should keep our eyes out for Phil Connors."

"I love that tone. I love that dismissal and that fucking smirk when you say it."

"Your eyes aren't even open. You can't tell whether I'm smirking. I just don't have a clue what you're talking about still."

"Maybe what I'm talking about is that our twenties are over, and what did we do? What did we miss? How did we *behave?* Who did we *become?*"

"All over an arbitrary number?"

"It's not arbitrary. At thirty you're basically halfway dead."

He shook his head again, but didn't address the math. Her mother had had a cancer scare at fifty-three. "What am I holding you back from? What am I not letting you be? Let's go do it. Let's get it out of our system today. Let's get it done this afternoon so that we can maybe go back to something standard-issue, seeing a fucking Gaudí park or whatever, without a crisis of life choices."

"Maybe I'm just hungry. Maybe this is just my insides talking. Maybe this is why we don't stay out late. Why I don't drink like that, *ever,* and why we don't do these things. This is why I'm no good at being young or fun or interesting anymore."

"We get older, we try to feel better about it, not worse. We live our lives. We do our best. We've never tried to keep up. Not so pathetically, at least. I don't get it. Why now?"

"There is just something going on up there," Whitney

said, serious as the sky. "I just have a sense for these things. All I'm saying is there's something strange that it happened when it happened, after everything we've done. The timing is just—"

"That what happened?"

"The volcano."

"The volcano 'happened . . . after everything we've done'?"

"I'm saying it's a strange coincidence, and maybe there's something to it."

"You're saying, what, exactly? That the volcano is somehow related to last month? You're saying there are ties between our sex life and earth science? You're saying: *It's a global response for 1-2-3? A ruling from the gods?*"

"I know you think that everyone who believes their life is tied up in something bigger is full of shit. But it would be a mistake not to at least *consider* it, just this once— what we did before we got here, and what happened once we confessed. And why it is we're trapped in the first place . . ."

"This is Sunday school talking? This is everything that was branded into you as a kid?" His mouth was tight, incredulous. Her eyes were open and fixed in the middle distance. He licked his lips waiting for her to snap out of the ancient logic, but she sat there patient. "There are more powerful forces in the universe than 1-2-3," he continued. "That's all I know. I want to make that knowing-ness super clear, okay? We are but specks of dust who decided to have sex with a couple other people before we got engaged. We even told each other about it. On the wide spectrum of humanity's transgressions, that's pretty fucking boring. That is *inconsequentially* boring. But not so boring that you should feel anxious about it! We're not being singled out for

1-2-3! You breaking your record with Adrien Green did not make an Icelandic volcano erupt!"

She pulled at the down on her arm. "I know that intellectually."

He laughed and her face held fixed. Then his smile faded. "But there's still a small part of you, on account of Sundays at Our Lady of Guilt, that makes you sometimes believe you're gnawing on the actual body of Christ, and that a series of record-smashing orgasms might serve as a catalyst for a natural disaster."

"It sounds dumb when you say it out loud."

"Yes it does."

"But the volcano, it erupted before we talked about it, you know? Before our dinner. When I was just holding it in, to myself? The secret. Everything that happened."

"But there was nothing to feel guilty about! There was nothing to be tied to it even in the most theoretical sense. The sex was the point! Fucking strangers was the point!"

"Look," she said, closing her eyes again, "my body did something it hasn't done before."

"We don't have to relitigate this."

"But I'm sounding crazy without you understanding what I'm trying to say."

"You're right."

"At one point, though—"

"Really, please, we did this already."

"—it wasn't that different from any other time, I just . . . felt something happening. Something from a different place in my body. I don't—"

"Like what?"

"It was like . . . I came, but, you know."

"I don't know. Either explain it or don't."

"It was…it's never gone that way before. And it happened three or four times in a row. And then not again."

"I still don't understand what you're saying. Are you saying you squirted?"

"Oh God, it's so gross!" She buried her face in her hands. "It's so, so gross! It's so embarrassing. Don't say the word."

"I didn't know that was something you wanted."

"It's not about *wanting*. I didn't know my body could—"

"And you're saying it's better, it feels better, and that's why the whole thing made you feel worse about it."

"It's not even *better*. It's just different. It's just a different spot or something. It's so embarrassing. It's just…it was intense. I don't know, but that's not—"

"I know some women squirt, I just didn't know it happened with you."

"Please don't say the word. It's so gross."

"A new record. And a whole new way of coming. This is kind of important. I take it back—the case apparently isn't closed after all. What else did you leave out?"

"Stop it," she said, swallowing heavy. "It was something I was embarrassed by. I wasn't happy about it. I just wanted you to understand where my mind was at. The connections it was making."

He was hot in the cheeks. He'd forgotten how they even got on the topic. And then his mouth opened wide.

"Ohhh," he said. "I get it now. What you're saying is you…erupted…and that caused the volcano to—"

"Will! Don't be a dick about this. I shouldn't have fucking said anything. You're right, my brain is mush. And I don't even know what I'm—"

"But isn't that your point? And because it was so

impossibly pleasurable, you're being punished by the universe? By the volcanoes of Iceland? Everything's sending a sign to you and to me, an imperative: *You two need to talk about this...* "

"I never should've said it. We should've gone home and gone back to sleep, and started today all over again."

" ... because for the first time in your life your body let down your ultimate barriers of inhibition and you gave yourself over to someone completely? Finally, so deeply, so un-Catholically, over to Sin, that you feel like your feet are being held to the fire for it?"

She sat there silent, her arms folded across her chest. She pressed her eyes shut again, and she licked her lower lip with a ticking compulsion.

"I shouldn't have said anything," she said. "Just please stop hitting me for it. I'm exhausted, and the whole thing obviously makes no sense. It just gives me a pit in my stomach when I play back what happened, that the whole thing happened in the first place, that it wasn't with you, that you were off doing the same thing with ... It makes me fucking want to throw up. And then we get trapped here after I didn't come fully clean the other night ... that I didn't mention this particular detail, I mean—"

"Consider yourself absolved," Will said, cutting her off and making the sign of the benediction. "And know, please know, deep in your soul, that you, Whitney, did not cause the volcano." He watched the lines in her forehead smooth over as she released all the tension she'd been holding in. "That your squirting did not cause—"

She threw herself at him across the bench and clapped her palm over his mouth. He made the muffled sounds of a bound hostage. He raised his arms in surrender. She wouldn't let go of his mouth. He pulled her hands from his face, finger by finger, until he could finally speak again. He opened his mouth wide and worked out his jaw with a heavy click. She waited for him to harangue her again. But all he said was: "Let's go eat. I'm starved. Let's go back to the Boqueria."

They stood and he shook out his body like a dog, snapping himself back into the logic of reality. He kissed the top of her head and they walked the crown of the mountain, through the parks and past the other Olympic venues. They took the tiled steps beneath the plane trees— the "Europe trees," as Whitney called them—to the base of the Palau Nacional. The palace was high on the hill, well back from the highway, with views of the bowl from several vantages. They passed through gardens and beside water-falls, each with royal proportions, the three-times-too-great scale. They watched the mighty fountain gushing, and Will nudged Whitney and peaked his eyebrows. She understood and she covered her face and collapsed on the ground into a cross-legged pretzel. "I should've never ever ever ever..."

"Just one more thing for me to shoot for," he said. "Another new benchmark."

He lifted her to her feet again and they gazed back up the hill toward the palace. From that perspective, there was a stark desperation to the grandness. Here was a structure built to say: *From this day forward, we, Catalonia, will be a country all our own.* That its architecture alone hadn't won the Civil War meant it now said something more like: *Please visit the gift shop so we can further explain our intentions.*

They passed the old bullfighting ring, long abandoned, now a mall.

"Did you know that Catalonia was the first place in Spain to ban bullfighting?" Whitney said. He knew what her knowing meant, the implication of it. It was her way of raising the idea of adopting a dog. She spent most weekend mornings reading scripts beside the dog run in Tompkins Square Park. Iced coffee from Ninth Street Espresso, eyes on the sporting breeds that wouldn't last a week in their studio.

"Dogs are for people in their thirties," Will said. "Dogs are for people with bedrooms and money."

"I didn't say anything about a dog," she said, smiling, and crossed the boulevard against the light. "All I said was that people here saved the bulls."

They zigzagged through Sant Antoni, past a couple of the other restaurants that Gwyneth had recommended and that they hadn't been able to get into. They pushed into El Raval and crossed the skateboard-infested plaza in front of the Museu d'Art Contemporani. Will promised no more museums for as long as they were stuck. They crashed into La Rambla and got swept into its raging current, downstream in the direction of the harbor, before turning into La Boqueria and finding their way by feel to the vendor where they'd had their favorite meal of the trip earlier in the week.

It was midafternoon and the late-lunch rush was on. Stalls on all sides. The silver steam of seafood and oil on griddles. Fresh fish mounted on walls of ice. Fruit juices spiked into ice mounds of their own. Nuts and seeds and berries for sale by the gram. There were gray birds cheeping in the vaulted roof that rose to the center of the marketplace like the canvas cover of a big-top tent. Their spot was smack in the middle. They didn't know the name of it and wouldn't have been able to find it if they hadn't retraced their steps precisely. All the stools at the counter were taken, but they spotted a middle-aged couple who looked to be paying, and hovered at their backs. They ordered two beers. They sipped slowly and did their best to keep out of the way. When they sat, they had a view through the glass partition that separated them from a bucket of baby squid, lavender and spilling slowly over the container edge like a lava slide. They ate shrimp, they ate razor clams, they ate seasoned mushrooms from the hills. They drank until their headaches were gone, instead dialing into the frequency of the cooks' meticulous operations, slipping into the day's first awe of post-confessional calm. They loved each other again.

On either side of them, English was being spoken. Beside Whitney was a family with Russian accents, calling for the attention of a server and failing to receive it. They clapped and waved their hands over the partition, and with each display of mounting impatience, they grew more invisible to the servers. Beside Will was a couple who he and Whitney discerned had arrived by train from Madrid that very morning and rolled straight to the counter because Jacqueline In Her Office had suggested it. Will felt the specialness of the spot diminish in big gluttonous gulps, even though he and Whitney had heard of it only because of their own email guide—a guide that seemed to have been forwarded over and over again, originating with somebody they and the person they received it from didn't even know personally. In fact, the guide had gone so wide that Will and Whitney had each received it independently from coworkers. Which meant there was but a single comprehensive email of suggestions from one unknown New Yorker that dictated the Barcelona experiences of dozens, hundreds, maybe thousands in their set. Will wondered if the guide had reached this couple beside them, too, or at least Jacqueline In Her Office. Will could've asked them, but he and Whitney had fallen into a private silence in face of all the English. They weren't like these tourists, they told themselves. They were return customers, after all. They understood how the menu worked. They knew how to order. They could pronounce the words by parroting them. They were practically locals.

They were also getting drunk. They'd done nothing yet to catch up on sleep. Their heads were full of static, and the impossible suggestion of sunlight was blasting in overhead through a crack in the roof. It was a beam from the sky like they hadn't seen in days. Whitney pointed and they squinted, wondering aloud if the clouds were breaking. But when they paid and found their way through the maze of vendors back outside to La Rambla, the ashcloud was baked over again—darker than ever, in fact—and Whitney and Will wondered if it hadn't been sunlight at all, if it was perhaps just another inexplicable sign from the heavens meant solely for them and their transgressions.

It looked ready to rain and they got within a couple blocks of the apartment before it started to dump. The initial downpour was of the heavy-dropped variety that they worried contained the worst of the chemical compounds that had been produced by the volcano. Black ash, black rain, dark spots on their clothing.

The doors to the apartment building were enormous—fifteen feet tall and ten feet across. But in one of them was cut a miniature door, through which their key permitted entry after-hours and on weekends and holidays, which maybe this was, at least for the superintendent of the building. It was Memorial Day back home, and a local holiday for at least some here. A volcano holiday. Catalan flags were hung proudly from every other balcony across the street.

They took the stairs, the four flights, and Whitney was in bed, facedown, before Will had locked up behind them. She flipped onto her side and opened her laptop and let out a resigned "Fuck..." A conference call had been scheduled for late morning, East Coast. She had an hour to sleep things off and sober up before dialing in.

It was an intrusion from the outside. A sign that the volcano wasn't cause for concern at home. And neither, apparently, was Memorial Day. She checked her personal email too, and sat up when she saw it.

"They want to know if we want to get dinner tonight."

The words disappeared into the living room and Will didn't reply. Whitney couldn't see him from the bed, couldn't see if he'd heard, couldn't read the reaction in his face. There was more silence. Will wanted her to stake out the first position.

"Did you hear me?" she said.

"What do you want to do?" he said, from what sounded to Whitney like the farthest corner of the apartment.

She was rereading the email. "One night and it's already this *we* and *us* bullshit..."

He emerged in the doorway and waited still for her to show her hand.

"I need to take a nap and then take this call and then we don't have plans," she said.

"Right. But do you even want to see them again?"

They were good to each other. They were often happy to shift to new positions to meet the other where they were. But Will had been mystified by Whitney's meltdown outside the museum, couldn't have articulated whether the ultimate thing she was asking for was more or less of Jack and Leonard in their volcano days.

"We just ate," he said, drifting back to the living room. "I feel disgusting. I can't even think about dinner. But if you—"

"I'm getting so gross," she said. "I got so soft this winter. These extra meals are only making things worse."

He let it linger, then tried again: "But we probably won't be mad about going, right? Isn't that the point you were making earlier? That you wish you and I wouldn't be so old and lame?"

He'd turned the television on and Spanish-language news suddenly filled the apartment at high volume.

"Jesus. Turn it down."

"What—you don't want to listen on full blast?"

"I didn't hear what you said."

He used it as an opportunity to soften the explanation. "It's totally up to you. But I feel like what you were just saying is that you might want to fill the rest of our time here with some things you might not ordinarily..."

"So what do you want me to say, then?"

"Why don't *you* decide if you want to—"

"I just can't believe they're still together," Whitney said.

"If she bugs you so much, maybe that's a reason to definitely not go?"

Will appeared in the doorway again.

"I could care less about her," she said. "The only thing that bugs me is your inability to say the words *yes* or *no*."

"*Yes* or *no*."

"The place they suggested is about a thirty-minute walk from here. I just looked it up. It's in the email guide, too. It's one of the places we talked about going the other night.

We might want to try it before we leave, anyway, with or without them."

"Then let's just go, okay?" he said. "If it's a place we should try, what's an hour or two?"

"So, yes?"

"If you're not gonna be super fucking weird about things again."

"I'm asking them when," she said, typing on her laptop.

"If you're gonna sleep, I'm gonna read out here."

"Can you turn the TV off, or turn it down at least? It's not like you can follow what they're saying."

"Check this out," he said. "I found a station that's solely coverage of the soccer club. Like, 24-7. They have one of the kids' teams on now. I can't believe they televise the Under-11s!"

"You're just gonna watch little-kid soccer?"

"They all have haircuts like the players on the big team."

"Close the door, please," she said. "I'm fucking dead."

He did as he was told, then started for the kitchen to grab a glass of water. On the way, he noodled out a few notes on the acoustic guitar in a corner of the living room, then returned to the couch and put his feet up. He reached for the book he'd brought along on the trip. A copy of *Homage to Catalonia* he'd picked up at The Strand. He cracked it in half and made it two pages deeper before he heard an excitable pitch on the TV and lifted his eyes to watch a shot go wide.

He was exhausted. His eyes burned. He butterflied the book on his chest and flipped the channel and found the news. There was an auto accident in the hills above the city. There were eyewitness interviews. There was white-and-yellow police tape and officers who looked confused by the paths in life that had led them to this horrific crime scene under this morbid sky. There was a teaser for updates on the volcano—the promise of photos out of Iceland. Will sat through the commercials and, resting there in the lapping pool of language, felt himself almost comprehending. The coffee ads. The cars. The food processor. It was either fluency by immersion or the onset of delirium. The photos of the volcano had been taken from a helicopter. The plumes of smoke and ash looked like cole crops from every angle. The volcano had apparently ceased emitting ash. But he knew that had little to do with the clearing of the cloud over Europe.

The news moved to updates on the fresh American crisis. The removal of the FBI director, the appointment of the Special Counsel—those flashed by as old headlines. But now, here was a potential exit from the global climate accord. Things had escalated all over again in twenty-four hours. The press secretary had been marched out to defend the tweets. Will couldn't follow entirely. He didn't have his daily dose of podcasts, the river of news that had made his commutes up to Grand Central assume a little more consequence since the election. According to the images on TV, the republic looked ready to implode at any moment. But he knew there was nothing he could do from this couch or this city. There was hardly anything he could do from home, either. He opened his laptop and donated twenty bucks to a congressional candidate who'd said something smart last week. They were all captives of the same machine. It had been a bad year. He panicked and then he calmed. He knew his body didn't dictate world events the way Whitney's apparently could. He just hoped there was an America to return to when his hiatus from American news was through.

The next story on the television was about a murder in Paris. The way the images cycled and the way the newscasters' faces spoke the facts, it looked like a breaking story. It seemed a young German woman had been killed by her boyfriend. They were students and the boyfriend was being questioned. Like an Amanda Knox thing, Will intuited. The days abroad were helping—he had a thimbleful of comprehension. Will was proud of what he understood to be true.

The windows of the apartment were unobstructed, waist to ceiling, but the light was pitiful and the rain outside gave everything inside the apartment the blue-gray hues of napping. He read another page of Orwell, about his training with the socialists, then fell asleep with the paperback bookmarked by his knee. He was drunk and stuck in Barcelona. He dreamed of the volcano and of the world spinning uncertainly around the fixed point of Will.

Whitney was put on hold and so snuck into the bathroom to pee and then hazarded to flush the toilet and wash her hands before the line clicked back over to the conference-call audience of six. She ran her wet fingers over her crown and threw her mass of hair over her shoulder. She put the phone on speaker and massaged the skin of her face, tightening, turning back the clock to two and then four and then seven years ago. She stretched the skin around her eyes, she frosted over her forehead like a Zamboni. She thought about her friends and colleagues at work who spent an hour a day with products, who were already getting injections. She'd always had good skin. But they were doing so much now, earlier than ever, the first leg of the long race. They avoided the beach, they avoided the sun. She shuddered to think of the afternoons of her youth out on her father's boat, the long lazy summers on man-made lakes, baking like a hooked trout. They all wore SPF 50 now. They bought machines for needling and sonic shocks. They worked out their bodies once or even twice a day. They rotated through eating trends. There was so much to know about and execute on. There was so much to do in addition to everything else. Whitney had assumed that they'd draw the line at anything involving a scalpel, just as they'd refrain from any food philosophy ending in an *ism*. But when just last month they told her about their injections, it had panicked her. She'd figured she might have another ten years before she'd have to wade into those waters. But now it was just another thing to stuff cash away for, another secret expense to add to the series of secret expenses that promised to eat up every incremental gain in income she'd make as a successful young woman in a growth industry.

During the years Will had been in law school, Whitney had found herself floating up to ceilings but failing to break through. She had, however, at least survived the gauntlet of the earliest days. There were so many assistants who'd been at the cable network when she started—each feeling lucky to have merely gained entry in the wake of the crash, and each to a number inevitably squeezed out. But she'd stayed aloft. Because of her brain, because of her conviction, because of her taste.

Also: the red dots she placed on her calendar. Three weeks was the max it ever was between red dots, and anyone could survive three weeks. Red dots meant a party. Red, as in carpet. Up-fronts in the spring, with the creators and cast. A celebration for the premiere of a season and a celebration for the finale. A celebration for the Emmys, a celebration for the Globes. Often in L.A., occasionally in New York. They were the carrots at the end of a long, hard stick. She stayed organized because of them; she never dropped a spinning plate. She took good notes. She gave good notes. But most of all—most essential to her survival—she just relished occasional proximity to a mid-list star. And a red dot on the calendar was never so far out that it was worth walking away.

Eventually, the gamble paid off. She'd been headhunted by a startup streaming service of an online marketplace that was suddenly in the business of developing new shows. She'd been recommended by one of her bosses, a woman who'd been helpful to Whitney for years but who had, Whitney knew, begun to resent Whitney's ideas, Whitney's ambition. The men asked for too many lunches, too many drinks out late. The women didn't like that Whitney spoke freely about wanting their jobs. So the move worked to everyone's benefit. And now was prime time for Whitney to make TV.

She was still on hold, a loop of the songs that scored the opening credits of a hit show. She googled *JJ Pickle* and scrolled through pictures of him in college. She googled *Leonard NYU,* but the only images that emerged were of bearded adjunct professors. She went to the kitchen to get herself a glass of water and found Will passed out on the couch. The terrible, familiar shape. Slung way down in the seat of the sofa, head balanced on the backrest and mouth gaping like a Pez dispenser. She'd never understood why he didn't just lie all the way down. It was the same resistance that made him believe he could stay awake later than she could at the end of the night. It didn't bother her except when he'd insist he could make it through another episode of whatever they were streaming, only to pass out minutes in, leaving her with the high-moral conundrum of whether to press on without him or not. She hated being out front alone with a series. She watched everything for work, and so only a few for fun. It was nice sometimes to just have something to share in, to mete out casually with him. She knew the inside word on the successes and failures of every show on every network, as seen through the eyes of the industry. She knew the fate of a show months before civilians had had the opportunity to rate it for themselves. So to have just one, every now and again, to experience purely, alongside someone who knew nothing about the takes of the trades, was a treat for her. But then each night: that dead face, that retired mass next to her in bed. He looked, in sleep, like every photo she'd ever seen of him as a child. Most people looked different over time, changed, but all of those people were not Will. That strange quality—that perpetual all-Will is now-Will—returned her frequently to a sort of lineage of their love, a proximity to the whole story of it, which flattened out the spikes and kept close for Whitney all the good from before.

When Will had moved back to New York from Washington, they'd picked out a place together: a second-floor studio apartment on the corner of 10th and A, across the street from Tompkins Square Park. It had exposed beams and high ceilings and it was a better deal than anything else they'd seen in the neighborhood. It didn't make sense, except that the owner was practically dead and wasn't concerned with market value. It was unlisted. Whitney worked with someone who lived in the building. Will liked the location fine, but loved especially that it was cheap, an outlier, a ninety-ninth-percentile steal.

The studio was a studio, but they rhetorically broke the space into the component parts of a larger home: they called the three shelves in the closet that held the scissors and thank-you cards *the office*; they called the corner near the park-facing window with the free weights and yoga mat *the gym*; they called the three-foot halo around the queen-size bed *the bedroom,* and treated that imaginary border like the line between territorial and international waters. It seemed like no time had passed since they'd been scattered across the city that first summer after college, surfing couches and subletting rooms without air-conditioning, sweating through sheets in four out of the five boroughs. Texting one another from hundreds of blocks away some nights and from within the same neighborhood on others. They'd lived apart for the first years, with roommates and then in other cities. But when they got to the same place again, they were ready for rootedness. Ready to read books and watch movies and roast chickens together. To receive the quarterly alumni magazine in duplicate. It was easy, at first, riding that conveyor belt of domestic life, easy and pleasurable and fun. When it wasn't, they fought hard with each other, but they forgave easily, too. The secret to making it work was that they were in love. They'd known each other since they were practically children. Three and then five and then seven years elapsed. They ended most nights beside one another in *the bedroom.* They'd never lived alone in their lives.

Whitney just hung there in the living room of the Airbnb, on hold, listening to Will breathe, the familiar faint wheeze from the twice-broken nose. She hated that unconscious mass, especially on nights when she couldn't sleep herself. And yet the thought of him passed out in their bed was the first thing that made her cry during the early days of

1-2-3. At eight or nine Pacific Standard, she would imagine the worst: Will with any of the thousands of young women in the neighborhood, with their elastic skin and flexible hips, every last young hopeless striver living life in the sliver of a chance that they might go to a bar after work and meet someone like her boyfriend. A good guy with a decent apartment and a little cash and white teeth and a Goldilocks cock—the mix of checked boxes those bees had been scouring the city for during happy hours since they'd graduated a few Mays ago. Whitney, alone, imagining all the possibilities, but knowing in her guts that Will was more likely than not propped up in their bed, trying to catch up with a show she'd long left him in the dust on, doing what he could to make a good-faith effort to get back in the game now that he had all this time to himself. Whitney, alone in L.A., checking their shared streaming account and seeing it had been used by another laptop, the elapsed-time bar frozen just after the opening credits, right where he always dropped off. It would melt her like microwaved butter; the relief was absolute. By 8:46 or 8:23 or 7:46 PST, the check-in would confirm it for her: he was Pezed out, exhausted and alone, hopefully missing her a little bit in his dreams, despite the experiment they'd designed to break the bones of their seven-year relationship in order to help it heal right. When she wanted to make sure he was asleep, when she wanted to confirm it beyond a doubt, she'd text him something stupid—a dog that looked like its owner on the sidewalk in front of her hotel, maybe—and wouldn't hear back, and so could lay her head to rest with that sleeping pill of certainty.

One evening, a week into 1-2-3, Whitney sent a text to no response, but that time, surprising herself, she cracked.

Her face went haywire without warning, she wanted to be physically next to that sleeping potato sack so badly. This was after a long day of a read-through, a few days after Adrien Green. There was probably some fatigue, certainly some guilt. There was that thing where her brain had been split in two along the cleave between her desire for Will to even the score and her desire for them to pack up the enterprise altogether and never exist in that idiotic in-between again. To make a date at City Hall and take care of things the easy way, the way they should have all along, and just get on with it, the way it was supposed to go. But she knew she couldn't do it. Not at that point. It wasn't fair if it wasn't even. And she knew it was too early for him, it'd take him longer than it had taken her. She knew she'd have to wait for the month-long prescription to run its course. It was dangerous to cut off medicine midstream.

So she busied herself making plans for their Memorial Day trip instead. They considered maybe Rome or Berlin or Mexico City or Peru. But they were ultimately pretty set on Barcelona. Neither had been before, and Whitney had just been forwarded an email guide written by someone she'd never met. Early one morning, after a few hours of sleep, she'd flipped over in bed and whispered to Will that her knee was throbbing again, that she'd run too hard that day, would he help her stretch her legs in the morning? But Whitney was in L.A. and Will was in New York. And at the moment of realization, emerging from sleep, her mind split again like a fault line in a California quake. She imagined herself on the wrong side of the chasm from Will—her fate of being alone until her dying days. She imagined him gone. She imagined him vanished. She imagined a lifetime of calling out to someone across the room about her clicky hips and busted knee, and the list of toiletries for him to order off Amazon, and her ideas for new shows—did he think it was a good concept for a half-hour comedy? That was the night she cried hardest, heavier than about anything since her mother's cancer scare, and then she fell asleep again with swollen eyes on a damp pillow that left a rash on her cheek.

"Whitney, you still there?" the call came back through the speaker into the bathroom in Barcelona, and she retreated to the bed to finish up her work.

Will woke up to Whitney's voice. She was on the call still. The afternoon news had turned over to a variety show with sequined dancers, and he reached for the control to cut the signal. He went to the kitchen sink for a fresh glass of water and crashed into the corner of the counter. He felt the disorienting face-fuzz of a daylight hangover and popped a new beer to sand off the edges. He halved the bottle and walked to the bedroom, where Whitney rolled back her eyes and stuck out her tongue and slashed her throat with her finger.

"Mm-hmm," she said into the phone. "We can one hundred percent try that."

Will passed the closet on the way to the bathroom. Whitney had unpacked the entirety of her suitcase again, just as she'd done their first day of the trip, hanging her dresses and folding her shirts and jeans and underwear into stacks in the drawers. Will, by contrast, had left all his clothes in his duffel, into which they'd been carelessly shoveled from the floor near the radiator the morning before. They lived together. They shared spaces and money and a projection of a future. But they lived differently still. Especially when left to their own devices or their own coasts or their own sides of a rental apartment.

He stood before the closet and ran his eyes over her clothes. They were expensive but they would last. They met the standard of what Whitney considered a justifiable cost-per-wear. She piped in on the call every thirty seconds or so. "That's exactly right. That was the plan all along, but we can hit that note harder." He strummed the edges of her dresses like a harp. He brought a cream linen hem to his nose. She'd left the dresses in New York during her month in L.A. She'd taken more casual clothes—jeans, and button-downs, and sneakers. She said it was more appropriate. She said it would be a waste to bring anything else along. And so these, the vestiges of functional and fashionable New York City professionalism, they'd stayed put. Will would come home after striking out at a neighborhood bar, and he'd just hang there in their shared space, their shared studio. He'd pour their shared bottle of olive oil into their shared frying fan. He'd boil their shared tap water in their shared tea-kettle. He'd strum the dresses in their shared closet and kick back atop their shared comforter to watch a TV show he'd fallen behind on. There was no escaping the togetherness. Temporarily untangling that inextricable life of theirs, for three discrete encounters, seemed an impossible proposition. He intended to marry her. What were they doing? He lived with her clothes.

He'd think about calling her before he'd jerk off. Why, though? It was earlier there, the workday still. They rarely talked dirty on the phone. And so he'd carry the buzz from the bars to *the bedroom,* settle in with the usual clips from the usual sites. He'd watch for five minutes, ten minutes, and then he'd find himself drifting. Imagining Whitney after work, Whitney after a run at sunset, the golden light of his home state pressing against the glass of the hotel room. Whitney riding the night where it went and finding herself like the girls on his laptop screen. With bosses or coworkers or neighbors or deans. Whitney being undressed slowly. Out of those familiar clothes, first off the shoulder, and then unzipped. Whitney down to very little material, to matching white or matching red or matching blue. Whitney on her knees, with something to prove to someone strange. Whitney on her back, Whitney with her clicky hips slung wide, and her eyes closed, and her body feeling the same old things but in new ways, maybe. And Whitney, ultimately, on her palms and her knees, her head between her arms, her hair spilled off her head into a puddle in the sheets. Whitney, from behind, always from behind, the way she most preferred. Whitney's face lifting when the pace shifted, when the force escalated. Whitney's face in the foreground, eyes tight in a centered-ness, 1-2-3 as a mental retreat, sure, but as a physical exhibition above all else. Devoid, for Will, of the specifics of feelings, of names, of thoughts. Just the image of 1-2-3 at its basest, Whitney as the lead actress, the whole thing transpiring in real time, right then and there, with Will at home and Whitney on the road. It made him sick. It always worked.

After he'd finish, he'd text. She wouldn't be able to talk. Always busy, always late. Hardly bothering herself with his same fruitless pursuits: bars in the neighborhood, bars at happy hour. Maybe they wouldn't go through with it, after all. He'd look around the apartment—the shared every-thing, intertwined for all time, maybe. Bureaus and books and lamps and framed posters that were uncuttable-in-two. But they were down this path already. There was no turning back. He'd smell her dresses. He'd smell the perfume. He'd reply to her reply. She was still working—didn't he understand it always ran late? She was working from the restaurant of the hotel, there was no one else around. It was quiet, she was alone. She would go to bed soon. He would probably pass out before she could talk. Everything in the closet in Barcelona reminded him of those nights.

"Of course, of course," she said into the phone. "You fold six into five, thread in the stuff about the sister beginning in four. So that when you reveal it, people feel like they knew there was something worth paying attention to there, even if they can't quite figure out how they sensed it coming all along."

Will returned to the couch and opened his email and was surprised to find forty new messages since he'd fallen asleep. A writer at one of the magazines was threatening a lawsuit. Will had been looped into the situation weeks ago. But they'd just learned that the writer was going public with accusations of coercion. The editor-in-chief needed to know what their options were to make sure it didn't become a big public mess. The first several messages in the chain were to Will's boss, asking him to advise. But Will's boss had snipped at the chain earlier in the weekend, complaining that he had already wasted "too much of his alleged 'vacation' on this garbage," and that he wouldn't be checking in again until Tuesday. Will knew his boss well enough to know that he'd meant it, that nothing would get him on the line from Nantucket, no matter how much money the media company paid him as lead counsel. Will felt the familiar pulse in his neck. A coursing of poison to his extremities. It was the feeling of the lobby mural all over again.

Will couldn't drown out Whitney's voice in the other

room. She was still on her call, sounding impossibly enthu-
siastic, offering recommendations that would make a thing
that was actually being made better. He clammed his laptop
shut. He hated this. He hated the pitch of anxiety. The work
was often meaningless and only ever had downsides, but at
least he was underpaid for it, too. He needed the money.
They'd been spending like assholes lately. And now the extension on the Airbnb. They'd budgeted for a specific length
of trip, not days and days longer. He listened to Whitney's
tone, that pleasant authority. She made 50 percent more
than he did, and now she was beginning to produce, too.
The apartment wouldn't be a problem for them, collectively,
but they'd booked it on his account, and these extra days
would go on his card. He couldn't leave his job. How had
he put himself in this position? How had he allowed it to
take control of his life? He wanted more than anything on
earth to snip the line of his contacts, to change his email
address by a single letter so that all correspondence would
bounce. Maybe he would never emerge from beneath the
cloud. Maybe it would be best to stay stuck in Barcelona
for good.

He checked his personal email, willing a response. He'd
been waiting all week, and still nothing. Before the trip,
he'd submitted the script he'd finished during the month of
1-2-3. He'd been working on it on the sly for a year now, a
side project for his own sanity, a pressure valve for when he
needed it most. He was certain Whitney still knew nothing
about it. He'd made a pact with himself to do it this way.
He must prove himself worthy on his own before asking
her to help fix everything that needed fixing, which of
course she would. Last year he'd run into a classmate from
law school who'd become a producer. They got coffee, they

caught up. The guy even offered to read the script Will had written in that college course his senior year. He enjoyed it, he told Will, before crediting ideas to the movie that Will hadn't even intended. The feedback shocked Will. He hadn't expected anything. And now the producer wanted Will to write something new.

Will wasn't an idiot—he knew every person in Hollywood with money fancied himself a producer. But this guy had a real job, a real office he went to, and everything. So it wasn't just a pipe dream when he sent it along. But now Will had been waiting ten days, and nothing still. He checked his email again. It was a holiday back home. Relax. He'd just never allowed himself to want something quite like this before. He needed out so badly. Away from everything that was transpiring in that other email box of his. But he needed the money. He needed the dignity. He couldn't let Whitney leave him further behind just yet. As ever, movies were his island, his salvation. But all he could do for now was tinker meaninglessly. He opened the software he'd downloaded for free. He read: *INT—BAR—NIGHT.* Then he changed it to something better: *INT—BAR—DAY.*

"Jesus, sorry," Whitney said, emerging from the bedroom. "That was an hour longer than it was supposed to be."

"All okay?"

"I can't stand it when executives misuse words. *Exegesis. Enervate. Epigraph.*"

"*Exigencies,*" he said. "*Equal pay.*"

Whitney smiled. "You get it. Will gets it. And that's the point of keeping him around..." she said. "The last twenty minutes was just Karen describing her house search, anyway."

"What neighborhood?"

"Oh, it doesn't matter. They're playing a much greater game than Westside-Eastside. They're looking for something that's *architecturally significant.*"

She was stripping down to take a shower. Off came her shirt and her bra and then her pants. He stood and pressed up behind her. She could feel him through his jeans.

"You're not so architecturally insignificant yourself," he said.

She looked at him with real or feigned disgust in the reflection of the hallway mirror.

"Are you calling me *sturdy*?" she said. "You're saying I'm what, a *brick house*?"

He dropped his hands from her hips and rolled his eyes and returned to the couch, to the fresh beer he'd just cracked, and she moved to the bathroom for a quick rinse-off since the moment was gone.

They were out the door by seven. They crossed Diagonal and zagged through the Eixample, the big corners, the wide intersections with their plane trees. They passed the 1-2-3 restaurant, set back on the chamfered corner beneath a black awning and black glass, no tables on the sidewalk, no invitation to come in without a reservation, as they'd done forty-eight impossibly long hours ago. They passed a Gaudí. They passed another Gaudí. It was the only thing they could count on in this neighborhood. The tree-trunk curves, the twisted wrought iron, the jagged colored tiles. Never more than a few blocks without a reminder of whose city it was.

They were up out of the Eixample and into Gràcia, squares with classical guitars and fathers dancing with young daughters. There were pedestrian alleys with empty restaurants and businesses with gibberish portmanteaus and big transparent windows framing two or three employees, younger than Will and Whitney, working on laptops with a single shared desk and a single shared printer, late on a maybe-local-holiday. They passed another couple their age speaking English, and both Whitney and the other woman did it to one another: They looked each other up and down and then in the eyes. *Do I know you? Do I like you? Do I hate you? Do I work with you? Did I go to school with you? Do I owe you an email? Do you owe me a call? Are you pretty? Are you famous? Are you a stranger? You're a stranger. You're nobody I know, goodbye.*

The slope grew steeper. They passed a man seated on a bench with a Walkman who was singing along with a heavy accent to the Beach Boys. The alley kicked back steeper still. If they followed it into the hills they would hit Parc Güell, the escalators that carried tourists to the top, to the palm trees and the salamander and the dreamscape and the view.

Instead, though, they found the restaurant, a stand-up thing with a stand-up counter and stand-up tables. Leonard had picked it. Whitney had cross-referenced it with their email guide, and there was indeed a consensus. The room was tight but the ceiling was high, and the walls were packed with wine and tins of fish. Golds and grays and strangely appetizing browns. The walls of liquor bottles appeared illuminated by a warm yellow source, shining through the vintage labels. They were on the early side, so there was still space to stake their claim. They spotted Jack and Leonard in the back. They already had glasses of wine. But they weren't speaking to one another as Will and Whitney approached. They were staring straight ahead. They had space between them, and Leonard's arms were crossed until she noticed Will and Whitney.

"Hola," Leonard said. Their standing up made her seem all the smaller, all the wronger in scale. Jack was wearing an oversize dark-blue shirt, an oversize collar spread like wings. The sculptedness of his hair made his head seem even smaller than the night before. Leonard was wearing a bright blue dress. In contrast with the dead laundered dark of Jack's shirt and jeans, the dress was alive with light. Whitney didn't know for certain, but she suspected it was Valentino. It reached her shins and was carved up in front, Miró shapes cut from the strained bust. Her hair was pushed back high on her forehead again, and fell exhaustively over her shoulders and down her back. There was so much blonde. She'd added hoop earrings and red lipstick since last night, and the whole picture made her look at least twenty-five.

"You look cute," Leonard said to Whitney, sizing up her shirt and jeans.

Whitney smiled politely and leaned into Leonard's kiss as Will and Jack shook hands. Whitney moved her mouth to Leonard's other cheek. Will always ribbed her for it at home. The way it'd catch people off guard. But it was natural here. Leonard took the second kiss like a pro, had in fact pushed it there herself. She'd spent the year in Paris, after all. Whitney moved to Jack and he bent over to receive one cheek and another. It occurred to Whitney in the instant she leaned toward him that she'd dreamed of Jack last night. She searched his face to see if he'd had the same dream, if he'd in fact shared in their shared experience. She kept tocking her head in strange ways on approach, trying to make knowing eye contact, to see if he remembered what they'd done together. From a few feet back, Will wondered if the moves weren't just a ploy to graze noses with Jack, to catch a corner of his mouth.

Leonard told them she'd been at the airport all afternoon, doing her best to get on a plane. But nothing had gone out. Not one flight. "It looked like a refugee camp," she said. "Some families had already been there for two full days. People with tickets were at least let into the terminals so that security could clear out the check-in and give the stranded folks access to bathrooms. The restaurants expanded their hours to stay open twenty-four-seven. Military guys were bringing in cots and water."

"What did they say?" Whitney said. "Did they have any guesses?"

"Now that it's at least stopped erupting, they just have to wait on the winds. It sounds like the week prediction is less likely, but it still may be a few more days. All they could really say was almost certainly not tomorrow. But I may go back again anyway."

"They changed my flight to Wednesday," Jack said. "But I have my apartment as long as I need it. I realize that's more than you all can say, so if anyone needs a place eventually..."

Leonard smiled without baring any teeth. It was a smirk that Whitney read to mean that she had already been there, that though she might be an *anyone* at this table, she'd already taken him up on the offer.

"We didn't even try today," Will said. "Which was maybe stupid. I got an email when we woke up that said our spot was still being held in line. That we'd be notified when there was anything new to report."

"Probably a smarter way to spend your time," Leonard said. "I just, well, you know...I'm ready to get out of here.

I need to get home." Jack shifted his weight weirdly from one leg to another. "But!" Leonard bit at the silence. "In the meantime..."

She explained how the menu worked. There were forty items in two columns on a single laminated sheet. You placed orders at the counter and they prepared the dishes on the fly' right in front of you. Toasts with cream cheese, brined salmon, and honey. Toasts with canned anchovies and peppers. Salted tuna. Sardines and urchin. A squid-ink something, black as a chess piece. The three behind the counter poured wine and prepped dishes and recorded orders in a dog-eared leather-bound book without looking customers in the eye. Everything was served cold.

"They ever screw up the tab?" Will asked, returning with wineglasses for himself and Whitney, and nodding with his head toward the vicinity of the bookkeeping system.

Whitney shook her head, and leaned into his ear, and slid him a big bill: "It's on me."

"Since everything's cheap, maybe nobody can tell when there's a mistake?" Jack said.

"Who likes what?" Whitney said. They pointed. They all pointed to the salmon, in particular. It was poppy-bright and looked to be the only fish that didn't come canned.

"Even though Jenna and I went to a sushi place for lunch," Jack said.

"Jenna?" Whitney said, looking at Jack, looking at Leonard.

"Well," Jack said, smiling at her patiently, "which is it tonight?"

"Today is a *Jenna* day," Leonard said.

"Well, pleased to meet you," Whitney said.

"*Enchantée*," Jenna said.

"What makes it a *Jenna day*?" Whitney said.

"I didn't wake up at Gram's," she said.

Jenna smiled softly at Whitney as though that explained something, or everything, or at least a couple important things at once.

"And so in spite of the sushi for lunch..." Will said.

"I know I should be used to it by now," Jack said, eyeing the grayer fish on the table adjacent to them, "but I still don't totally love the tins."

"It's no grilled chicken," Whitney said.

"Exactly," Jack said, smiling widely at her.

Jenna lifted her glass and puffed a low laugh, an *at,* not a *with.* Jack noticed and his cheeks showed that he'd been drinking for a while.

"Look at this shit," Jack said, a little loudly, to Will and Whitney. "Nothing is cool enough for the coolest chick in town."

"I'm gonna get a refill," Jenna said, ignoring him, already edging toward the bar. "Should I just grab a bottle?"

They watched her squeeze between two sets of male shoulders and place her elbows and the top half of her torso, the loosely trestled window of the chest of her dress, on the counter. Behind the bar were a woman who looked like she could've fought beside Orwell in Will's book, and two men as tall as Jack, each with dusty hair and glasses. One of them was quick to take Jenna's order, quick to take a generous glance at what she'd presented on the other side of the partition.

"So just...*Jenna,* then," Whitney said to Jack, when she was still out of earshot.

"I've been going with the flow," Jack said. "There's a lot to get with, turns out."

"Oh yeah?" Whitney said.

"I mean, that's probably no surprise, given all...given all this and that. But even more than you'd think," Jack said, stooping a little to conspire, then catching himself and laughing. "What am I doing? Two drinks in and I'm blah-blah-blah-ing already."

"Did you guys stay out much later last night?" Whitney said.

"Probably an hour after you. I was dead by the time we left. I don't know how anyone can do that. This week's been so surreal."

"And was it a good rest of the morning after that, then?"

"I don't know what you mean," Jack said, innocently.

Whitney held fixed, arching her thick eyebrows like a gossip columnist.

"We walked around for a while."

"Us, too," Whitney said. "We walked home."

There was an unnatural lull, the sort that can derail a group of relative strangers. They sipped their drinks and then perked up in unison at the sight of her.

"Well that was fast," Will said as Jenna fell back in with the bottle and four fresh glasses.

"I cut the line," Jenna said.

"Saw that," Will said. "They hopped right to."

"You do what you can to survive," Jenna said.

Will poured the wine. They clinked. They swallowed big swallows.

"Jenna, what'll you do this summer?" Will said. "Summer before senior year....Internship? More travel? L.A.? New York?"

"I have this job," Jenna said. "I did it last year. You'll

actually appreciate it, knowing what you know about the Westside."

"Elbow model?" Whitney said. The first sip had gone straight to her head.

Jenna examined Whitney's face to see if she was amused with herself, then turned back to Will and said, "I buy books for people to put in their house."

"Like a personal shopper?" Will said.

"More like an art adviser, but for bookshelves," Jenna said. "Pick books that make people seem like the sort who would actually read those books."

"I've heard of that," Whitney said. "Somebody was telling me about it when I was out there last month. I've just never met anyone who—"

"These people with, you know," Jenna said, cutting her off, "the six-thousand-square-foot homes, and the countless rooms, and the miles of shelves—they need decorating help. It's not like it's *my* business. I just work for the woman who does it. She finds the clients. She conducts this personality test. She prepares the lists: mix of classic and contemporary, used and new. And then I go shopping."

"Local booksellers must love you," Will said.

"They always insist on taking me out to lunch," Jenna said.

"I bet one big client's enough to float a store for a month, right?" Whitney said.

Jenna shrugged and poured herself another few fingers of wine.

"I helped deliver boxes to students when I was home for summers in college," Will said. "A friend of mine from high school ran a dorm-moving business. I thought *that* whole thing was rich L.A., as far as seemingly unnecessary services go—pick up the boxes for you, stick them in storage, bring the boxes back to campus in August—but yours has got it beat by miles."

"She gets five bucks a book," Jenna said.

"Same as what an author gets," Whitney said, laughing.

"And some of these guys—and they're obviously mostly men—they're in it for thousands and thousands of books."

"I don't get it," Jack said. "If they're just for decoration, what does it matter which books they are?"

"Simple Jack," Jenna said. "You sweet, beautiful boy. So sensemaking. So pure."

"All right, all right," he said.

"The clients study up to have passing familiarity. She forces you to memorize the title and the author, to be able to move among them. So that if some guest browsing at your party says, you know, 'Oh, *White Teeth*!' he can get in a 'Zadie? I love Zadie.'"

"Does she give them flash cards?" Whitney said. "Slides?"

"Spreadsheet included," Jenna said. "PowerPoint for another buck a book."

"It's like an art history class!" Whitney said. "Painting to artist. Artist to painting. Incredible."

"So what's your cut, then?" Will said.

"I get a dollar a book," Jenna said. "Plus lunch and gas. Lunch, if the booksellers don't bribe me first with a sandwich. I made a couple grand one week last summer. I buy, I deliver, I buy, I deliver. Sometimes it's less specific. Sometimes it's: *Pick fifty at random from the New Releases tables at the front of the store.*"

"And then you just swing them by the house, one box at a time?" Will said.

"However they please. She gives them choices for arrangement. Author name. Country. Language. Era. Color."

"Obviously color is an option," Whitney said.

"One guy last summer wanted a thousand blue books—that was it."

"No significance beyond blue?" Jack said.

"It's the easiest of all. No personality tests. No manufactured taste. Just *blue*. And hardcover...the older the better was the preference. I went to twenty stores. I picked up the final hundred from the *Used* bins at Vroman's."

"Maybe I move to L.A. instead of going home," Jack said. "Learn the real ways of the world."

"You can live with my dad," Jenna said. "He'll love it. Someone to watch Lakers games with. Someone to play golf with."

"It's settled, then," Jack said. "Cali, here I come."

"Ugh," Jenna said.

"What now?" Jack said.

"Never say that," Jenna said.

"*SoCal*?" Jack said.

"Will: *Cali? SoCal?*"

"*California. Southern California,*" Will said.

"Got it?" Jenna said to Jack.

Will smiled and Whitney squinted. There were shifting tethers, fluid alliances.

"But it won't get you in trouble like how San Franciscans feel about *San Fran*," Will said.

"No good, either?" Jack said.

"They'll run you out," Will said.

"This is great," Jenna said. "This is why we travel. To meet strangers and suck out of each other what's worth sucking out."

There was a halt. Three of the four wineglasses elevated. Whitney looked at Jack to see if they were sharing in a conspiracy; Will was watching Jenna to see if it had been a joke. The temperature rose in their corner of the restaurant.

"You know," Jack said, running right through it, "some people think I'm pretty cool."

"Maybe in your athlete days of yore," Jenna said.

"Maybe that's right," Jack said.

"But now," Jenna said, "you're just another bro from the North Shore who's ready to start his life all over again in L.A."

Jack's mouth smiled, but not his eyes.

"JJ Pickle is still pretty cool," Will said. "Just not as cool as...Jenna Saisquoi."

Jenna's lips were flat and her eyes were still.

"Isn't that what that guy said last night?" Will said, flailing a little. "That whole weird thing?"

"I forgot about him," Jenna said.

"Anyway..." Will said. "Does anyone want any more of these?"

"The salmon," Jack said.

"Two," Whitney said.

"Two and a half," Jenna said, undercutting her, so Will got four.

While Will went to the counter, Jack went to the bathroom and Whitney tried her best to keep things normal with Jenna. She asked if there was any place she'd liked more than any other during her time in Europe.

"When I was abroad in Paris," Whitney said, "we traveled almost every weekend. I don't totally know why, but I'm the same way now. I'm all excited to get to the one place, but then as soon as I'm there, all I can think about is where I want to go next."

"I liked Copenhagen," Jenna said. "I liked Berlin. I didn't go all that many places, though. I guess I was the same as you heading into the program, but I didn't change in some big way once I arrived....I'd waited all my life to live in Paris, so I didn't want to waste it. There were the trips down here. But those were typically just a couple days. And then some trips with some friends, with my...with my roommates."

Jenna stumbled over the mention of *my roommates* as Jack returned. There was a shard of something that had emerged when Jenna had seen Jack. Jenna laughed a low, full-throated giggle, remembering something else.

"The three of us got stuck in Copenhagen for a couple extra days in November," she said. "It wasn't even Thanksgiving yet, and it was already dark and snowy. I got what the big deal was about that place, though. We rode bikes around the lakes as it snowed. We drank in dark bars and ate pizza down near the waterfront in an old warehouse. It was outrageously expensive—Fantas cost, like, seven bucks. And so until the tracks were cleared, we mostly lived on hot dogs from the 7-Elevens that were everywhere."

"What about Jack's top three?" Whitney said.

"What's that?" he said, drying his hands on his jeans. She explained. "Besides the places I played, it was really in and out. We'd get to a city in the afternoon and leave that night if we could. Buses and trains. I could tell you my favorite buses and trains? And the places I lived: Bergen, Frankfurt, here obviously. I guess I liked Oslo. I liked Munich. We got a day off for Oktoberfest. A two-beer limit at Oktoberfest is not exactly the point of Oktoberfest, but it was fun to hang with teammates in a different context. Berlin, too, I guess. But it was the middle of winter and I stuck around the hotel most of the time, stayed near the big gate, near the memorial with the stones."

Will was back with the salmon toasts and another bottle.

"The Eisenman," Jenna said. "The Murdered Jews of Europe."

"Hmm?" Whitney said, regretting her show of ignorance at once.

"The memorial he's talking about," Jenna said. "I went there, too, with those roommates. There's something especially strange about being an American Jew walking around that thing with two blond Germans."

"You realize you have blonde hair, too?" Jack said.

"We come in all shapes, sizes, and colors," Jenna said, placing her finger on the subtle curve of her nose.

Will and Whitney watched Jack and Jenna. Pinwheels spun behind their eyes. They possibly loathed each other, but craved one another nonetheless. Will and Whitney saw images passing between Jack and Jenna from their previous evening, from their morning, images of their bare bodies and whatever they'd done to each other. There was a taffy-stretched thickness of silence between them. Words only ran the risk of derailing the rest of their thing.

Whitney opened her mouth to tell Will it was probably about time for them to head home, but he started talking before she could.

"So I'm always thinking about this thing," Will said. "And lately I've tried to get my boss to try it out in interviews, but he doesn't want to fuck around with HR. I'm not long for that place, so what do I care anymore—but have you guys ever seen *Bull Durham*?" Jenna hadn't. It was one of Jack's favorite movies, of course. Whitney winced because she knew where this was going. "Well, there's this famous speech. This speech where Kevin Costner's character monologues to Susan Sarandon's character about the stuff he 'believes in,' the stuff he truly lives for. We'll show you.... Who can pull it up? Mine doesn't have..."

Jack reached for his phone. His international service.

"The benefits of stardom..." Will said. "Anyway, I've always believed there must be no better way to do a job interview. Your résumé says where you went to school, where you've clocked in. But the point is to actually learn something about someone, right?"

The clip loaded slowly and they watched it: *I be-lieve in the soul...the cock...the pussy...the small of a woman's back...the hangin' curveball...high fiber...good Scotch...and on and on.*

All four of them laughed at the hamminess. They were a little lit up by the wine.

"So, Whitney," Will said, turning to her stagily, "what do you believe in?"

"Oh, I like this," Jenna said.

"Someone else start," Whitney said, still ready to leave. "How 'bout you?"

"Jack?" Will said, deflecting.

"I can't do it off the top of my head," Jack said. "Can I take a minute and write something down?"

Jenna moved across the crowded floor and squeezed be-tween the elbows at the bar again. She put her chest on the counter. She returned with two pencils.

They stood at their table scribbling for several silent minutes, taking breaks to sip wine, to refill glasses. They made lists. Will proclaimed there'd be a buzzer in five more minutes.

Jenna was left-handed. Her wrist cupped over in a claw and she held the pencil like a murder weapon. She had a neat, angled script that stood tall in a mix of lowercase and capital letters. Jack focused completely, his tongue piercing his lips ever so subtly, like his hero's, like Jordan's. Will scratched away in a tight, tiny, twelve-point font. Whitney wrote like she was icing a cake. The lightest loops and verticals. Jenna marveled aloud that Whitney could get any of her lead to stick, as she'd already torn through two of the wax-paper napkins.

"Whit?" Will said when time was up.

"I still don't want to go first."

"I'll go first," Jack said. "I didn't know how many to do?"

"I'm sure whatever you've got is the exact right amount," Will said.

Jack held his napkin to his nose so he could read his scrawl.

"Okay," he said, stuffing the smile back into his face, like a seven-year-old steadying to present a science project. "I believe in the jump shot," he began. "The pick-and-roll. The alley-oop. I believe in grilled chicken. And fried chicken. And chicken *à l'orange*..."

Will and Jenna burst out laughing, and Jack raised a long index finger to quiet them, to signal that he was just getting started.

"...I believe in the Loop, the lake, the Bulls, the Bears. I believe it's better when teams win titles at home rather than on the road. I believe that Wrigley Field is probably the most important structure on earth. I believe in Christopher Nolan. And the *Batman* with Heath Ledger. I believe in brown-haired girls—and blonde-haired girls who are Jewish. I believe in *Breaking Bad*. I believe in big beds. I believe in

175

imported cheeses and meats. I believe in the Father, the Son, and the Holy Ghost—at least for my mom's sake. I believe in America. I believe in basketball still. And . . . " He looked up. "That's it, that's as far as I got."

They whooped. They'd been smiling the whole time. They couldn't believe it. He'd taken it so seriously.

"Holy shit," Will said. "I wrote down, like, five things."

"Look at that stack," Jenna said. "He went through an entire napkin dispenser."

"See what I mean?" Will said. "You're hired!"

"What do you do again?" Jack said.

"Don't worry about it," Will said. "Follow any path besides mine."

"All righty, then," Jack said. "Who's up?"

They were silent. Jack grabbed an olive pick in the shape of a plastic sword and dropped it from his height onto the table. The blade pointed to Whitney.

Will looked at her and jutted out his lower lip expectantly.

"I don't want to go," she said. "Mine's stupid compared to that."

"Nobody cares!" Will said.

"C'mon," Jack said.

"He's right, literally nobody cares," Jenna said, flat.

Whitney looked at her, put off, then stared at her napkin, then stared at Will.

"Whitney," Jack said, doing his best Susan Sarandon, "*What* do *you believe in, then?*"

"Well," she said, seeing no way out but through, "I believe in the Met . . ."—she looked up to clarify—" . . . the museum, not the baseball team. I believe in the essays of Joan Didion. I believe in the paintings of Helen Frankenthaler and Lee Krasner. I believe in Julia Louis-Dreyfus, Elisabeth Moss, and Nora Ephron. I believe in Shondaland. I believe that the television shows of Aaron Sorkin and David Milch are—what's Costner's line?—*self-indulgent, overrated crap.* I believe in *The Daily Mail.* I believe in *Us Weekly.* I believe in *The New York Post* and *TMZ.* I believe in Ninth Street Espresso, Momofuku Noodle Bar, autumn in New York, and the MoMA corporate rate. I believe in MTV reality programming. I believe in dogs that look like their owners. I believe in Lorde and Cat Power. I believe in barre classes, even though they're getting a little basic. I believe in RBG—and Hillary, still. And I, uh, I believe *Save the Cat!* ruined a generation of Hollywood screenwriters."

She looked up, a snapping to. She'd resisted the wave, then ridden it into shore until the words on her napkin ran out. They looked as though they weren't certain she was through. But Will was smiling. Hearts were spilling out of his eyes like coins from a jackpot.

It was halftime. They killed the bottle. Jenna flipped a euro and told Will to call it in the air. Will lost.

"There's a lot of pressure," Whitney said, "given that you proposed it. That you must've thought this through before. That you weren't coming to it blank like the rest of us."

"Honestly?" Will said. "I've never had the opportunity. I've never actually gone through with it. So lower your expectations. It's as impromptu as all of yours, and a tenth as well-executed."

"I can't wait till you get fired for harassment when you try to impose this on an applicant," Whitney said, laughing loosely for the first time since they'd started.

"They'll be doing me a favor," Will said.

"C'mon, get on with it," Whitney said, rolling her eyes.

Will cleared his throat as a joke.

"Ready?" he said. It was all for Whitney at this point, it was just the two of them again. "I believe in the taco, the burrito, the tostada, and free chips when you sit down. I believe in point breaks, grommets, and beaches in Baja. I believe in the Pacific Ocean and palm trees and the Sela del Mar pier. I believe in L.A. people who live on the East Coast and East Coast people who live in L.A. I believe that California can secede from the Union but shouldn't. I believe that if it does, New York should turn into the capital from *The Hunger Games*. I believe in good governance, due process, and the Ninth Circuit. I believe that libel-law litigation is out of hand. I believe in William Goldman scripts. I believe in women who make way more money than men. I believe in summer-dress season in New York. Especially in the East Village. Especially at Young Lawyers happy hours..." He smirked without looking up and could feel the pleasant heat of Whitney's face. "I believe hot weather is better than cold. And I believe that *Boogie Nights* is the only perfect film."

He turned up smiling.

"Oh c'mon, that's it?" Jenna said, with a new edge.

It wiped the grin from Will's face.

"When's someone gonna bare their *soul* here?" she said. "I don't have a sense of what's in your *heart*. It's all *surface*, it's all cute little *jokes*."

He couldn't tell if she was kidding. She was clearly drunk, but he felt wrong-footed all the same.

"Consider mine kept a little lighter, then," Will said, his face changing before their eyes, his temples graying, his wrinkles dredging. "I guess there's plenty of ways to skin it."

"But what about *fate*?" Jenna said. "What about love and sex? What about *her*?"

"I didn't say anything about any of that, either," Jack said, stepping to Will's aid.

"You've been together, what, seven years?" Jenna said. "That's a long time."

"You're right," Will said.

"And so you must have *something* to say? We just want to *know*," Jenna said. She was in control of the table now.

Will shrugged. Whitney shrugged. They were at least a united front.

"I'll just come out and ask some questions, then…" Jenna said. Her eyes were bright, turned all the way up all of a sudden. They reflected the overhead lights like carved stones, and they were trained on Will. "People talk about the seven-year itch, right? So is it a real thing, or is it bullshit?"

"Must be one of those things they made up for a Marilyn Monroe movie," Whitney said.

"Really?" Jenna said. "I thought it might've been like taste buds, you know? The way I don't like the same food I liked when I was fifteen."

" 'I believe in the taste-bud theory of relationships,' " Will said, smiling, trying to lighten things again. "Is that the sort of thing you were looking for?"

"You tell me?" Jenna said, looking at Whitney. "All three of you are a full iteration of taste buds further along than I am. What changes?"

"You're up next, aren't you?" Whitney said, her own bright eyes dialing in a little now. "Don't you still have to go?"

"C'mon, let me in on it, Whit," Jenna said. "Do you feel like a different person than you did when you were my age? Different ideas? Different desires, different kinks? It's gotta *evolve,* right? To keep things fresh, to keep things hot? I just think about it a lot, you know: What happens to your brain? What happens to your code? What happened to your skin and your tits and your ass?"

She'd shifted tenses. Whitney heard it if no one else did.

"Guess you'll have to see for yourself when the time comes," Whitney said. "Some people know themselves right away; some people spend their lives figuring out who they want to be when they grow up."

A woman climbing a ladder for a bottle of wine bumped the light overhead, and they all strobed a little.

"I wonder which one of those people I am," Jenna said.

"Like whether you're Jenna or Leonard on any given night?" Whitney said.

Jenna didn't react. The men may as well not have been there anymore.

"C'mon," Whitney said. "Quit filibustering. You're up. The floor is yours."

"I went in a little different direction," Jenna said. "It's a different sort of . . ."

Whitney opened her arms wide, like: *Please, proceed.* She'd seized the table back.

"Well, uh . . . " she said, yanking a strap of her dress, maybe feeling the strain of the fabric. "I believe in life after death. I believe in the Buddhist's conception of reincarnation and Dante's conception of Purgatory and the secular Jew's conception of Heaven and Earth. I believe time moves faster sometimes and time moves slower other times. I believe that marriage is a fallacy and that monogamy is obviously unnatural. I believe that women have all the power but that most are too weak to use it. I believe seduction is sexier than sex. I believe that Paris is sexier than L.A., which is sexier than New York. I believe in Picard frozen foods. I believe in *cafés noisettes*. I believe in Michel Houellebecq. I believe people have more control over their lives than they give themselves credit for. I believe that people deliberately make themselves miserable by making bad choices. I believe I could kill a person if I had to. I believe most people are fucked up in the head and that feet are super gross. And I believe"—she'd stopped looking at her notes, even though there were plenty left; she was bored suddenly—"in the taste-bud theory of relationships."

"And there you have it," Will said. "A-pluses all around."

The four of them stood there breathing dumbly, a little worn out, a little beyond the threshold of amusement. They were out of wine but they'd already had way too much. The half-eaten salmon toasts were buried beneath the grave of crumpled napkins that they'd used to keep the honey off their hands. The air shifted around them. Behind their faces were four distinct temperatures, but each was ready to get out of there. Jenna moved first to retrieve the check. The same routine. Straight to the counter, into the in-between spaces. It was getting crowded now. There was a stack-up outside on the street. Whitney made a silent appeal to Will, but Will's face was following Jenna. It made her want to murder him.

When the bill landed, Will did some frantic accounting and determined it was somehow exactly right. The handwritten tabs hadn't failed tonight, and maybe they never had. They settled up with cash—twenty-five euros each—and they bused their dishes and wiped down their table, erasing the evidence that they'd ever been there.

They fell from the tight quarters of the restaurant into the cool alleyway and the breeze of the street. It was still May—

the temperature was still diving in the early evenings. The men pulled on light jackets, Jack's tenting him, twice the size of Will's. Jenna wore nothing but her dress and looked entirely unbothered by the breeze. The bones in Whitney's shoulders poked through her cotton sleeves and she huddled herself up in her arms.

"I should've brought something," she said to Will, privately.

"You can get a sweatshirt here," Jenna said, without looking back, pointing to a tourist shop on the corner. "Look, this one has the salamander from Parc Güell on it."

Whitney's mouth cracked wide, a little disbelieving.

"It looks warm," Jenna continued. "And actually kinda like the new Gucci…"

"I'll be fine," Whitney said.

They weren't off in any direction in particular, but Jenna and Jack were in the lead. They were walking up the alley, not down. They were following the alley to its end. Will and Whitney hung back.

"What the fuck is her problem?" Whitney said.

"What do you mean?" Will said.

"That pretentious bullshit in there," she said. "That fucking list and those smirks and knowing little laughs. The way she went after you two. The way she was nipping at me the whole time."

"I mean, I know she says some obnoxious stuff, but that just seems to be what you get with her, right? It's non-discriminating, at least."

"That Buddhist bullshit. That Houellebecq crap. That line about getting older—my skin and tits and ass? And now this fucking sweatshirt?"

"I think she just was saying that you could get a sweatshirt there if you're cold. She's a little much, but I don't think there was anything that was more than—"

"You're kidding me."

"Am I? I don't know, I just don't really think there's anything malicious going on."

"Every little thing's a provocation. That shit about new kinks and keeping things hot? Did you fucking blab to her last night about what we did?"

"Whit, Jesus. Of course not. I haven't told anybody, let alone a loony tunes chick we met at a party."

"Then what the fuck was that about? Just another dig? *What about fate, what about love and sex?* What a precocious little twat."

"All right, well, I guess that's that, then. Don't need to do *this* again."

"I know you can't see past that tight little body, but there's some serious bullshit going on, and it's getting me a little—"

"You're making way too much of this! I don't think there was anything there that should be perceived as direct, specific shots at you. Okay? I thought it was super nice and fun most of the time. She needled me, too. Right after my dumb list. And if anyone has grounds, isn't it Jack? She's especially vicious to—"

"Right, right. Defend him, not me. You're an idiot. *Jenna Fucking Leonard.* She's got you both by the cocks. Her legs wrapped around your neck like a fucking femmebot. Sweet Jack and Predictably Susceptible Will. Stuck with this old crumpled bag. I always forget that that thing up there has been your fantasy forever. Manic Pixie Dream Bitch behavior that you've always had a weakness for. Someone to slap you around a little and get you off with some fucking

Snapple-bottle philosophy. I'm surprised that wasn't one of your freebies, a girl like that. Find someone to tell you about all the books she's bought but never read, and then step on your balls."

Will laughed incredulously. "You're unbelievable. It's un-fucking-believable to me how quickly you escalate this shit. How quickly you get to the red rage without a warning bell. You always do—"

"I don't *always* do anything. This isn't my fault. Don't start hitting back at me with shit like that. I'm glad you found a compadre in Jack, and that you both find it all so irresistible. But she's gonna destroy him. And she can destroy you, too, for all I care."

Will started up the alley in their direction. They were pulling away, and they'd notice if he and Whitney didn't start walking soon.

"I'm gonna go home," Whitney said, staying put.

"What are you doing, seriously?"

"I don't want to go that way. You're more than welcome. I'll take the key and you can buzz up when you get home and I'll let you in. I'm exhausted. And I really don't want to go wherever they're going."

"Please don't make this more than it is. She's a bitch. Does that do it? We're on the same page now? She's a needling pain in the ass who knew some spots to go to the last two nights. But I don't understand why you're letting her get to you. I don't know why you can't just ignore her. C'mon. Let's not make a scene right here. Please just come along."

Jack and Jenna were two blocks ahead of them now and they still hadn't turned around. They strolled slowly, Jenna taking two strides for each of Jack's. Jack rested his open hand on the top of her head. From distance, it looked like he was palming her like a basketball.

"Let's please not make this a thing," Will said. "Let's just catch up and say good night and then walk our own way. Just please don't make me go up there alone."

"Always so concerned with what others will think. Quaking at the thought of someone perceiving conflict."

"Whitney, c'mon. Jesus. *I* didn't do anything. Don't lash out at me because some fucking college chick hurt your feelings."

Whitney laughed and shook her head. "Give me the keys, please."

"Strike that last line from the record," he said. He couldn't help himself. Each time he'd climb up to the edge, he'd fall back down and wind up deeper in the hole than before. "Just walk to the intersection and say goodbye. You don't even have to walk home with me. I'll stay behind you and won't say a thing. Please just go up there and say good night."

"Give me the keys."

"I'm not giving you the keys until you come up the hill."

She one-eightied and started down the alley in the other direction.

"Whitney, Jesus," Will said, and chased her a quarter block and stood in her way. "Remember what this is over! This is over a fucking *sweatshirt*."

"Don't make me sound trivial. Get out of my way."

"This is my least-favorite version of you, period."

"Move."

He moved with her like a lineman. "This is the part of you I *can't stand*." He said it sweetly, softly, to keep his voice down.

"Then all the better that we're parting ways. Have fun with them. Hope you end up at a nightclub again. Hope you meet your third."

"This is ridiculous! Have you lost your fucking *mind*?"

"Maybe you guys can both take her home tonight. Maybe they'll let you watch. That's the ultimate dream for you, right? You don't even want to be involved. Your dream basketball player. Your dream blonde—built just the way you really like them. Grapefruit tits and a *parfait* French accent. I had to hear it for years, how the girls at college were nothing compared to the girls back home, right? The California girls, *wowweeee*. Congrats on proving your point. You can watch to your heart's delight and jerk off in the corner."

"Just tell me what this is really about," Will said. "Find a way to articulate it, please. Is it just the wine? Is it the fucking salmon toasts? Is it the fact that she, and not you, gets to go home with Jack? What is it?!"

"Fuck you," she said.

"The worst version of you, period," he said. "Sloppy logic. Dripping envy. You're fucking drunk."

"Get out of my way," she said, and she grabbed him by the shoulders to force him aside. He held his ground and she lowered her head and butted him in the chest, hard as she could. His feet pedaled backward and he grabbed her by the arms. They locked and started stumbling down the alley. They found their collective footing and stood there straining against one another, Will stronger by enough to contain the effort, but needing to focus to do so. He felt the flash in his chin before he saw it coming. She'd lifted her head swiftly and uppercut him with her skull. He stumbled backward again, stunned. She stood there with alarm in her eyes, her head ringing loudly. They hadn't fought like this in years. That's when they heard it.

"Hey!" It was Jack. They were coming back down the alley. But they were far enough away still to have missed it. "What happened?" Jack shouted.

"I dropped my wallet," Will said. He said it quickly, softly, still at the volume of their low-volume fight. He pulled it from his pocket and shook it in the yellow light. "Found it, though."

Will wouldn't look at Whitney, and he didn't hear her sandals moving away, either. He didn't notice Jack and Jenna noticing her, and so figured she must still be steps behind him, in the shadows of the alley.

"What is that, anyway?" Jenna said, as she approached. "Tom Ford?"

"Give me a break," Will said.

"You guys still cold?" Jenna said, a tone like a Rorschach test, sweet or sarcastic depending on how one intended to hear it. "I know an outdoor bar with some heat lamps."

"I'm actually...I think we're gonna head home," Will said. "Don't know about you guys, but we got a little beat up last night. Not sure how you do it, but we're too old now."

"Don't exclude me from that," Jack said. "I actually booted this morning."

"You're kidding?" Will said. His chin pulsed from the blow. But he acted genuinely surprised. He acted as though nothing was wrong between him and Whitney. He'd had the month of 1-2-3 to rehearse the illusion.

"I hadn't puked in five years," Jack said.

"December," Will said, raising his hand. "Office party. November, that one..." Will said, thumbing over his shoulder, then turning to look at the face he knew better than any other. She was still there, but farther away than he'd expected. There was an organs-deep impertinence blaring back at him from down the alley. The temporary disdain was real; it was always genuine when it came for him. Color and temperature and shadow, those were the variables he keyed in on at the edges of her facial features. The hang in the hair that swept across her forehead. The weight of the slashes of her eyebrows. The mouth a little fuller and redder, just then, a puffiness from the rage that was boiling an eighth of an inch beneath the surface of her skin. "Election Night. She was up sick all night Election Night. Ruined the Thai place we'd ordered from. Haven't been back."

"Actually, last month," Whitney said, looking at him. She'd intended it to sting. "When I was in L.A. Out too long, up way too late..." Her face was razor blades. She was speaking loudly and moving in closer, and her eyes were suddenly fixed fiercely in Jenna's direction. "What about you?"

"I can't," Jenna said, yawning. "I've got"—she waved a hand in front of her throat—"no gag reflex."

"That shocks me," Whitney said, taking several additional steps in her direction. "I would've taken you for a morning, noon, and night type."

"What does *that* mean?" Jenna said, twisting up her face.

"You just check the boxes of someone familiar with the inside of a toilet bowl."

Jenna laughed uncertainly, and looked to Will and Jack to see if they'd registered it as a bad joke. "Hate to disappoint you..."

"But...no gag reflex. That's cool. Is that true?" Whitney said, looking at Jack this time.

"Hey," Jack said, raising his hands. "Leave me out of whatever this is."

"Yeah, Whit," Jenna said, flexing her eyes. "What is this, exactly?"

Whitney stepped closer still to Jenna, and this time she didn't stop short. Whitney had six inches on her and she'd thrown her shoulders back into the posture of a ballerina. She tossed her hair and threw a long languid arm around Jenna's shoulders and pulled in even closer and squeezed. For the first time all night it was Jenna who shrank, shorter and smaller than she'd been in the short, small history of their twenty-four-hour quartet.

"I'm just joking with you," Whitney said, smiling with cold control. "We're all just joking around with each other, I thought? Isn't that what this has been?" Jenna stared at the paving stones and Whitney shifted Jenna in her arm. Whitney's dominant hand traced Jenna's neck and crept around the baby fat of her cheek. Then her fingers fondled the gold hoop that fell from the lobe of Jenna's right ear.

Whitney tugged and Jenna flinched. The earring popped off easily.

"Oh, jeez," Whitney said. "Is this a clip-on? You of all people?..."

Whitney still had Jenna in her arm. She leaned her back ever so slightly and tilted Jenna's head up to hers, looking for something in her face.

"Why do you look so nervous?" Whitney said. "We're all just having fun with each other, right?" Whitney clipped the earring back in place and Jenna flinched again. "Lighten up, Leonard. Not everything has to be life and death and theories of reincarnation."

Just as Jenna looked like she might crumple to the street,

she lifted the arm that was trapped behind Whitney's body and slipped her fingers into Whitney's hair.

"I don't want to be all mushy," Jenna said, meeting Whitney's eyes, two faces locked in an angle, locked in a negotiation of wills. "But I just love this. I love how coarse it is. I wish mine was like it. Instead of this baby hair, so fine you can't do anything with it. Yours, though, it reminds me of horse hair." Her arms rose over Whitney's shoulders and she ran the blue-black mane through the whole of her hands.

"I always wished I'd had a little sister, you know?" Whitney said. "Just a different thing than with a brother. A little girl to look after all your life. I always wanted to be the guardrail for someone like that. Girls can be so smart and so fucking stupid."

They existed for each other and only for each other. Will and Jack stood silently, watching without breathing, on the outside of the bubble that seemed to have sealed itself around the two women in the alley.

Will's arms were crossed. He watched the two of them wordlessly. But if he listened closely, he could hear a low groan slipping from his lips.

"So do you guys want to go to this bar or not?" Jenna said, unlocking from Whitney, using the words as a wedge to separate from her.

"No thanks, I've really used it all up," Whitney said. "Like I said...like *you* said: I'm not twenty-two anymore..."

"But you've got our numbers and email..." Will said, from a distance now, having slithered down the alleyway some himself.

"And looks like..." Jack said, pointing to the heavens, to the starless black, the black without holes, "...we're gonna be stuck right here all over again tomorrow."

"Until mañana, then," Will said. And Whitney waved with both hands, and showed them her widest wide smile, a thick red ring of twenty-nine-year-old lips, lit up with pleasure and neon.

When Will turned back down the alley, pocketing his own waves, Whitney was already a storefront along, the gap widening, so that he was forced to lengthen his stride.

Jack's "Bye!" barked in delay. For all the professional reflexes, for all the legendary hand-eye, his reactions were always a beat behind, like sound in a stadium.

Whitney turned the corner at first opportunity, down a darker alley that ran parallel to the boulevard. She kept a distance Will couldn't collapse, in space or in spirit, for the entirety of the walk back to the apartment. Will had the keys still, but Whitney knew he wouldn't dare be anywhere but right behind her when it was time to unlock the front door. He called her name, just once, and without stuttering a step, without missing a stride, she threw two middle fingers with bright painted nails up over her shoulders in reply.

Ljósmyndari

The photographer arrived by boat with four fishermen. The docks were burned badly and the harbor was filled with new rock. They anchored offshore and dinghied in. He dragged his hand in the water. The sea was cool again. As they reached the black beach, they could see the rivulets of basalt that had burned their way into the surf. He poked some with a stick. When it pressed back firmly, he smelled the end of his poker and it smelled like rotten eggs.

They tied down the boat and the fishermen set off on foot for the village. The photographer trained his eyes skyward, to the flowering of black clouds above Holudjöfulsins. The air was still warm and dense with particulate. When he waved his stick, a fine ash swirled around him. He uncapped his water bottle and took a swig. He pulled a piece of wintergreen gum from his vest. He had two cameras with him, and he pointed the first one up.

He shot for an hour. He shot the volcano and the ash-cloud and the burned-up homes and livestock. The lava had descended the mountain in spokes that carved the valley floor into ribbons of fortune and misfortune. This home had been turned to ash, but the neighbor's stood unscathed. He took pictures of good luck and bad luck.

The cloud illumed every now and then, crackling from its center, a weather system all its own. Against the protests of the fishermen, he set off up the slopes of the volcano for a closer look. He climbed for half an hour, pausing only when the rumblings beneath his feet froze him in his boots. The cloud was an impenetrable trap, a light-suck composed, he imagined, of every element in the periodic table. It was black, but marbled. It was so outsize in scale that it was like its very own idea—a tropospheric mass he'd heard was now the size of a continent. It was less than a week old. Astonishing.

He shot from the slopes for an amount of time that was impossible to measure. There were none of the typical reference points. It was an alien landscape at alien altitude, the up swirling imperceptibly with the down. It was a place of pure science, of chemistry and physics, of solids that looked like gases and gases that looked like solids. It was a place he was convinced must be devoid of life altogether. He felt himself moving closer to the cloud. He felt his body lifting from his boots and rising toward the mass above him, as though in the tractor beam of an alien ship. He felt light and he felt small and he felt he would never worry too hard about anything ever again now that he had had his perspective shifted, now that he had come face to face with the ashcloud.

He was returned to his body when he heard the clamor in the valley. The fishermen were whistling at him. They were waving their arms. They were a mile away, but the sound carried up the slopes. He fixed them through his viewfinder. They were pointing back toward the shore. He gathered his equipment and packed his lenses. He slung his cameras over *his shoulder and turned to start down the slope. But before he set off, he gazed up one last time at the belly of the cloud. At the graveness and the density. At the infinite-seeming blackness and the immeasurable weight.*

"Do you have any idea how much bloody trouble you've caused?" he shouted. And he laughed like the last man on Earth. Then he turned his back to the ashcloud and trotted down the slope beside the runways of rock to the sea.

Tuesday

Will spent the first part of his morning on the phone with the airline and got a human for the first time yet. It would be another day of nothing. But, as they were sure he'd heard, it wasn't a matter of accumulation anymore so much as dispersion. Things were socked in. It was still heavy. They needed some assistance from the heavens. A high-pressure system could make tomorrow a possibility. Tomorrow or the next day or the day after that—just don't hold your breath.

Whitney had left for a run over an hour ago. She'd woken up before Will and jumped out of bed and cut over to the arch and down past the zoo and over the tracks they'd crossed the other night as a company of four. She ran along the beach in one direction, then back again in the other, all the way out to the promontory with the hotel that sat raised like a sail.

Will waited for Whitney to return. He read and reread the same dumb pages of his book. He checked his email: no new nothing from the producer. Maybe today, now that everyone would be back from the long holiday weekend.

He went out for coffee but didn't go far—just across the street, worried that Whitney might get home and, finding him out with the key, grow only more incensed than she already was. He brought his book with him. He drank a *café con leche* quickly. He ate a chocolate croissant and then a second. He swept up his mess of flakes and felt sick with sugar and walked back across the street with his head down and almost got hit by a garbage truck. Two men hung off the back and another drove. They were handsome and tan and had clean uniforms and the same haircuts as the soccer players. Will bet they made a living wage. He bet it was enough to get on happily, pridefully, in this city of extreme reasonableness. He couldn't quit his job, could he? He'd made more than she had at first, and then she'd rocketed past him. She'd deferred her loans but had been paying them off quickly now. She was just comfortable in a way he wasn't. She didn't think about it incessantly anymore. But even with the gap, he insisted on splitting everything down the middle. He couldn't afford to regress to zero. The two men on the back waved at him and hopped off to clear the human-size recycling receptacle on the forty-fived corner of the city block. Everywhere people looked pleased with the temperature, with the state of the city's sidewalks and trees. They didn't seem bothered by the volcano. He finally understood in his gut—unless that was just the sugar surge—their collective desire for secession. He understood it on some level in California and it was beginning to make sense on another in Catalonia. It was beautiful all around. Everyone seemed content. Fucking Whitney. Fucking Will. Why were they wasting their morning apart in this place of immeasurable pleasantness?

Whitney stretched on the beach in front of the hotel. She

watched three women with a decade on her spread out on mats near the water and salute the steel-trap sky. She spread her legs and pressed her palms into the sand and heard a wolf whistle behind her. She ignored it and then heard it again and flipped around with acid in her eyes, only to find a woman whistling at her daughter to get away from the gulls in the garbage can. The mother recognized that Whitney had turned, and she smiled sweetly. Whitney smiled back and then brushed the sweat from her exposed stomach. She wrung out her ponytail and took a deep breath. She spread her feet to match the width of her shoulders and straightened her spine as though she were being reeled in by a fisherman. She dusted the sand off her legs. They were thicker than she liked—soccer legs still, only stiffer in the joints. But they were effective, thirty miles a week. She brushed off her stomach again, some sand stuck to her sticky skin. Her stomach was hard and flat, and possessed a pleasing deflated-ness—she hadn't eaten since the snacks at dinner. She put her hands on her ribs, finding their individual frets beneath her skin, fingering their notes. She breathed deeply and felt her cage expand. She felt hungry and it was energizing. She'd woken up ashamed of how the night had ended. The rage on the walk and then the silence that had choked them to sleep in their shared bed. She'd burned it off in the first hour, running it out of herself, but then she'd pushed it farther, harder, pushed herself into the ground, and now she felt good and empty, but a little sick, too. It was growing darker by the minute. The yoga women were rolling up their mats. The ashcloud was about to break open, she could tell. She was several miles from the apartment. She would be caught out here and need to hail a cab. She followed the women into the lobby of the hotel.

Will made coffee. He checked in with work. He reviewed his boss's careful recommendations to the magazine now that his boss was back from his island and willing to do his job again. Will proposed changes to some new contracts. He sent a response to an agent. He read the next email slowly, without comprehension. He started on another and then, as though tied to the crack of thunder out the window, he realized that he might not ever be able to read another contract again. It seemed he might not be able to read and comprehend anything at all ever again, all those electronic words were so scrambled as they traveled from his eyes to his brain. There was zero sensemaking. There were rights and there was money and there was Will in the middle, with not a drop left in the tank. He couldn't do it for even another day. It had started to pour outside. Where the hell was she? He was worried now. He was enraged.

It was cool inside the lobby. It was pink and purple, lit like a bachelorette party. She went to the bathroom to dry herself off with some paper towels. She admired her stomach and arms in the mirror—different, she was certain, from what she'd seen in the mirror when she woke up. Nine miles of sweat. Nine miles of compression. She needed a glass of water and took the elevator to the sky lounge. It was ten in the morning, but the place was half full. Because it was morning, because they were serving breakfast, she didn't stick out as sorely in her workout clothes as she suspected she might have. The woman behind the bar filled a glass with her water gun and Whitney took a seat by the window. They were on the twenty-eighth floor. It felt like the same raw height as the terrace at the Miró. But the rain seemed to have brought the ashcloud closer. They were amidst it, inside the cloud, mixed up with the Icelandic ash that had traversed thousands of miles. She felt like she could reach out and touch it through the window. From her side of the lounge, it was water and cloud forever; but from the other side, she saw as she approached the glass, it was a look back toward the city. Through the black mist she could make out the Nouvel office building with its rainbow scales, the unfinished cathedral, the towers near the water that had been built for the Olympics, the ones she imagined Jack living in. Jack and Jenna probably weren't so far away. She tried to guess which floor they were fucking on.

Will stretched out full-bodied on the leather couch in front of the television. The blackness from the storm pressed heavily against the windows. He felt unpleasant pricks on his skin each time a new email pinged his inbox. He needed something to airlift him from the corner he'd painted himself into. But he knew he wouldn't solve it now. Now was a time for staying hidden, for huddling up beneath the ashcloud. Now was a time for watching the ten-year-old girls' soccer game on the FC Barcelona channel. The game was slow, but they held their shape on the field. No swarming. Long lanes, diagonal balls, rapid one-touch passes in crowded space. He imagined little Whitney, dominating on the wing, and he loved her again. Precision crosses from the flank. Crunching tackles in open play. He imagined the long flat eternities in Euless and Richardson and Haney, running, lifting, training each day in pain and solitude for the opportunity to get out of Dallas. Barcelona scored twice in fifteen minutes and he flipped it off. He couldn't do anything for longer than fifteen minutes anymore. He went to the bed and dialed into their streaming services, but none of them apparently worked in Spain. He tried to sleep but was wired from the coffee. He flipped out of bed and did three sets of push-ups and then connected to the Wi-Fi to text Whitney. A message popped up from a number he didn't recognize. It was Jack. They were getting a bite in the early afternoon, if they wanted to meet up. Even after last night, even after all that. Still nothing from Whitney. He stared at their last text exchange, a packing list from before they left New York. Converters. Passports. Swimsuits. Shades. They hadn't needed to text while they were here; they'd been together the whole time. He listened to the rain pound the window. He texted: You okay?

You okay? The text popped up on her screen as her water glass was refilled by the bartender. She was young and extra friendly and she looked a little like Jewel. Whitney was tapped into the hotel Wi-Fi, checking her email, composing a reply to a message she'd received overnight. "Would you like anything else?" the bartender said, lingering, and Whitney looked up a little flustered, and reflexively said no thank you. But before the bartender went back to chopping her limes, Whitney said, "Actually..." and ordered an Aperol spritz. It was voluminous, filled to the brim with ice, and bright in ways it seemed the outside never would be again. She was so thirsty still. She watched the waterline recede as she sucked her straw. Got caught in this rain and waiting it out in a hotel. Be home when I can. She watched his bubbles. They'd appear and then disappear and then appear and then disappear, and finally what came through was: K

He did push-ups again until his arms failed. He did sit-ups until his tailbone was sore. He had the taste of stale butter and chocolate and steamed milk in his mouth. He finished a set and burped and felt like throwing up. He had a buzz in his extremities, a healthy strain. But he had a new surge in his blood as well, the new anxiety that no battery of body-weight exercises could neutralize: *Would he get what he needed at another law firm? Would he get it anywhere in New York? Who hadn't he thought of yet that could use a lawyer, or at least someone with a law degree?* He could serve a startup, a place with equity, a place where his long hours meant skin in the game. He'd rest and vest. He'd cash out. He'd be tethered to the new economy rather than the old, dying one. He wrote an email to the producer asking if there was any news. He sent the email and regretted it instantly. The stink of desperation. He'd broken his own code. Maybe it was time for the nuclear option. Maybe it was time to ask Whitney for help. To hand over the secret project to the wife-to-be who knew more than anyone else about what worked and what didn't. She had her things. She had her things that made him crazy. But she was going to be one of the best there was at the thing she'd chosen to do. He knew it. It made him impossibly proud. It made him corrosively envious. It was like his father had bored into him: *It didn't really matter what work you did, so long as you were great.* Talent above all else. God, Whitney. It made his heart beat faster. He couldn't hand her a draft and sit there through her polite defanged criticism, her pulled punches, her encouraging nudges. He didn't have any business touching those rails. He'd been good at law school. He was good at the rules, the regulations, the statutes, even the interpretation. But he'd had no business writing the script. He was a lawyer. He could at least do something with it. He could work trials. He could clerk for a judge. He was smart enough, he believed. He could *be* a judge someday. But first he needed to get back to basics. He needed to remember how to read emails and documents and finish the job he still had. He couldn't walk away cold. Not yet. They were to get married soon. They might even try to buy an apartment someday, if anyone their generation was able to do that still. He must contribute half, no matter what. He must finish his work the right way before blowing things up. Maybe he could get fired. Downsized. Severance and all, he'd been there almost three years now. He knew it was important to tune in to the frequency of the universe—to listen to where it said he should go. He thought of the rules of growing up in the ocean, of swimming in riptides: Let it pull you, don't fight it, don't tire yourself out paddling against the insurmountable currents. Let the forces push you to the better place you're meant to be. God, he loved California. Maybe that was what was next. He went to the fridge and cracked the last beer. It would soften things. The fuzz would make him focus. He halved it. He opened another counterproposal from an agent. He read two pages. He opened a new browser. NYTimes. ESPN. SCOTUSblog. He googled *Jenna Leonard,* but weirdly nothing on their Jenna Leonard came up. He opened a different browser and went to one of his porn sites. The videos streamed slowly. It would never load all the way on the weak Wi-Fi. He toggled back to the marked-up contract, made it another couple pages. He did some more sit-ups. He started the shower. He brought his beer in with him, finished it while the water heated up. He jerked off in the shower, imagining the girl from the Young Lawyers Night slowly turning herself around without his asking; imagining Kelly Kyle making eye contact from between his legs; imagining Whitney in the body-slackened haze of her Santa Monica hotel room and, in a surge of useful jealousy, knowing that he needed to work harder from here on out or else he might lose her for good—to world-famous actors or Euroleague basketball stars or whoever else might turn her head. He toweled off and went to the fridge and found zero beers remaining. He looked outside and it was raining harder. He couldn't even cross the street to the *supermercat* without getting soaked. He found some ice and a bottle of whiskey hidden in an otherwise-empty cabinet, and made himself a mixed drink with a 250ml Coca Lite. He texted Whitney an emoji of a raincloud. And then he sat back down with his work.

Whitney texted back three emojis of lightning. She'd ordered a second drink. She googled *Jenna Leonard* and still couldn't find a picture of her online. Jenna reminded her so much of the girls she'd encountered her freshman year of college, the girls she couldn't have fathomed before arriving on campus—girls, in particular from those cities from the show that she'd admired so feverishly as a teenager. Girls from Los Angeles (season 2) and San Francisco (season 3) and New York (seasons 1 and 10). Girls who'd lived entire lives already, it seemed, by the time they arrived on campus. Girls who'd had so much to drink in high school that they were already practicing moderation on behalf of their bodies. Girls who'd done all the drugs there were to do, and were already over most of them. Girls who'd had so much sex that they were more focused now on their relationships with one another than on any boy in a Polo shirt or Nantucket reds. These girls knew the names of directors and playwrights and gallerists; they'd gone to prep school with their children. They knew the books on the bestseller lists and had opinions on which ones didn't belong. They knew about things not just in their home cities, but in other cities, too. They knew the neighborhoods, the street names, the restaurants, the stores. They had boyfriends in those cities. They had boyfriends, somehow, with jobs in office buildings.

Whitney had been watching girls like that from behind glass for practically half her life. She sat at the window of the hotel lounge facing the sea and the storm. They were very much in the ashcloud now. The room jumped with the next flash of lightning. She finished the email she'd started at the bar, and sent it. She looked exhausted, a little flushed. When she drained her spritz, the busser approached and asked in English if she was finished with her drink. She turned up into his face and said she still had some left even though they could both see that she didn't. He was wearing all white. He had slick black hair and strong tanned arms. He looked college-aged, Jenna-aged. She imagined Jenna in a place like this, in a place like this or any other place like it in Barcelona or Paris or New York or L.A. The same general outlines, the same purple and pleather. The sort of place no one wanted to see with the lights all the way up. *Jenna Saisquoi.* What the hell was that the other night? Some double life. Some party life. It had never been Whitney's scene. And it never would be again. The darkness. The anonymity of it. The slipping into corners, into bathroom stalls. The scumminess of the whole thing. The danger, the needless vulnerability. The pit that she'd experience the next morning, in daylight, at the office, seated at the conference-room table during a meeting, knowing what she'd done the night before and how and where and with whom. That guilt. Always that guilt. It lived inside her like a broken gene. The busser returned and he had another fresh drink with him. "She says it's on the house, third one's free at brunch, her special rule for you," he said. "Wow," Whitney said, waving thanks to the grinning bartender, "lush life." "Hmm?" he said, and Whitney smiled the full width of her head and pulled herself higher in her seat. He lingered there and she felt his eyes on her body. On her exposed stomach and waist, on her neck and arms and chest, on her legs that stretched all the way up into the running shorts that had ridden up practically to her hip bones. She let him hang there and her skin felt like oil in a skillet. She met his eyes and he was waiting for an answer to something. "What's that?" she said. And he said, "I just wanted to know if you'd like me to take the empty one now." Her face felt hot and she laughed stupidly and nodded and ran her hand through her hair. He smiled and took the glass and left her alone at the window. She had to pee and the bartender pointed to the bathroom, touching her shoulder as he showed the way. Her skin was humming, turned all the way up. She caught herself in the mirror again. It was the best her body had looked all trip. She felt empty, her stomach felt coated with spritz. She hadn't eaten all day and now she wasn't even hungry. The lines of her body shimmered in her reflection thanks to the sparkling wine. The room smelled like the honeysuckle of her summers growing up. The doors of the three stalls were ajar but she bent herself over, looking for shoes. She tested the air with an "*Hola?*" and nothing replied but the drone of the centralized air. She pulled the edges of her shorts up farther than they'd been in her seat near the window. She pulled them way up and admired the tautness of her ass, clenched like fists, hard and soft at the same time like boxing gloves. Her face was losing some of its snap—she knew she had only a couple more years before she'd have to double the effort. But her butt looked good and it dialed her up further. She looked at the door that led back into the bar and when it didn't move she slowly peeled down the front of her shorts and admired the way the plane of her stomach fell flatly into her pubic hair. She slipped a hand down the front of her shorts and was surprised to find herself as wet as she was. She moved to the stall farthest from the door and locked herself in. She dropped her shorts and sat on the hard plastic seat and lowered her longest finger between her legs. She felt the busboy's eyes on her body again. The sizzling skin still. College-aged, Jenna-aged. She imagined the busboy watching her now. She imagined the bartender watching him watch her. She imagined the two of them slipping her into one of the hotel suites. 1-2-*Tres*. She imagined herself in a hotel suite that looked like the hotel suite in Santa Monica. She imagined Adrien Green. She imagined herself with Adrien, in all the ways it had gone. She felt that surge in her body she'd never felt before that night, the suspicion that it was going where it was going, the rush. She couldn't push it to that place again herself—it was a door she didn't have a key to. And so as it backed away from an edge, the images shifted. She imagined Will with a faceless young associate at a Young Lawyers Night, his hungry mouth and hungry eyes and hungry fingers moving across her body the way they rarely moved across hers anymore. She imagined him with Kelly Kyle, doing whatever men did with tits that were that much bigger than her own, whatever it was that boys in school had been dreaming about since they were nine years old, fantasies she'd never understand and would never be able to grant someone herself. She imagined herself back with the busboy, the busboy and the bartender, less anything specific than his watching her, his walking in on her now. Him or the bartender. Either of them: college-aged, Jenna-aged. She imagined Jack and Jenna. She imagined Jack and Jenna in that skyrise apartment down the rainy beach. She imagined them there now, screams and laughter. Jenna Saisquoi. Whitney knew she'd

be loud. Whitney knew she'd be a performer. That blonde
hair thrown around like a sparkler. That perfect little taut
body put to good use. Curling up inside the shape of Jack,
consumed, subsumed. All the work to earn her place in
that big bed. She imagined Will this time, Will with Jenna,
back at their Airbnb. Will with a look of concentration, of
gratitude, like she'd never seen on his face before, a sense
of having leveled up to something extra special, forbidden
and golden-glittered, a taste of something made with lots of
butter and chocolate and steamed milk. Someone who, at
the very least, knew what she was doing in a youthful and
unmoored kind of way, who might rub off some lavender-
scented lotion and leave the smell on his skin for a few days.
Who would leave a hole in him that couldn't be filled the
old way ever again, certainly not by the likes of Whitney.
That was enough, that thought. That emptiness, that hole
at the center of each of them that might not be satisfied by
the other anymore. That was enough to do it. She sat there
breathing heavily, her eyes still closed, her brain a little
dizzy, her bladder still full. That final thought—that help-
lessness, that powerlessness, that realization that it might
be something they'd have to cope with for the rest of their
lives—almost made her cry. She peed and she washed her
hands and her body looked back at her in the mirror, and it
looked slacker to Whitney than it had even ten minutes ago,
her skin splotchy and red, lines everywhere she looked. Her
head was empty. She was getting so old. She was almost
thirty. She was drunk. She walked back to the bar and sat
back down in her seat near the window. She sipped her
drink and checked her work email. She typed out responses
without reading them through and sent them having forgotten where the responses had begun. She looked up and out

the window. The rain had stopped. There was still the thick ash, but it wasn't pouring anymore. Will texted a sun and a running girl. She texted a thumbs up. She paid her tab with two twenty-euro bills that she'd slotted into her cellphone case for an emergency. The bartender thanked her for the tip and wished her a pleasant afternoon and smiled one final time. Whitney hit the street, she mapped the distance, she balked at the mileage. A cab was waiting at the curb. She gave the address with practiced pronunciation. She got carsick on the way and shut her eyes.

Will woke up to the buzzer. He'd nodded off after he'd poured a fresh drink. He couldn't have drifted long—ten or fifteen minutes. His head was scrambled when he pressed the intercom and met Whitney at the front door. He couldn't tell for sure but she seemed loose herself. She smiled at him dolefully and moved past him into the kitchen, where she steadied herself on the counter.

"Are you okay?" he said.

"I had some drinks at the hotel," she said. "I don't know why."

"*Really...*" he said.

"Really," she said. "Is that okay?"

"Sure, whatever you want."

"That's what this is, right?" she said. "A big old vacation..."

"I guess that's right."

"I had one, and then I had three."

"What if I told you that I had one and then I had three, too?" he said.

"You've been drinking here by yourself?"

"So were you."

"I was in a hotel bar. I was waiting out a storm. Not just..."

"What is this? What are you doing? I was hoping we could start today fresh."

"I just didn't know that you...never mind, this is dumb, forget it."

"So, what then?" he said, and he could tell that she knew what he meant.

"I don't know," she said. "I'm sorry. I don't know what's going on. I don't know what that was last night, or what any of this is. I'm just ready to go home."

"I'm ready to go home, too. I'm very ready. I feel like I've had too much time to think about stuff while we've been here. I feel my brain dying. I can't even answer emails without getting anxious. I need to figure this out. I need to find something else for real."

"At least you know for sure."

"If a consequence of being stuck here is finding something a little more—"

"Sounds like a positive thing."

"It'll make things better for me and it'll make things better for you."

"How can I join in? What reckless decision can I make?" she said.

The slackening of tension came as such a relief to Will that he mistook the détente for resolution, as a new and welcome invitation to walk through the un-walk-through-able door.

"Well, to start," he said, "you can finally say *yes* to me. We can start telling people that we're engaged. I don't know why we'd put it off any longer. I mean, I know the reasons. And parts of all those reasons are maybe still there. But what is putting this off another month in the scope of all time? Why put it off when what we're doing is committing to, you know, forever?"

She looked at him sadly, like she wished he'd said anything but this.

"But the logic works the other way, too..." she said, moving to the kitchen to pour a glass of water. "What *is* another few months if there's sixty years on the horizon?"

"You're saying you're still not ready to tell people," he said.

"I'm saying I'm still fucking pissed about last night. And now is not exactly the primest moment to be asking me this, don't you think? Nothing seems to be going the way it normally does. With last month, and this trip, and, I dunno, I just feel like things are gonna be so much clearer when we get home. Can we just hold off talking about it till we get back? Last night made me mad. And you know I'm not like you. It's not: *Sleep it off and everything's good to go.*"

"I know that," he said. "And it's too bad for you."

"So at this point, why would I pretend I'm any other way? I don't exactly love this about me, but it's not so easy for me to just sweep everything away. Just: a little space for a little longer, okay? We'll be home soon. Then we'll know..."

"You at least realize this fucking hurts, right?"

"I'm sorry. It shouldn't hurt. It really shouldn't. It should be right where we were a month ago, and a week ago, and a day ago. Same as before that bullshit from last night."

"It still...Even if I understand what you're saying."

"I'm *really* sorry? I don't know what you want me to say. You know where I've been with this. I just, my head's a mess right now. Last night, that wasn't great. Not just what happened, but where I went, what it made me do. It's scary to see where my head goes sometimes, what effect certain people can have on me."

"Then I probably shouldn't mention that they want to get lunch. I guess they think everything's A-OK. Or at least didn't pick up on anything serious."

"I grabbed her and pulled an earring off her head. What the fuck is wrong with her that she wants to get lunch with us the next day?"

"It was from Jack, but it was filled with your favorite *we's* and *us's*. Maybe it happens all the time to Jenna Saisquoi. I don't know. I realize it's not how it works for you, but I woke up this morning and just thought: *That was dumb, let's discount the last part of the night.*" Will hadn't liked how things had ended with Jack. Jenna he'd never see again, but Jack was their age, they had each other's phone numbers, they texted now. Wouldn't it be weird if that was the last they ever saw of him? What if they were just getting started? "Anyway, it's just lunch. What's another lunch in the scheme of all the future time of No-Jenna-and-No-Jack?"

"I hope you're kidding. Did you already say we were going to meet them, or something?"

"I didn't say anything. I didn't respond. I know better. I'm just thinking out loud."

Whitney felt her clammy running clothes on her body in a self-conscious way. The way she could live for stretches without noticing her heartbeat, until she suddenly couldn't not sense it. She felt the straps around her shoulders and neck. She felt the salt and dampness at her hairline. She tore off her shirt, she kicked off her shoes. Her socks, her shorts. She was standing there in a sports bra, naked from the chest down.

"If you want to fuck her just get it over with," she said.

She stood there almost naked with betrayal in her face. She stood there like a child who'd just been scolded for playing in a mud pit.

He frowned and shook his head. "Why do you want to have this fight? Why do you say things like that? It's like you think your only move right now is hopping back into the same old tired bullshit."

"I'm just saying you still have a freebie."

"All I did was ask about lunch! We can skip it. We can read and walk down to the beach. We can keep drinking all day, it's as good as anything else to fucking do."

She started in the direction of the bathroom, taking an extra-wide line past the giant windows that looked out onto the street. She stopped, then stood before the windowpane and waved at a woman clipping towels to a line on the roof across the way. The woman glanced at Whitney's naked body, then returned to her business.

"Come fuck me against the window," she said.

"What?"

She stood on her tiptoes and reached around and body-gloved her ass cheek.

"There are people out there," he said. "There's an old grandma on the roof."

She fell back down onto flat feet and sighed and completed her journey to the bathroom.

"Do you really want to marry me?" she said, as she started the water.

He followed her and placed his hands on her narrow waist, on her tight hips.

"We know the real question is: Do you really want to marry *me*?" he said.

She slipped through his hands and stepped into the shower

and neither of them answered, or both of them answered, or it was a little of each.

"What are you going to tell them?" she said, eyes closed beneath the stream.

"What?" he said. "You're talking directly into the water."

"I said, *What are you going to tell them?*" She opened one eye and it peered at him through the fogging glass.

"I'll tell them we appreciate it but we already have plans."

"Fine," she said.

"Or I'll tell them we'll see them at two."

"I can't tell you how little I care either way."

"In that case, I'll flip a coin."

"Just make a decision. There's no wrong answer. Don't be an idiot."

"Heads is *go,* tails is *stay,*" he said, searching the bathroom counter for a euro.

"You can lie to me, I can't see through the glass anyway, I'll never know."

"Our fate is now in the hands of Icelandic volcanoes and Catalan spirits and the hard currency of the Eurozone."

The water rushed, he disappeared from the room.

"Found one," he said, returning within earshot.

"I'll never know either way," she said.

"I'm flipping the coin now," he said. "What do you think it's gonna say?"

They met Jack and Jenna on a stretch of Passeig de Gràcia bookended by Gaudís. Gaudí everywhere. Gaudí strung from buildings and balconies and trees like prayer flags.

The restaurant had no presence on the sidewalk. It was narrow inside and had a horseshoe bar. They served only *jamón ibérico,* but served it twenty different ways.

Jack and Jenna were already seated at the bar, always first somehow. They waved Will and Whitney over casually, without getting up for greetings this time. Jack was wearing khaki shorts that showed off his muscular legs. He wore a pair of high-top Jordans and a bull-red Toni Kukoč jersey. Jenna had on a tight black shirt tucked into jean shorts, and her hair was tied back in a ponytail. He looked baggy and she looked vacuum-sealed.

It was hot after the rains, and Will and Whitney were sweating now in their clothes. Whitney wore one of her heavy cotton peasant dresses that made her look like an extra in a Botticelli. She kept her credit card and passport in one of its loose pockets. Will wore jeans and one of the seemingly forty-five button-up J.Crew shirts he'd packed for their five-day trip. Correcting for the night before, they'd overdressed for the afternoon, and were all wrong again for the restaurant and the company.

Will sat next to Jack, Whitney and Jenna on either side of them at the bar. Will asked Jenna what she recommended and she raised both hands and an eyebrow at Jack because it was his choice, his place, it turned out.

"I used to come here after games if I didn't want to go straight home," he said. "It's a little out of the way but I like it."

"What's your go-to, then?" Whitney said to Jack. She was eyeing Jenna's defiantly clipped-on earrings and the skintight fabric of her top. As Jenna turned to the side, Whitney saw that it wasn't a shirt at all, but a leotard. Snug to her chest and scooped in the back all the way down to the waistband of her shorts. Whitney's eyes searched Jenna's body for its flaws. For an unevenness of tan, for the fanny packs of fat Whitney had been sure she'd been concealing in her dresses the last two nights. But nothing. Jenna caught Whitney in the eyes, and Whitney knew she knew what she was looking for. They signaled their intentions to each other down the bar in ways that were obvious to them and invisible to Will and Jack.

"Get the sandwich," Jack said. "The simple one. The *classico*. It's ham and this tomato mush and crusty bread. I obviously don't know anything about food, but this is real good."

They ordered four. Five euros apiece. They each ordered two-euro beers in succession, too, and then, after Whitney ordered hers, Jenna changed her order to a sparkling water with lemon. Whitney laughed. Everything meant something.

They ate quickly. They savored the crunch and the salty tie-dye swirl of the cured ham. There was a slickness to the meat that the four wore in a glisten on their lips. They dabbed up crumbs with their fingers and carried them to the tips of their tongues. It was over before Jack had even finished describing the long night he and his teammates had spent there, the night they'd found it. How they had disappeared for an evening into a crack in the city where the people who spoke the language and understood its movements actually lived. It was, he said, as though he'd stepped into this place and ended up in a secret version of Barcelona where he could finally see everything that had been hiding in plain sight. That was maybe more like how things looked to everyone else, everyone who wasn't an American here just to ball.

"That's really cool," Jenna said, impatiently tapping out a beat on the bar. "So we should probably head down there now unless you guys need an espresso or a dessert or something?"

She looked at Whitney and Whitney laughed again, and shook her head.

Will ordered an espresso and asked what she meant—where were they heading?

"I thought he mentioned in the text?" Jenna said. "We're going to this festival thing down at the Fòrum." She described the lineup of musicians. It sounded deadly to Whitney but featured acts she remembered Will mentioning Sunday night, stuff he'd been trying to describe to her after she'd accused him of not knowing any new music.

"How'd they all get here for the concert?" Will asked.

"They were supposed to play Sunday, but couldn't get in. The tour's moving on next weekend, but they decided to try to resurrect something. Half the lineup was in Lyon, and so they were able to drive here. Then they're off to Italy next, I guess. But Volcano Fest today."

"It's just on for, what, this afternoon? A weekday afternoon?" Will said.

"You know how it is here," Jenna said. "Weekend, weekday..."

"Where is this place?" Will seemed genuinely interested.

"The Fòrum's, what?" Jenna said to Jack. "Forty-minute walk, twenty by metro?"

"Yeah, it's closer to where I live, down on the water. It's this big weird concrete park. Not far from that club we went to the other night, actually."

Will received his espresso and drank it as he stood up.

"Is it the sort of thing where they maybe still have tickets?" Will said.

Whitney froze at the question, at the notion that he might want to tag along.

"Oh," Jack said. "Probably? The tickets were all her. She

bought a couple last night, but I'm sure there'll be people selling more at the—"

"It's sold out, but there'll be scalpers," Jenna said. "You coming?"

"I don't want to, you know . . ." Will said, looking at Whitney. "We have some stuff we were trying to do, and I don't want to butt in. It just sounds . . ."

Whitney held neutral-faced and steady. She didn't want to overreact, and so forced herself to consider the alternative. Maybe this wasn't such a big deal. Maybe this was exactly the sort of thing they were meant to do, exactly the sort of impulsiveness she'd asked for in the park yesterday.

"I guess we can at least head down there with you and see something new," she said.

They took the metro. The subterranean station was gleaming. The tiles were scrubbed. The sides of the escalator issued crisp reflections. The tracks were free of rust and garbage. The electronic signs on each platform announced the time of the next arriving train down to the second.

They moved as four in a comfortable quiet. They clustered there in equilibrium, surfing the smoothness of the ride. Eight stops, twenty minutes. They talked about their glimpses of the news—the president, the special counsel— and Jack read updates to them off his phone about the latest on the ashcloud. They could expect rain again soon, but a clearing following the rain. Meteorologists were predicting flights could be up and running as early as tomorrow now.

They exited the station at the base of Avinguda Diagonal. A light-rail tram split the boulevard the way the trolley in New Orleans split St. Charles. The streets hummed like trees in summer, taxis and buses carrying workers to and from indistinguishable glass office buildings. Down this way, things clipped commercially. There were trim suits and Bluetooth earpieces and frameless eyeglasses and pointy shoes. Down here, it was less Barcelona, more Brussels—or any other European city that didn't have Gothic buildings and beaches and mountains on the water.

Jenna led them in the direction of the gate, and was at once in negotiation with a scalper. It was forty euros apiece, Jenna told them. She'd talked the man down from sixty. Will and Whitney exchanged a wordless look that neither could read definitively, and so, one beer deeper into the day, and sick of Whitney's unhelpful indifference, Will stepped forward and opened his wallet and before thinking through the consequences of what he was about to do pulled out his last hundred-euro bill, a bill he'd tried and failed to rid himself of at any tapas bar or café—and, in exchange, received the tickets, printed out on real-live ticket stock, printed with red and black ink, like the kind he'd received in the mail all through high school for the shows at the Troubadour and the Palladium and the Hollywood Bowl he'd attended with the pink-haired girls of his early-driving years. The scalper gave him his change. He reached back for Whitney's hand, who took the pair of tens like someone neither pleased nor displeased, like someone with nothing better to do on a trapped afternoon.

They were at the edge of the continent. The sea and sky were gray. The Parc del Fòrum, Jack said, was only maybe fifteen years old. It was a reclaimed industrial slip on the waterfront that had been transformed into a provocation of concrete planes and angles. It looked to Will like the models he sometimes spied in the windows of the Cooper Union on his walk to and from the subway. There were primary colors and blocks, cement and steel the way Olmsted used grass and trees. It reminded Will of the few days he spent in Berlin during a summer of law school, the concrete that had been poured after the Wall fell, the concrete Oz of the government buildings on the river.

At the water there was an enormous solar-power panel soaring above the Fòrum like a pergola. It rose at a disconcerting angle, summoning the sun through the blackness of the ash veil. It looked built to power an entire city. Before it, made miniature by the scale, was the band shell, around which were gathered the masses, the flashing signs of underemployment and of endless summer. Life went on beneath the volcano. There were thumpings of a DJ beat all around.

Will handed his newly purchased tickets to the attendant at the gate, and a pit fixed itself in his throat. He never trusted scalpers. He always presumed that he was getting screwed. But the pleasing green sound of *go* followed the scanning of each of his tickets, and he and Whitney filed through the turnstile.

Jenna handed the attendant her printouts and waited for the same sound. Whitney watched Jenna's face hold its lineless liquid form while the moment distended and the attendant fumbled around, spraying the red laser on the bar code over and over. Whitney moved her eyes between the tickets and Jenna's face, and saw Jenna's lips part uncertain and her eyes flutter scared.

The attendant said something quickly in Spanish and Jenna had to ask her to repeat herself. The attendant was holding out the tickets as she said it again. And all Whitney and Will heard Jenna say was: *"Qué? Qué? Es imposible."*

"She says they're counterfeit," Jenna said, incredulously. "She says they're no good."

Jack put his arm on her shoulder and she flinched.

"Fuck," Jenna said. "I guess we'll go see about those guys back there, see what else they have. This is fucking insane. This has never happened before."

She stretched the elastic straps of her leotard off her neck and shoulders, as though her clothes were beginning to squeeze too tightly. She turned and had taken a marching step in the other direction when Whitney said, "Wait...wait, Jenna. Just take our tickets. It's your thing. It's not worth spending even more money. Just take—"

"No, no, don't be ridiculous. I mean, thank you," she said. "But that's not—"

"How 'bout this, then," Jack said. "I'm in the same boat as you guys, you know? I mean, I don't *need* to go. I'm behind on packing, anyway. I have plenty else I *should* be doing. How 'bout you three go, and I'll meet you afterward?"

Jenna stared at him. Whitney's face was stony.

"Or in that case, what if, Jenna, you just take mine?" Whitney said. "A one-for-one swap."

Whitney didn't want to be here. She wasn't at all interested in the music and she was still a little sick of Will. She felt a rush of relief at the prospect of getting out of it.

The attendant asked Jenna and Jack to move to the side so that she could scan the tickets of the kids behind them in line.

Whitney looked at Jack, and Jack smiled at her, proud that the two of them had arrived at the same simple solution.

Will looked at Jenna, and Jenna jutted out her plump lower lip, in recognition that it wasn't such a bad idea if everyone was on board.

Will looked at Whitney, and Whitney's face betrayed

nothing. He smiled disdainfully. He loved her still. She was so predictable. She would give him zero to go off.

"I'd pay for my ticket," Jenna said.

"Don't be silly," Will said. "You already did. This is just a lame situation. But this is a nice solution. We'll go for a couple hours and then meet you guys at…"

"Yeah, I mean, there's only a few hours left anyway," Jenna said. "We can meet you around here, or near wherever? It's not like it'll be too late. The ones I was hoping to see are up soon."

Will and Whitney looked at each other again, and Whitney could tell that Will would never be the one to make the definitive call—he wouldn't give her that, it was his way of giving it back a little. He knew better than to gift her anything that could be held against him later, given every last misstep lately, given last night and this morning and all afternoon now. So Whitney put an end to it herself:

"Sound good to everyone?"

Jenna waited for the catch and they held there one last long moment, the two women communicating at their own encrypted frequency. Then, when there was nothing but static—no trap, no nothing one way or the other—Jenna nodded gratefully and explained to the attendant what they were doing, and the attendant said she'd have to explain it to her boss, who would have to explain it to *her* boss. But after five minutes they were finally at an exit, swapping Jenna for Whitney and thanking the hordes of employees who had been required to approve the ticket exchange.

And that was how it happened. How they'd broken the links and re-paired. How Whitney wound up watching Will and Jenna lean back ever so slightly as they took the low concrete slope toward the band shell, and how Will turned to see Whitney and Jack disappear over the high hill of asphalt in the direction of the city where Jack had once appeared on a billboard looking as handsome and famous as the most handsome and famous Americans sometimes can in advertisements in European capitals.

Whitney and Jack found their way back to the base of Diagonal, to the metro stop, to the stairs that led underground.

"Does this get you home?" Whitney said. "Or, more relevantly: Does it get *me* home?"

"It all sorta, you know—" He threw both hands forward like airport ground crew, up Diagonal, back into the heart of the city. She was already on the steps, but he stood there squinting up the road, toes pointed toward the beach.

"But it looks like you're maybe not coming down here..." she said.

"I don't know quite how far it is," he said. "But I thought I'd maybe try walking."

"Is it nice?"

"It's a lot of this," he said, indicating the walkway with the trees and the tram.

"I might come with you, if you don't mind?" she said, casting her eyes up at him.

"Of course. Sure. I wish I was a better guide..." he said, as the tram approached. "This thing here is kinda cool."

"Are you sure you want to walk? I feel like you're maybe not all that close," she said, smiling.

"If it starts raining, we can grab a cab."

Whitney still had a foot on the first step. "Doesn't it seem like it's gotten darker?"

"C'mon," he said, "I'll give you a ride home if it gets bad."

They found the walkway, the canopy of plane trees and palms.

"So the team or whatever, they're helping get you out of here?"

"They say they're working the angles. But everyone's in the same boat. It seems silly to push too hard until the all clear, until they start sending the first flights out. They take care of shit....I just still can't believe it's over!"

"I can't imagine..." she said as a thing to say.

"But you can, right? I mean, what was it like for you— you said you were on the soccer team?"

"Uh, hardly..." A little shock ran through her. She was surprised he remembered. "My knee exploded in the second game of the season freshman year. I spent the whole semester on crutches. Sat on the bench for spring workouts. And then, I dunno, I just didn't want to do it anymore."

"Just like that."

"I'd never loved it like it sounds like you love it. There were years there, for sure. But it was mostly a way to get out, you know? It was a way to get way away from home and have it paid for—at least until I pulled the plug."

Jack nodded. "I knew some of the soccer girls my year. I must've seen you at parties, or overlapped at some point, right?"

"I mean, when I was out, I was really out. I just kinda disappeared into the stacks. I'd never had that kind of free time before. I couldn't believe what it felt like to use my brain without soccer, too."

He laughed. "I wouldn't know a thing about it."

"Without the scholarship, I had to work a lot. It was pretty full-on. Not much time for...just really busy..."

"Still, I can't believe we didn't cross paths at all. I mean, who were your friends?"

Whitney stiffened at the question. "I—I kinda kept to myself, you know? Like, Will and I were the same year, and we didn't even meet each other till the last six weeks of senior year."

"The gardens."

"Right." She felt a little beat in her temples. "But, I just...I guess if I'm being honest, I think I kinda missed the boat on a lot of friend groups because of what happened with the team. Like, by the time I quit, everyone had found their people. I was the odd duck out. The team had the team. Other people had...It's not like I didn't have fun, or whatever....But by the end, it was mostly me and the museum café and a bunch of old movie scripts."

Jack nodded. She looked up at his face.

"I'm sure you can't relate," she said. "Given that you're the king from jump."

"It's weird, though. You're never really a part of it for real, you know? You're taking classes during summer, you're missing absolutely everything on campus during the season. It's not like I got all that close to anyone, either."

"I don't want to make it sound like I was this pathetic..." she said, trying to force a laugh. "It's weird, we just moved around a lot when I was young, never in the same school for, like, more than two or three years. So I just never found a super-close group of girls, you know? It never felt like it was 'worth it' or something. I just knew we'd move on. That's what I liked most about soccer at first, I think. The club team, at least. That I was gonna be with those girls for years and years. I think it's why I gave so much to it. I didn't want to lose those new friends..."

He was thinking about himself as she spoke, she could tell. She could see it in the drift of his eyes. He shook his head and then sniffled and then laughed at his sniffle. "You know it has to end. That's been the case forever. It ends in high school and college and in Norway and Germany. But they don't tell you about the *real* end, where, like, your body and soul are put on fucking ice."

"It was who you were for a really long time."

"Who I was, but also just what I *did*. How I spent my time, you know? Every day since I was six years old, I've woken up knowing that the goal of today is to get a little bit better. I took it for granted, that even without anything else going on, there was always that main thing to turn to. If plans fell through like back there, I'd go steal a few hours in the gym. Now, though, I'm..."

"*Well*," Whitney said, teasingly, "it seems like you've found plenty to do with your days this week..."

"You know what I mean," he said, pink-cheeked. "She's...she's fun. But she's a girl I probably won't see again after we leave here. I don't see her making it out for Christmas in Chicago."

"Is that such a bad thing?"

"I didn't say it was. You're the one with that grin on your face, like you know something, like I have to explain myself."

"No grins. No explanations required."

"You don't like her much, I can tell."

"I like her. She's fun. She's just young. She can be kinda needling. To me, to you. Which is ridiculous. She has that attitude that maybe I had at her age? But I dunno, it's a little *extra* with her," Whitney said. "*At her age*—like I'm a hundred fucking years old."

"So you were a Jenna in college, then?"

"Hardly. I just, I got caught up in some stuff. I started reading some heady things and watching some good movies and thinking I had my finger on something. I'm sure I was insufferable."

"You probably hung out at that coffee shop, huh? What's that one off campus? I had to go there for a class once, a documentary class with that one professor who actually makes documentaries?"

"That's funny. No. No, I wasn't much in that crowd, either. I really was pretty solo, just kinda figuring stuff out for myself. But sophomore year, I found this boy. Really, the one and only serious one before Will. And I glommed on. Became obsessed with his thing. He was from New York and looked like he was in the Strokes and all his friends were in college film festivals and things like that, and the one time I went home with him, he knew all these... He knew this taco shop where you'd go in the front door, then down the stairs and through the kitchen and into a dining room..."

"Sounds like *Goodfellas*."

"Exactly! That's what it felt like. And, anyway, I was pretty much ready to marry him on the spot. We were inseparable for a bit. And I was counting on spending the summer up there with him. Staying at his mom's apartment. Waitressing like I had back home. Making movies for fun. I dunno, it was just, like, this thing I'd never wanted but suddenly very very much wanted. Then he broke up with me on the last day of classes and I spiraled pretty hard, and ended up having to go back home for the summer. I was... I was really down, like scarily down. I was humiliated. I was drinking too much. I was hooking up with anyone who looked at me. I was just a total fucking mess. I didn't think

I could go back to school in the fall. Truly. And so I basically called the study-abroad office every morning, trying to
squeeze my way into a program. I would've gone anywhere.
But nothing. And then as I was packing for the semester, I
got a call that some kid had broken his leg in a boating accident and a spot was open in Paris. It was...very important
for me just then. It was, like, life-alteringly important for
me to have a place to escape to, where I could figure myself
out all over..." She looked up at him. "And so, anyway:
voilà. That's how my Jenna phase began in earnest."

"That thing last night..." Jack said. "What was that?
That was super bizarre, I'm not gonna lie."

"Well, good, I'm glad my new friends are so honest."

"I'd never seen that move before. I thought you were
gonna get her in a triangle choke and drop her to the
pavement."

"Nah, just checking out her earrings."

"She was a little shook. Whatever you did, I don't think
she saw it coming."

"Oh yeah?"

"But when I tried to talk to her about it, she acted like
it was nothing. Like she's cool with everything, like she's in
complete control. I just never know what to make of any
of it. One minute she's having a nice time, the next she's
saying something insane. A lie for lying's sake. Like she's
deliberately trying to see how big an idiot I am."

"A lie like what?"

"She's just, I dunno, always saying shit, and then if I
look at her funny, she says I'm so gullible, like, *Who would
believe that?* Like—here, perfect—yesterday, she started to
tell me that one of her roommates in Paris had been fucking
murdered last week! And that was one of the reasons she

had to get out of town—so she wouldn't be dragged into talking to the cops and have to spend more time in France. Then when I looked at her all shocked and concerned, she started laughing hysterically, like I was so fucking dumb, how could I believe her? And then she just snaps back to being totally normal."

"Normal, then, as a baseline of two or three fake names goes, right?" she said.

"Right. Which, to be fair, is maybe more normal than dropping MMA moves on someone," he said, grinning.

"What can I say—that's how they teach you to defend when the attacker's back is to goal," she said, smiling. "Just checking out her earrings, seeing if she dyes her hair..."

"She's harmless. Just a little weird sometimes. I can't crack it."

"So," she said, a little drunk still, and desperately wanting to know, "what is it about her, then? I mean: What's it *like* with her?"

"What do you mean? You know her."

"I mean, is it just unadulterated in its greatness?" She watched his face change as he caught on. "Or is she one of those who's all show until the bedroom and then is actually kinda timid and quiet and sweet and deferential when it all comes down to it? I know girls like that. All this big talk and then a different person once you get her back?"

"Um," he said, kicking a seedpod. "Not really that one."

"So she's into it, she's loud, she's what she seems?"

"You're just gonna keep pushing, huh?"

"Gimme one thing! I've always cared more than is polite. But we're bros now, right?"

He laughed. "I dunno, she...she's young. It's not over till she says it's over. One of those."

It hit her sharper than she'd anticipated. She'd brought it on herself but hadn't expected it.

"She really gets to you, huh?" he said.

"I don't know why," Whitney said, quickly. "I did it, too. The acting-older thing. The projecting yourself forward a few years in an effort to, I dunno, get there faster. It's so dumb. She's just gonna piss some people off along the way, she's gonna burn bridges. Then she'll graduate, get a job, get beaten down in some useful ways and probably some ways nobody should. And then she'll wish she'd just shut her mouth and made some more friends along the way. My boss used to say, 'I wish somebody had told me when I was your age: These people, they're going to be in your life forever—on the way up, and again on the way down.' It's a long road. Then again, she can probably blow up her life and land on her feet in New York or Paris, or go back to L.A. and settle into whatever. Or better yet: Chicago, with the basketball star of her dreams."

He chuckled half-heartedly. He was checking over his shoulder to make sure they didn't get hit by the tram.

"Or," she continued, wading into the non-reaction, "maybe I don't know anything about her, or you, for that matter.... We're all strangers."

"No, no," he said. "You're probably right. I was just thinking about that advice from your boss. Just coming up in an industry or whatever.... I'm basically in the same boat as her, when you think about it. Seven years older, but nothing to show for all this time over here. I'm starting at the bottom again. I'm going home, probably for good. Back in the house.... Have you ever gone back to live at home?"

"Home's not—I mean, when I left, I really tried to leave.

I go back now and again to check the boxes with my folks, make sure people know I'm still alive and that I still like a few of them. I drink beers with my brother and his idiotic girlfriend. But I don't have a ton that's left there. The old teammates I do keep up with, they have different things going. Husbands, dogs—fucking *babies*. I sit through stories about hunting trips. Updates on their yards. Long recaps of the after-work kickball leagues they play in. It's different than being from a place where people from my work wind up, you know? It's different for Will, or even how it'll be for you."

"The kickball thing, that's what makes me most nervous. Well, not *nervous*..." He looked genuinely distraught. "I always pick the wrong word...I just know I'm gonna be playing in that league. *Crushing* it. *Dominating* at the park where my brothers and I grew up playing Little League. Then the same bars. Lollapalooza every August....Honestly, that part—that might be why I was okay ducking that scene back there. I had this sudden feeling of: *Am I really doing the same thing I've been doing since I was a teenager?* Same jersey, even. But then I feel guilty about it, because the thing I'm worried about becoming is the life my brothers and my best buddies are living. It's not like it's horrible—it's my favorite place in the world. But up there, up near the house...I'm gonna get sucked into all that because it's my world to a T."

"Who would've thunk there was all this existential *roiling* going on in that noggin!"

"It'll be a good way to get back in with people. But when you were just describing it—the games under the lights, like when we were little—it's this weird full circle, and I don't know, dude...erasing the old memories with new ones. I like the fact that I've lived other places. I've been proud of that. I don't have all that many grown-up memories there, and I just worry I'm gonna replace all the old stuff. When I was a kid, I'd see the old guys—who were probably, like, our age now—waiting with a case of beer to take the field after our game ended. I remember thinking that was the saddest thing I'd ever seen. It's just gonna be weird to be one of those dorks hanging around the park, smashing beers on that field. That field's for Gatorade and orange slices."

"What a protector of innocence," she said. "Jack Pickle: catcher in the rye!"

"Maybe I've just been over here too long," he said, plodding ahead earnestly. "Alone for nine months out of the year, six years in a row. It's been hard sometimes—like, really really hard. But I've also gotten used to it, these cities, these languages I can't understand, the unfamiliari—"

"The grilled chicken."

"Ex*act*ly."

The pleasant lull that followed was filled with the screech of children in a park close by. An ivy-covered wall with portholes, and through the portholes, Whitney could see, dozens of kids scattering about. They couldn't have been out of school yet—they seemed to stay in session until five each afternoon. But in this city, she'd learned, every day was meant to feel like Saturday.

"You need some *work*. You need some boring-ass office job to distract you. By Week Two, all these concerns will be behind you."

"You hiring?"

She smiled sweetly. Then after a pause, she said: "Actually, want a distracting homework assignment?"

He glanced down at her from way up high.

"Once you get back this afternoon," she said, "write down three ideas. Three movie pitches. And send them to me tonight? I'll help you on the next steps."

"I appreciate that, but I don't know if you know what you're getting into. I truly have no clue what I'm doing. You don't need to take pity on me."

"I'm getting as bummed out by all this talk as you are imagining you all fat and sad on the kickball field, raising up the trophy at the end of the season like it's the best win of your career. At least here we'll have something to keep you busy, right?"

He mimed hoisting the depressing trophy. "This is getting too real!"

"Gotta keep you focused, engaged. Nobody wants to see that body go from elite BMI to, I dunno, what I imagine most guys on the North Shore look like by thirty, after too many imported sausages and cheese wheels from Pickle Products."

"Ah, you refer to the standard-issue physique of the older Brothers Pickle. It's not a bad bet, given what's come before me."

"Just keep a couple abs, huh? Not necessarily eight, or whatever you've got going on in there now..." She exaggeratingly peeked down the armhole of his jersey, a deep gap that showed off some ribs.

He laughed and the laugh made her fully recognize what she'd done. She'd not only peeked, but touched his arm, right above the elbow, at the base of his tricep.

"Well," he said, "I do appreciate it. I'm embarrassed, but you're probably right, it might cut against the...the way I'm taking this whole thing, like it's an injury. Maybe that's what I'm trying to say: This week's been like waiting to hear how bad an injury is. Waiting to hear if you're okay, or if you're gonna be out for the season—or if your career is over for good. The difference is I already know the deal. I know I'm never playing again. I know it's a career-ender."

Will followed Jenna to the edge of the body-spill that spread out from the stage. The band shell opened away from the water, so the mass, with no natural corral points, was just a thumping shifting whorl that beat like a pulse. They pushed into the rear of the crowd. Will would have stopped there and made camp on his own modest swatch of concrete, but Jenna pressed deeper into the jungle, hacking away with her machete.

She didn't so much reach back for him as flash an expression of clear intention. She was going in and he could follow her or not. She edged into the mass with one shoulder forward. Perturbed male faces snapped hatefully to the source of pressure at their backs, only to see the eyes and the height, only to sense the smell of the blonde bountiful hair, and to acquiesce, to step aside, to make a narrow gap to pass. If Will left too much space between them, the gap would close before he had the chance to draft, sealing shut like a wound.

It went like that for an interminable stretch of awkwardnesses and apologies, as Jenna pushed in closer and closer to the band shell. Then, at a seemingly arbitrary point stage right, she pulled up and stopped, having determined that the spot satisfied some triangulation of sight lines and acoustics and space, at least enough for her to dance around the way she wanted. Will was proud to have stuck close enough in her wake. He would never have made it otherwise. Never dreamed of attempting it. He'd received his share of grim looks, but he would never see these people again. He could act a little selfishly for once.

It was inarguably better up there. He'd paid for two tickets and only used one. He was entitled to a little something extra, wasn't he? It had been his last hundred-euro bill. He still wasn't sure why he'd pulled it out of his wallet, who he was trying to prove something to—Jenna or Jack or Whitney or the scalper? It was as though an idea beyond his own calculus had popped his wallet from his pocket and produced the cash. Or maybe he just genuinely wanted to go in. To follow the jean shorts and the black leotard into the crowd, exactly as it had gone. Maybe he had known Whitney and Jack wouldn't make it through together. And that it might do him and Whitney some good to spend a few hours apart. After last night. After this morning. She clearly needed some more time alone. As he perhaps needed to stand before some speakers and blow his face off for a couple hours. They could use the jostle, they could use the fresh air. He could use a pulse in his body that was different from the dumb little skittering heartbeat he'd been living with these past few days. *Go ahead,* he appealed in the direction of the stage: *Change up the rhythm of my blood, please.*

As though sensing the plea, Jenna's hand reached down the front of her leotard and emerged with two tiny tablets between her thumb and forefinger, tablets that had been concealed between her breasts. She placed one in her mouth and reached toward Will with the other.

"What is it?" he said.

She opened her mouth wide and said *Ahh.*

"Don't be a baby," she said. "It's mild."

He kept his teeth clenched, and then opened, tentatively,

and her fingers were in his mouth before he could retreat. She kept her fingers there until he swallowed, and then she removed her hand and smiled contentedly. She turned back to the stage and found a gap between the male shoulders in front of her. He looked at the sky and waited.

The ashcloud gave the outdoor show the sensation of indoor-ness. The thump beat back from the clouds like an echo, like the reverb of a cathedral. The lights on the stage reflected off the low belly of the silver sky, and the blue lasers disappeared up into its wool. It seemed the ashcloud had grown denser since lunch. Like it had added a dimension. The way a school of fish balls itself into some-thing enormous when under attack. It was as though, Will thought, the ashcloud knew its days were numbered.

"It's definitely going to rain again," Will said at a lull.

"Huh?" Jenna said.

He pointed at the cloud and she shrugged and kept moving in her four square feet. Her arms were at her side, but she'd found a way to dance maximally in a small amount of space. He gave in. He tried it himself. It was steamy. The air was thick. He was still wearing his dumb jeans and he was starting to feel the heat in his pants. The heaviness. They would be stuck here forever, wouldn't they? He had no choice but to let it in. He opened his pores. He opened his mouth and his nostrils and the rest of the holes in his head. Then he closed his eyes. He accepted an exchange, a passing of something important from the stage into his body, and something important of himself into the concrete and the crowd. It was probably just sweat, but it felt significant. He couldn't have checked his phone if he wanted to. He couldn't have escaped this place if his life depended on it.

Jenna was lost in something all her own, a field of consciousness she seemed to have no trouble turning on and up and into. All this was normal for her. But it was something else for Will. He'd resisted at first. But now he melted into it. He was down the road, wherever it was heading. It made him feel more interesting. He was keeping up with the beat. It was effortful, it was work. He'd reached a plane that resembled that floating point of a long run. The lights were pulsing now. They were fixated on something new—not just the DJ pumping the air, but a team of dancers or singers or models, somebodies dressed as kangaroos, moving in unison. Hopping and boxing. A master choreography that had been worked out for months. There was narrative. There was a war with winners and losers. There was enough of whatever it was in his brain to elevate him to a still higher floor. The dancing had brought it back out of him. He had fallen into it and now he was out of himself, watching himself, watching the way he had let himself slide into this place, the furthest he'd been gone in a long while. It was a much-needed loss of control.

There was a sudden flash of light, greater than any of the pulsing blue lights onstage. It didn't take Will long to spot the lightning in the low clouds, the warning shot. The branches of electricity didn't reach out for the land or the water, but bounced around wildly up into the mass, a rubber ball in an empty apartment. Because of the nature of the music, the ability to hand off the beat from one DJ to the next, nothing changed at first. The music kept coming, even as the kangaroos scattered. A stagehand came out and waved to the engineer at their backs. And still, due to the hit of the interminable beat, only some of the crowd seemed to have noticed.

Then, all at once, the crowd started moving away from the stage. Will turned and there was a great pressure at his back. Will held his ground, but the mass was collective and impossibly forceful. There were groans and then some shouts and then some screams. Then there was an ear-splitting boom—an explosion. There were new screams, hordes fleeing up the incline. A woman in front of Will tripped and fell and the people behind Will nearly pushed him down on top of her. Will was able to hold off the others from trampling forward, and to lift the woman to her feet. But there was still the pressure of the stampede at their backs. He found Jenna's eyes and she looked terrified. She was being sandwiched between torsos. She looked like she might not be able to breathe. Will lost her behind a wall of bodies, and he thought he heard her cry out for help. There was another crack from above, gunfire this time. Will was suddenly cold with terror. There was a gunman somewhere, wasn't there? On the stage, most likely. It was the perfect venue, the perfect opportunity—all these hundreds trapped beneath the ashcloud like this. He'd always wondered when it would be his turn. When he would unsuspectingly make a hasty decision that would lead him into the crosshairs of a mass shooting. He felt a forceful shove at his back again and he nearly lost his footing. He slammed into the person in front of him. He felt his phone in his pocket connect with the studs of the man's belt. It sent a shock through his system. It cracked Will's hip. But more than the pain, he worried about his phone. He couldn't lose his phone in this mess. He needed to call or text for help. He needed to let Whitney know what was happening, and that he loved her. Though there was still shoving and groaning all around— the full force of the stampede—he didn't hear any more shots, and he didn't see anyone crying out bloodied. He found Jenna again and lunged toward her and grabbed her hand, then tucked her head against his body. They took one step forward at a time, and before long they were through it, emerging as though from beneath a giant wave after wiping out.

It had been nothing, it turned out. It had been a little thunder and a little lightning, and then a rush to the bathroom as the band cleared the stage.

They were at the end of the bathroom line and Jenna acted as though practically zero had transpired, as though there hadn't just been a terror scare—that it had all been in Will's head.

"Fuck," she said, "I should've gone before we went in."

The line looked a quarter-mile long. Will was breathing heavily still, body still cold.

"While we have the time," she said, "want to get a couple beers and meet me back here?"

He obeyed. He knew she knew he would. He thrilled to the simple tasks. He was perfect for so many new jobs. He floated to the concession stand dazed. His head was pounding and he was ready for a drink. In line, Will turned on his roaming and checked his phone. Nothing from Whitney. Still, he was grateful to have it in working condition. He noticed his battery was low—he'd forgotten to charge overnight. After everything that had transpired. He quickly tapped out a text saying he loved her, but then deleted it. No need to stoke suspicions. No need to act like the decision they'd made at the gate was anything but ordinary. No need to mention that the object of her envy and scorn had forced a party drug down his throat and that it had made him overreact to a little weather. No need to make her think that there was any reason to worry about Will and Jenna being all alone together in the rain.

"Let's hang a left down through here," Jack said. "You may have been over this way after the club the other night. It's a little sketchy, but there's a few places I like. My movie theater's over here."

Off Diagonal, the blocks were gridded but narrow, somewhere between the octagons of the Eixample and the slot canyons of the Gothic Quarter. There were abandoned buildings and operational warehouses. There were Laundromats and cafés serving espresso and Moritz. And there were the standard-issue drying lines and skin-colored stucco of everywhere in Western Europe. Of Avignon, of Bologna, of Porto—and apparently of here, too, in the Poblenou of Barcelona.

"It really is wild that after three years on the same campus it took meeting thousands of miles away at some random party, right?" he said.

"'*Fate,* man...' Should I get ready for some of Jenna's dorm-room philosophy?"

He smiled, but she could tell she'd embarrassed him. He was so sensitive about his brain. He had reached out, raw-nerved, and she'd swatted down the offering.

"It is, you're right," she said. "None of this makes any sense. I know what you're doing here, but I have no idea what I'm doing here."

"Vacation."

"Yes," she said. "But why? Why these days, of any days? And why here?"

Jack shrugged. "Memorial Day? And it's nice?"

She smiled. "Yes, good answer. Half right. Half point for

239

the half-right answers. But it makes even less sense if I really think about it. You, I get. But why us?"

He narrowed his eyes, a little suspicious of the rhetorical questions. He obviously didn't have the answer, and she obviously did. He shrugged again, impatient.

It was growing darker still and looked very much like it might start raining any moment. They passed beneath awnings that covered the sidewalk and each time they stepped out there was a bit of the thrill of being between seats in a game of musical chairs. Red neon—a Spanish red, the red of muletas and mashed tomatoes and cured ham and rioja—blared from the window of a cheap seafood restaurant, with shrimp and lobsters visible in the tanks through the glass. The red ran over Jack like a highlighter and seemed to lift the Kukoč jersey an inch off his body. His skin was red, the fur on his arms and legs was red. His head of dark hair lit up red, too. Something about the ethereal vision—a break from the monochrome of the ashcloud—made her think it and say it and give into it:

"Beautiful . . ." she said, almost without meaning to.

"Hmm?" he said. Her cheeks went hot. What this vision before her had to do with the forces that had trapped them there she couldn't say for sure, but she'd connected them, and the picture of this bright beautiful body awash in light had made her say it. She didn't want to say the word again, though, and so in burying the first slight embarrassment, she offered up another—but one she desperately wanted to share with somebody.

"Can you keep a secret?" she said.

He smiled as he'd done with every other silly thing she'd said on the walk, and when he stepped out of the light, they crossed another street into new darkness.

"I mean, you can't tell Jenna, or Will, or anyone at the

alumni association," she said, smiling as though there might be a joke coming. "This is just between you and me and the laundry hanging from that balcony, 'cause I think I just need to tell someone, 'cause it's kinda rusting away inside of me. Besides, it's the other reason we're here, the real-er reason, the other half point—and I probably should just say it to make sense."

"Okay..."

"So, as you know, Will and I have been together since the end of college. That's a great thing most of the time, and not great other times."

"Sure," he said.

"And a couple months ago—back at school, actually— we got engaged. Or, rather, Will proposed, and..."

"Oh!" Jack said. "I hadn't realized. That's amazing."

"Well, this is the between-you-and-me part, because it goes a long way to explaining... We both, or, I don't know, that's probably up for some debate, but we both decided to try something because it didn't feel quite right. Something wasn't sinking in the way we thought it would. Something was just not certain.... And if there's one thing the married people I work with seem to agree on, it's that if there's something bothering you, it's not gonna get better with marriage, it's not gonna be fixed by marriage, right? Not that I usually care what those people have to say. But we decided to do this thing.... We decided to go on, like, a quasi-break. Not to date other people, but to sleep with other people. I was in L.A. for a month for work while he was in New York. And, so, we each gave each other three freebies. And the idea, then, was to come here at the end of it, to come clean, and then go home engaged, all the better for having, you know, gotten it out of our system."

She'd been looking straight ahead, trying to put words to something she hadn't had to describe before. She turned to Jack. He wore a neutral expression. She couldn't tell if he thought it was scandalous or boring, or if it reasonably explained everything.

"And so..." she said, and he looked at her expectantly, searching for a line to guide him to the next part, "that's what we're doing here, and that's what we've been sort of dealing with these last couple days. We thought we were getting out of here, we were ready to put everything behind us, and then these days keep on coming..."

"And so you did it?" Jack said.

"What's that?"

"You went through with it? You had your three each? And everything's okay?"

"Is that awful? I haven't told even my close...I haven't told a soul. Does it sound terrible?"

"I mean, I feel about as far away from getting married as possible. But when I've dated girls—which, you know...but when I *have*—I guess I'm the jealous type. The thought of even someone I've hooked up with a couple times, if I really like her, the thought of her being with someone else...That's very mature of both of you, I guess."

She laughed softly. "I don't know. I mean, hearing you say it back, it gets me all tied up in knots again. And it makes me wonder why I think it'll all be okay now. I never was the jealous type until I met Will. I didn't die for boys the way other girls did. I didn't usually get caught up in crushes the same way. I just tried to act above it all. And then things changed. I was so crazy after I met him. I'd finally found this person I could settle into. Then, I don't know what happened—I mean I *do* know part of what happened.

He hooked up with some girl his first year of law school, that's what happened. And it short-circuited me. It seems trivial now, but when it happened... Anyway, eventually all that went away. And by the time he proposed, I just, I don't know, I felt totally numb to it. It didn't hit me hard one way or the other. It was terrible. And so this other idea, the three, I guess I wanted it for him, but I wanted it for me, too. I wanted to wake up a little. I wanted it to be fair, and that was the only way, even if it would be excruciating. I got tweaked when he told me about his ones the other night, when we confessed everything. But that was some-thing that was missing even a few months ago—me feeling *crazy* again. That's actually what got me excited all over. This is how you're supposed to feel about this. *Strongly.* It's like it snapped me out of my whatever. And then we tried to get out of here and put it all behind us. And, yeah, you've basically had a front-row seat to everything since..." She looked at him. "Does this all sound totally insane?"

"I'm just impressed that you were able to go through with it. I know people who've gone on breaks, or whatever, but it never *works.*"

"Well, I guess that's TBD. I think we thought we'd reached the end of something, then realized a bunch of other shit was just starting up."

"So three each?" Jack said. The premise of 1-2-3 was finally sinking in.

"Well, he actually only did...*we* only did two..." She flinched as she said it. "To be fair to the facts....But all that's behind us now."

"Does Will know it's behind you?" he said. Jack was tuned in in a way she hadn't seen before, like she'd found a station with a song he liked.

243

"I believe so...yes." She looked up at him. "If you're suggesting what I think you're suggesting, I don't think you need to worry about him making any moves on her."

"That's not what I meant," he said. "I've just never met someone in that situation. I'm legit curious. It's totally cool if you don't want to talk about it anymore, but you can understand why it piques my interest."

"How 'bout this?" Whitney said. "Three more questions and then we change the subject, never to speak of it again. I'll answer honestly, unless I lie. In which case you won't know the difference anyway. What do you most want to know about 1-2-3?"

"What's *1-2-3*? You call it *1-2-3*?!"

She'd never encountered a fellow human looking so pleased.

"Are those your first two questions?" she said.

"No way!" he said. There was a new energy all around. It was as though the red neon had clung to them, a spiderweb stuck to their skin and clothes. She felt a heat in her hair. She felt static in her stomach and thighs.

"Can I ask a pre-question?" he said. "Like a warm-up question?"

"In addition to the ones you've already used up?" she said. "How 'bout I decide after you ask?"

He smiled. "You really hadn't been with anyone else for the whole seven years?"

She breathed in through her nose. "I guess it's related to what I was saying before. It wasn't even just that it wasn't something I'd considered, it's that I was crazy about cheating for a long time.... After that thing I mentioned, after that one shit-faced slipup of Will's, I just became this zealot. I couldn't stand the thought. I couldn't hear stories about cheating. I felt sick when I'd watch shows or read scripts with affairs. I'd stop talking to friends if they were screwing around. It just…twisted me up in a way I can't even articulate. Then as the years built up, something relaxed. Or maybe it was more like deadened nerves. I started to think of 1-2-3 as this very adult thing. This hedge against future problems. Mitigating the derailment of the relationship down the road by going through with the arrangement now. I'd never have done anything without being on the same page as Will. But it made me realize how dumb it had been of me to project onto other people for so long. Nobody has any idea what's going on in someone else's relationship. I guess that's one thing to come out of this: I don't know shit about anyone else's sex life, just like they don't know about mine."

"Except me, now…" He smiled. "And I'll take that as a…*no*—one person in seven years?"

"Is that your second question?"

"No way, you didn't even answer definitively!" he said, grinning. "I'm just looking for some context. If one since senior year, then how many before that?"

"Is *that* your second question?" It had started light, but the way it was going was starting to irritate her. "What's so interesting about a girl's number, anyway? I've never understood it. Nobody gives a shit the other way around so long as it's, like, more than two and less than a thousand."

"I withdraw the question, then. I didn't mean to waste one."

"No, no. It's out there. There's gotta be some penalty for this sloppy line of questioning."

He zipped his lips with his fingers. He wasn't going to waste another shot.

"Six before," she said.

"Oh—" he said.

"Is that *Oh* a question or *Oh* an exclamation?"

"It's neither, it's just: *Oh.*"

"I can't tell if that's too few or too many for you," she said. "It can't possibly be either?"

"I have no idea," he said, raising innocent hands. "We're talking about numbers at twenty-two? Who cares?"

"Exactly, yes," she said. "It's one of those questions that means everything for a while and nothing after a certain point. Every year I realize there are things like that that killed me for what felt like eternities, and that are meaningless now."

"Like what else?"

"Well, let's see: going back, you know.... Did you make varsity or junior varsity? Did you make the Haney Hawks travel team? Have you ever kissed anyone? Have you ever given a hand job? Then, you know: virginity; college admissions; GPA; career; title; salary; what you've made; where you've been; where you're going. Then you get to a point, and I feel myself hurtling toward it, where nobody seems to give a shit about anything anymore. About what boxes you've checked, about how high up you got or how pure the work was or wasn't. It's just less important. It becomes about comfort. About doing what it takes to just be happy enough. Fewer concerns about whether something's cutting edge, or cool, or art, or *selling out*. At least in TV. But also for other jobs, for other friends.... Everyone seems to just want to be content enough. And you know what? That's okay with me. Because nobody knows *anything,* it turns out. Most people are just feeling around in the dark, trying to do their best..."

"*Haney Hawks travel team,*" he said. "I love it."

"I lost you way back there, huh?"

"No, no," he said. "I hear you on the rest, too. At least, I think I do. I just—I can't relate, totally. I feel completely removed from so much that's going on with my friends. I wish I knew more about it—about titles and promotions and office gossip or whatever. When I'm home, I'm embarrassed how much I like hearing about people's dumb problems at their offices. They care so much! They catch themselves and say they'll stop talking about it, but they really want to keep going on about the boss, their reports, the guy who does less work and gets paid more. They talk about it all night. And I'm totally into it! It's just not my world. Not yet. *Senior Associate. CMO. PowerPoint deck.* It all sounds goofy to me, but I love it. They probably say the same thing about my world."

"*Slam dunk. Bottle service. Jersey chaser.*"

"Oof, you make me sound like Gronk," he said. "Anyway, back to the matter at hand....I feel like I'm maybe only more confused now. Can I at least use up all three? Unlike you...."

She smiled. "Get on with it."

"After seven years with the same person, was it...like, was it super weird?"

She smiled. "Uh. It's not like the technology changed. It's not like the last time I was with someone else it was a Razr and now it's an iPhone."

"Okay, okay..." he said.

"But I dunno, the thing that made it the most different was the guilt of the whole thing..."

"But you both had agreed to it, right?"

"You still just kinda feel deeply deeply wrong for it to not be the person you're used to it being with, even when you're in the clear. Or at least I did. There's the obvious stuff that makes you feel it, the things anyone knows from being with someone for the first time. You don't know what they look like with their clothes off. The moment before everything comes off when you're wondering whether you're going to be impressed or disappointed. It's the way it's all sort of the same, except when…I dunno, when it isn't…" She was playing with her hair, looking increasingly uncomfortable. "You think it's the relationship that's made it rote. You think it's the familiarity with the other person. But maybe it's something else.…Besides, there was this famous actor, so that might've been at play, too."

"A famous actor? Which actor?!" he said, lit up fresh.

"Sorry, you're out of questions."

"Seriously?"

"That's another question. You're digging yourself deeper into debt."

"Okay, how 'bout this…" he said, pointing a finger to the marquee a couple blocks away. "If he's on one of the posters out front of the theater, will you tell me?"

She didn't think he was in anything that was out. It was safe enough.

"Fine," she said, and they walked the rest of the way, eventually edging up to the posters, where they started scanning.

He kept naming actors. Practically every actor he recognized, and then the last names of some Spanish actors he read straight from the posters.

She smiled at his enthusiasm. Then she stopped smiling and said, "Oh God."

"What?" Jack said, excitedly covering the distance to her side in a single stride.

She didn't move.

"I stepped on a bug," she said. "It surprised me."

"No way," he said. "I saw what you were looking at, you were looking at this one, and you saw something."

He scanned the poster in front of her. It was a space movie with an ensemble cast. *The Right Stuff,* but for a mission to Mars. There he was. One of the astronauts, second from center. She watched Jack's eyes scan the poster frantically, trying to decide which one. Then she gave in and thumbed at him.

"Oh, yes..." he said. "Oh, this is awesome! This is the best thing I've ever heard. And Will knows?" He was jumping up and down a little bit. He was purely delighted. "And you've seen that *one* movie, right?"

She knew which movie he was referring to and why. She felt her throat getting pink and she raised her eyebrows and smiled through tight lips.

"Oh my God, that's awesome. I've never known someone who's had sex with a movie star. This is great. I'm so glad we met! I'm so glad we didn't go to the concert and that we wound up here instead. So that I can finally say I know someone who—"

He was bobbing up and down a little recklessly and spilled over into the gutter as a car was passing by.

"Easy..." she said, as he hopped back up onto the curb with a doofy grin slopped across his face.

"What was he like? Did you know him from before?"

"You're out of questions. You're well into the red. We're on to other things now."

A warm storm gust blew through. She heard the weather in the trees. The sky was getting evening-colored. It wasn't raining yet, but it couldn't hold off forever.

"Should we see it?" Jack said. "Should we go in?"

"You want to see a movie?" Whitney said.

"I mean, look at that," he said, gesturing at the ashcloud. "Might as well not get caught in it. And besides, it'll give us an opportunity for you to break it down for me."

"My time with Adrien?"

He smiled widely again and pulled the hair on his arms. "No, no," he said, giddy. "I mean, that too, sure. But I meant we can talk about the movie afterward. I'm sure you pick up on a million things I don't even know to look for. Maybe I can ask you some more questions if you're not sick of me yet."

She hadn't planned to see this movie and she hated seeing movies that weren't on her lists. But where else was there to go? What else would she do with the borrowed time? The concert was meant to last another two hours.

She turned on roaming and checked her phone. She'd forgotten to charge it last night or after her run, and it was already in the red. She watched the signal announce itself. She checked her email first. Then she saw there were no new texts from Will. He was either crammed in with a bunch of teenagers pretending to enjoy the music or he was fucking Jenna in a Porta-John. Neither of which she had much say over from where she stood, anyway. She wondered what might happen to the concert if it started raining, but she let the thought consume her only a little.

"Sure," Whitney said. "But let's get a couple tallboys from over there and hide them in my pockets."

She started across the street to the *supermercat*. She thought he heard him say, "My kind of woman."

And then she paid for the beers and he paid for the tickets and they disappeared inside the theater to watch a blockbuster movie on a weekday afternoon and to get drunk in the dark together.

They hid under a tree and then an awning and then a sculpture, squeezing in with several dozen other concert-goers. They were getting wet—not directly, but by mist, by diffuse exposure like secondhand smoke. From what Will could see over the tops of heads and down into the bowl in front of the band shell, there wasn't any movement toward more music. So they got their hands stamped and split through the turnstile and found a bar off Diagonal, a couple blocks away.

They sat at the corner of the bar and ordered two beers. The air from the cooling unit chilled Will's shirt on his back. He felt his skin clam up. Jenna wrapped her arms around her ribs and when she turned toward him, Will could make out the width of her nipples. They dabbed their faces with waxy napkins. They dried their hair with their hands.

Will activated his roaming again and texted Whitney to let her know they'd left. He checked his email, too. There might be news. No word on the script, of course, but there was a message from the airline: flights would start back up in the midafternoon tomorrow. They still had their place in line, so they should stand by for further updates. He cycled back to his texts. Nothing in response.

He placed his phone on the bar, screen facedown.

"You don't have to hide it," Jenna said.

Will glanced at the black rubber case, touched it with his finger, flipped it over.

"I'm a big girl," she said. "I know she's probably not thrilled that you're alone with me. And certainly not psyched about that move you pulled back there. If I were her, I wouldn't have been so chill about splitting off."

"It's no problem," he said. "We can do some things apart."

"But it's not just doing *some things apart...*" she said. "She obviously doesn't, you know...she doesn't seem to like me much."

"What makes you say that?" he said.

She shaded toward him in her seat, and instead of answering the question, ticked her head from twelve o'clock to two.

"I don't know..." he said. "It hasn't come up. I think she likes you fine. We've all just been a little stressed these past few days. If you're referring to last night, that was just booze and exhaustion. That was as weird as anything I've seen her do, but nothing to read too much into."

"You're sweet," she said. "Defending her. Defending me. It's a lie, but it's a lie with heart."

She sipped her beer and wore the foam on her lip. He smiled. The length of her long pink tongue removed the foam like a windshield wiper. He watched a little too fixedly and his smile dialed back.

"I sometimes wonder if I'll ever have something like that, you know?" she said. "Someone who'll lie helpfully on my behalf. Someone who'll *lie with heart* for me."

"Well, you're twenty-two," he said.

"Which means, yes, you think so?" she said.

"You have endless time. You'll meet your share."

"But I'm not just talking about meeting boys, going out. I'm talking about dinners and vacations and real fucking. I'm talking about *years*. I'm talking about something built-up, like...living in a conspiracy with someone."

"You're very early days in this whole thing," he said, smiling. "I wouldn't worry too much about it. I think if you asked Whitney, she might say she could've used a couple more years in your shoes. Could've used a couple more years in her twenties, as a person in the world, before getting in too deep with someone else."

"And what about you?"

"I don't think about it much anymore because it doesn't change anything at this point. But, I mean, it's always easier to look back from a nice position and say, *Hey, I should've taken more advantage of being single.* That it would've been nice to screw around while I had the opportunity.... But you never know what's in store, right? You never know when you're out of time."

"That's depressing," she said.

"Then maybe that's not the way to put it. But you get what I mean. When you've found the person—"

"The person *for ever and ever...*" she said.

"Something like that," he said.

"Is there ever any pressure? I mean, seven years? Don't people ask you about it?"

He laughed a little and clicked his nails on the bar to the bass line. "Are you asking as a follow-up to your taste-bud theory? Or because you believe so deeply in marriage that you can't imagine waiting?"

She shrugged, though he saw the answer in her face.

"I don't know about it," he said. "We don't know about it. I know we seem ancient to you, but in some circles we're thought of as young still."

"I know that..." she said. "It's just impossible for me to imagine what I'll be looking for in seven years. Especially given that seven years ago I was at camp just praying each night that Davy Rothman would feel me up before the end of the summer."

Will finished his beer. It came in a small glass. He felt his scalp lift a centimeter off his skull.

"And were your prayers answered?"

"They certainly were," she said. "Unwavering faith here."

The waiter brought over two more. Will was wondering about Whitney again, and he could feel Jenna reading it on his face. He glanced at his phone and she caught his eyes.

"No response?" she said.

He moved his phone to his pocket.

"I wonder if she's still with Jack," she said.

"Don't know," he said, sipping his fresh beer.

"And you don't worry about her with other men like that?"

"Should I?" he said. "Do you worry about him with other women like that?"

"Oh, I could care less. We're just, you know...I'm going home. He's cool. And I like the way he looks with his clothes off. But we'll never see each other again after we get out of here."

"You've got it all figured out, huh?"

She shrugged again.

"You're right, that's not giving you enough credit," he said. "But that's a pretty mature way to think about this stuff."

"If I was convinced he was my Whitney, maybe it'd be different..." She'd said her name out loud and it sounded to him like a provocation. "I like him fine. And his place is better than Gram's."

"A big bed..." he said.

"It's a nice bed."

"And so you're just staying with him till you catch your flight?"

"I actually got a hotel this morning. I needed some space of my own, even for a day. I haven't had my own place in, I don't know, since being home last summer, maybe. Which: nothing like the Valley in summer, but still..."

Will flexed his eyebrows. She hadn't said anything about the Valley before.

"I had some leftover cash. I got this place this morning—and after hauling my stuff up to the room, I just lay there on the covers in the quiet. It was paradise. Even if it was just for an hour."

"I traveled in Europe the summer before college. We went hostel to hostel, four or eight or sixteen people to a room. Me and my buddies from high school. They left before I did at the end of the trip, so I was alone for a few days when I'd totally run out of steam. I hadn't asked my parents for money the whole time, but I wrote them from an internet café and splurged on a hotel in Amsterdam those last few days. I basically didn't leave the room for forty-eight hours. It wasn't even nice, but I was finally alone. Air-conditioning. A bathroom that wasn't way down the hall. It felt like staying at the Ritz compared to what we'd gotten used to for ten weeks. Point is: I get what you mean."

"I never meant to end up at Jack's, you know? I just really couldn't go back to Gram's."

"No more swinger parties."

"There was that. But there was also, he just...when I went back there to get my stuff that morning after the club, there was a whole scene. He said I hadn't had his *permission* to be out all night. He didn't like me skipping out on the party and coming back in the morning. He was treating me like I'd been hired to spend the night with him. Like I was his girlfriend. It was awful."

"What did he say?"

"I don't know, it was all very intense. He yelled, he threw some books around."

"Jesus."

"I grabbed my bags and he stood by the front door and tried to block me from leaving. Curtis the Cook had to intervene. He popped up in the loft and asked if everything was all right, and Gram sort of straightened up, shocked— he must've thought we were alone. And so I squeezed past him and out the door into the courtyard. I waved good-bye to Curtis over my shoulder and he had this horrified look on his face. Like, *What kind of monster have I been living with?*"

"God, I'm sorry. That sounds awful."

"I knew what was going on," she said. "I just didn't think it'd come to that. I knew he was an asshole. I knew he was possessive. But he paid a lot for practically nothing. I never let him touch me, okay? That time I took my shirt off, he tried, and I made a big deal out of it, and he seemed genuinely sorry and ashamed. I thought he'd be able to handle his shit. Which is fucking naive of me."

"How did you even meet him initially?"

"I was writing a paper in the fall about Picasso. The class spent time with the collections in Paris, but the professors encouraged us to come down to use the research library at the museum here, too. I was all set up at a hostel, and then someone at the museum told me about the Sunday dinner, and so I went to check it out, whatever, and then he offered me a bed and blah blah."

"Blah blah foot model blah blah."

"That's how it usually goes, right? It seemed fine enough at first. I can look out for myself. It was money and it was easy work and it was free trips down and it was no big deal. I love visiting here. Obviously. I just never thought of it as crossing a line, even when it probably did. It was never...I was never made to feel like I was yesterday. But as I was rolling my bag across the courtyard after the whole blowup, he yells after me—with all those open windows, he says it in Spanish for people to hear—*You ungrateful little whore.* I hadn't thought of it that way before, silly as that sounds."

"I mean, you shouldn't have. You were modeling for money and a room—so what?"

"But then, later that day, there I was in this deluxe apartment with this guy I've just met, propped up on the bed, putting out for my room and board again. I don't know, it just begs the question..."

"I don't think that's how it really works. I don't think that's how people classify someone hooking up with a person they're into."

"He was just so nonchalant about it," she said, reliving it in her mind, clearly. "Just another one of many for the basketball star....Not ungrateful, but not exactly *surprised* by his great good fortune." She smiled. "He's been there before, he knows what he's doing."

"Ah, of course," Will said, wincing a little. "Lucky you....Lucky Whitney..."

He was drunk. He didn't know why he said it or what he meant.

"So you *are* worried about her with him..."

"No, not that. I just meant Whitney and this..."

"Whitney and *what*?" She leaned forward on her stool.

The slipup had boxed him in. They'd been sealed here

by the ashcloud, scooted inside by the rain. His shirt was sticking to his skin still. His hair was matted down flat on his forehead. He was trapped in this comfortable corner of the bar with this beautiful young woman with whom he was conversing more easily than in their previous encounters. She was sharing secrets, and maybe so should he. His beer glass was empty again and his head felt light, light all over, this morning's whiskey melting again and dripping down his shoulders and arms into his static fingers. He felt his heart beating carefully, deliberately, beating like wings. He hadn't spoken to friends back home all week. He hadn't spoken to family. He had spent time with Whitney and with Jack and with Jenna. That was it. Here was this woman, one of the few now in his immediate orbit, and maybe just maybe she was becoming one of his favorite people to talk to in all the world. Maybe here in this city was where they were supposed to meet some new people who might displace the old. Maybe with a few more years he and Jenna would become close, as proper adults, the age difference growing less substantial each year. She was intelligent, independent. She was good-looking and had figured out lots on her own already. She was extremely impressive in her way. Maybe this was his *brand new friend* beside him now at the bar. He certainly enjoyed being in her presence. She was full of life, overripe with energy, and he could use some proximity to that from time to time. Like a battery-charging station. Not an everyday sort of companion, but an after-work-beers-once-a-season kinda thing. She had interestingness in surplus. She had living to spare. She lowered the angle of her face, and her lips pressed together into an expectant node, deliciously, flirtatiously egging him on into telling her precisely what he'd meant. She had shared some of her secrets. It was only fair that he might share some of his. They were confidants now, after all.

"So the thing to know," he started, "and this is very much between you and me, like *deeply* between you and me, because our closest friends and family don't even know this.... But Whitney and I are engaged."

"Oh?" Jenna said, shifting on her stool again and leaning back a little. "Congratulations, then. I didn't—"

"We're sort of engaged, kind of engaged, TBD engaged."

"I don't know what that is."

"I don't really, either. But something happened between our maybe becoming engaged and this trip. And that something was—seriously, please, you can't even mention this to Jack—but we decided to give each other a couple freebies before setting things in stone."

"Like, freebie freebies?"

"We called it...well, it doesn't matter what we called it, but she went to L.A. for a month and we decided to go on a break, with the intention of meeting up here after and coming clean. And then just having that be a thing we did while we still could, while we still had the chance to get it out of our systems, and not hurt each other terribly, and still be honest about it, and just sort of take care of something that felt necessary."

Jenna was sitting up straighter now. She wore that pucker again, and her eyes and nose and mouth all seemed to be compassing toward a space a couple inches in front of her face. Her eyes were thrilling to the new information. She looked to have so many questions, so many questions that they'd logjammed the flume and nothing was coming out, and so there hung between them a silence that Will just kept filling.

"And so we did. She in L.A. Me in New York. And then on whatever night it was, Saturday, we told each other about it."

"This past Saturday? The day before the party? 'Cause by then, you're saying you were back to being together? Or at least that's how it looked from the outside..."

"I guess that's right," he said. "It was weird. But so was a lot about that night. So I guess the only reason I'm telling you is, just, there was more going on than it maybe seemed. There's been more reason to be jealous of her lately."

"And—I have so many questions, *but*—you were both, just, *okay* with it? That was something you were cool with?"

"I think so. I mean, she's still here, I'm still here, right?"

"But, like, these other men were fucking your fiancée?"

"I hate that word."

"*Fuck?*"

"No. Too many syllables."

"*Fiancée?*"

"The whole thing sounds not great when you say it...and it wasn't great, don't get me wrong. But, I don't know, I had mine, too. It was even. It was fair. And, besides, haven't you ever taken a break with someone?"

"No."

"Well, things get interesting when you get super old like us. Stuff happens. Things end up different than you expect."

"And here I thought...here I was with all my presumptions about how *boring*..."

"You thought you had us all figured out, huh?" Will said. "Well, that's it for us, as far as that stuff goes. No more swinger parties in our future, I don't think. No more flings. Those were it."

"*Those*...how many, exactly?"

"The rules were three each, but we took two."

"You had free passes for three and you left one on the table?"

"We didn't realize it until the other night. We each did two independently."

"How adorable," she said. "How perfect. Was it amazing, though? After all those years—"

"It was...I had fun."

"Sounds like it."

"I dunno, it was sex with strangers."

"And so never anyone else that whole time?"

"I hooked up with someone my first year of law school."

"*Hooked up?*"

"We made out."

She laughed. "So? That doesn't count."

"Well, it counted with Whitney. We were just starting out, we were young—well, we were your age—and so the scale of everything just...it felt different."

"I mean, that doesn't count. Even for a high schooler that doesn't count."

"Well, you weren't on the jury at my sentencing. I wish you had been."

"She really held that against you?"

"It was pretty dumb. But I should've..."

"What happened?"

"It was the first semester of 1L. Some stupid mixer with the business school. You know the nickname for MBAs, right? *Married But Available?*"

"No, but that's pathetic."

"Well, yes. Now you know. Regardless, it's a fucking snake pit. You're around all these people in this pressure cooker. Most MBAs are coming in from the real world and then suddenly it's like all the rules are suspended, nobody seems to give a shit who's from where, how old he is and how old she is, who's coupled up or what. They've already gotten a taste of how shitty life is at most jobs, so they're extra out of their minds. I ended up in an empty classroom with this not-even-great-looking British chick."

"And you told Whitney?"

"I told her within the week."

"Why?"

"I'm a terrible liar. I'm terrible at holding shit in."

"You must be a bad lawyer, then."

"Not that kind of lawyer," he said. "But, yeah, I melted down over the course of the week and came clean."

"What'd she do?"

"She made me point her out. She, like, made me hunt her down at the library just to give her a look. Then she mercilessly trashed the way the girl dressed and her haircut and my taste and my pathetic lack of restraint, et cetera. It was interesting, she was always sort of too cool for school about everything up to that point. Nothing seemed to phase her. Never jealous about other girls. Never worried about me. She had it all figured out when I met her. But then from that point forward..."

"What do you mean?"

"I dunno, it just took a while to get back to normal. It was terrible. It's one of my strongest memories of law school. Just being on the phone with her in between classes. Worrying that I'd miss a call and she'd come after me. It was like I was wearing an ankle monitor. You know how when people get struck by lightning it changes their pH levels, or whatever? That's what happened to her—and that's how

I thought it was gonna maybe be forever. This one stupid fucking thing had changed her chemistry. I thought about ending it almost daily, and it killed me, because I knew I didn't want to, but maybe I had to. I just couldn't keep living under that cloud. Then gradually things got better. Returned to normal. But, man, I was not gonna fuck up again. I was so conditioned against it. Not even because I thought it was the most horrible thing you could do to a person—it's not like I'd had some long-standing affair. I just couldn't fathom dealing with the fallout again. It was like extra-bad food poisoning, or something. You're not gonna tempt fate eating raw tuna again even if it was just one fluke piece that made you sick."

"Tuna or fluke?"

He shook his head. He hadn't heard Jenna make a dad joke before. The glasses of Moritz were framing this new version of her. "So yeah," he said, "you especially don't test the fences if you think you're gonna end up with the person in the long run."

"And yet you orchestrate this scheme."

"Well, right, that all happened a while ago. That was during the first year we were dating, and I guess everything was more fragile. Then everything changed. I know on paper it looks like I've been with the same person all this time. But in reality, for both of us, it's like we've dated several different people. At least three Whitneys. Probably three Wills. You lock into new routines, new comforts, new ideas about things. You change a lot, especially when you're together in your twenties. It's just different, I dunno. And, yeah, things had just felt extra right for a while, and so I asked her to marry me, and she had these...surprise reservations. And she was the one who suggested the whole thing."

Jenna's eyebrows flinched.

"So I went along. And, you know, once you're in it, it's not exactly twisting your arm to be out there talking to cute girls again, but there was still a part of me that was deeply deeply conditioned to feel nothing but guilt about putting myself in that position. I just felt properly trained off of tempting myself with situations like those. It took a little while to be okay with it, to sort of deliberately expose myself to it."

"And now what? You're just back to where it was? You're free for a month and then able to snap right back to normal?"

"I guess so? I hadn't thought too hard about it. We had this name for it—*1-2-3*—and when—"

"Even though it was *1-2-*" She smiled at her cleverness.

"Yes. Exactly." He felt his phone in his pocket but didn't pull it out. "Doesn't have the same pop, does it? But when we came clean, I dunno, I thought we'd just return to how things were. Hop on a plane, get back to New York, everything behind us. But instead we're stuck here in whatever this is."

"And did you like being out there? I mean, once you were *deprogrammed*?"

"It's funny," he said, "I didn't even tell Whitney this, but the first thing that happened—and this is ridiculous to say out loud—but you just start to see women in the world a little differently again when you're single. I mean, there's this thing for so much of your life where you just can't help but picture women naked, in their underwear, getting undressed, whatever. At least that's how it was for me. Maybe it comes from growing up at the beach—the constant bodies, the constant bikinis, the bathing suits on every size, age, whatever. And so wherever I went for years, it was just a thing, it was wiring. But then, as I got older, busier, it sort of faded away. I hadn't noticed for a while. Most of the time I'm riding the subway I've got my nose in paperwork, or I've got a podcast distracting me. But Day One with Whitney out of the house, I was riding the train to work, and there it was, that long-lost filter—all I saw was every woman in her underwear. My age. Younger. Older. Non-discriminating. It was one of those New York spring days when people were losing their minds, just skin every-where. Pasty legs in sundresses, sleeves off the shoulder. But I could see straight through everything, too."

"Sounds violating."

"Sure," he said. "So, apologies to everyone. It's not the most conscientious way to walk around in the world. But April and May in New York...I mean, you get it. The next thing that happens is I find that I'm noticing wedding rings, engagement rings, I'm looking for them in a way I never have before. Everywhere I go, my eyes shoot to the ring finger. That was obviously never a consideration the last time I was single, but it was something that happened unwittingly this time. It's weird: There were far fewer than I'd expected. Especially on the trains. And so I realize it's just: *single everywhere.* Availability. Bodies, bare fingers. All these possibilities."

She sat up straight, her beer was almost gone. "It sounds like a dream, then."

"But it should be very much said that I don't have what-ever the skill is. Or at least I don't have it anymore. Maybe I only ever had it one time.... The conversation-with-strange-girls skill, the willingness-to-be-humiliated skill. And so it almost became doubly frustrating. All these women, and I don't have an angle in on any of them. I can't download the apps, because we can't have people we know seeing us on there, right? So the whole thing is, like, walking up to these women and putting it out there cold. That gives me hives. I don't have any of those superpowers."

She smiled. "Just your X-ray glasses."

"Exactly," he said.

"So, do you still have them?"

"What's that?" he said, smiling back and reaching for his beer.

She sat up straight again and twisted in her seat so that her legs dangled off the stool, dark denim and a long brass zipper facing him squarely, the black of the leotard up under her arms, up over her shoulders. Will's eyes involuntarily down-and-upped her. It was still very cold beneath the AC unit. He caught himself lingering and squinted instead, as though he'd been testing out the glasses, as though it were a bit.

"I guess the powers ran out at the end of the month," he said.

"Too bad. I was gonna test you to see if they really worked."

"Oh yeah? Test how?"

"Just a quiz, you know, colors, that sorta thing."

"What kind of colors?"

"Like: What color is my bra?"

Will smiled but Jenna's face was serious. His smile faded slowly and he heard himself breathing.

"Well, Jenna, that would be a trick question," he said.

"Oh!" she said. "So they *do* still work. I knew you were a liar."

"A liar with heart."

She'd picked up a cocktail straw and was chewing it. She smiled in appreciation of the callback.

"You know, hearing you say that just now," he said, "that was the thing I think I enjoyed the most. About the month. About the whole thing. Was just the ability to *lie* again, and the lying being okay. You spend all these years, or at least *I* spent all these years, trying to do the right thing—bending it sometimes, but knowing I'd be caught out if I didn't just spill the complete truth to Whitney. That it was just easier to cut the crap and say it straight. But this whole thing was different. Stuff like: *I'll call you.* And: *I just got out of a long relationship.* And: *I'm going out of town next week, so won't be around for your party, sorry.* And obviously the small ones lead to bigger ones, and soon you're doing nothing but lying—purposefully, consciously, spooling out these elaborate whatevers. But with these little interactions, these little rendezvous with women, there were no consequences. And so: a hundred little lies—*who cares?* The lightness of that, the ease and the lack of consequence. I loved it. I'd never given myself over to it before."

"So there were lessons learned," she said. "And now you get it."

He smiled into his beer and squinted at her again. "Bear with me for apparently stating the obvious to an old pro..." he said.

"I'm not advocating for it, Will Who Cannot Lie. I'm just saying: *Yep, that's part of the game.*"

"Jenna Saisquoi..."

Her face deadened, and then she bit down on the edge of her glass with both rows of teeth, and started laughing her biggest laugh yet.

"*Exactly*..." she said. "Now he's starting to understand."

*   *   *

The theater lobby was stained with the scent of popcorn butter, and when they saw the rain through the windows, they stopped short of the doors.

"I guess we made the right call," Whitney said, pressing her hands to the glass and peering up into the blackness. It could've been the middle of the night, but according to her phone, they were still an hour out from sunset.

"I wonder if they got crushed by this at the festival," Jack said.

"I just saw a text from Will. He said there was a rain delay but that they were gonna stay close by, and that he'd let me know if things change. But my phone's about to die. Should I tell him to just text you instead?"

"Sure, but I wonder what's up with my service, too. Couple things popping up all at once," he said, and they stood there staring at their screens. "Wow. The team says they have me on a flight tomorrow. That they've started booking people out for the afternoon and evening."

"Let the countdown begin, then," Whitney said. "Twenty-four hours left of..."

It turned down the corners of his mouth.

"This is a good thing," she said. "We all need to get on with it, and, you know, lucky you to have a seat. I wonder if Will heard anything for us."

Jack had a little glisten in his eyes. He was such a lightweight and he'd been drinking those big beers. He was hanging there in the space and light of the lobby, almost like he was underwater.

"Let's get out of here," he said. "The smell of this place is making me dizzy."

"You have an umbrella?"

"I'm not that far from here. Five or six blocks. Want to make a run for it?"

"I guess? It occurred to me during the movie that Will has the fucking key—and I need to get somewhere to charge my phone. But it's actually really raining, you know?"

"It'll be, like, five minutes of exposure. It'll barely touch us if we're quick."

"I don't think that's how it works..." she said. "But, okay, I'll be right—"

He opened the door and eyed the storm as though it were a raging river he intended to ford. Then, on some private mark of *go,* he hit the street like a golden retriever. "Now!"

They splashed along the sidewalk and were drenched at once. By the second street crossing, Whitney was soaked through. By the third she couldn't get any wetter, and so slowed to a stroll and watched Jack gallop along in the direction of the beach, toward the glass high-rise she'd eyed that morning from the hotel bar. Just the one she'd suspected. Her feet were slipping from her sandals and she worried she might break a strap if she didn't remove them. So she went the rest of the way barefoot, careful to avoid the broken glass that showed itself every so often. The wet-ness gave Whitney the feeling of swimming in the rain, no amount of water making a difference, the temperatures of the water on her body and the water in the air close enough to be indistinguishable.

He was waiting for her in the lobby with a towel. It was a luxury building with a doorman who kept freshly laundered linen beneath the front desk. She searched with her eyes for the lobby bathroom, but he'd already called the elevator and was holding the door.

"Sorry," he said. "Because the building's big, I always think it's a little closer."

She flexed her eyebrows and dried her hair silently.

"I have a washer and dryer, so you can at least get your clothes back in shape. I'm really...I just needed to get some air and get back here. I think it sorta hit me all at once."

She saw his muscles decompress as he stepped through the door of his apartment. The unit wasn't huge but it was sleek. It had the sharp lines and neutral shades of a boutique hotel room. He offered her a robe with the name of the building stitched on the breast. He pointed her in the direction of the bathroom and told her she should feel free to warm up in the shower if she wanted.

Her hair was dripping wet. She hurried to the bathroom and the lights came up automatically when she stepped inside. There was a shower with a glass door and oversize black squeeze bottles of male shower goop. There was shaving cream and antiperspirant gel and toothpaste streaked in the porcelain bowl of the sink. She peeled her clothes off and felt her skin grow pimpled, the light air from the vent above the toilet dropping the temperature just enough to frost over her skin. Her nipples were shades darker than she'd seen them since winter and her fingertips were already withered. She wrung out her hair on the shower tiles and decided to turn on the hot water.

She rinsed quickly and then wrapped herself in the robe. She felt instantly better, lifted, her head high from the terrycloth and the lingering suds sloshing around her brain.

In the living room, he was sitting enamored with his phone, shirtless in a fresh pair of shorts. He was dry on the surface but still clearly waterlogged. His hair had been combed back on his head by his hands.

"You know what bugged me most?" he said. He was reading about the movie, she could tell from his face. He was reacting to reviews. "The way it was so thirsty for, like, every country to have their star in it. I didn't know the Chinese guy, but he's their biggest movie star right now, apparently. And the Russian woman. And the Nigerian woman. And the Italian. It's one thing if it makes sense— like, I get it, you bring together this dream team of pilots from all over the world, and yes, there are going to be some from other countries, not just Americans. And that's great. But then you just leave them in there to say dumb shit?"

"I could barely follow it, either way," Whitney said. "But I'm not entirely blaming the movie—I got up to pee three times. I think I missed every explanation of the science and how the jump to Mars worked."

"I promise you you didn't miss anything helpful. They just sort of skipped over it, assumed we'd go along with whatever. Anywho..."

"*Anywho?*"

He was skimming around on his laptop, too, several tabs pulled up.

"No fucking way..." he said. "That makes it even funnier." He looked up at Whitney. "Jenna's dad was one of the executive producers."

"What do you mean?" Whitney said.

"He wasn't the sole guy, but one of a dozen or whatever."

"I thought her dad was a stay-at-home something or other—a part-time caddy."

"Yeah, that's what she told me that first night, too. Another one of the...Her dad's this guy Bob Silverstein. He—"

"*Bob Silverstein?*"

"He's a—"

"I know who he is. What do you mean that's her dad? She said her mom's some businesswoman and her dad's a deadbeat layabout."

"I don't know what to tell you. I heard a bunch of different versions....She said she doesn't like people to know. She said she started doing it when she was little, telling the other stories. She didn't want people to know about him. I guess the caddy guy is her stepdad, maybe? Or who the fuck knows, maybe he doesn't exist at all."

"Isn't her name Jenna Leonard?"

"Mom's name. After the divorce. Started using it in college."

"You're kidding me. What a ridiculous person. So all that stuff...all that stuff she said the other night was bullshit?"

"I dunno...some of it?"

"Bob Fucking Silverstein."

"He's a big deal?" he said.

"You have no idea."

So she was even more the thing that Whitney envied and loathed. Admired and detested. Attraction, repulsion. She'd been born to the professional caste Whitney most strived for. It was Jenna's for the taking. She could leapfrog the Whitneys of the industry at will, when useful, just by dropping her name.

"And seems like some people are gonna see this one, huh?" Jack said. "Though maybe it's not the best movie to start our lessons on. Maybe I'll email you sometime when we're home and we can discuss something better."

"Why me, when she's got the real keys to the kingdom?" Whitney said. "Remember, I'm not anybody when it comes to this stuff. I'm just getting my feet wet."

"Well, that's obviously not true, or else you wouldn't have your job. She's probably never gonna talk to me again, anyway. But I like you—I hope that's not the case with you..."

She stared back at him. She couldn't decide whether to respond to what he was saying or stay stuck in the mud, piecing together the puzzle of Jenna Silverstein.

"And come this time two days from now," he said, his eyes still glassy, buzzed, "I'm gonna be a little shaky about the end of all this. Summers at home always used to restore me, but this year—"

"What do you mean *restore*?"

"I dunno, it's related to this other thing, it's not important, it's just...The first few seasons, I'd think about home at all times. It would be December or January in Norway or Germany, and there wouldn't be any sun, or any way to go outside, it was so cold."

Whitney lifted an exaggerated eyebrow.

"No, I realize where I'm from, but it's somehow worse. It's hard. It's bad. Plus, practice all day for a coach who didn't speak English. The only other American on the team resenting me because of stuff from college, because of the tournament run and the magazine covers, because they thought that supposedly meant I was given more opportunities than they were. I had a good thing on those teams, but I had stretches of terrible weeks. You start getting run-down in practice. You catch the flu, can't eat anything. Entire months like that those first few seasons."

He paused and closed his eyes and shook his head.

"And I can fall back into that place pretty easily. It's scary. I've done what I can about it. I saw doctors, I saw shrinks, and, you know, they never put me on drugs, but I was *there*.

I know that place. I mean, you said you had something like it, right? It sounds like maybe you know..."

She listened to see if he was going to continue, and then she spoke slowly. "I do. You're right. It was bad. It was really really bad."

"But then it went away?"

"It was...everything changed for me after that."

He nodded and looked at her and she felt a compulsion to explain herself.

"I don't want it to sound like it was just over a bad breakup," she said. "That's what started it. But then that summer at home, I fought constantly with my parents. I really think I hated them for those months, and they hated me. And, like I said, I got...I was working, but I was going out a lot. With these people from this restaurant I was waitressing at. There was this bartender. I didn't even know it until it had happened, but...I somehow got pregnant and miscarried."

His face didn't move. She had his attention.

"I didn't know what was happening. I just had the worst cramps of my life. I was in the bathroom one night. And— It was terrifying. But that wasn't the worst part. The worst part was that I couldn't tell anyone. My brother—he's four years younger, we'd been at each other's throats all my life. I don't think I'd had a single serious conversation with him up to that point. My dad was away, there was just no way to...over the phone. And my mom, I just couldn't imagine facing her. Just having to live the rest of my life with that look on her face. That flinch of shame...I...I couldn't do that. So I handled it by myself. I just refused to give them that piece of me—I didn't want that ordeal to suck me back down into some sort of indebtedness to them. I don't know—I'm sure it wasn't the right thing to do....Then I quit my job. I didn't leave my room for two weeks. My mom was on me the rest of the summer for being lazy. But gradually it got better. I stopped drinking. I started running again in the evenings. And that's when I started calling the study-abroad office every day. I couldn't stay at home and I couldn't go back to campus, but all of a sudden I had this escape. And that was everything for me. When I was gone, when I was in Paris, I was finally able to start figuring out what the hell I was meant to be doing. It worked, I guess. That pivot. That fresh start. That was the beginning of something important. And I haven't been back to that place since..."

She'd pushed him into silence. She hadn't intended to give so much, but she hadn't been this open with a stranger about any of it in seven years, and it felt good.

"What happened to you, then?" she said.

"It was nothing like that," he said, sheepishly. "It was nothing real."

"Don't be ridiculous."

He looked at her squarely, searching for some stoplight, and when he couldn't find it, he must've felt free to proceed. "Those winters, I'd just walk around scared sometimes for what could trigger it. People called it *homesickness*—that's just not what it was. Or it was that times one hundred. I'd hear a song in a restaurant, and it'd remind me of being in a car cruising around in high school, and I'd practically start crying, I just felt so fucking alone. They said it would screw up my game if I took something to help with it. I didn't know better, I just knew I was struggling. They gave me this lamp. They gave me a subscription to a juice service, to up my fruits and vegetables. But it only does so much.

There was just this ache, at all times. I dunno, this perpetual off-ness."

It was Whitney's turn to sit quiet. She gave him everything she had.

"During those stretches, though, the one thing I could fixate on when I wasn't on the court was getting back home for summer. To the swimming pool in the back, to the concrete court off the yard where my brothers and sister and I played two-on-two everything you can think of.... It's always been about my brothers and sister and mom and dad. When we would fly somewhere, it would have to be all of us on board, or max two of us together. So that if the plane went down, no one would be left all alone. It was always that sort of thing, those sorts of considerations. So, yeah, just getting back home, to that house, to that block. They pave the streets with bricks there. Wide sidewalks with cracks from tree roots. Streetlamps. Big old elms on both sides of the block, and branches that meet in the middle of the street like the roof of a church or something."

"There's the good Catholic bringing everything back to..." she said.

He smiled. "That's what I'd think about when I was feeling sick, when I couldn't get myself out of bed in Norway...those trees in summer. The heat coming up, the trees buzzing. For weeks with the team, I'd throw up I ached so bad. But then I'd get home and everything would just settle again. Even Christmas worked. The week off at the holidays. The snow piled up in the gutters. The way—I don't know what the word is, but the way I used to tell my mom that the smell of the snow had different colors: green and black and blue. The blue snow compacted in the yard."

She'd taken a seat on the couch, wrapped tightly in her

robe, listening close, watching him melt into the bent shape of a child.

"*Blue*," she said. "I love that. Reminds me of visiting my grandparents in Colorado. That clean cold like we never got at home. *Blue cold.*"

"So, anyway, I love it there," he said. "I'm just afraid, I guess. It's dumb. But I really am afraid that I'll get back tomorrow, and just never leave again for the rest of my life."

"But that doesn't have to be the—" Whitney started.

"I've been away six years and coming back without knowing *any fucking thing*. Here I am at the end of this whole time away and I'm returning with what, exactly?"

"Well, at least you know what you don't know," she said. "And so what? It's the same for literally everyone. I thought I knew some things, and now every day the universe informs me that I don't. That's how it's apparently gonna go from here on out. You're still trying to decide what kind of person you want to be? Okay. Welcome to the club."

Her face went a little haywire, a jolt of recognition, having heard herself say it. She watched his face react, and then he said it back to her: "Right. Exactly. I'm still figuring out what kind of person I want to be…"

"But before we get too squishy," she said, "I just want to point out that when you had me on your block, outside your house, that was good. That was the establishment of a world—of a very specific, emotional place for you. You have this place, and it punches you in the chest. You've got a house on this block in a town where the weather rolls around. You've got something you love, but something you maybe yearn for beyond it. That's the first five seconds of a movie, right? Maybe that's something that could be useful to you. That set of images to open on. So: *now what?*"

He was biting his nails, something she hadn't seen him do before. His legs were slung out in front of him.

"*Now what?*" he said.

"*Now what?*" Whitney said, smiling stupidly at her dumb repetition, and she felt herself drawing in slightly to his sprawling roots of bone and muscle and skin and hair. She wasn't wearing anything beneath her robe and her mind began to fixate on the ease with which she could drop the robe to the floor. Some decisions require patience and care and an order of operations. Others require nothing but the act itself. It could be achieved in the simultaneous snap of her shoulders, arms, and hands. A choice could be deliberately plotted or reckless—the point was she was in control of it.

"Now what," he said, "is I'm gonna hop in the shower." He stood. "You can throw your clothes in the dryer down the hall, if you want. Mine have been in for five minutes, or however long I've been blabbing. But shouldn't be a problem to drop yours in now, too."

"Great," she said, and smiled through the pinkness of her cheeks, the steam still in her face, the tension between a decision and a not-decision still taut in her mouth.

"Make yourself at home," he said, before disappearing into the bathroom.

She put her clothes in the dryer and then walked in tight lines around the parts of the apartment she could see from the living room, never veering too close to a wall or a closet door or anything that might be disturbed or intruded upon. The window curtains on the far side of the living room were drawn and she pulled them aside to peek at the view.

They were on the eighteenth floor. The apartment had an unobstructed look out onto the Mediterranean. Below them, to the right, were the residential buildings of Barceloneta. Way out on the promontory was the hotel where she'd holed up that morning. Farther still was the considerable altitude of Montjuïc, and the Miró museum. Directly in front of her was that stroke of beach and palm trees they'd walked through that first night together a million years ago on their way to and from the club.

The city was coming together for her. Even in its blacks and grays, even in the illness-colored hues of the ashcloud, the city made its intentions obvious. Its tight coils. Its proximate logic. Its complementary, puzzle-cut edges. The city was modest in size and meant to be known. The whole thing was right there in front of her.

The windows stretched from the ceiling to her knees. There was an empty sill, and on the empty sill was a bright blue hair tie. She picked it up and stretched it with her fingers. She sniffed it as though it might have an answer to her question, which it did.

Jenna Fucking Silverstein. It was all so perfectly designed to get her goat. She still couldn't quite believe it. But it made so much sense that she laughed out loud.

Smiling still, she lifted her robe off her shoulders so that she could dry her hair with it, and then she combed her hair back with her hands and drew the bright blue band around her ponytail. It was *hers,* Whitney knew. It was hers and now it belonged to Whitney.

"So, now what?" Whitney whispered to her reflection in the windows of Jack's apartment, and to the city outside, sooted over in shadow and rain. Her phone was some-where in the apartment, probably dead. But containing all the new texts and emails that were always waiting for her. She lowered her robe back down onto her shoulders and loosened the knot around her waist. "Now what?"

As Will walked Jenna back to her hotel, he slipped off a curb and ended up on his hip in the gutter. They'd had five or six little beers each, on top of whatever it was she'd given him earlier, and his body was humming when he went down. He didn't appear to have broken any bones or done much but scrape up his ankle and wrist, but his heart was beating hard and he felt the blood in his brain. Then he sensed the crackle in his pocket, like a plastic baggy. He understood the implication at once. He carefully slid the mess of his phone out between two pincers. The screen was lit still but splintered in a dense web. He couldn't comprehend anything on it but the power bar in the upper right-hand corner, which was running out anyway.

His mouth was slack in incomprehension. He stared back at the curb as though it was the curb's fault. They were on a walkway that split Diagonal. The curbs were gleaming. The result of the healthy and happy-seeming street cleaners he'd admired that morning. The civic pride, the reasonable cost of living, the halfway decent hours. He had them to thank for the cleanness of the curb.

"It's decimated," he said.

"Throw it out," she said.

"I'm not throwing it out. I can't just throw away a phone."

"Then at least try not to cut your hand. Look at that thing."

He held it a foot from his body, the way dog-walkers hold a bag of shit. Jenna was off down the sidewalk, up Diagonal. He was drunk and rattled and his head was flooded with adrenaline, contemplating all that he would miss now that his phone was busted. His mind was elsewhere, which was how he started absently answering all of Jenna's questions about 1-2-3.

Once he'd started, he worried that he shouldn't have said anything to begin with, and knew it was a double betrayal of Whitney that he was blabbing to someone who irked her so intensely. But it was out of the bag, and so he decided to go fishing for a big laugh. He told her things he had told Whitney at dinner on Saturday—the bloody nose, the litter box. But he told her things he'd forgotten to tell Whitney, too. He told her about how he'd gone empty-handed to Kelly Kyle's, how they'd had to go on a scavenger hunt for condoms in her closet, and how they'd found a single glow-in-the-dark something called a "Night Light." He told her about how Whitney had taught him some new moves before she'd gone to L.A., "tricks" she'd picked up from somewhere but never suggested he use before, not for them, but that she figured might come in handy when he went out there all alone in the world. He told her that, in retrospect, one of those new moves might have prevented the bloody nose. He told her about prowling the East Village, the way he'd walk into bars to case the joint, the way he wouldn't even buy a beer sometimes, but would just sweep around for realistic targets. He said he didn't even know what he meant by that—*realistic targets*—but it's what it felt like. He told her how he'd look for girls in the East Village whose dresses weren't zipped up all the way to the top, who evidently didn't have a helping hand at home in the mornings. He told her how he'd look for girls reading alone on benches in the park. How he'd look for girls in bars whose friends were coupled off with other guys. It reminded him of something

Whitney had said before: that she wished her single friends from work could hang out together like Will and his friends could, where the hanging out was the point, rather than just a means toward the be-all-end-all mission of getting picked up. Every night she went out with them, Will said, Whitney would be traded out at the earliest opportunity for the first cute guy who approached their table. Jenna shrugged like it was nothing surprising, like everything he'd said made obvious boring sense.

Her hotel wasn't far, just a few more blocks, and it was a good thing, because the rain was starting to come down again. It would be warmer there, at least. The AC in the bar had practically given him the flu. He could use the bathroom in the lobby before checking in with Whitney, if he could even remember her number. As they approached the front steps to the hotel, Will took in the building. It was considerably grander than he'd imagined, and on a plainly luxurious stretch of Diagonal. Maybe she'd gotten a deal off one of the night-of apps. Maybe the foot modeling paid more than he'd imagined. A bellhop appeared in a suit. Will watched Jenna move past him from behind. He remembered the summer Whitney wore jeans over a leotard. Maybe Jenna was just a younger, more thinly drawn version of the woman Whitney had been, the woman he'd long loved.

He dashed to the bathroom in the lobby without fully taking it in, and looked at the inscrutable screen of his phone again. No texts, as far as he could tell. He'd have to call Whitney from the lobby to figure out where they might meet up again. He had the keys to the apartment, after all, so she couldn't get inside without him.

He found Jenna in a plush leather chair near the elevator

bank. The lobby was decorated with the sort of dark velvets and fresh-cut flowers one might find in the country estate of a monarch.

"I'm gonna make some coffee," she said. "I'm gonna change my clothes."

"Got it," he said. "I'll just wait down here to see—"

"Don't be silly," she said. "You just fell in a gutter."

"I'm fine, really."

She looked at him sweetly, pitifully: "You're not doing anything wrong, you know? Nothing's gonna happen that you're gonna have to lie about later."

He hadn't been suggesting that. He hadn't presumed anything.

"Okay," he said, carefully. "I could probably wash these scrapes out better, you're right."

As they passed the front desk, the concierge beckoned for her at a casual volume: "Ms. Silverstein, your father asked that you return his call at your earliest convenience."

Jenna nodded and waved thanks.

Will waited for the elevator doors to shut to ask, frozen up as he was by the ever-revealing luxury: "Who's *Ms. Silverstein?*"

"*Moi,*" she said.

"Leonard. Jenna. Ms. Saisquoi. *Ms. Silverstein.*"

"That about covers it."

The doors dinged open and she led him down the hallway and they were inside quickly.

The room was small and dark but hung with the same velvets as the lobby, voluminously appointed around a single king bed and a mahogany table. There was a leather luggage perch at the end of the bed, where the oversize suitcase that had lasted her all year rested. She'd barely unpacked anything. This room was clearly as she'd described: a place to escape to, a place all her own to breathe. But this was of a different order than what he'd expected. The price was all Will could think of.

When the door latched shut, he felt suddenly nauseated. He'd had too much to drink and his head was heavy. His ankle and wrist were throbbing—maybe he'd sprained something. He felt the sand filling up his skull and he felt a shock of alarm in his stomach. There was nothing good that could come of this. And yet: he was in control here, all he had to do was the right thing.

She ran the water in the bathroom to warm up her hands. She handed him a small laundry bag to wrap his phone in. Then she started fiddling with the coffee maker—an old American drip-coffee model with grounds and everything. He sat on the edge of the bed. She took the pot into the bathroom and filled it with water and dumped it down the back of the coffee maker.

"Well, that's a nice perk," he said, trying to bait her into acknowledging the hotel and the room.

"Every morning for, like, ten years, I watched my mom work one of these," she said. "Six a.m. with her at the diner before school. Black pot, regular; orange pot, decaf. I usually can't drink this stuff 'cause of it."

Will sat on the edge of the bed, narrowing his eyes. She'd said her mother was a businesswoman who worked in Asian markets. It reminded him of the thing she'd said about the Valley, about hot summers in the Valley. The quicksand of facts.

"Where was the diner?" he said, tentatively.

She was operating mindlessly. She had to have been drunk, too. She was speaking without thinking.

"Uh...on Magnolia. Magnolia and, like, Lankershim, I think."

North Hollywood. The Valley. Not Santa Monica. Not Rustic Canyon.

He made a sound of unsurprised understanding. Maybe they'd moved from one place to the other at some point. Maybe this was a stepmom.

The coffee maker was burbling and she turned, snapping out of the routine, and told him she was gonna hop in the shower.

The water started, he heard her clothes hit the floor. The door wasn't closed all the way, but he didn't try to sneak a peek through the crack. It all felt like a setup for something. Concentrating on not looking, he looked, but he couldn't see anything, anyway. He stood and walked toward the coffee maker to check on its progress, and couldn't see anything through the crack from over there, either.

He could have pressed her on the discrepancies—either the old story was a lie or the new story was a lie, or none of it was true. He didn't know her. The only thing that was certain was that it was all some ruse. And at this point he didn't even want to catch her out. He didn't want to trap her in the corner. What would be the point, anyway? He hated confrontations that exposed people, that wrong-footed them. How had he become a lawyer? He so very much needed a new job.

The water was running. Jenna was humming something. He sat back down on the edge of the bed and pulled out his busted phone. It was still alive. He touched the cracked screen tentatively, as though it were a pan handle straight off a stovetop. The shower knobs screeched off. He could hear the showerhead dripping, the slide of the curtain on the rod, the infamous feet padding out of the tub, one and then another. He could hear a brush running through hair. He could hear a brush untangling knots. He could hear a towel drying skin, and then he heard the door open and was confronted by the bright white lights running the rails of the bathroom mirror.

Jenna was burrito-wrapped in a towel. Her hair was wet and wavier than he'd seen it, and it fell over her shoulders and down her back.

"Help yourself," she said, squaring up to him, her feet wider than her shoulders, hanging there like a provocation.

"What?" Will said.

"Help yourself to the coffee," she said, smiling. "Did you pour yourself any yet?"

"No, not yet," he said, swallowing. "But thank you."

He stood up and grabbed two porcelain mugs, and she poured expertly, thoughtlessly, like a diner waitress.

"Any gross cream?"

"No thanks," he said.

He was still wearing his shoes and so towered over her. They were sharing the tightest quarters of a small hotel room. The "kitchen." Will thought of the many rooms of his and Whitney's studio.

He sipped his coffee and it was hot and terrible.

"Don't forget to call your dad or whatever," he said.

"I'm sure it's just about my flight," she said, moving back into the bathroom. "He's been helping to get me on a flight. Earliest available is tomorrow morning. I'll call him in a little bit."

"Just like that, the skies clear up and everyone's outta here, huh?"

He wondered if she could hear him from the bathroom.

She'd vanished from sight again, but the shampoo cloud enveloping her had found its way into every corner of the room. She reemerged, sipping her coffee and smiling at him, the electric blues peering over the rim of her mug, pools in the smooth, liquid face, a creamy pink without makeup.

He felt the full length of his cock straining against his jeans. She sipped again and didn't drop her eyes.

He turned back to the edge of the bed and sat, crossing his legs, concealing himself.

"Are you sure you don't want to just call your dad now to get it over with?"

She smiled again and sipped.

"I wonder how much longer it's gonna be for us," he said. "Clearing Zone 6—Jesus."

"I haven't told you yet the real reason I'm so eager to get out of here, have I?" she said, walking back to the coffee-pot for a warm-up. "You know my roommates in Paris— I mentioned them? Something insane happened, and I still don't totally know what the truth is. But she's dead and I think he killed her."

Will felt at once like he wasn't living his real life. His mind went somewhere fantastical, as it had during the concert. He was drunk or high and his body hurt and he couldn't tell for sure if he had maybe fallen asleep already. All he could say as his heart beat faster was: "*What?*"

"Yeah, I'd moved out and everything, and then I saw it on the news while I was waiting at the train station, and it just freaked me the fuck out. I just don't want any part of that, you know? I don't want to be caught up with the police up there. It's this whole thing now that's unraveling. I keep reading about it online, and they think he killed her."

"Your roommates? Literally *your* roommates."

287

"Wild, right?"

"You seem not as freaked out by this as I would be."

She shrugged. "I mean, I've known for several days now. I just don't want to have to go back there and be questioned, you know? The French police. The German police, too, probably. They were both from Cologne. They'd met there and come to—"

"Wait, I saw something on the news about this! Yesterday afternoon, I totally forgot. This guy was a suspect for the murder of his girlfriend? In Paris. Those were your *roommates?*"

"You saw it on TV? So you saw what a big deal it is, then, right? You get why I need to get the fuck out of here."

"But...but maybe you can help the police, right? Maybe you can help them with—"

"I just want to leave. I need to leave. I've been here too long. I can't get caught up in a thing where I'm here for another month while they try to figure this thing out, and interview me about what I know, and then I become a suspect, and blah blah blah. I didn't even know them that well. It was their place for the year, and I rented a room for the spring term when I got out of university housing, and that was it."

"But you're not worried about, I don't know, seeming like you're uncooperative or whatever? When they *do* look for you, and you're back in L.A. or New York not talking to them? I mean, I bet they're looking for you right now, don't you think?"

"Well, maybe that's why I got rid of my cell phone, then."

She widened her eyes, as though testing to see if he was following the plot.

"It just might be helpful if you, you know—" he said.

"Well, maybe I don't want to be around for when they

figure things out. Maybe *I* was the one who killed her, and that's why I wanted to get out of Dodge."

The look on his face wasn't something he was in control of anymore, which is why he was surprised to hear her laugh at the sight of it. He felt his features come into focus—the slack mouth, the wrinkled forehead, the eyes with their chill behind them.

"Relax! Will! Jesus! You must really fucking think the world of me," she said, laughing. "I didn't *kill* her—my God! But...I did fuck her boyfriend the night before I left. So I'm feeling, you know, I'm feeling a modicum of guilt..."

He eliminated the look of shock on his face, deliberately trying to draw it down to neutral. The drapes were closed. It was so dark out anyway with the rain and the ashcloud.

She started laughing again. "I'm kid-ding! It was a *joke*. C'mon! All of this is a joke. You're such a *stiff*. There wasn't a fucking *murder*. There wasn't anything. And certainly nothing *I'm* involved with. You're ridiculous!"

But Will knew the news report. He'd seen it, plain as anything yesterday, before he'd fallen asleep. Or had he dreamed it? He'd been drunk and beat then, too, and had been drifting off. He couldn't remember anything after it. He'd seen the report about the murder in Paris, the apartment building, the two young Germans. But he couldn't tell what was real or not anymore. She'd scrambled the baseline of fact. Then again, what was he doing thinking a baseline of fact existed at all? He didn't know a thing about her. And he'd known less than nothing until two days ago. It had been just forty-eight hours. He couldn't believe it. He knew nothing about her except what he'd seen and heard in her presence, and she was doing her best to make him question the certainty of even that shared reality.

She was still smiling and then she was rolling her eyes, like he'd taken the joke way too seriously again. The cold blood coursing through his body had choked off any arousal, and now he was sitting in damp clothes, working too hard to make sense of what was true. She might've killed someone, or she might've seen the news and made the whole thing up. Who knew if she'd even had roommates in Paris? Who knew for certain if she'd even studied abroad there? Or if she'd gone to NYU at all? Or if she was twenty-two or from Los Angeles or named Ms. Leonard or Ms. Silverstein—or lived a single detail of the life she'd described to him at Gram's party?

This woman was the body before him, but that was the only thing he could say for sure.

It was at that point that she walked slowly toward him. It didn't take all that many steps to cross the room. The steam had moved from the bathroom into the bedroom, the steam and the scent of the shampoo. She was ten feet away, facing squarely toward him as before. She had an idea written on her face and he understood it clearly. He didn't move. She ran her tongue over her teeth, beneath her lips. He sat on the edge of the bed and she stood in the center of the room. Neither of them said anything. She kept her mouth shut and her tongue moving. He heard himself breathing through his nose. He heard himself swallow. She cocked her head to the side and then dropped her eyes to the floor, and her whole body slackened, like the audition was over.

"You have remarkable restraint," she said, and chuckled, and then turned toward the bathroom, dropping her towel as she went, so that it was the whole of the back of her— wet blonde, firm butt, park-blackened pads of her feet— that Will watched slip into what was left of the steam.

Endurkoman

For thirteen days they'd waited out the volcano, slept on floors in nearby villages, cooked in strange kitchens with pots and pans that were in all the wrong places, with ovens that ran too hot and too cold. They'd read the papers. They'd seen the photographs in the foreign magazines. They'd consumed radio broadcasts and television programs and internet websites with updates. They'd prayed for their neighbors, they'd prayed for their cows, they'd prayed for resilience of spirit. They'd tuned in each night for the assessment by the volcanologists at the Department of Civil Protection and Emergency Management. All while they waited patiently for the all-clear to return to the valley. When it finally came, it came via robocall from the President herself.

Much of what was left in the valley was stone and ash. Entire plots were slurried black and still smoldering. Some homes stood untouched, soot on the windowpanes and side paneling, but interiors preserved in a panorama of aquamarine light. Gardens, even, were blooming casually, complacently, from autumn-buried bulbs. For most, though, it was an end of things. Entire material lives ceased to exist, *worldly possessions swallowed by liquid flame. But as far as anyone could count, no neighbors had been killed. And, in that way, nothing had truly been lost at all.*

They'd known it had been coming. They'd known it had been near time. They'd fled before the worst of it, lifted out as though by valkyries, and were set down in their purgatories up the coast and down the coast and inland. But then the President lowered the threat of further activity to green. The eruptions were through and they had survived. So the angels set them right back down where they'd been before, where their grandparents had lived and their grandparents before them, and they puzzled through how to move forward. How to lay new foundations in the ashes.

Wednesday

"Where the fuck have you been?" he said.

"Where the fuck have *you* been?" she said.

He was at the apartment when she buzzed up, six-thirty in the morning, bright light through the windows, a broken ashcloud at last.

"I've been here all night," he said.

"Bullshit," she said. "I was here at six *and* eight last night. Buzzing up. Beating down the door. Waiting around in the street. Calling over and over. Nothing. Just that same straight-to-voicemail over and over."

"My phone broke," he said.

"Your *phone broke,*" she said.

"Screen's shattered and it's been dead since last night. But I was home by eight. If you were really here, I must've just missed you. I even tried you from a pay phone around then. Three or four times. It was *your* phone that was dead. And your mailbox is full, as always. How can you possibly be putting this on me? I thought something terrible had happened. I didn't fucking sleep."

"I was at his apartment," she said. "After you weren't

here, *twice,* we walked all the way back and I went to sleep. I don't know what you want from me. You weren't here."

"I don't know what you want *me* to say, either. I'm certainly not the one at fault here."

"I know you were with her. I know you were at her hotel," she said. "Your phone's allegedly broken, but what about hers?"

"You were there when she said it: she threw her fucking phone in the Seine!"

"*Riiiiight.* Right right right. How could I forget? And so no way to be in touch until you got to a pay phone. No other solution."

"You don't have the high road here," he said. "I'm sorry. You're giving me shit for being at her hotel. You're hitting me for not figuring this out sooner. I waited till the rain stopped and then I walked straight back here. You're the one in his apartment. You're the one who could've walked right back over again, who doesn't pick up when I call because you're passed out in his big fucking bed."

"Don't do that," she said. "There's only one side of this where the person's eyes are falling out of their head every time the object of his greatest desire slips into the frame. Don't try to put that same shit on me. I went back to his apartment, I slept on the couch. In the living room. A *different* room. Who knows if the same can be said for…whatever the fuck you did last night. Whatever fantasy you played out before you got back here—if you're even telling the truth about that part."

"What are you doing?" he said. His face was stricken with a hot rictus of disbelief. "What is it about her? Seriously, what is it about her that makes you so fucking crazy?

I would never ever ever do that, okay? It makes me insane that you're making me even say that to you."

"It wouldn't matter if you had," she said. Her face was strained in its own characteristic ways: pink, puffy, brittle around the eyes. "I hope you know that. You had one left. We're still here, it's not technically over. I couldn't say anything if it happened, so just tell me the truth, okay? Just tell me the truth, and there's nothing I can say about it."

"Whitney...What is wrong with you? I don't even know who the fuck I'm talking to right now. *Nothing happened.* Nothing would ever happen. We did this already. 1-2-3 is over. I would *never*—" He stopped himself short. "Or is this just your way of giving yourself cover for what actually happened between *you two* last night? Is there something you're trying to tell me?"

"Don't put it on me to take it off you."

"It's okay, Whit. You only had your two as well, right? Apparently by your understanding of the rules, your third is still on the table. Still free to cash in your third until you get on that airplane? Fair's fair. But you'd have to tell me about your third. You'd have to say it, 'cause that's part of the rules, too."

She was silent. It was the first time either of them had drawn a conscious breath since she'd walked in the door. She hadn't even sat down yet. They'd been standing the entire time near the entryway. She moved to the couch.

"I understand that," she said.

"Well?" he said.

"You think I fucked him."

"I have no idea. I truly didn't until you started getting weird about it."

"I didn't."

"Okay," he said, "then why do I feel like you did all of a sudden?"

"You don't believe me?" Her eyes were bloodshot. Her face had a sort of directionless disdain.

"You tell me: Is there anything else I should know?"

"What are you trying to say?" she said.

"I'm saying: You have a third guy waiting for you out there unless you spent it last night. Or unless you already spent it before, in which case JJ Pickle is way off—"

"*1-2*. Two guys," she said emphatically. "Just like I told you the other night. Can *you* say the same thing to *me*?"

His eyes were redder than hers. Red lightning, red saucers. He hadn't slept for longer than thirty minutes at a time all night, cracked phone on the pillow beside his head, committed to not missing her call if it miraculously sprang back to life. It had made him go nuts. Hour after hour after hour after hour. He was scared for her at moments. He hated her at others. Now, he was so dehydrated. He moved to the kitchen. He poured two glasses of water, and two glasses of whiskey.

He sat at the opposite end of the couch from her, just out of arm's reach. He stretched forward to give her her drinks. She sipped from the water glass. She smelled the whiskey and her eyes articulated that it was the last thing in the world she wanted, and then she took a mouthful anyway.

"Well?" she said. "Answer the question."

"What question?" he said.

"What happened between you two?"

"Nothing happened."

"How do I know that?"

"Because I'm telling you."

"But how do I know she didn't hypnotize you? Didn't just put you under her deceitful little spell? How do I know she didn't turn you into a pathological liar, too?"

"She is a confirmed pathological liar. But I didn't have sex with her. I would never do that to you."

"You didn't *have sex*.... Did you kiss her? Did you get to feel up those glorious tits? Did she suck your cock?"

"Whitney."

"Do you know who her father is?" she said. "It's not who she says, you know."

"Is it a Mr. Silverstein?"

"You knew all along?"

"I don't know anything, I just know that was the name she was under at the hotel. That's what she responded to when the concierge called to her."

"That little twat. All that crap she spun to you the other night, to all of us, everything's bullshit. Bob Silverstein. She's Bob Silverstein's daughter."

"Come on..."

"It makes sense, even if you don't think about it too hard. The way she moves through the world. All the dots connect."

"The hotel was way nicer than I expected. I thought it must've been some deal, some last-minute clearance. But that means she was lying all afternoon, too. This new shit about her mother being a waitress in the Valley. It's like she forgot she'd already told me a completely different story. And this thing she said about her fucking roommate being *murdered* in Paris? She really committed to it, and then made me feel like I was an asshole for believing what she was saying. How she'd been running from the police, and that's why she came down here. I have no idea what's true or what's not from any word that came out of her mouth these last few days."

"She said the same thing to Jack."

"Really?"

"The same story about the roommates."

He nodded and rubbed his forehead.

"Why should I believe you about what happened with her?" she said.

He looked up, incredulous again. "Because I have no reason to lie. Because, you're right: I could've. That could've been my third. But I didn't, it wasn't. It would've hurt you. And I wouldn't do that."

"But you wanted to."

"I didn't want to. I'm just explaining that I have nothing to hide because it was technically inbounds. I'm not hiding anything."

"Did you take a shower in her room?"

"No."

"But you were in fact in her room. You were at the concert in the rain—and so you went back with her."

"Yes."

"And you didn't take a shower at the hotel?"

"No."

"Did she?"

"Yes."

"And so you took a shower together?"

"I didn't take a shower."

"Why do you smell like her shampoo?"

"Because I was in her room for a few hours. Because she took a shower."

"Did you see her shower? Did she let you watch?"

"I didn't watch her take a shower, no. Jesus."

"All those hours in her hotel room and nothing happened."

"Whitney."

"I don't know what to believe," she said, staring at the black hole of the television set. "What would it matter, anyway? What would it change?"

"Everything. It would change everything. If I did anything, it would change everything. But I didn't."

"Me neither."

"Okay. I believe you."

"I didn't do anything, but I took a shower. And he took a shower. Not together. We ordered cheeseburgers. I slept on his couch." She took a longer draw of her whiskey.

"You said that already."

"I need you to believe me," she said.

"I do," he said.

"I need you to believe me because I don't believe you."

"Well, that's not very fair, is it?"

"I just don't see it happening the way you say it did. You just sitting there in your wet clothes, all content and unbothered by everything, resisting, while she's there for the taking. I know she doesn't give a shit about what happens to us, what trouble she causes in other people's lives. And I'd kind of be insulted if she didn't try.... But I just don't get why it wouldn't have happened, why you wouldn't have...after all this, after last month."

"Because I wouldn't. Because last month is last month, which means it's over. Because we don't do things like that to each other."

"Just tell me you fucked her. Just please do it now, and get it over with. It's fine. You have immunity. It's in the rules, it's okay. But I just can't find out later, okay? It can't be a year from now and I see some text come in on your phone and it's a picture of you getting dressed in her hotel room, afterward. I need to hear it now so that I never have to be surprised by anything."

"We didn't do anything."

"Just tell me, Will. We're still here. We're still in it. We haven't left yet. It's okay. Please. Please do this for me. Just tell me the truth."

The shock was still in his face. He squinted at her and then lowered his head, trying to see up through her mouth and nose and into her brain, trying to get a look at what was really going on in there. He finished his drink. He sighed. And then he spoke. "Fine," he said. "But it goes for you too, then. I'll tell you, but you have to tell me what really happened, too. And you have to go first."

"I told you the extent of it," she said. "We split off with you two at the Fòrum. We walked around, the storm caught us, we went to a movie, we drank some beers in the theater, we went to his place in the rain. I took a shower, the rain eventually stopped, we came here once, you weren't here, we ordered cheeseburgers, I came here again. That was the second time. You were still gone. You still weren't here. I went back to his place again and passed out. It had been a long day—a long several days—and I felt like shit and just needed to get some sleep. I slept on his couch. I woke up. I walked here. This time, you were home."

"I believe you about Jack," he said.

"No you don't."

"I do. I really do. Why wouldn't I? It's better for everyone this way. But do you believe me?"

"I don't know."

"Just believe me. It's better all around. For you, for me, for us. It's easier—and it's true."

"But I'm telling you," she said, "it would be fair, okay? It would be inbounds. It's okay if it happened. I just need you to tell me now and not later."

"Why do you say it would be *fair*?" he said, maneuvering to peer inside her head again. "You keep saying that. Like you want it to be the case so badly. What are you not telling me? There's something right up in the front of your brain. There's something that you're clearly getting at, that you want to tell me. I really believe you didn't do anything with him. But what is it?"

She shook her head. "There's nothing," she said. "What is it that *you* really want to tell *me*?"

He shook his head as well. "That nothing happened," he said. "That she's as crazy as we thought. That she's out of our life forever now. That she's fucking bonkers, but sometimes fun to talk to, and that she'll go on with her blessed life, and never think of us again, and be extremely A-OK in the end. Besides all that? There's nothing to add. Do you understand?"

She sucked on her teeth and watched his head nod, as though he might coax her into nodding along with him. She finished her whiskey and rubbed her head. She closed her eyes and exhaled and let a string of *Okay okay okay*s trail from her lips as they both drifted into silence.

The buzzer woke her. It didn't make sense. She sat up on the couch and it spun her and it made her nauseated. It was still bright out, certainly not evening yet, but was it today or tomorrow? White sunlight and crisp shadows shone on the walls opposite the windows. She hadn't seen crisp shadows in days. She hadn't remembered dozing off. She sensed Will moving from the bedroom to the door.

There was no intercom but he buzzed the buzzee up anyway. They heard the heavy tread on the stairs and Will peered through the eyehole.

"Who is it?" Whitney said.

"It's Jack," Will said.

Will put his hand on the dead bolt and turned to Whitney. There was a new starvation in his eyes. "Tell me now, once and for all: Did you or didn't you? Just tell me before I open this door."

"No! For the last time: *No*."

Will held on her, and licked his lower lip, and then turned the bolt and swung the door wide.

"Hey...Will..." Jack said, stopping short of the threshold, a look on his face that suggested he was counting on it being Whitney. He had a stuffed travel duffel over his shoulder, striped in the green and black of his team colors.

Will scoured Jack's face, searching for confirmation of Whitney's assertion. But it was blank and blameless as ever.

"Hey," Whitney said, emerging within sight of the doorway. "I thought you had to catch a flight?"

Will moved aside and Jack stepped tentatively into the apartment. He reached for his back pocket and pulled out Whitney's passport and credit card.

"Jesus," she said. "I hadn't even noticed. What would I have..."

She took them from him and he explained, "They were on the floor of the bathroom. Must've fallen out when you took a shower."

As the words were coming out of his mouth, Jack seemed to be comprehending them, and he looked at her, panicked, with the question all over his face: *Had he said too much?*

He kept his body pointed in Whitney's direction, relying on her to lead.

"Thank you, thank you, seriously. What a pain in the ass you've saved me. Imagine us getting to the airport after all this time only to...I really hope this didn't delay you too much. You said your flight's at—"

"Nah, plenty of time. Just wanted to make sure you didn't have another problem, since it'd be hard to get it back once...Anyway, at least I knew where to find you."

He looked as unrested as they did. It had only been the final night of the first part of his life.

"That's not all you're taking with you, is it?" she said.

"I have a car downstairs. Couple bags. But the team's shipping the rest. Shouldn't be too—"

"Well, thanks," she said.

"Hey, before I go," Jack said, turning to Will but only glancing at him, not holding him in his eyes, "you haven't heard from Jenna this morning, have you?"

Jack's face was cautious, but Will could tell he wasn't capable of concealing whatever it was he wanted to say, whatever he was getting at. Will could see that more than concern, there was even a little disdain creeping into Jack's face.

"Not this morning," Will said. "Just for a few hours after the festival yesterday. I was back here by eight. Why?"

"I got this crazy email this morning. Right as I was packing up. It was from that guy Gram. He had my email from when I made the reservation for Sunday dinner. He said he knew that I knew where she was, and that he needed to get in touch with her. I have no idea what he was getting at, if it was some trick or something—I didn't respond. But he said the police were looking for her. They'd been in touch with him, they'd somehow got his address because she'd written it down at some point coming into the country. I don't know if she told you, but he kinda came at her after she stayed at my place the other night. Called her names, really made her feel uncomfortable. That's why she wound up crashing with me. I guess you never know, with the stuff she says, how much of it is...But if any part of it was true, it sounded bad. Anyway, this note from Gram, I didn't know if it was some kind of trap or what. She didn't mention anything about police when you were together, did she?"

Will's eyes were still, his mind rolling through the half-true stories and the half-fake ones, but all he did was jut out his lower lip and say, "She didn't mention anything, no."

Jack nodded slowly. "Well, all right, then. I sent her an email saying Gram had been in touch, and then I got a second email from him in the car on the way over here, but no response from her. Not even a call from the hotel to say *Nice knowin' ya* or whatever. I guess you can't expect...Anyway, maybe she's already at the airport. Maybe she's even already in the air."

Jack was watching Whitney for a cue and Whitney was watching Will. Her face was still humming from her nap, her head wasn't screwed on straight. What did Will know about it, really? Will shrugged again: innocent of knowledge, unhelpful.

"All right, well," Jack said, "I guess I'll see you guys. Sorry to barge in like this, I know you're getting ready to go too, and have stuff to...I just wanted to make sure you got—"

"No, no, thank you," Whitney said, looking back and forth between the two boys, trying to key in to whatever it was that wasn't being said. "You just saved us *days,* probably, at the embassy. I think I would've lost my mind looking for it."

Jack waved off Whitney's gratitude but didn't move to leave yet.

"Fly safe, then, huh?" Will said.

Jack snorted—*message received*. He adjusted his bag on his shoulder and started toward the door. Will could tell that all of a sudden Jack maybe hated him.

"And you have my email and Will's email?" Whitney said. "I'm dead serious about you being in touch about ideas and scripts and—"

Will snorted this time and looked at the floor to conceal his grin.

Jack adjusted his bag again, and his eyes drifted toward the stairs in the hallway.

"Yes, thank you, I really appreciate that," Jack said, smiling stiffly at Whitney. "It was really nice getting to hang. And please look me up if you're ever in—"

"Before you go," Will said, cutting him off, his smile wiped away. "Just one final thing for you, JJ. I don't want you to think about your answer, I just want you to hear my question and respond—"

"Will," Whitney said.

"—There's nothing you can say that will change anything here, I promise, I just want your unvarnished opinion on something."

"Will..." Whitney said.

"Okay. Shoot," Jack said.

Will squinted and shot: "Did you two fuck last night?"

Will leaned in toward Jack the instant he said it, running his eyes across his mouth and forehead and cheeks, his pure lineless face. Will examined his jaw, his throat—he waited

for tics. What he registered instead, though, was wounded-
ness and pure contempt. Jack did hate him. Now Will knew
for sure. "Of course not," Jack said. "No. Jesus."

Whitney received a look from Jack with all the pity it
possessed, pity for her having to deal with Will and his
accusations for even a moment longer.

Will watched them watch each other, and then he shook
his head, as though he were disappointed in both.

"That's not what she said," Will said.

Jack's head snapped back to Will. "*What?*"

"What the fuck are you doing?!" Whitney said, practically
lurching for him.

"She told me already," Will said. "She confessed. Just
please confirm it so that we can end this. It's not a big deal.
We have this game we're—"

"*What the actual fuck—?!*" Whitney was moving toward
Will now. She had a half-full water glass in her hand and
looked prepared to hurl it at his head.

Will put his hands up, innocent, as though everyone was
taking things too seriously all of a sudden, as though he
hadn't meant to elicit such a grand overreaction. "All right.
All right. I believe you. I believe you both, I was just trying
to, I needed to—"

"What is *wrong* with you two?" Jack said, mouth gaping.
"This is about that experiment of yours? Is that what you're
talking about? Jesus Christ. Leave me the fuck out of it,
okay? I don't want any part of it."

Will turned on Whitney now, smiling, satisfied as a
prosecutor by the new revelation. Whitney's eyes bore right
back into Will's. *So what,* they said. *She'd told Jack what
they'd done.*

No one was paying attention to Jack anymore. But he

hadn't noticed, and so he kept going: "Or is directing all this shit at me just a way to make you feel better about what happened with you and Jenna last night? She—"

Whitney flipped back to Jack: "What do you know?"

"He doesn't know anything because there's nothing to know," Will said.

A window opened through which Jack might submit the next evidence. He looked ready to say something, to stab them both, but then he swallowed his tongue. He shook his head, seething, and reached for the door handle instead, ready to march out, but still not all the way ready yet.

"You two are *fucked up.*" Jack was cracking, his eyes were wide. He whipped to Whitney one last time—with an apology in his face, it seemed, as well as an offer to get her out of there.

She was stone still. "Thank you for everything," she said coolly. "Thank you for bringing me my stuff, okay?"

Jack looked stunned, hot in the cheeks, the initial accusation still branded onto his forehead. "Whatever," he said. "If you're into this, you two deserve each other. I hope it ends up great!" He was out the door and down a couple stairs, but he couldn't stop himself; it just kept coming, the exasperation flowing like a gusher that might take days to cap. "Best of luck with it! Get home safe!"

Jack pounded the stairs. Whitney didn't say anything as he descended and neither did Will.

Will shut the door with a gentle *click.* He was shaking his head and rubbing his temples, but Whitney could see in his jaw that he wasn't wound tight. She was the one who was shaking, shaking there silently. Will rubbed his eyes, but she was wider awake now than she'd been in days. They were both still drunk from the morning, and the night before, and the night before that.

"I don't even...I don't have a clue who you are right now," Whitney said.

"He was lying," Will said. "He obviously just made something up about Jenna because he was offended. Or maybe she made it up and said something—who knows? I don't know what to believe about anything right now."

"*You* don't know what to believe? *You?*"

"*Nothing happened with her,*" he said. "He was fighting back. He was throwing sand in my eyes because I'd offended him. I'd accused him of lying and doing the most dishonorable thing there is. I don't blame him. If nothing really happened between you two, I get why he was offended."

He was so plain about it. He yawned. Their limited stores of energy were reducing back to zero.

"You're telling me that was completely baseless."

"I don't know how many times I can say it. I had my chances last month. I took two. I played by the rules that you established. I did what you told me to do. I told you about it. And that was it for me. It was hard enough. It never felt right for me to play around like that. I didn't feel comfortable. I mostly didn't enjoy it. *I don't want that.* I never asked for it. I wouldn't bring that around again for anything, and I would never hurt you."

He moved to the kitchen and poured a fresh drink, just one, and then handed it to her instead of taking it himself. Her hands were shaking, her face was red. She seemed fixed still on what he'd just said. She took a large sip, warm whiskey, then he took a sip.

"Why don't you believe me?" she said. "I just don't get

why you did that to him, why you said that. He had nothing to do with any of this, and now he thinks we're fucking insane."

"So what?"

"So, you're the one who's cared this whole time about keeping up impressions. You're the one who couldn't stand the thought of them finding out we'd been arguing the other night in the alley, who practically got on his knees to beg me to join them before going home."

"I just don't care anymore. It doesn't matter. It's over. None of the last three days was anything, none of it was real. The trip's over."

"No. I don't believe that," she said. "What is it, *really?* Why do you keep acting like this?"

"Because there's *something else,*" he said, looking hard into her. "I can just tell, okay? There's something right there that you're not telling me, but I can't figure out what it is. I've been staring at you for seven fucking years and I can tell when there's something else there. That every time I ask the question, you're considering *something else.* I guess it's not him. Or it is, and you guys are good together, you're synced up with the story. But I believe you. I really do. Then again, if it's him, and you two both lied, that's fucked up...just know that. But if it's not him—it's *not* him, right?—then I believe you. I believe you unless I don't, but I believe you, which means it's something else."

While he was speaking she'd closed her eyes, and they were still shut. She sipped again, swallowing hard. She wanted to go back to sleep and start over again. She clenched her eyes tighter, in a strain, as though fighting off inertia, some inevitable inconvenient reality that was closing in. Her cheeks glowed bright like electric stovetops and she squeezed her eyes tight enough that tears, real live tears, appeared at the corners.

"Who do you think is lying?" Will said, retreating to the kitchen again. "Do you think it's Gram? Do you think he's trying to lure her back? Or do you think the police really are looking for her? What if, after all the lies she told, the one about her roommates is actually true? What if that really was her roommate who got killed? What if the police really are looking for her? What if she really did tell Jack something happened between her and me, just to fuck with us?"

Her eyes shot open, filmed over, wet. "Then what would it be—another true story?"

"It would be a lie. Another lie. But maybe he's not the one who's lying, is all I mean. Just something to fuck with him and you and me on her way out of here. One last little dagger before leaving."

"Why should I believe that explanation?" she said.

"Because it's exactly the sort of thing she'd do. Not the sort of thing he'd do, but the sort of thing she'd do. Why do I have to accept your explanation, but you're not willing to accept mine?"

"I guess that's the fundamental question, huh?" she said. "I guess the answer to that is the answer to everything."

She sipped from the glass, and swallowed hard, and squeezed her eyes shut again.

"What if the police come looking for us next?" Will said. "Asking questions about Jenna? Or what if she can't get out on her flight? What if there's a red notice or whatever at the airport to hold her for questioning? And then what if Jack can't get out? What if *we* can't get out?"

"Who knows what name they're even looking for..." she said.

"What if there really was a murder and she actually knows something?"

"What if she knows the whole story?"

"She said she slept with the boyfriend before leaving town," Will said. "That could be yet another lie, or it could be the truth. And, anyway, it would give sufficient motive for fleeing. Insane as that is."

"In that case, what if she's the reason the boyfriend killed the girlfriend?" Whitney said. "Or…what if she really is the killer?"

They were standing fifteen feet from one another near the front door still, sort of arranged around the dining-room table. It was as though they sensed themselves fully in the apartment all of a sudden—their staging, their scale—and were seeing the whole scene from a fresh perspective, the implication of the stakes of the conversation, the incredible predicament they'd engineered for themselves.

"Let's not do this," Will said. "She didn't do anything. This is ridiculous."

"And now she's missing," Whitney said. "Gone without a trace. Phone in the Seine on her way to the train. A first-time killer on the lam. Never to be heard of again, except for one final tryst."

Will shook his head and finished their shared drink. He was so beat. He shook his head and closed his eyes and now he was eyeing the bed in the other room.

"Just fucking tell me the truth," Whitney said, eyes shut now to the unfamiliar blazing sunlight in the room, speaking in his direction without looking at him.

"I get this sense that you almost want it to have happened," he said, searching her all over again, looking into the fresh seams in that well-manicured face, searching for a reason, for an answer, but still not finding it. "You want it for some reason. For cover, or something. It's all related to what I was saying before, to the fact that there's something there that you're not saying. What do you want it so bad for, Whit?"

"No cover. No hiding. No nothing. It would make sense if it had happened, is all I mean. And Jack wouldn't make it up himself. I just want to know why he said that."

"I would never."

"*Please.*" Her eyes were shut again, but they were especially tense now, so tight they looked painful, and the tears were back at the corners.

"You want it to have happened. *Why?* I'm getting the feeling there might be a good reason."

"Please just say it," she said, eyes still shut, mouth now falling at the corners. "Say what really happened. I need you to. I need it."

"But why?"

"Because I need it." A tear slipped down her cheek.

"What happens if I give it to you?" he said. "If I say something happened, even if it didn't. Do you get to tell me the truth, then? Do you get to tell me what it is you're holding back?"

"No," she said, her eyes shut like steel gates, her mouth a full frown. She needed to go back to sleep. She found the edge of the couch with her hand and sat. "I just need to know."

"Open your eyes," he said. "I want to look at you."

He moved to the couch and sat across from her. There were single streaks out of each eye. She held them pressed tight.

"Whitney, open your eyes," he said again.

She shook her head *no*.

"Why are you crying?"

She shook her head *no* again.

"Open your eyes and look at me."

This time she did as she was told. Her eyes were their light-hoarding silver coins at their centers, but they were wet all over and ringed in red. They found Will's face and he smiled sweetly at her, generous Will, conscientious Will, the man she'd loved for seven years.

"I fucked Jenna," he said.

She inhaled like she'd been stabbed in the lung.

"No you didn't," she said. She did it again, the sharp inhale. And then again. And again. Like a hiccup.

"I did. Last night. It was quick and it wasn't anything." He was as calm as when he'd been denying Jack's accusation.

"Don't lie to me," she said. *Inhale. Inhale.* "I just need to know the actual truth."

"There was nothing I could do," he said. "She dropped her towel and disappeared into the bathroom, and it was just this body, and I had one more, and I knew it would hurt, but I was drunk, and I wasn't thinking straight, and I knew that as hard as it would be, you and I could get over it."

"Don't." She'd slammed her eyes shut again. She had her hands over her ears like a child with a siren. She'd sealed herself off from the light and the sound. "I don't want to hear any more."

"The truth is she was like any girl that age. All talk, all body, hardly knew what she was doing. Once it finally happened, it was quick. It was nothing."

Whitney was pulling at the ends of her hair, doing it mindlessly. "You're a liar," she said. "But if you're not, I fucking hate you forever. If you're not lying, I'll never forgive you, and this is over now. I'll never ever ever forgive you. Her of all people—"

"I'm not lying. And I'm glad to hear you say all that. I want you to feel it. I want you to know what I did. And I want you to think about it until you want to kill me. Just think about it, think about what I did, think about me with that girl you hate so much, think about how much it makes you hate me, think about it until you can't take it anymore—and then tell me whatever it is that you did."

She was heaving now, in heavy convulsions. She was upright, but her body had folded into a strange shape he'd never seen before. Her head was between her knees. He was looking at the top of her head between her legs. She shook her head *no*.

"No?" he said.

"I can't," she said, shaking her head *no* and *no* and *no*. Her mouth was full of snot. He could barely distinguish the two words. Her head was still shaking *no*.

"You can't what?" he said.

"I can't tell you," she said, eyes cinched, tears streaming down her cheeks. "I can't ever tell you. I can't I can't I can't..."

He moved closer to her on the couch and grabbed her hands and she let him take them. She had no fight. He squeezed her hands, kneaded them.

"Whitney," he said. "What is it?"

"No," she said, shaking her head, rocking her whole body side to side.

He let her rock there, folded unnaturally still, eyes closed, shaking, sputtering, failing to breathe. He held her until she turned up back into his face and opened her slimy wet eyes. She was breathing again, but there was terror in her face.

"Please..." he said.

She'd been pestled into mush. There was nothing whole left of her. There was nothing formidable. She breathed unevenly, her breath skipped like a seizure, she stared possessed into a vague zone several feet behind his head. And without refocusing her eyes, without turning back from the middle-distance nothingness, the words came out, thin as the first indication of a pinhole leak in a hose.

"There was," she said, severing the statement with a breath, "a third."

He didn't say anything. His cheeks filled with blood. He'd known. He'd known the whole time there was something else. She'd had her chance and lied about it for days.

"Okay," he said, frozen, speaking as little as possible so as not to spook her out of confessing.

"There was a third," she said.

"You just said that," he said.

"There was a third person," she said.

"You told me on Saturday that there were two, just like me."

"I told you on Saturday that there were two guys..."

"Okay."

"But I also had sex with a woman."

"Okay..."

"A woman in L.A."

"Okay...that's okay...I don't totally...I just wish you would've...why didn't you say something?"

"I know it was okay, within the rules, within everything, it wasn't stipulated. But, Will...*fuck*. Will. Will. Will..." She was spinning out again. "I don't know what to do."

"What do you mean you don't know what to do?"

"I've been seriously messed up."

"You were allowed three. Those were the rules. We didn't specify that it had to be—I just don't get why you've been hiding th—"

"I don't mean...you're not understanding. Because I'm not really saying...It was, I don't know what to do. My whole...my head. I don't know. I haven't been able to...and I don't know....I've been fucked up by...I'm fucked up, I'm fucked up..."

Her eyes were shut again and her body rocked with the record skips.

"You're saying...you liked it." He stared at her.

"It's not *liking* it. It's that...something happened. To me. And I'm just so fucking *confused*."

"What are you trying to say? Just say it to me. It's just me. You've already said most of it..."

"It's why I've been so...this whole time, this whole trip....All the shit that's been making me feel so out of control. I haven't been able to think straight. I've barely been able to sleep. I haven't been myself at all."

"But not just because you had sex with a woman. You're saying something else."

"I don't know what I'm saying."

"Are you saying that you enjoyed it more than you expected?"

"I don't know what I'm saying."

"Are you saying that you think you might want to have sex with women again?"

"I don't know. I don't know I don't know I don't know."

"Are you saying that you think you might be gay?"

"No! God! I'm not gay...I don't know. Will. I just...I don't know what's going...It was something that just, the entire thing was completely different than anything else....I'm not even talking about the sex. I just felt...I don't know what I'm saying. I felt nothing for the other two. I felt nothing, I felt weird but not so guilty or bad about the other two. I just didn't think about them for a minute afterward. But this one...it fucked me up."

"Fucked you up how?"

"I just...I've thought about it a lot. I've thought about it constantly..."

"You fell in love."

"No! Christ. No no no."

"You said you felt guilty about Adrien Green. The other day..."

"Not...that's not..."

"After the museum, in the park...that guilt. All that Catholic volcano shit. But it was actually..."

"All those things that happened to me, the new things. And the staying up all night, that wasn't...it just...I don't know what I'm trying to say to you! I'm so sorry. I'm so so fucking sorry for not telling you at dinner. But I don't know what to do now. I don't know what to do I don't know what to do..." She was gummy-mouthed, the skipping record again.

"Whit, we don't lie to each other. What is happening? This whole thing, the whole point of it was that we'd be straight up, that we wouldn't pull this shit on each other."

"I know. And now you know..."

"But how do I know that's it? How do I know what's real and what isn't?"

Now he was the one who was rocking a little. His eyes were locked on the top of her head. She still had her head between her knees, and she was wiping her nose with her forearm.

"Why didn't you just tell me?" he said.

"I just hadn't figured it out yet," she said. "I didn't know what to make of.... And then when you said you hadn't had a third, I didn't know what to do. I just knew I couldn't tell you then."

"And so you broke the deal."

"I didn't know how to say it. I *still* don't know how to say it."

"So you just straight up lied."

"No, no—at dinner, I said two *guys.*"

He looked at her and she made the mistake of looking up at him. She shouldn't have said it again, she shouldn't have underlined the calculated loophole.

"This is so fucked," he said. "You lied and then you kept lying and then you accused me of all sorts of bullshit on top of everything else to make yourself feel better about what you'd done and how you'd withheld it. To try to drag me down into it with you."

"You fucked Jenna!" she said. "You betrayed me, too. Don't put this all on me."

"No, I didn't," he said, shaking his head softly, calmly, sadly again. "I just said that to get you to fess up. I didn't touch her. I didn't do a goddamned thing, because I never fucking would. I swear on everything in my life and yours. You just weren't going to tell me unless I said it."

She saw something in his face that convinced her unequivocally. She knew he hadn't done it. She'd known deep down all morning. She crumpled further into herself. She was weeping this time, the heaviest tears yet. He let her bob there in heaves and sobs.

She heard him moving from the living room to the bedroom. She was so exhausted. She wanted to die, but first she needed to sleep. She stood up to join him there, and she saw him smile at her softly for the first time in an eternity. But as she approached the threshold, he gave the door a shove, and it closed with a *click* in her face.

She heard music coming from the bedroom. The door was still shut. She'd lain down on the couch with a pillow over her face to shade the blaring sunlight, but hadn't been able to sleep. Her laptop was in the bedroom and so she couldn't even catch up on queries from work—not that she would've been able to draft a cogent email anyway. It was all her fault, she knew. It was her body's fault and her mind's fault. Her head hurt badly. She was on the other side of being drunk again. She poured herself a glass of water in the kitchen and collapsed on the couch. She was a part-time corpse now who lived in a perpetual hangover state.

It had been well over an hour of failing to nap by the time the music started through the wall. He never ran his music player anymore. It had been years since she'd heard music through the tinny speakers of his laptop. In fact, she could've sworn he'd blown out those speakers last year and refused to pay to get them repaired. Maybe it was coming from his busted phone. She knew he subscribed to one of the streaming services but rarely used it. It was one of those recurring monthly charges he always talked about needing to eliminate. At least she'd assumed he still subscribed. But did they know anything for certain about each other anymore?

No, she knew these songs. What was coming through the wall was older—the stuff from high school and college and the years right after they'd graduated, the years when they'd imprinted one another's music onto each other's brains. The result of having run a cable from one laptop to the other that first summer to make mirrors out of one another's catalogs. In which case, maybe it was *her* speakers. Maybe the music was coming from her laptop, not his.

The thought made her heart flutter. The thought made her feel like she might faint.

She stood up and quietly moved toward the door. She heard him scrounging around on the other side, packing maybe. Packing instead of reading the open tabs on her laptop. Had he been able to sleep? Or had he been awake this whole time? She didn't want to barge in just yet. And so her feet carried her through a series of moves her mind was entirely indifferent to. She ate some almonds. She drank some more water. She adjusted some framed photos of La Sagrada Familia on the wall. She walked circles in the living room, into shadow and then into light. She sat back down on the couch. The music was louder now. She knew every inch of every song. It must've been her laptop. They'd seen so much of the music live together. At the Mercury Lounge. At the Bowery Ballroom. At Terminal 5. She'd taken those shows for granted. She'd never perceived them to be things she'd never have again. Experiences that could burn up and blow away. She puddled up on the couch again and closed her eyes and concentrated on her breathing so as not to throw up.

She heard the toilet flush off the bedroom. It roused her alert. She thought of her laptop and her heart spiked again, making her head hurt with the pulse. She couldn't just sit out here forever. She couldn't take it any longer. She knocked on the bedroom door and then opened it delicately.

The blinds were drawn and it was dark in a way she thought it never would be again in the apartment. Will folded a shirt and placed it in his bag and then looked up at her. The rictus had returned to his face and it made her feel like they'd never met before—like he was looking at her as though she were a stranger. It made her dizzy. It terrified her. She read his face in the instant as a sign of being, at best, heartbroken—at worst, indifferent.

"I'm sorry," she said.

He looked back at her again with that blunt vacancy.

"I'm sorry, Will," she said.

"We're officially on a three a.m. flight. Seats confirmed."

"Okay...great..." she said, trying to lock his eyes. "Listen, I need you to know that I'm so—"

"There's nothing to be sorry about," he said. "I'm sorry that you're going through what you're going through. I'm sorry that I've put you in this position."

"You haven't put me in a...it's not a big thing. I shouldn't have kept it to myself, but it's nothing."

He looked up at her. "I just don't know if that's true. If it were nothing, you would've mentioned it. You would've said it right out, and we would've had a big laugh like we did about the others. *Those* were nothing. I could tell. They were obviously as meaningful to you as mine were to me, which was...not. And that's why you were able to talk about them, to laugh about them. Those were about sex— that was it. But you couldn't tell me about this one."

"I don't know why," she said, swallowing. "I'm sorry, but I don't know why. I just don't want you to think this is a bigger deal than it is, okay?"

He nodded. He leveled his eyes at her. He inhaled and then spoke it so casually that it caught her off guard. "Who was it?"

"What?"

"Who was she?"

"Nobody. Some girl who came by the set for one of the days of shooting."

"Some girl."

"A woman, I dunno, she's mentored a bunch of the writers on our show."

"A writer. A big-deal writer."

"I don't know. I guess so."

"You guess so."

"Yes...she's a big deal. She's a very talented writer and she's helping all these other writers."

"And so you just...hit it off? How did she know you were available?"

"She was direct. She came up to me after we wrapped for the day. Asked if I wanted to get a drink. I was busy, but I thought it might be about pitching something to the—"

"But it wasn't. You knew it wasn't."

"I knew it probably wasn't."

"You were busy, but you went anyway."

"We had a drink, and then another, and nobody ever had to say anything."

"You brought her back to the hotel."

"I went to her apartment. It was closer. We had another drink. I played with her Weimaraner."

"Just like that," he said.

"It was nothing to her..." she said, swallowing again. "It was easy, it was casual, it was nothing. That was the whole thing. There was nothing special about it."

"Except of course there was."

"I mean, there was nothing special about it for her. It was just...routine for her."

He looked at her blankly again. "Did she know it was your first time?"

She looked right back. "She understood what the situation was."

"And so she got what she wanted, and then moved on," he said.

"I guess so," she said.

Will nodded slowly. "Meg..." he said.

"What?" Whitney said. She swallowed hard.

She stared at him across the ocean of blond hardwood. He saw the reaction in her face. Of course it confirmed everything.

"Meg Herrera," he said.

"Right..." Whitney said.

"Her production company's involved," Will said. "So she has lots of ideas, lots to share with you guys all the time, right? And so even if it didn't mean so much to her, she's helping shape the show, and so has to be in touch a lot afterward. She has to send lots of emails and you have to send lots of emails back—to Meg, I mean."

Her vision actually whited out. She hadn't fainted, because she could feel her feet on the ground, and her legs beneath her hips, and the cold clam of her palms. But her sight was all powder.

"I went to check on the status of our flight and accidentally opened your laptop instead of mine, and your email was up," he said. "There were a handful of unread emails at the top."

"And so you went ahead and read them." She had said it or she hadn't. She couldn't distinguish between what was happening inside and outside her skull.

"There was a little 73 next to her name. And just a few words in the preview of the email."

Whitney had collapsed into a pretzel on the floor. It had

made an enormous noise. Her head had fallen against her chest, and her legs were bent out to the sides like they might be broken.

"I don't think you'd seen the latest one yet, but its first few words probably won't come as a surprise."

"Will."

"Care to know what it said?"

She lifted her head and looked up at him.

"Hmm?" he said.

"No."

"Okay, cool. Let me know if you're curious. Sounds like you won't be totally surprised by the sentiment, either way."

Whitney felt the hot tears on her face.

"The previewed part wasn't actually that bad," Will said. "All it said was: *Three weeks?? You're going to make me wait three...* That could mean anything, right? That could be feedback on a script, an answer from your boss—any number of plenty reasonable things, really."

She looked up at him with tears in her eyes.

"But I didn't answer you a minute ago, did I?" Will said. "I probably *did* click through, huh?"

"Will."

"I didn't read *all* of them. Given that there were 72 emails before this one. But I can confirm: the latest doesn't deviate much from the previous... from what she's been sending, or from those responses of yours at four a.m., five-thirty a.m. No wonder you're so tired all the time, sweetheart."

"I didn't ask for this to become a thing," she said. "I didn't know it would turn into this."

"Of course you did," he said. "You absolutely did. This whole fucking thing was literally your idea."

"I mean, I didn't ask for this situation with this woman."

"With *Meg*. You can say her name. We're finally getting to a place of legitimate transparency. At least I think we are."

"After it happened, she sent me an email. I didn't know what to say."

"You didn't need to respond."

"I work with her on this thing. There might be things in the future. She's a big deal. I didn't want to slam any doors shut."

"People don't respond to emails all the time."

"I didn't want to be rude."

"God love you," Will said. "I'm so glad you didn't hurt Meg's feelings. We both appreciate that, me and her. But obviously her a little more than me."

"I'm sorry. I'm so so sorry."

"So, what, then?" he said.

"So, it ends," she said. "I don't talk to her again."

"Is that so easy? Wouldn't it be *more* rude now to just cut it off? After 73 emails? After all, she seems fairly eager to have her tongue on your clit again ASAP."

"Hey..."

"Oh, please. Her fucking words, not mine. I love how quickly you turn into a scandalized little prude when it suits you."

"I was just trying to...I don't know, Will. I don't know about anything anymore."

"Here I was suspecting Jack," he said. "Poor sweet simple Jack. When you dozed off before he got here, there was this slew of texts for you from a number I didn't recognize. Figured it was him. Figured something was going on between you two. I almost feel bad about what I said to him. Good Jack. Honest Jack. Unless it *was* him, after all..."

She was still on the floor. "I haven't checked my phone since I plugged it in."

"It doesn't matter. It couldn't be more explicit than what she wrote you in those emails."

"I didn't ask for it. I don't care about any of that."

"But Whitney, you do. Do you not realize that your responses are in there, too? That this isn't, like, a one-sided shoebox of letters?"

"I was just...I was just playing along. I had sex with a woman. That's it. So what?"

"That's right," he said. "So, what? What now? What the fuck are we supposed to do?"

She stared at him.

"What does this mean?" he said. "What are you actually saying?"

Her eyes were closed, but she picked at her cuticle, picked it to the point of blood.

"Hey!" he said. "What am I supposed to do with this, Whit?"

Will moved to the kitchen and poured himself a fresh glass of whiskey. He halved it in two long gulps as he walked back to the couch. She was staring aimlessly across the street at the roofs of the other buildings, to the drying lines. The sun was brighter still through the windows. When he got back, her face was wet and streaked with salt and bright like a sidewalk after a spontaneous shower.

"So is this it, then?" he said, so plain it made her choke. "Is that all there is for us?"

Her face spoke for her, the horror in her mouth and eyes. "Of course not...what are you talking about?"

He'd done it purposefully, hadn't he? He'd done it to hurt her in a new way. She stood up and threw herself at him, grabbing his body, her limbs out of control, seizing his shoulders and arms and knees with every last appendage available to her, grasping for any point of contact. "I love you. *I love you.* I've never stopped loving you. God, Will!"

"But is this all supposed to be okay now? What are we supposed to do?"

"I don't know...I don't know I don't know I don't know..."

"Besides the lies, besides the deception, besides the fucking emails behind my back—what is it that made you not tell me? Why couldn't you tell me? Why couldn't you just say it and then move on from it?"

He drank again. He was asking the essential questions but he was sublimely still. It terrified her. She shook her head slowly again.

"This all makes sense when you start to think about it, right?" Will said. "Why you wanted the break in the first place, I mean. Why you wanted 1-2-3, why you were resisting everything, why you couldn't imagine being engaged. What you *needed* in the meantime...I just wish you'd—"

"That's not true," she said, grabbing hold of him again, searching his face for his eyes. "That's just not true at all. Please don't make me feel worse about this than I already do. It's not like I've been living with this desire for years, or something...it's something that just happened."

"I don't believe that. I just don't anymore. I read those fucking emails. Did you forget that again? The lying's over, okay?" he said, and she pulled away from him slowly. He understood so much more than she probably even understood herself. "How long have you been feeling this way?

Just tell me. Please. Whitney. There's nothing else to hide anymore. There's just two people left."

"But there's one person who's the same and one person who's fucking changed. And I don't know what to say to you about it. I don't know what this was about—or why."

Will finished his drink. "You're telling me all it takes is one hot fuck to turn you inside out like this? You're saying that's all this is. That there's nothing else going on . . . I just don't buy it anymore! I'm sorry. I love you. But I'm getting sick of you bullshitting me like this. I just don't believe that there's not something bigger going on."

He was talking so much. She was getting fed up. "What do you want me to say?! That I've known all my life that I wasn't pegged at one hundred on the spectrum or whatever? Nobody is!"

"I think some people are, actually? I fucking am!"

"Well, that's fitting, right? Reliable, dependable, conventional Will."

"Are you suggesting my heterosexuality is too boring for you? Are you saying—"

"I'm saying you're *lucky,* okay? But this actually isn't about you for once. Not everything's about how fucking glorious your gloriously uninteresting life is."

He chuckled darkly and shook his head. "You and I used to sit around talking about how nice it was to just *know.* To just know that you were the one for me, and I was the one for you, and that we didn't have to worry about that stuff, because only movie stars like Adrien Fucking Green could come between us. About how lucky we were to have survived growing up and figuring ourselves out, unlike so many other people we know. But now you're saying, what— that that wasn't the case, after all?"

"I don't have the answers for you. Or for me. I'm sorry. I just can't explain any of this right now . . . I'm saying it's never been one hundred percent for me, things were never quite the way you had it for yourself. It's never been all the way, and lately it's been harder . . . different . . . shifting. It's been *louder.*"

"Lately."

"These last few months. These last couple . . . years."

"*Years?*"

"I don't know what to tell you. I don't know why and I don't know how. Growing up, I mean, obviously it wasn't a possibility. There was nothing to do but shove it down into the deepest drawer, and never acknowledge its existence. But then in—"

"You're saying you've felt this way since you were a *kid?*"

"I don't know what I'm saying! *Okay?* I'm saying there have been things at times that don't feel like I feel with you, or with the other boys I dated, or the—"

"The other *three* boys you dated," he said.

"I don't know what you want me to do with that fact. What you intend for it to mean."

"I just mean you weren't exactly serially out there, boy crazy, even in . . . so it actually makes sense when you think about it, if you've just been—"

"Please don't start turning over every rock to find convenient explanations. Connecting everything to this one fucking thing."

"I can't tell whether you're saying that this is the smallest thing or the biggest thing in the world. If this is nothing or if it's everything. If it wasn't a big deal, you just wouldn't have kept it concealed like this. And there wouldn't be 73 emails with you and this woman drooling over the prospect of fucking each other again."

"I just don't know."

"She's quite striking. Not what I would've expected. But it's interesting to see where you went when you had the opportunity."

Her nails were making the soft sensitive flesh in her webs turn red.

"And that's a hell of a deal she signed last year," he said. "I guess I get it. But just know that it makes me fucking crazy, okay? That this epistolary romance was going on this whole fucking time…"

She was crying again.

"Every time you had to rush home for Wi-Fi," he said, "or get up in the middle of the night to respond to 'work emails'…"

She was heaving and her breath was skipping.

"See?" he said. "I knew it. I knew it was more than nothing. More than you just not wanting to be rude."

She whispered it: "I just don't know what to tell you."

"Please do your fucking best."

She pulled at her hair. She pulled it hard and Will could hear some of the strands click from her scalp. "There've been things for a while, little things in the back of my head," she said. "Same as when you see a beautiful woman cross the street in front of you, the things you've said that jump into your head. But my things were nothing I didn't think everyone experienced."

He looked back at her, so very calm. It was as though he was hearing her clearly, at last.

"So what has *this* been, then?" he said. "The whole of these past seven years?"

"*This* has been my life," she said. "The relationship of my life. With the love of my life."

"Was being with me, like, a cover-up for something else? Or an alternative to something you kept yourself from pursuing all this time? Was there anyone else?"

"No. It never even occurred to me to think about it too hard. As more than just a fantasy. It was just a thing that would never happen. That's the truth. That's the deepest true thing I can tell you. I was with you. I was in love. I loved you. I love you. It's simple. That's all it is."

"What if we hadn't been together? What if you'd been single?"

"I probably would've dated some other boy, or several other boys."

"Really."

"Yes, of course I would've met somebody else."

"Other boys."

"Maybe I would've dated a girl. Is that what you want me to say?"

"No wonder getting married is so terrifying to you. You don't even know if... No wonder marriage is the scariest thing there is."

"It's what I want," she said. "It's what I want more than anything. It is."

"It's not," he said. "And it's okay that it isn't. Really. Just be honest with me. Finally. Please, Whit. Just please start helping me understand what any of this actually means."

She lifted her head but her eyes were shut again now. "Everyone's a little afraid of marriage," she said. "But it's not you that I'm afraid of. It's... letting the fucking state... and St. Luke's... and whatever else into our lives, into our private personal situation together. It's so fucking official, and legal, and none of their business, really."

"Don't do this," he said. "You don't have to do this for

my benefit. Letting the state into your life is not what twists you up inside."

"That's all there is. That's all there was and is to it."

"Just tell me what this thing is now," he said. "You can't say that it's nothing, that it changes nothing. You know that doesn't make any sense. Just tell me what—"

"Stop saying the same thing over and over! *Okay?!* I don't know what to tell you! I just don't know who the fuck I am right now, okay?!"

He let her hang there breathing. He'd pushed it there and it wasn't satisfying to him in the least. He knew he was bullying her and it disgusted him. Despite everything. Despite everything she'd done. He loved her, even if it was over, and he was making things worse for her. He reached for her hands. He pulled them from her knees.

"You're Whitney," he said.

"And who is that?" she said.

"That's the person I love more than anyone in the world," he said.

She started crying again, swellingly grateful, relieved that the inquisition was over.

He nodded and stood. "Okay."

"Okay."

"So, what now?" he said.

She shrugged and her mouth was small.

"So, we pack," he said, folding another shirt.

She sat there on the edge of the bed, waiting for more, waiting for anything else from him.

"I didn't do this to hurt you," she said.

"I know. How could you have known that it would mean something, right?"

She paused and swallowed. "I couldn't have expected

this, whatever this is," she said, swallowing again. "But I should tell you, because...I should tell you that it wasn't my first time with a woman."

"Ah." He shook his head.

"When I was abroad junior year. When I was all alone and all fucked up after everything that had happened that summer. There was a girl from Paris. It happened a few times over a few weeks. Then I saw her again spring break senior year, when I went back alone. But it was nothing. And I never even thought about it again, really, but—"

"So, right before we met. You went and saw her, like, a week before we got together."

"I didn't *go* to see her. I went to Paris and she was there."

He licked his lips and shook his head again. "And you never thought about it all this time?"

"I don't know. I don't know what to tell you. It didn't mean anything to me then. I guess I could've told you in the beginning, but I didn't think it was all that important. I was doing everything to make this work. I didn't want to risk anything.... It's not like I was hung up on it or something, or had all these feelings for her. It was just something that happened. I know a lot of women who..."

"You're right, everyone's done it, I forgot," he said. "Anything else to report?"

She shut her eyes and was pulling her hair again. She had her hair twisted around her longest finger and was yanking mindlessly. "I...I don't know how important or not this is...but I need to tell you so that we never have to talk about it again. To just...say everything about.... It happened on a Friday, a weekend, and so..." Her voice caught on a hitch. "...it happened again in the morning."

He stared back at her.

"It happened again in the morning," she said, "and then again the next day."

"Whitney," he said. "C'mon."

"I'm sorry," she said. "There's nothing else."

"How could there be?" he said.

"There's nothing else, I just wanted you to know."

"Okay."

"I would've never in a million years done it if I'd known this is how I would feel afterward."

"Okay. I'm sorry you're confused."

"But it doesn't change anything, okay?"

"If you say so," he said, packing still, eyes on his crumpled boxers and shirts.

"I couldn't have known..."

He looked up at her with ice behind his eyes. "Right, but, like, maybe just a *little*..." he said. "You maybe knew just a fucking *little*, right?"

Her face was rolling to a boil again, on the verge of tears all over.

"No," she said, shaking her head faintly. "The only thing I know is that I can't figure any of this out without...I just can't live my life without you, okay? I can't not be with you."

He looked at her, tears in his eyes now.

"How can that possibly be?" he said.

She inhaled like before. A fresh blade in the other lung. "What do you mean?"

"It's very clear that you've got some shit to figure out."

"Okay, but what does that have to do with—"

"I just assumed," he said, twisting a shirt in his hands. "After all this, after all the secrets, after everything you've just said you're feeling—how could we possibly be okay?"

"Will, what are you talking about?" she said, moving toward him suddenly, reaching for him. "Of course this doesn't mean that we aren't—"

"Stop," he said. "I just…I don't know right now, just like you don't know. What am I supposed to do with all this? All the fucking *deception*. Do you have any idea how horrifying it is to realize that the single person you think you know best in the world you don't actually have a fucking *clue* about?"

"I hope you don't mean that."

"It's true!"

"Imagine how it is for *me?!*" she said softly. "How much scarier it is for *me?!*"

"What do you want me to do, Whit?! *You* broke the rules. *You* didn't tell me about it. And you obviously *loved* it. You obviously couldn't get enough—and neither could she. It's fucked you up. It's changed you. You're telling me you have no idea who you are or how you feel about any of this stuff. *Everything* has fucking changed. *Everything*."

She stood up and grabbed him, grabbed his body but also picked up the arms that were hanging at his sides and slung them around her shoulders, forcing him to touch her, to wrap her up.

"Will, please," she said.

"What do you expect?" he said.

"What do you mean, *What do I expect*?"

"We're fucking *broken*," he said. "We are forcing something like we've never had to force it before. There is something clearly not right in this relationship. This whole thing is obviously off the rails in ways we've never acknowledged, and it's making us insane."

"No," she said, grabbing his face and shaking her head.

"No. No no no no. Don't say that. Don't you dare say that. I can't not be with you, okay? Not a minute. You're my *family. You* are my family...I can't imagine living—let's just finally do this, okay? Let's tell our parents today. Let's tell our friends. Let's set a date. Let's do it this week. Let's do it right here before they close the courthouse tonight, okay? We survived. We made it. It's time now."

He shook his head. "No. No way. How can you say that with everything else you're saying? With everything else you're feeling? The *fundamental* things you're talking about."

She collapsed onto the edge of the bed. On her face was the dawning realization that she'd perhaps ruined everything. The delicate balance. The even score. The precarious framework of 1-2-3 and the fragile architecture of a seven-year relationship. She'd poisoned the order of things with her confession, and the implication was coursing through her veins.

"Please..." she said, sprawling over the comforter to meet his downcast eyes. "Will, please."

He slipped her gaze and started throwing laundry into his bag again.

"We don't have to do any more of this right now, okay?" he said. "Let's just pack and get to the airport and get home. We have time to figure this out."

"No," she said, desperate. "I need you to tell me you understand what I'm saying. That nothing needs to change. That you understand and that we're okay. I need to know, Will. I need to know right now that we're going to be okay, or I'm gonna fucking die."

"Look: *I* didn't do anything. I'm not the fucking liar here. I'm not the one who's changing the rules as she goes along.

I'm the boring one—you said it yourself. With me, you know what you get. You're the ground that's shifting, Whit. *None* of this was my idea. *None* of it was my decision. *You* made the choices. You tell me what the new reality is, and I'll decide on my own fucking timeline whether I want a part of it."

"I can't possibly..." she said, tears slipping from her eyes again. "If this ends, then what? *What,* Will? What am I? If this ends, you're going to tell people, aren't you? Somebody's going to find out what happened. I can't tell my friends about this. I can't tell my parents. I can't fucking tell my *mom,* Will!"

"We're not with your mom right now. We're packing our bags."

"We don't have to leave for hours! You don't have to pack right now!"

"Maybe I don't want to talk about this anymore. Maybe I can't talk about this anymore without breaking a fucking window."

"There's nothing else," she said. "Nothing. Nothing has changed. Nothing is broken."

"Okay," he said, stuffing, folding, stuffing.

"Nothing changes. Nobody besides you and me has to know a thing. We go home, we put it behind us, life is as it was. Please."

"Please, what?"

"Please believe me."

"I don't even know what you're asking me to believe."

"I'm the same as ever. I'm me. Everything is okay, okay?"

He moved to the other side of the bed to retrieve a pair of pants.

She could tell he was dismissing her, finished, deferring to the place beyond today. She could tell she'd lost him, and so she sat on the edge of the bed and started heaving again.

Which is when the music turned over from one old song to another.

"I'm so sick of these shit-ass speakers," he said, walking out into the living room, searching for any better way to amplify the music. He pressed some buttons and banged some switches, but couldn't get the sound system going. He'd just needed out of the room. Whitney heard her own breathing and then she heard him clattering around in the kitchen. She heard the sound of freezer-burned ice cubes. She heard the threads of the bottle top. He returned with a fresh glass of whiskey.

"This is all that's left if you want some," he said, placing the glass on the side table. She'd collapsed again on the bed. Her face was slick. She was puddled up in the rumpled comforter.

The next song started. Something essential unearthed by the algorithm. It was a song from that first spring seven years ago. A song from another era; they'd spanned eras together. Something from the first concert they ever attended together, at a small club half an hour off campus, a concert for which they'd borrowed someone else's car, stayed out all night, listened to this very record again and again on the way there and on the way back, and again while they made out in the front seat on a poorly lit wooded road.

Neither of them had reacted to the music at first, except in their faces. Then, suddenly, unexpectedly, he laughed, a sick bark, and he shook his head in acknowledgment of the unwelcome ways the world was nosing in on their business. Why? Why this song just now? Her mouth was fixed in a frown, drawn down at the edges by the weight of her face. She wiped her eyes again and tried extra hard to draw Will's gaze back toward hers. It was something they could do to each other, a power they'd had since the beginning. He sensed the request, the heat and the signal, the silver lights flashing up at him from the bed.

He sat down and looked at her. And then it happened the way it sometimes happened for them. He didn't want it just then, but he couldn't help himself and she couldn't help herself. Since the beginning, it had gone that way: He'd look at her and she'd look at him, and there would be something chemical. A syncing-up. A pure meld. And now, as their eyes locked, it knitted them in place, sewed them right there into the comforter. The two minds behind the four eyes became one for an instant—it was all just chemistry—and the whole movie started to play in reverse:

A clink of two wineglasses. A bar without a menu. Will with his eyes over the rim of the butcher-red something from Penedès. Whitney's freckled face distorted through the bleeding legs that ran down the windows of her wineglass. Alone in the world with one another. Wrapped up tight, rubber-banded together on those barstools, in an elastic closeness, as each waited to hear what the other had done, and who they'd done it with. To understand how much damage had been inflicted, and whether it was the beginning of something or very much the end.

A beach outside the city, a week ago now. Palm trees rooted in ancient stone. Brown bodies arranged like glyphs on the sand, no one at work on a warm weekday afternoon. Will's face turned up into the sun, throat exposed, the posture of a defiant executionee. White feet, white thighs, white arms from the elbows up. Flesh spilling over the edges of his shorts, stomach muscles concealed by the dough of an uncooked piecrust. Whitney propped up like a waterslide beside him, legs crossed at the ankles, palms dug into the sand on either side of her towel. Eyes drifting to the women with the exposed breasts, the heavy breasts spread out across the sand, eyes scanning through the lenses of her shades to watch Will's eyes, to watch him watching, wondering what he was wondering about. Whitney wondered what Will had done while she'd been in L.A. She dreaded the dinner they'd planned to have at the end of the trip, when they'd spill all their secrets. She wondered what he'd seen, what he'd taken, what he'd experienced that he hadn't even known he'd been missing for those seven long years with her. All around Whitney, Mediterranean breasts, Mediterranean tan lines. Beauty. When the women got toasted, they turned over. When they got hot, they went swimming. Everybody watching everybody else. Will breathed shallowly beside her, drifting off to sleep. Whitney breathed sharply and un-knotted her top. Her fingers fell back to the sand, clenched around the weightless fabric. The sun stung her nipples. She'd done something she'd never done before, just like that. Will stirred and turned to Whitney, Whitney turned to Will. There was a look between them. Two faces that expressed the pleasant realization that there was still room on their seven-year-old island for surprises.

A call from Los Angeles, a month ago now. Will well asleep, Whitney sleepless. She'd tried three times already, and on the fourth he picked up. Nothing but uncertainty in the story of their affairs, nothing revealed yet. He might've been with someone that very night, she might've just as likely, too—there was no way of knowing. But she sounded alone in her hotel room, and he sounded asleep in their bed. Whitney asked for the old thing they'd done in the early years. When they'd been living in separate apartments, in separate cities, to help her get to sleep. *My feet on the back of your feet,* he'd say. *My shins on the back of your calves.* Spoon on spoon. All the way up the body, until her breathing would shift and she'd be dead to the world. She relied on the routine most nights, whether he was at home or with friends. He'd step out of the bar into the cold of a snowy night and run through the evolution, whispering into his phone beneath an overhang near a dumpster—the same lines, the same order, like a prayer. It had been forever since she'd asked for it. But that night, it was like old times.

A childhood bed, last Thanksgiving. A bed Whitney's parents had never swapped out. Will scanning the corkboard of memories above her desk for the pictures of her dates to high school dances, to the acquaintances she'd mostly kissed off, to the boys he'd always assumed she'd kissed. The bulletin board filled with the quaint tendernesses from a life lived long ago. Her shrine to those souls—the wilting corsages, the cracked petals that meant there was always a past no matter how much they both tried to overwrite it with one another.

A shared couch they'd purchased together for their shared "living room," their first month off Tompkins Square Park. A grown-up couch with a grown-up chicken roasting in a grown-up pot, the scent slipping from the kitchen and wrapping them up in a blanket of maturity. A new home. A new chapter. They lived together now. Sometimes they worried about growing too old too fast. Here, though: two faces of contentment wed in that instant to the scent of responsibility, of roasting chicken, a scent that they could welcome for the rest of their lives.

An argument, too much to drink, too much talk of long-term plans. About cities they might live in. About parents who might need them around someday. About where life could take them, and about where they'd never let it. They used to drink more and they used to fight harder. When everything was still possible, even the theoretical felt consequential. Will would yell. Whitney would punch and bite. Will would shove. Whitney would weep.

An unexceptional window of an unexceptional restaurant on an exceptionally cold morning during the first days of a new year. Will in D.C., Whitney down for the weekend, off the Washington Deluxe bus, twenty bucks each way. Drinking before noon, fighting off the crush of playoff football fans crowding in around them. Eating *croques madames* and *monsieurs,* and ordering rounds of Belgian beer until their brains unsealed from the walls of their skulls and relieved them of their hangovers. Pinned in by Redskins jerseys on all sides, shoved into the center of the table toward one another, in no hurry to return to the single digits outside, or the tiny room he rented from strangers on the sunnier side of U Street. It was one of the times they'd looked at each other in the midst of the chaos of a crowd, and cinched off their own fate from the fates of everyone else, speaking aloud across the table the sentiment, if not the exact words: *I think we're destined to win this thing together, I think we're meant to make it.* It happened often in those middle years, but this one stuck with both of them, maybe because of the cold outside. It was eight or nine degrees, and it made a mark like frostbite.

The raw, filthy fucking. Fistfuls of hair. Choking and gagging. Bruises and burns that wouldn't vanish for days. Broken bed frames. Snapped straps and torn fabric.

Tequila and whiskey and mushrooms and molly. Gratuitous volume through temporary walls. Retroactive apologies to roommates. Video functions on outdated digital cameras. Blackmailable photos. There were months and then years when they were mostly apart. He bought her a lavender vibrator before he moved to D.C. She bought a blue silicone dildo that roughly resembled the shape of his cock. They traveled hours on Friday evenings and Monday mornings in order to break each other's bodies, and then answer emails side by side beneath the sheets. They knew other couples in long-distance arrangements who'd lose entire weekends in bed. That wasn't them; they did other things together, too. But when they fucked each other, they were obscene. And as the years went on, as they grew more anxious spending all their time with single friends whose twenties were playing out the way they were meant to, the more seriously they took the imperative to prove something to one another. To treat each time like a first time, with effort to make it memorable. They auditioned for one another—physical arguments that said there was nothing else out there worth ending what they had.

The toast for graduating from law school. The toast for convincing a strange adult in a job interview that she was exactly what the streaming service was looking for. The toast for setting their lives on a course. It all happened in the same week. And so: six beers each in a grimy bar with tall windows on the hottest night of the year. The two of them at the corner table where the windows touched, projecting their lives forward into grand, sweeping plotlines. They disappeared the pint glasses and decided that it was worth the little money they had between them to keep new glasses coming forever. It was one of those nights in a bar in New

York, one for no one else but them. They couldn't tell you the faces of the people in the place, but they remembered for years the particulars of those who passed by the windows. There was a late sun. There were bare legs. There was chest hair. There was every last sweating skinny beautiful body that night in a hurry to somewhere sexy.

The sleepovers in the law-school dorm. A Friday evening that first winter when both his roommates had gone home for the weekend. They'd bought groceries and tried to cook themselves dinner for the first time in their lives. They boiled pasta and made grilled cheeses. They smoked one roommate's weed from the other roommate's pipe. Whitney scavenged the fridge for snacks. She found a tube of Toll House and spread the dough around a ceramic plate. She burned her forearm on the oven door but didn't notice the infection until the morning. They fell asleep on the couch, watching the ocean episodes of *Planet Earth* and testing out names for their future children.

A one-star hotel room with blood and wine. A young American couple in Europe, their first big trip together. And so they skirted the hostels they'd stayed at in college and splurged on a proper private hotel room instead. The second day they walked themselves dead, stayed in at night, opened three bottles of wine and a playlist on her laptop. They woke up at an indeterminate hour to half a bottle tipped into the bed, the sheets doused and stained maroon. They sprang up, he to the bathroom and she close behind. He barfed in the tub, she slammed the door on his foot. A screw in the door separated his big nail from his big toe. He bled out on the tile and the carpet and eventually in the bed when, after running out of towels, she wrapped his foot in the soiled sheets. They slept on the bare mattress and woke again to the carnage of a murder-suicide. They spent the next day at an American hospital, a vacation day devoid of new sites. They left a guilty tip for the maid that equaled the price of a night. They left the city forever and never returned. But on the train that afternoon, they confessed to one another that they'd never been more in love.

The first visit to California with his parents. The first visit to Texas with hers. The ease with which they became the new addition to each family. They said and did the right things. They cleaned their dishes and dusted up their crumbs. They didn't stay out too late, didn't wake anyone up when they trundled in at night. They laughed at things that were funny and were interested in stories even the second time they were told. They didn't throw up from drinking too much. They didn't fool around within earshot. They felt comfortable lazing about and comfortable asking for a glass of water. Before leaving town, they made sure to leave a full tank of gas in the car that they had borrowed.

The polyps they found in her mother's colon after graduation. The body they found of a friend of his near the pylons of the pier that first summer. The astonishing sense that they didn't know a thing about death but had said mostly the right things to each other anyway, confirming that those first couple months weren't just the product of a bottled-up experiment, of the Stockholm syndrome of the end of college, but rather of something worth paying attention to. Still, they'd considered what it might be like to break up over the summer, that it might realistically be too hard to preserve whatever special thing they'd started, even if they both planned to end up in New York. But then the news, the two shots of heaviest reality right away. They comforted one another and they realized that no one in their lives, even those they'd known for considerably longer, could have said the right things any better. They didn't just want each other, they needed each other now. They needed each other to keep the world from intruding too quickly.

The day before parents arrived. The day before graduation weekend. A party at his house. Up all night, drinking and dancing to live Talking Heads records and working their way through a molehill of cocaine. They'd been upstairs in his room with their share, spread out on the carpet, faces nearly touching and hovering above an old issue of *Rolling Stone*. They'd been in the room for ten minutes, or an hour, quieter up there, the music contained to the basement floor. They were screwing around, shouting *Boogie Nights* lines into each other's faces, that they *must never leave this room,* while feeling the sentiment elementally too, in every cell from their soles to their scalps. He asked her what she wanted more than anything in the world and she told him her most private ambition, and she asked him what he wanted more than anything in the world and he told her his. And then he started tearing up and he grabbed her by the face, and told her he didn't know quite how or why, but he just knew they were destined to hold each other to their dreams, and that together they could make them happen. That even though they'd known each other for just six weeks, they owed each other their assurances right then and there that no matter what, no matter what happened in the future history of their long lives and their destiny with fulfillment, they must always hold each other to it, whether they were romantically linked or not, to make sure neither ever forgot what they'd once desired and what they were meant to make of themselves, what they'd confessed in this room on this very last night, when life was still okay, and everything was still possible, before the real world came crashing in. They pinkie-swore and then snorted a line each off the magazine cover, and he tackled her as their brains and bodies sparkled like Pop Rocks, and he pinned her down and stuck his tongue up her nose and they stared into each other's eyes, and she said *Yes* to a question that hadn't been posed.

The week of their final finals. Will buried beneath books, secreted away in the fourth-floor stacks, hidden well enough that only Whitney knew where he was. Whitney out in the open, on the first floor, near the entrance. In the late afternoons all week long, he could count on her being there. Once her papers were submitted, she didn't need to show up. But she kept coming anyway, to be there in case he walked by. She'd sit beneath the high windows lit up with Southern spring from morning until dusk, reading scripts, waiting for it. Will knew, even as he was seeing it for the first time, that he'd never lose that image: Whitney in the soft swirl of book dust, Whitney in the library light, the first true love of his life.

The moment of linkage on that bed in Barcelona, it went back further still, almost all the way back. A late night in the hammock on the porch of his house. A bus ride to a formal at a farm with dairy cows. The big bright afternoon of the last day of classes, when they'd been swimming in the buzz of a long morning of shotgunned beers, and wound up fucking in the public shower of a freshman dorm neither of them had lived in. They were clear memories, crisp incidents, because there were photographs commemorating so many of the moments. Photographs taken by his housemates who knew that what they were witnessing was dangerous. A futile pairing-off during the home stretch, right before it was all meant to end. They took those pictures without faith that it could last. But they saw the way Will and Whitney's eyes locked amid crowds, as though they were the only ones alive at a party, the way their hands found each other's cheeks on overstuffed dance floors, as though the hourglass was draining down a little bit slower for the two of them than it was for everybody else. It was a joke that every last class-mate at the bars on Sweetgum Street those last few weeks could share in—watching the ill-advised enterprise lift off. But not even they were there to witness Will and Whitney sitting alone together in a parking lot outside a bar on one of the earliest nights, as she held the back of his head in the crook of her elbow, petting his feathery hair, whispering "Can I keep you?" into his ear.

The end of that long first night together, seven years ago. A bar closing down. His friends winking as they left them together to order one final drink. A cab, even though his house was walking distance. A cab, even though she didn't have any cash left. A kiss in the back of the cab. A hot spring night that began in a garden—a denim skirt for her and cotton shorts for him. A pair of hammered twenty-two-year-olds. One hand each on the other's face. Eyes sealed shut. She crept her free hand to the fabric in his lap and felt his smile through her lips. He moved his free hand from her knee to the hem of her skirt and felt her legs part micro-scopically. His fingers traced the inside of both sticky thighs. She was dripping wet, heat radiating from the thatch of hair. The driver braked abruptly in front of the house and Will opened his eyes to peek out the window. He pulled his hand and reached for his wallet and then looked at Whitney's face in the sallow streetlight to ask her if she wanted to come see that DVD collection he had been talking about all night.

And then finally, at last: a garden. The campus gardens in early spring. A boy playing catch with a friend who'd brought two baseball mitts to school all four years. A girl reading a 1970s movie script in the shade of a dogwood tree. A boy with gym shorts and a Dodgers hat and a T-shirt printed with a pun on the name of his freshman dorm. A girl with a green camisole and faded blue boyfriend jeans frayed at the knees, a revealing window on a gnarled scar from an athletic injury. Both without shoes. It was a shoeless kind of day, during a shoeless time of their lives. A boy who spotted the cover of the hardbound script, the poster for a movie he knew better than any other. A cover on a book in the hands of a girl he maybe recognized but whose name he didn't know, a girl with a body stretched out like a leaf in the grass, a body with a head that was still, and legitimately reading, unconcerned with anything swirling around her. A boy who'd just handed back the mitt and the ball, telling his friend he'd see him downtown in a few hours to watch the game, to watch JJ Pickle play in the Sweet Sixteen of the tournament. A boy, therefore, with nothing in the world requiring his attention at that very instant. A boy who thought: *At worst she'll politely acknowledge that it is indeed the movie script the cover says it is, and maybe roll her eyes at him for making a move in the gardens, of all places.* A boy who thought: *At best she'll politely acknowledge that it is indeed the movie script the cover says it is, and maybe smile and sort of applaud him for making a move in the gardens, of all places.* A boy taking a chance, out of character for him, truly. A boy just feeling lifted by the green and the breeze, and killing time before the big game. A boy who noticed her freckles come into focus on her yogurt-smooth skin and couldn't help but say something. A boy who noticed her plump pink lips and her thick black brows and the blue blackness of her hair, and then the flush of her throat, the roundnesses beneath her shirt, the narrow slot of skin between the bottom of her top and the top of her jeans, the brass button there catching the sun like a gold coin. A boy whose head inadvertently cast a shadow across the face of a girl, dirty-blondly knocking the sun out of the sky. A girl who felt the shadow and lowered her book and, coaxed by some force beyond her comprehension, decided to look up into a stranger's face and start things off with a spring-sweet smile.

Smiður

The carpenter's home had been saved. It was a good joke. He'd returned to find it musty and worn as ever, but still standing, impervious. The fire had split at his gate—he'd raised his foundation to ward off flooding—and the lava had flowed like a forked tongue around his property. The flames had licked his iron fence but left the rest intact.

For all the houses he'd built in town, he hadn't made improvements on his own in twenty years. It was the last thing he could bring himself to undertake after long days of framing and finish work—to buckle up his tool belt, knot his boots, and perform repairs in his downtime. His twins had left five years earlier for university, and then work in the capital. His wife had left the summer before for another man, in another town, on the other side of the island— a man she'd met online. She said she left him because of their fundamental incompatibilities as human beings, but he knew she left him because he'd refused to work on the house. Rotten beams. Eroded insulation. Electrical wires chewed through by mice. And that was just the stuff inside the walls. The house was a decaying heap, a tomb bereft

351

of life. He could've used a clean start, he told the neighbor with whom he'd feuded for years. He wished it had been his home that had got burned up instead of all of theirs.

But it had gone the way it had gone—that fateful indifference of the volcano. And so he went to work as never before. He foremanned a crew composed of all the capable hands in the valley. Neighbors put their property-line disputes aside, forgave differences in Christian doctrine, erased financial debts since the ledger at the general store had been destroyed, too. They scrounged for materials and received lumber and steel and concrete mix from the countryside. They borrowed tools from villages up and down the coast. The carpenter led them like a wartime general through the meticulous stages of a lengthy siege. Foundations. Framing. Windows and doors. Roofs and siding. Electrical and plumbing. Insulation and drywall. And, at last, his beloved finish work. Hand planes. Band saws. Dovetail joints. He cherished the words and the tools in his toolshed.

Up they went, thirty-six houses in sixty days. The displaced slept in the chapel, high on the hillside. When the weather warmed, some slept outside in tents and sleeping bags donated by an American manufacturer of environmentally conscious outerwear. By the middle of summer, when the sun barely set, they were back in their homes, and the carpenter was back in his. It had been chaotic, but never hasty. It had been urgent, but never rushed. They had done what was necessary, and they had been blessed with occasionally sunny skies.

Their lives had been upended, but no one was dead, at least not yet. They were small, and the volcano was large, immeasurably so, and one day in the future it would come for them again. That compact between villager and volcano was the one intrinsic truth of their existence. How inconsequential were the lives of the citizens of the valley, how insignificant their free will. And yet they would persist collectively, choosing to exist in the shadow of death and destruction, so long as they could live out their lives in the land of their ancestors. They would look upon the volcano, day and night, and thank it for its presence, for the perpetual charge it provided them, those in close proximity to that judgment. Their lives, after all, were solitary notes in a universe of ceaseless symphony; they were minuscule and fleeting, and it was useful to be reminded how soon they would all ring out and resolve.

And yet still: before bed each night, the carpenter would look out his kitchen window to the looming mass he'd known all his life as the horizon, and, like so many before him in the valley, and all those who would follow, make his negligible appeal for mercy. He'd pray to the volcano on behalf of himself and every neighbor who'd found a way to carry on with life in the wake of disaster. He'd smile and tap the glass with a defiant finger, standing up for the living in a world composed overwhelmingly of rock and metal and swift-moving fire, and whisper to Holudjöfulsins, the volcano through the pane: "Ekki enn. Ekki enn." Not yet. Not yet.

He still had the repairs to his own house to make. He needed to win back the love of his life. He needed more time. They all needed more time to figure things out and to live the right way, at long last.

"Ekki enn. Ekki enn," he'd say. Let's not end this quite yet.

III.

After Volcano

Thursday

They woke with a start to their simultaneous midnight alarms, Whitney locked to her side of the bed, Will to his. It was morning all over again, but blackest morning, night-morning. The airport had stacked up the departures so that the flights were running all through the night. They'd drawn their pair of seats on the three a.m. back to New York. Clearing Zone 6. Limited status. But today was the day they'd finally be going home.

The shock of the alarm made Will want to barf. They'd slept for four hours, and he was at the peak of a fresh hangover. Whitney looked worse than when she'd gone to bed. Her skin was leached of color. All that work, all that self-care, was no match for the fallout of blowing up one's life.

They'd packed in the afternoon to give themselves some-thing to do besides talk about what had happened. When they were through packing, they'd gone for a long walk up to Parc Güell. They'd walked beneath the corridors of twisted-stone tree trunks, they'd looked out from the gener-ous heights over the city from the terrace of broken tiles, and taken a picture together with their one working phone, the one phone left between them. They hadn't taken a picture together the whole trip, and in this one they smiled gingerly. They were drunk and hadn't eaten much—but neither of them had a huge appetite. Later, they bought some sticks of salami and two cans of Coke at the Mercado de Santa Caterina, and ate together on a wooden bench beside a dirt soccer pitch in El Born. Then, with the sun still up but the shutters closed, they got in bed, turned out the lights, and kept to their sides. That was it. That was how they spent the last night of the trip.

He asked her if she wanted coffee and she didn't and he said he didn't really, either. They didn't have much food left in the refrigerator, anyway, it'd be better to get something at the airport at this point. They cut wide lines around one another as they moved through the apartment in the surgical light. They moved with an underwater slowness. They glanced at one another to take in the ghostly stranger they'd seemingly never encountered before. They packed their stragglers, they kicked orphan socks across the floor toward the other's bag. They made sure the lengths of their showers weren't inconvenient. They made sure their toothbrushes didn't touch. They carved up the apartment with invisible incisions. They knew that what had happened couldn't have happened—that was two other people in a whole other time and place. They left the keys to the front door on the dining-room table. They shut up the apartment one last time.

In the cab it was wordless, just the rush of the silent streets and the occasional tick of the meter. Will mouthed his goodbyes to the city as they passed through. Goodbye apartment. Goodbye Eixample. Goodbye mountains, goodbye beach. Goodbye *cafés con leche* and *pans con tomate*. Goodbye Gaudí, Columbus, and Miró. Goodbye seaport, cemetery, and Montjuïc. Goodbye yellow ribbons and red-and-gold dreams of separatist rule. Goodbye Neymar, goodbye Messi.

As they pulled into the war-zone lineup at the departures curb, Will opened his mouth and spoke finally. "I'm glad you told me," he said. "Thank you for telling me. Seriously. I don't want you to think I don't understand, or that I don't believe you that you don't really know what's going on, or that I don't appreciate how hard that must've been to say all that out loud. I just…I'm pretty confused myself, and I'm just fucking *sad*. Not because I don't get what you're feeling—but because I *do*. Something has happened, and it's messed you up. That scares me. And it hurts me. And it just really, really bums me out. And it makes me wonder about what happens with a lot of things."

"I'm sorry," she said. "I don't know what to say."

He paid the cab driver with his single leftover bill and pulled their bags out of the trunk.

After the zombie routines of check-in, they moved like husks across the crowded gleaming floors of the international terminal, where most travelers had lived in a pop-up refugee camp while the two of them had carried on with their charades in the city. It was Thursday now. It had been just four days since they'd been here last, just ninety hours since they'd been denied their initial escape. A village had been built in the terminal in that time, and now they were pushing through it—the packs, the stalls, the new order.

They had a suitcase each—Whitney's rolling bag and Will's duffel—and a bag each with their laptops and their chargers and their unread books. Whitney listened to a gossip podcast while they waited in the security line; Will plugged his headphones into his laptop and listened to some music. When they were through to the other side, Will went to the bathroom and Whitney waited with their things, and then they traded. They didn't speak except to tell the other that passport control was to the right not the left, and did she want a coffee and croissant, or a proper breakfast from a proper restaurant with the thirty euros in coins they had left?

They went to McDonald's. Two Egg McMuffins, two hash browns, two black coffees. The food was gone before their coffees had cooled. Will got in the long line again and ordered seconds. They had time to wait in all of the lines. They'd never flown out in the middle of the night before. They'd heard about the airports in the Middle East, the midnight flights to beat the heat. But this was a clearing-house now. They couldn't move. The line at McDonald's was tangled again, which was fine with Will and it was fine with Whitney. It meant another break. It meant acceptable silence. It meant she could keep her headphones in until Will returned with a fresh tray.

They drank their coffees. They felt better, gradually them-selves. A woman sat down next to them. She was long, reedy, olive. From Barcelona or Rio de Janeiro or El Paso. She was precisely the size and shape of female species that Will had always found a little alien-seeming but that Whitney had long admired. She was six feet tall. She was runway-thin. Her skin was the tone of all future citizens of Earth, circa 2350. They knew the type from their neighbor-hood. She looked like seemingly all of them looked: white T-shirt, no makeup, beautiful but brittle.

Will crumpled up the wrapper of his second sandwich and flexed his eyebrows at Whitney.

"What?"

He did it again, this time with an exaggerated nod in the woman's direction.

"What?" she said again.

"Is that..."

"What are you saying?"

"Is she your...you know, is she your type?"

Whitney was on her feet at once. Will stood from the table to cut her off, reached for her waist and then her hand. But she snapped it from his grip and shoved him back down into his seat with the strength of a former college athlete.

The model looked up, innocent and alarmed. Whitney clopped away down the concourse. Will didn't bother chasing her and sat with the trash on the table.

He knew she wasn't coming back, not for a while. He sipped his coffee, scalding still. He looked around at the swarms, as crowded as he'd ever seen an airport outside of a snowstorm. His eyes caught the television—some soccer highlights, some news from home. The endless stream. And then, astonishingly, there was the familiar B-roll of the murder in Paris. Of the apartment, of the police tape. But over the images, a decipherable chyron: an arrest. New footage of a young man in glasses and a quarter-zip sweatshirt walking in cuffs beneath that familiar shadowless silver of the ashcloud in Paris. Will stood up and walked toward the monitor. Sure enough—charges. *Su novio*. Her boyfriend. Jenna Leonard Silverstein was off the hook. Will shook his head. He couldn't believe he'd believed her. He couldn't believe he'd believed any part of it. But as he turned his head from the monitor, Will wondered all over again if Jenna had maybe gotten away with murder.

Will grabbed Whitney's bags, stacked his on top of hers, and slowly, awkwardly, wheeled their collective haul to the gate. No sign of Whitney there, either. He found two seats near the window. They would be boarding in twenty minutes.

She monitored him from the adjacent gate, concealed by the camp of hundreds who'd been holding out at the airport for days. She didn't have any money of her own. She didn't have her suitcase or her bag. All she had was her passport and her ticket, and that couldn't get her anywhere but on her flight, next to the same person she'd flown over with. She never should've told him. Of course she shouldn't have. She should've known better. He would never understand all the way, what it had meant to her. Or, worse, he would. He would understand that it might change everything. That something had happened, that something was happening, and that she alone would have to decide what to do with it.

She approached his terrible shape, his wrinkled clothes and mussed hair and week-old stubble. He was so thick and heavy and meat-filled. And after one week abroad, there was more hair now. The correlative stink of his pits, the swamp of his crotch, the wiry sprigs on his shoulders, the mess of his ass crack. There were things all over his body, growths and blemishes and scourges of irritation that a woman would never get away with. How fortunate for Will. Always and forever, favored. How fortunate for him that he could do nothing at all and be just fine. He was going to quit his job when they got home, she could sense it. They'd been here before, but he seemed over the edge now, he seemed to really mean it this time. And then what? She'd cover their costs, she'd help with his loans. All while he floundered and toiled in the fantasy of writing that movie he thought she wasn't aware of. The stubble would get thicker. He'd waste his days on infinite subsequent drafts. She knew the current version of the script was with a C-minus production company, this guy he'd gone to law school with, and that he'd find out soon, if he hadn't already, that there wouldn't be interest until she introduced him to some real people herself. When he finally came to her asking for a lift, she'd have to tell him the truth about what he'd written, but not all the way. It would be a phase—maybe just the summer. And then he'd go back to an office, a better job. Enough money to bring him back in line with her, at least for the time being. But for now, there was that future beard for her to worry about, that haggard thatch. She'd have to tell him the truth about that, too. How much she hated it. How much less handsome it made him when he grew it out. How much less serious he looked. How much rougher it was on her thighs, how much it had always bothered her, for seven years, how much she'd always detested it, if he wanted her to be honest.

But, no, she couldn't say all that, either. Not given everything she'd just revealed. Not with the subtext. Everything now would be seen through the new lens. The eggshells of what it might mean, of what might really be going on inside her heart and mind. She could live with it. She would have to. Because she couldn't live her life without him, that was all she knew. They'd come this far, a lifetime it seemed, and there was certainly no one else on earth as much for her as he was. No man in the world who could know her better. She felt something on her face and caught a tear with her tongue. She wasn't even in a crying mood, she hadn't even felt it coming. Her face was just leaking now, it had been so warped out of shape—it just did it on its own. It had been a terrible run of days and nights. She couldn't take full responsibility for the involuntary tears.

She knew she would have to decide. If it was even up to her, if it could even be her decision. Of course she knew it was the sort of thing one couldn't decide, but she would have to. Today, though, all they had to do was board a flight. They had to keep it going for now. It was okay. Okay, Whitney? It'll be okay.

She approached him, sat in the empty seat, appealed tentatively with her eyes.

"Sorry," he said, looking up at her. "I was just kidding. But I realize this isn't the kidding kind of thing right now, is it?"

She smiled softly in appreciation.

They sat there next to one another in the airport of the strange city where they'd been trapped by the clouds.

"Let's just . . ." he said.

"Okay," she said.

"I know everything that I shouldn't have—"

"I know. Me, too," she said.

"I'm sorry about the things I did that made this worse."

"I am, too. I'm sorry for the things I said and the things I did and the things that made this what it became. I never meant for this to—"

"Okay," he said.

"Okay," she said.

They didn't touch hands. They didn't kiss. But they smiled teethlessly at one another. It was the first time they'd really looked each other in the eyes since they'd woken up. There was an agreement in the look, some sort of temporary contract. Or maybe a toast, something more like: *to safety, to gratitude, to comfort, to pleasure, and to the unthinking lightness of just getting along for now, okay?* Traveling companions. The dearest of friends. It was a shared look that was of no place or time, of no context, except a cilial comprehension that there was still plenty of good left here. One-Two. Him. Her. That was all there was to understand as they heard their zone called to board the plane. *Not yet,* the look seemed to say. We can't destroy each other all the way, at least not yet.

Before they stood, Will turned in his seat and Whitney turned in hers. Then he grabbed her head with both palms and framed her face. He held her firmly, as though it were everything there was in the world. Then he moved his own face toward hers and, as she turned her mouth up to meet his, he plunged his tongue into her nostril. She shoved him away and punched his arm, hard enough to leave a mark, they both knew at once. Like the old days. It flooded them both with relief. He pinned her hands to her sides and attempted to restrain her with one arm. Her nails ripped into his flesh, drawing out two threads of under-skin. She grabbed a fistful of his hair, yanking his head back like the Pez dispenser that it could sometimes be, and licked his hairless forehead. She released him, and they were breathing heavily. Not smiling. Not laughing. Exhausted. Relieved.

Eyes traced in at them from several vantages. They were being watched. By passengers in the lineup, by the brittle young thing from McDonald's, who was of course on their flight.

"Truce?" she said.

"Truce," he said.

"Even?" she said.

He looked at her, conceding nothing, and then she nodded, understanding.

"We're up," he said.

"Okay," she said.

It was finally time for them to get out of there. It was finally time to go home.

They boarded slowly. They had a pair of seats on the left side of the plane. Will unlatched the overhead compartment and the door thumped open. He put their bags up. He sat in a clatter near the window, giving her the aisle to stretch out her knee and hip. The standard routine. She pulled a script from her bag and plunked the brass tacks with her nails. He crushed his knees into the seat in front of him. He plugged into the armrest and screwed in his earbuds. The masses came streaming up the pair of aisles for twenty minutes, the hundreds on their flight. Out the window the planes were lined up, ready to roll out all through the night, dozens upon dozens of previously unscheduled flights, the collective effort of their great escape.

They'd been trapped, Will and Whitney. It had been the most essential fact of their lives these past five days. But all the rest of them had been trapped, too. Each person on their flight and in the airport, and the millions well beyond the limits of the city—each individual, a life disrupted, broken, recast, redirected. The volcano effect. It had affected them, all of them here, more than they would ever fully comprehend. And yet somewhere far away, they knew in the logic parts of their brains, some lives had been truly destroyed, human beings burnt up like insects. The indifferent volcano. The volcano that didn't give a shit about the billions walking its planet, and about Will and Whitney least of all. The indifferent volcano that didn't care about 1-2-3 or a murder in Paris or the end of a basketball career or the lies twisted up amid them. Their lives were small. Smaller than small. All their lives, with all their adorable little inconsequential human concerns. The only thing Will and Whitney knew deep down was that in face of the volcano, in face of that geological scale, none of it, none of them, mattered one smidge.

Only they had to matter. They had to. Otherwise what was the point of getting on the plane? What was the point of leaving here and getting on with it at all? In the wells of their solipsism, they knew that they had to matter, that everyone did—but the two of them most of all. They mattered to each other, at the very least. Will and Whitney. What they were and what would become of them mattered to Will and mattered to Whitney. Him. Her. Now. Later. They were of consequence. They were of importance. They mattered they mattered they mattered. They had to. They mattered to each other. They mattered to Whitney and they mattered to Will.

Will listened to the classical music channel and felt like he might drop off to sleep right away. It had caught up to him—everything, the hours of the last few days, the math of it all. The betrayal. The bone exhaustion. The ways they'd wrung each other out. He drifted through the boarding announcements. He was dead to the safety demonstration. He startled at the blasts from the PA and got bopped in the head by a carry-on stuffing in behind him. He woke more widely at the first sudden lurch of the plane, ninth for take-off, and then sixth, and then third. It was three-thirty in the morning, blacker than black out, and it was finally time. Whitney was beside him. He could feel her heat and her weight, and he wanted to see her without letting her know that he was looking. He saw her flip from page 32 to 33. She had a red pen in her hand, a red pen he'd never seen before. She had a life of pens he knew nothing about, separate from him, out there in the world.

She felt his eyes out of the corner of her own. She felt him watching her read, watching her mark up the draft. She had nothing to prove to him, she was as good as anyone at what she did. She didn't need to write something in the margin to show that she had notes to make, that she had thoughts. It was only Will, after all. It was Will, who she knew better than anyone in the world, who knew her better, too. And yet she felt only his scrutiny, felt him like a stranger. She hated the script, they'd never make the show, it was a waste of her time. But she'd been away so long, she needed to do all that was asked of her for at least the first week back. She'd go straight into the office this morning, even. She knew she'd be asleep by the time the cabin pressure settled, and so wanted to get as much done as she could before the full reality of her new situation flooded her. Before she realized that everything would be different from this point forward, that there was no turning back ever again, and that this—this here— was the very first moment of the rest of everything else. She turned another page, she'd skimmed it, she couldn't track what she was reading anymore. They would figure things out tomorrow or the next day. They would go home to the apartment they shared, and after talking about anything else, they would sleep it off. And then, and only then, after really thinking it through, for a few days or maybe a week or two or three or four, they would try to figure out what the rest of their lives were going to look like.

They were up next. They could feel the airplane turn its

big wide ninety. She'd forgotten her seatbelt and so buckled in. He heard hers and buckled his, too. *Click. Click.* They were next to each other but as distant as they'd ever been, operating on discrete frequencies all their own. It was over, wasn't it? She knew it was probably the case and so did he—but only probably, not certainly. They would figure it out when they got to New York. The only thing to think about now was getting off the ground, getting turned back west, back in the direction home. Things would never be the same, she knew. They would never return to the way things were, yet they must. But that was a riddle for tomorrow, or some day next week. She would never stop loving him. She really did love him more than anyone in the world. She felt his breathing next to her, his face flanged open. She hated the shape of his head just then, but she knew that she would love him forever.

She crept her hand beneath the armrest and placed it in his lap. He was out. He probably hadn't even noticed. But then she felt it. She felt his hand grab her hand. She felt his fingers thread her fingers. His palm below, hers above. His eyes were still closed, so she closed hers, too. They might not survive another day beyond this one, but this was okay for now, wasn't it? They heard the surge of the engines, felt the thrust at their backs, were pressed into their seats as though commanded by hypnosis. They could decide to be happy, they both knew it was their choice. They knew that's what they had to do, or at least that it was an option. They could be helpful still, they could be generous and gentle and kind. They could provide for one another the outcome that each desired most deep down. They could be happy—all they had to do was decide.

But the decision was for tomorrow, or some day next

week. For now, it was simpler than that. It was as simple as two hands. Two hands, clasped. Him and her. Will and Whitney. They would be okay, after all. They would be okay they would be okay they would be okay. They felt the wheels separate from the runway. And then, on a silent shared count of 1-2-3, somebody squeezed.

Acknowledgments

Utmost gratitude to the book people in my corner: Josh Kendall at Little, Brown and Kirby Kim at Janklow & Nesbit. And everyone else in their halls who had a hand in getting this novel into shape and out the door—in particular, Reagan Arthur, Ira Boudah, Nicky Guerreiro, Alexandra Hoopes, Sareena Kamath, Maggie Southard, Elora Weil, Ben Allen, Allan Fallow, and Eloy Bleifuss.

To the writers and editors in my life, especially in magazines. Magazines are more fragile than ever—read them, subscribe to them, indulge their paywalls, please.

To early readers on this project: Angelica Baker, Sarah Colombo, Sarah Goldstein, Alice Gregory, Alyssa Reichardt, Patti Riley, and Claire Stapleton.

To the many friends who tolerated the weekends of writing.

To Mom and Dad and Patons and Pattisons and Rileys and Glenns and Goulets, for basements and beaches and understanding the difference between fiction and non-.

ACKNOWLEDGMENTS

To Icelandic volcanoes (c. 2010) and European Air-bnbs (c. 2017–19), for inspiration and accommodation, respectively.

To Barcelona, for letting me drop in from time to time.

And to Sarah Goulet. I love you even more than visiting Europe.

About the Author

Daniel Riley is the author of *Fly Me* and a correspondent at *GQ*. He grew up in Manhattan Beach, California, attended Duke University, and lives in New York City with his wife.